A TALE OF ELEVENTH-CENTURY JAPAN

A Tale of Eleventh-Century Japan:

HAMAMATSU CHŪNAGON

MONOGATARI

Introduction and Translation

by THOMAS H. ROHLICH

 Princeton University Press

Copyright © 1983 by Princeton University Press
Published by Princeton University Press, 41 William Street, Princeton,
New Jersey 08540
In the United Kingdom: Princeton University Press, Guildford, Surrey

All Rights Reserved
Library of Congress Cataloging in Publication Data will be found on the last
printed page of this book

Publication of this book has been aided by a grant
from the Bollingen Foundation

This book has been composed in Linotron Electra

Clothbound editions of Princeton University Press books are printed on acid-free
paper, and binding materials are chosen for strength and durability. Paperbacks, while
satisfactory for personal collections, are not usually suitable for library rebinding

Printed in the United States of America by Princeton University Press,
Princeton, New Jersey

For My Parents

Mary E. and Gerard A. Rohlich

Contents

Preface

THIS TRANSLATION is based on the text found in Endō Yoshimoto and Matsuo Satoshi, *Takamura Monogatari, Heichū Monogatari, Hamamatsu Chūnagon Monogatari*, Nihon Koten Bungaku Taikei, no. 77 (Tokyo: Iwanami Shoten, 1964). The annotation for *Hamamatsu* was done by Matsuo, and henceforth all references to this basic source will be cited under Matsuo, *Hamamatsu*. For the readings of Chinese names written in *kana* and for corruptions or lacunae in the text I have generally followed the readings suggested in Matsuo's notes.

Acknowledgments

I WISH to express my thanks to a number of people for their encouragement, assistance, and understanding during the years I spent working on *Hamamatsu Chūnagon Monogatari*. Professor Akira Komai was my first teacher of both modern and classical Japanese, and my decision to enter Japanese studies was largely due to his inspiration and encouragement. I am indebted to Professor Inaga Keiji who introduced me to the Tale and offered patient instruction while I was at Hiroshima University as a Mombushō research student from 1974-75. My deepest thanks go to Professor James A. O'Brien, my dissertation adviser at the University of Wisconsin. His careful readings and thoughtful suggestions on my work in different stages of its development have been important to me both scholastically and personally. I would also like to thank Professors Marian Ury, Earl Miner, Masao Miyoshi, and an anonymous reader for the Princeton University Press for their suggestions and encouragement during the period I was revising the work for publication. All of the above gave helpful advice and I alone bear responsibility for any errors in the work. Finally, I wish to express my gratitude to my wife, Wakako, and our children, Nina and Mary, for their patience and understanding the many, many hours spent writing, revising, and preparing the manuscript for publication.

A TALE OF ELEVENTH-CENTURY JAPAN

Introduction

THE WORK, THE AUTHOR, THE DATES

THE BRILLIANCE of a masterpiece often serves to dim the pleasing but less arresting luster of subsequent works of the same genre; such is the fate of *Hamamatsu Chūnagon Monogatari*, which has historically suffered in comparison with *The Tale of Genji*. Although the exact date of completion of neither work is known, *Hamamatsu* was most likely written some time after the middle of the eleventh century, approximately twenty-five to fifty years after the completion of *Genji*. The influence of Murasaki Shikibu's masterpiece on subsequent *monogatari* was pervasive, for not only did *Genji* demonstrate possibilities of and set new standards for the genre, it also described characters, scenes, and realtionships that served as models for the author of *Hamamatsu* and many other post-*Genji* works.

But while *Hamamatsu* is heir to the legacy of *Genji*, there is no reason to expect it to measure up to the excellence of its illustrious predecessor. *Genji* is a work of supreme genius, one of those rare works that stands out so eminently in a literary tradition as to render any comparisons in terms of quality pointless. There was little in the *monogatari* tradition prior to *Genji* to anticipate its arrival, and, in the opinion of many, nothing in the history of all Japanese literature since then to equal it. Perhaps because *Hamamatsu* is of the same period, the same genre, and was produced, presumably, by the same court society as *Genji*, more than other works in different genres or later periods that also show obvious parallels to *Genji* without achieving its greatness *Hamamatsu* has borne the stigma of being labeled derivative and second-rate for failing to live up to the potential of the genre demonstrated in *Genji*. Unfortunately such a judgment obscures the intrinsic value of *Hamamatsu* as a work of literature and its importance as a source for studying the nature of *monogatari* literature. To judge *Hamamatsu* on its own merits is to afford it the attention befitting a secondary masterpiece of Heian literature. This will also enhance our understanding of the *monogatari* in general, for *Hamamatsu* and the other post-*Genji* tales—*Yowa no Nezame*,

3

Sagoromo Monogatari, Torikaebaya Monogatari and a host of *monogatari* no longer extant—represent the continued development of this genre in the history of Japanese literature. That *Genji* represents the *monogatari* genre at its best is indisputable, but it did not mark the end of the genre. If anything, the success of *Genji* stimulated the creation of many more works, and while the vast majority is no longer extant, those that do remain deserve our careful scrutiny.[1]

One measure of the esteem in which a work is held through succeeding generations is the care shown in the physical preservation and transmission of copies of the text, and on this count *Hamamatsu Chūnagon Monogatari* has not fared well. By the middle of the sixteenth century both the first and last chapters of the text had disappeared; two copies of the final chapter were rediscovered in the 1930s, but the first chapter remains lost. While the question of when and why these chapters disappeared is somewhat of a mystery, we do know that the ravages of the Ōnin War (1467-1477) and subsequent fighting during the *sengoku* (country-at-war) era left Kyoto in ruins. Virtually all the buildings from the Heian period were destroyed, and most of the fragile paper manuscripts undoubtedly went up in flames with the city. Although *Hamamatsu* is still missing part of its original text, its fate was more fortunate than most *monogatari*: of 198 *monogatari* mentioned in the *Fūyō Wakashū* (1271) only 24 are extant in some form today.[2]

The earliest mention of *Hamamatsu Chūnagon Monogatari* is found in *Genji Ippon Kyō*, compiled by a monk named Ankyoin

1. In the past ten years work has been done in English on the major post-*Genji* *monogatari*. See, for instance, Carol Hochstedler, *The Tale of Nezame: Part Three of Yowa no Nezame Monogatari*, Cornell University East Asia Papers, no. 22 (Ithaca: China-Japan Program, Cornell University, 1979); Kenneth L. Richard, "Developments in Late Heian Prose Fiction: *The Tale of Nezame*" (Ph.D. diss., University of Washington, 1973); Rosette Friedman Willig, "A Study and Translation of the 'Torikaebaya Monogatari' " (Ph.D. diss. University of Pennsylvania, 1978); Thomas H. Rohlich, "*Hamamatsu Chūnagon Monogatari*: An Introduction and Translation" (Ph.D. diss., University of Wisconsin, 1979).

2. The *Fūyō Wakashū* is a collection of poems taken exclusively from *monogatari*. It was compiled in 1271 by order of the Empress Mother Yoshiko, also known as Ōmiyain, Consort of the Emperor Gosaga. Although two of the original twenty chapters are no longer extant, 1,412 poems from 198 *monogatari* remain today. Ogi Takashi, "Monogatari," in *Shimpan Nihon Bungakushi: Chūsei*, ed. Hisamatsu Sen'ichi (Tokyo: Shibundō, 1971), pp. 111-12.

4

Chōken around 1166.[3] Written in Chinese in the form of a sutra, the *Genji Ippon Kyō* is meant as a prayer for the repose of the souls of Murasaki Shikibu and the readers of *The Tale of Genji*. They were presumed to be suffering in hell for having spent their idle hours with frivolous works of fiction. *Hamamatsu* is listed under its original title, *Mitsu no Hamamatsu*, along with eleven other *monogatari*. Nothing is said concerning the nature of *Hamamatsu*, and the mere mention of the work is important only in that it indicates *Hamamatsu* was written sometime before this date.

Hamamatsu was dealt with extensively and for the most part favorably in the *Mumyōzōshi*, an early Kamakura work devoted primarily to critical evaluation of characters, scenes, and poems of the major works of the *monogatari* genre. Although its author and exact date of completion are uncertain, the *Mumyōzōshi* was probably written sometime between 1196 and 1201, possibly by the adopted daughter (natural granddaughter) of Fujiwara Shunzei. Since some of the *Hamamatsu* poems quoted in the *Mumyōzōshi* are from both the initial and final chapters, it is probable that the work existed in its entirety at this time.[4]

Further data confirming the existence in the thirteenth century of the complete *Hamamatsu* are found in the *Shūi Hyakuban Utaawase* (also known as *Gohyakuban Utaawase*) and the *Fūyō Wakashū*.[5] The former is a mock poem-matching contest in which one hundred poems from *The Tale of Genji* are matched against one hundred poems from ten different *monogatari*. The *Shūi Hyakuban Utaawase* is actually the latter half of a two-hundred-poem *utaawase* known as *Teika Monogatari Nihyakuban Utaawase* compiled in 1219 or thereabouts by Fujiwara Teika (1162-1241). The first half of the *Nihyakuban Utaawase*, known as *Genji Sagoromo Utaawase*, matches one hundred poems from *Genji* against one hundred poems from *Sagoromo Monogatari*. Of the one hundred poems matched

3. Abe Akio; Oka Kazuo; and Yamagishi Tokuhei, eds., *Kokugo Kokubungaku Kenkyūshi Taisei* 3, *Genji Monogatari Jo* (Tokyo: Sanseidō, 1960), pp. 37 and 421.
4. The *Mumyōzōshi* comments on *Hamamatsu* are dealt with in more detail on pp. 12-23.
5. The entire text of the *Shūi Hyakuban Utaawase* can be found in Hanawa Hokinoichi, *Gunsho Ruijū*, Volume 11 (Tokyo: Keizai Zasshisha, 1906), pp. 278-98. The *Fūyō Wakashū* is in Nakano Sōji, *Kōhon Fūyō Wakashū* (Kyoto: Yūzan Bunko, 1970).

against the Genji poems in the Shūi Hyakuban Utaawase, fifteen are from Hamamatsu, the second most frequent source after Yowa no Nezame, which provided twenty poems. Fifteen poems were also selected from Mikawa ni Sakeru, but it and the seven other monogatari cited in the Shūi Hyakuban Utaawase are no longer extant. Of the fifteen Hamamatsu poems, two are from the missing first chapter.[6]

Fujiwara Teika was perhaps the most eminent scholar of monogatari prior to the Edo period, and the inclusion of so many Hamamatsu poems in an utaawase he himself compiled is indicative of the esteem afforded this work in the Kamakura era. If the order of presentation (as in the Mumyōzōshi) and the number of poems chosen (as in the Shūi Hyakuban Utaawase) is any indication of the reputation of a work—and it probably is—then Hamamatsu would appear to rank right after Genji, Sagoromo, and Nezame.

As to the Fūyō Wakashū, twenty-nine Hamamatsu poems are found in it, five of which are from the missing first chapter and two from the last chapter. Inclusion of these poems would seem to indicate that the first and last chapters were extant in the late thirteenth century.

From that point on, however, the fate of Hamamatsu is sketchy and difficult to follow. The only solid evidence of its existence is found in a few commentaries on Genji which refer to Hamamatsu only incidentally. In the Kakaishō of Yotsutsuji Yoshinari, written around 1367, there is a commentary on the technique of describing in two separate chapters events that happen at approximately the same time (nami itchō, "concurrent chapters"). The commentary concerns the "Utsusemi" chapter of Genji which takes place at the same time as the first part of the following chapter, "Yūgao." Hamamatsu is mentioned as follows: "There is a concurrent chapter in a work called Hamamatsu Monogatari. . . . In the Hamamatsu sequence, events which occur at the same time in China and Japan are written about sequentially. These events are parallel."[7]

6. A summary of the content of the first chapter and translations of the extant poems from this chapter are found on pp. 48-51.
7. Quoted in Matsuo, Hamamatsu, p. 144. Some scholars have interpreted these comments as indicating that there are actually two chapters missing from the beginning of Hamamatsu, but most of the evidence argues against this theory.

Although the *Kakaishō* note is the last solid evidence pointing to the existence of the first chapter, the final chapter may have been in general circulation among scholars in the fifteenth and possibly the sixteenth century. Once again the evidence comes from commentaries to *Genji*. In the *Rōkashō*, compiled in 1476 by the *renga* poet Shōhaku, passing mention is made of the abduction scene which occurs in the final chapter of *Hamamatsu*.[8] A similar note is found in an early sixteenth-century commentary, the *Sairyūshō*.

It is clear that over one hundred years later in the early Edo period the final chapter was not in general circulation among scholars of the classics. A *Genji* commentary known as the *Kogetsushō* notes that the *Hamamatsu Chūnagon Monogatari* mentioned in the *Rōkashō* and *Sairyūshō* was not to be found in the present day, i.e., the last half of the seventeenth century when the *Kogetsushō* was compiled.[9]

Although there are over thirty hand-copied manuscripts and one printed version of *Hamamatsu* dating from the Edo period, the work seems to have been largely ignored by scholars and the reading public.[10] With the discovery of two versions of Chapter Five in the 1930s, *Hamamatsu* once again became a significant object of study for Japanese scholars of Heian literature. It is a mystery as to why only two manuscripts contain the final chapter and why the existence of these copies was unknown for so long. In both cases the final chapter was apparently copied from a different manuscript from the

---

8. The pertinent *Rōkashō* comments are quoted in Komatsu Shigemi, "Kaisetsu," *Kōhon Hamamatsu Chūnagon Monogatari* (Tokyo: Nigensha, 1964), p. 24. It should be noted that the *Rōkashō* commentary erroneously implies that *Hamamatsu* predated *Genji*. The commentaries of the late Muromachi age were often based on oral transmission, and the fact that such an obvious error could be made suggests that the commentator himself might not have had access to the *Hamamatsu* text.

9. The *Kogetsushō* is a collection of earlier commentaries compiled by Kitamura Kigen ca. 1673. For the quote concerning *Hamamatsu* see Matsuo, "Kaisetsu," *Hamamatsu*, p. 125.

10. Scholars of *Hamamatsu Chūnagon Monogatari* generally divide the manuscripts qualitatively into six groups. Not a single text predates the Keichō (1596-1615) era, and most date from the end of the seventeenth century or later. All of the manuscripts apparently stem from a single source since they each have seven separate blank spots occurring in the same location within a few brief pages of the first chapter. For more detailed information on the quality of the manuscripts see Matsuo, "Kaisetsu," *Hamamatsu*, pp. 136-39; Komatsu, "Kaisetsu II," *Kōhon Hamamatsu*, pp. 34-60.

one used for the other four chapters. In one case the copier of Chapter Five was a different person from the copier of the first four chapters. [11] We can only assume that somehow or other a copy of the chapter was discovered and added to the four-chapter text already in the possession of the person who made the copy.

The inclusion of *Hamamatsu Chūnagon Monogatari* in the Iwanami Koten Bungaku Taikei Series (1964) made a well-annotated text available to scholars and the general public. Two other works have greatly enhanced the scholarly study of this long-neglected tale: Komatsu Shigemi's collated text, *Kōhon Hamamatsu Chūnagon Monogatari* (1964), and Ikeda Toshio's general index of words, *Hamamatsu Chūnagon Monogatari Sōsakuin* (1964).

It is difficult to determine the authorship of many Heian *monogatari*, and *Hamamatsu Chūnagon Monogatari* is no exception. Traditionally it has been attributed to the daughter of Sugawara no Takasue, the author of *Sarashina Nikki*. [12] The earliest evidence supporting this attribution is the following colophon found in *Gyōbutsubon Sarashina Nikki* (*Imperial Book, The Sarashina Diary*):

Diary of the daughter of Sugawara no Takasue, Governor of Hitachi. Her mother was the daughter of Lord Tomoyasu, she was the niece of the mother of Fu no Tono. People say *Yowa no Nezame, Mitsu no Hamamatsu, Mizukara Kuyuru,* and *Asakura* were written by the author of this diary. [13]

Mitsu no Hamamatsu is one of several traditional titles for *Hamamatsu Chūnagon Monogatari*. Even though the copy of *Sarashina Nikki* which contains this colophon was transcribed by the eminent scholar Fujiwara Teika, there are good reasons to doubt the accuracy of this attribution. The grammar of the colophon itself raises some doubts. It ends with the particles *to zo*, which indicate that a subsequent verb of saying or thinking has been omitted, the import being that what is recorded is not to be taken as a statement

---

11. Komatsu, "Kaisetsu II," *Kōhon Hamamatsu*, pp. 45 and 47.

12. English translation by Ivan Morris, *As I Crossed a Bridge of Dreams* (New York: The Dial Press, 1971).

13. Suzuki Tomotarō et al., eds. *Tosa Nikki, Kagerō Nikki, Izumi Shikibu Nikki, Sarashina Nikki,* Nihon Koten Bungaku Taikei, no. 20 (Tokyo: Iwanami Shoten, 1957), p. 535. "Fu no tono" is a title, "Lord Guardian of the Crown Prince." Here it refers to Fujiwara no Michitsuna. His mother (aunt of Takasue's daughter) wrote *Kagerō Nikki,* Edward G. Seidensticker, trans., *The Gossamer Years* (Tokyo and Rutland, Vt.: Charles E. Tuttle Co., 1964).

of fact but rather as something "people say." The fact that the colophon was copied by Teika lends a sense of weighty authority to the content, and one leading scholar of *Hamamatsu*, Matsuo Satoshi, contends that even if Teika was not vouching for the accuracy of this colophon, the absence of any positive expression of doubt by Teika indicates that the attribution to Takasue's daughter of the four works mentioned therein was generally accepted as true in the early Kamakura period (thirteenth century). [14]

An equally acceptable interpretation, however, is that Teika was simply recording what was written in the text he was copying. [15] Most of the colophons which are taken to be Teika's personal opinion on the work he was copying (such as those found in *Tosa Nikki*, *Ise Monogatari*, and *Kokinshū* manuscripts) were written in *kambun*, while the one cited above was written in *kana*. Since *Sarashina Nikki* has a *kambun* colophon following this one in *kana*, it is reasonable to assume that the one written in *kana* is copied from another text and not Teika's own studied opinion.

While the colophon itself cannot be taken as proof that Takasue's daughter wrote *Hamamatsu* and the other works mentioned therein, it has led scholars to examine these works carefully in hopes of finding similarities in terms of style, content, and conception that might indicate they are the work of a single author. [16] There is, of course, no argument about her authorship of *Sarashina Nikki*: the question is whether or not she wrote the other works mentioned in the colophon. Of the four, *Mizukara Kuyuru* and *Asakura* are no longer extant, and the copies of *Hamamatsu* and *Yowa no Nezame* that have survived to the present are not complete.

There are a number of interesting similarities in *Hamamatsu* and *Sarashina Nikki*. For instance, the relatively large number of dreams in both *Sarashina Nikki* (eleven) and *Hamamatsu* (eleven in the extant text), the peculiar treatment afforded these dreams, and their importance to the narrative of both works are salient features distin-

14. Matsuo, *Hamamatsu*, p. 129.

15. This argument was made by Inaga Keiji in "Keishikiteki Shori ni yoru Hitotsu no Baai—*Nezame, Hamamatsu* ni Kanshite—," *Kokugo to Kokubungaku* (December 1950), pp. 38-40.

16. A useful summary of the arguments favoring Takasue's daughter as author of both *Hamamatsu* and *Sarashina Nikki* is found in Matsuo, *Hamamatsu*, pp. 125-34.

guishing these two works from other Heian works of prose.[17] Dreams are not, of course, unheard of in other Heian works, but the actual descriptions of the dreams are more vivid and their importance to the plot more pronounced in these two works than in other Heian *monogatari*. The author(s) of these two works obviously puts a great deal of faith in the significance of dreams.

Further arguments supporting the single author theory are as follows: the relative lack of sophisticated humor in both works;[18] the obvious importance of *The Tale of Genji* to the author of both works; the acceptance of reincarnation as a demonstrable fact of life in both works; the unusual sentimental attachment to one's father depicted in both works; and finally, the use of similar phrases and allusions in both. While all of the above parallels do, in fact, exist in both works, they are not necessarily peculiar to these works, and it would seem a bit hasty to conclude that they are the creation of one person based solely on these similarities.

While the presence of similar allusions in *Hamamatsu* and *Sarashina Nikki* has been cited as support for the single-author theory,[19] a strong argument against this theory has been made by Inaga Keiji based on a single poetic allusion found in *Hamamatsu*.[20] Inaga argues convincingly that the presence of an allusion to a poem by Suō no Naishi would most likely place the dating of *Hamamatsu* in a period in which Takasue's daughter was no longer writing *monogatari*, and was possibly no longer even alive.[21] In any case, the arguments supporting the traditional attribution of *Hamamatsu Chūnagon Monogatari* to the daughter of Sugawara no Takasue are not without their shortcomings, and the best we can do at this point is to say that while the traditional attribution remains a possibility, it is far from a certainty. For formal purposes we should perhaps

17. The use of dreams in *Hamamatsu* is discussed in more detail on pp. 34-47.

18. See Matsuo Satoshi, "Sarashina, Hamamatsu, Nezame ni egakareta Kashōmi ni tsuite," *Kokugo to Kokubungaku* (August 1935); reprinted in Matsuo Satoshi, *Heian Jidai Monogatari Ronkō* (Tokyo: Kasama Shoin, 1968), pp. 399-430.

19. See, for instance, Masabuchi Tsunekichi, *Monogatari Shōsetsuhen Jo*, Nihon Bungaku Kōza, No. 3 (Tokyo: Kaizōsha, 1934), pp. 202-224.

20. Inaga Keiji, "Suō no Naishi Denkō, Tsuku: *Hamamatsu Chūnagon Monogatari* Makkan no Hikiuta to no Kankei," *Kokugo to Kokubungaku* (August 1954), pp. 17-26.

21. For a more detailed discussion in English of the argument see Rohlich, "Hamamatsu," pp. 21-24.

accept the usual attribution of this work to Takasue's daughter. However, the whole notion of authorship of such works is perhaps anachronistic and misleading since we have little knowledge as to whether the works as we know them today are largely the unaltered creation of one person or, for that matter, whether the idea of personal creation and authorship was at all significant. The "problem" of authorship may well be a conceptual one of our own creation.

Dating the completion of *Hamamatsu* is a question closely related to that of authorship. If we accept the proposition that it was written after the composition of Suō no Naishi's poem (ca. 1064), and that it was written by Takasue's daughter (b. 1008), then it was probably finished some time shortly after 1067, allowing three years for Suō no Naishi's poem to circulate and become sufficiently known for Takasue's daughter to allude to it meaningfully.[22] Assuming that Takasue's daughter even lived so long (the last datable entry of *Sarashina Nikki* is in 1059), it seems unlikely that Takasue's daughter would write a work such as *Hamamatsu* much past the age of seventy. In fact, one of the entries in *Sarashina Nikki* suggests that she was ready to abandon such interests altogether. Shortly after her husband's funeral (1058) she laments the time wasted on frivolous pursuits: "If only I had not given myself over to Tales and poems since my young days but had spent my time in religious devotion, I should have been spared this misery."[23] Assuming Takasue's daughter wrote *Hamamatsu* some time after the composition of Suō no Naishi's poem, it would probably be safe to say the work was completed some time in the late 1060s or early 1070s.

If Takasue's daughter is not assumed to be the author, then it is quite possible the work was written even later in the eleventh century. An attempt to date post-*Genji monogatari* based on linguisitic evidence—specifically the use of the auxiliary verb *saburau*—implies that *Hamamatsu* may have been written in the last quarter of the eleventh century or the first decade of the twelfth century.[24] As was

---

22. Given the margin for error in Inaga's calculation of Suō no Naishi's dates, it is possible her poem was written as much as five years earlier than 1064. Matsuo, "*Hamamatsu Chūnagon Monogatari, Yoru no Nezame,*" in *Shimpan Nihon Bungakushi: Chūko,* ed. Hisamatsu Sen'ichi (Tokyo: Shibundō, 1971), pp. 585-86.

23. Morris, *As I Crossed a Bridge of Dreams,* p. 119.

24. Sakakura Atsuyoshi, "*Yoru no Nezame* no Bunshō," *Kokugo to Kokubungaku* (October 1964), pp. 144-56. Although the focus of this work is *Yoru no Nezame,* the

stated earlier, the listing of *Hamamatsu* in *Genji Ippon Kyō* (1166) is the first mention of *Hamamatsu* in an unrelated work. Some scholars who are not persuaded by Inaga's dating based on the allusion to Suō no Naishi's poem argue that *Hamamatsu* was written when Takasue's daughter was still relatively young.[25] Their arguments are largely impressionistic in nature, and different scholars use the same evidence to reach opposite conclusions.

It is probably impossible to date exactly the completion of *Hamamatsu Chūnagon Monogatari*. The best evidence seems to point to the decades of the 1060s and 1070s, but even this tentative conclusion would be contested by many knowledgeable scholars of late Heian *monogatari*.

HAMAMATSU CHŪNAGON MONOGATARI IN THE MUMYŌZŌSHI

Since the modern reader's approach to *monogatari* literature in general and *Hamamatsu Chūnagon Monogatari* in particular inevitably differs considerably from that of the contemporary reader, our understanding as to what are the important aspects of the *monogatari* genre and how *Hamamatsu* manifests these aspects will be enhanced if we familiarize ourselves with some ways an earlier audience viewed this work. Examination of early criticism of a text, even if that criticism is no more than a listing of likes and dislikes based on the ability of the text to fulfill certain expectations, is one way of discovering what was implicitly understood by the audience to constitute the important elements of a genre. To this end the *Mumyōzōshi* ("Untitled Book"), an early Kamakura work devoted primarily to criticism of works of the *monogatari* genre, is a valuable source. It was written approximately a hundred and fifty years after the com-

---

tentative dating of *Hamamatsu* is a logical conclusion of the evidence he presents. For a more detailed discussion in English of Sakakura's evidence, see Rohlich, "Hamamatsu," pp. 38-42.

25. Summary and analysis of a number of arguments concerning the dating of *Hamamatsu* in relation to *Nezame* can be found in Suzuki Hiromichi, "Yowa no Nezame, Hamamatsu Chūnagon Monogatari no Seiritsu Junjō," *Ronkyū Nihon Bungaku* (June 1945); reprinted in *Heian Makki Monogatari ni tsuite no Kenkyū* (Kyoto: Akao Shōbundō, 1971), pp. 171-244. For a summary in English, see Rohlich, "Hamamatsu," pp. 28-38.

pletion of *Hamamatsu* and contains revealing comments on it and other *monogatari*. Although the author and exact date of completion are uncertain, the *Mumyōzōshi* was probably written some time between 1196 and 1201, possibly by the granddaughter of Fujiwara Shunzei. Written in the same classical language as the Heian *monogatari*, it was obviously a product of the same aristocratic society that created and enjoyed the *monogatari* genre.

The *Mumyōzōshi* is told in the form of a conversation between an eighty-three-year-old nun and a number of young ladies she meets while looking for a place to rest after picking flowers for the Buddha. The ladies first discuss cherished things of this world: the moon, letters, dreams, tears, the Nembutsu, and the Lotus Sutra. This section is followed by discussion on *monogatari*, almost half of which is devoted to outstanding chapters, characters, and scenes from *The Tale of Genji*. The *monogatari* section is followed by a perfunctory analysis of Imperial and private poetry anthologies and finally by brief descriptions of famous female poets and writers.

In discussing *monogatari* the author of the *Mumyōzōshi* apparently took the best (*Genji*) first, and the rest in their order of importance or preference. Of the twenty-eight *monogatari* mentioned, *Hamamatsu* is dealt with fourth, after *Genji Monogatari*, *Sagoromo Monogatari*, and *Yowa no Nezame*. Following is a translation of the entire *Mumyōzōshi* section devoted to *Hamamatsu*:[26]

And then [one of the ladies said]:

"Mitsu no Hamamatsu is not as highly regarded as Nezame or Sagoromo, but the style and descriptions are outstanding and the entire work is quite moving and impressive. It is the kind of work one would think to emulate in writing a *monogatari*. All told, the depiction of events is unusual, the poems are well done, and the characterization of Chūnagon, his sensibilities, demeanor, and such, is as one would want it to be. How splendid that he seems so much like Captain Kaoru.

"On the morning after having a dream in which he learns that his father is reborn as a Prince in China, Chūnagon is visited by Saishō no Chūjō who recites this poem:

> Surely she did not expect
> To spend the night alone,

26. The translation is based on the text found in Tomikura Tokujirō, *Mumyōzōshi Hyōkai* (Tokyo: Yūseidō, 1954), pp. 189-210.

But now the unexpected sound of waves
Echoes at her bed.

The events beginning with this scene until Chūnagon leaves for China are particularly impressive.

"At the banquet in China on the fifteenth day of the eighth month when the Emperor tells Chūnagon that he will have the Hoyang Consort play the *kin* for them, without replying Chūnagon smartly adjusts his robes, taps his baton and fan together, and begins to sing 'How Grand the Day.' As the Emperor watches the Consort and Chūnagon together he thinks, 'The Consort is the most beautiful woman in our land, and Chūnagon seems to be a superior gentleman of Japan. How magnificent it is to gaze at them and feel as though I am watching sunlight and moonlight joined together.' Indeed, this sequence of events is truly magnificent.

"The incident with Wu Chün, daughter of the Prime Minister, is a very hasty affair. She does not seem so attractive when she rises to look at him from her sickbed, jewels sparkling in her hair while she toys with her fan. But when Chūnagon is about to return to Japan she laments his departure with this poem:

Though every night I watch the moon
And think it a reminder of you,
How could only half a moon
Satisfy my longing?

This scene is particularly moving.

"Chūnagon sends a poem to Wu Chün from Tsukushi:

How sad indeed!
When will we meet again
To watch the early morning moon?

It is very moving just to imagine Wu Chün's feelings on receiving this poem. Indeed, a profoundly impressive scene is the final one in which Wu Chün cuts her hair, dyes her robes, and goes into hiding deep in the mountains with this poem:

I long for one not in this land;
What good is a jeweled crown to me?

"Although Taishō no Kimi's behavior was neither dignified nor thoughtful, it is very moving and quite sad when she cuts that beautiful hair of hers and recites these poems:

What am I to do,
What can I do?
To renounce the world grieving
Would be sad;
But to stay on is also regretful!

14

My parents' loving care
Was not for this:
How wearisome the short clipped ends
Of my black hair.

"Daini's daughter is somehow a pitifully touching character. She recites her poem 'The wind that turns the ivy leaves' and later this poem:

I did not forget our vow,
But what now can be done?
If only the past were retrievable . . .

When told by Chūnagon that he would like to take her and hide away she nods gently in assent. When it comes to young women of not much depth, a woman like this is quite attractive.

"Yoshinohime is also quite a pitiful character. It is astonishing yet pathetic when after being kidnapped by the Prince Shikibukyō she says, 'Please inform Chūnagon.' It is also pitiful when she recites this poem:

I lost the strength
To cross the mountain of death
While waiting when
You could not find me;
Now I have returned."

Another lady replied,

"It really is a wonderful tale in which everything happens as we would expect it to, but still, there are some parts where I think, 'If only this were not included. . . .' The section in which Chūnagon is told that his father, Prince Shikibukyō,[27] has been reborn in China, and when he sees his father in a dream and then travels to China is splendid. But this Prince's mother is the Hoyang Consort of the Emperor of China, even though her mother is Japanese and she has a younger sister living in Yoshino. This jumbling of China and Japan into one is too unrealistic. And even though the treatment of Chūnagon as a serious, responsible person is very impressive, we are quite disappointed that he never really takes a proper wife but ends up spending each night sleeping alone wherever he may be. The section in which he hears a voice telling him of the Consort's eventual rebirth as the Yoshino maiden's child is nonsensical. Unfortunately we cannot help but think to ourselves that life in Trāyastriṃśa is said to last so very long, how could something like this happen so quickly? We never pay much attention

27. "Shikibukyō" means "Minister of Ceremonies," the position Chūnagon's father apparently held when he was alive in Japan. He should not be confused with another character known as "Shikibukyō no Miya" (Prince Shikibukyō in the translation) who plays an important role in the last two chapters of the story.

to a work which is not any good to begin with, but because this is such a fine work we occasionally think of these minor flaws."

Hamamatsu Chūnagon Monogatari is mentioned once more in the *Mumyōzōshi* after the ladies discuss three stories (*Komamukae, Otaenonuma,* and *Hatsuyuki*) which were closer to the time of the *Mumyōzōshi* than to *Hamamatsu* but are now no longer extant. "An extraordinary number of works have appeared in recent years, and while some seem to have more impressive style and descriptions than the older stories, I have found none as fine as *Nezame, Sagoromo,* and *Hamamatsu.*"

The *Mumyōzōshi*'s evaluation of *Hamamatsu Chūnagon Monogatari* is brief and simple, but it does reveal some interesting ways in which a *monogatari* was viewed by its audience. It is indicative of the reader's interest in the language and mode of expression found in a *monogatari* that the criticism should begin with comments on style (*kotobazukai,* "usage of words"), descriptions (*arisama*), depiction of events (*koto no omomuki,* suggesting the tenor or purport of things), and poems. After this the *Mumyōzōshi* notes reassuringly that Chūnagon, the hero, is a man much like Kaoru in *The Tale of Genji,* a handsome gentleman sensitive to and ever solicitous of the needs of the women with whom he becomes involved. The hero of a *monogatari* is expected to manifest the Heian ideals of physical and spiritual beauty in the mold of the *Genji* heroes.

From these initial comments on the general impression of the work as a whole, the *Mumyōzōshi* criticism moves directly to particular characters and scenes, classifying each example cited in terms that are a familiar and important part of the *monogatari* lexicon: *imiji* (impressive), *medetashi* (magnificent, splendid), *aware* (sad and moving), *itōshi* (pitiful). The characters and scenes cited by the *Mumyōzōshi* are stereotypes or highly stylized variations of familiar *monogatari* patterns, and it is no wonder that the well-known descriptive words of *monogatari* fiction—*aware, medetashi, itōshi, imiji*—seem to come so naturally in describing them. There are certain unique or at least unusual aspects of *Hamamatsu Chūnagon Monogatari* that set it apart from other *monogatari,* but in the *Mumyōzōshi* criticism it is the presentation of the familiar, well-known patterns that is implicitly praised. To the contemporary reader surely part of the charm of *Hamamatsu* is that many of its character types and plot segments were easily recognizable as falling within the stereotypical patterns of the genre. This is particularly important in Chapter One where the setting is China. The potential strangeness of the locale is fully neutralized by the fact that the characters and scenes are not only very Japanese but very much in accordance with familiar *monogatari* patterns.

In most instances the *Mumyōzōshi* also quotes a poem. This is in recognition of the fact that in a *monogatari* a poem will often serve to capture the mood of the scene or character being described. As in real court society, poems in a story sometimes are used simply as a means of communication, but their role is not limited to this alone. In addition to expressing the immediate sentiments of a character, many of the poems in the narrative highlight a scene by representing the essence of the emotional tenor of that scene. And while poems serve on occasion to supplement the prose in a summarizing or concentrating manner, there are also instances where the opposite seems to be the case, where the only explanation for the presence of a particular scene is that it leads up to, gives context to, a poem which the author wished to include in the narrative. This would be the case in Chapter One (pp. 73-74) where one moonlit night the hero comes upon an old Chinese gentleman and a child by a pond. The scene as described in *Hamamatsu* seems very much like a Chinese brush painting and has little significance other than to provide a context for the exchange of poems that follows. Such scenes of gratuitous beauty, not uncommon in a *monogatari*, are perhaps vestiges of the *uta monogatari* (poem-tales), progenitors of the *tsukuri-monogatari* (fictional tales), works in which the prose is clearly created specifically to give a context to a collection of poems.

The first sequence of events described in the *Mumyōzōshi*, that leading up to Chūnagon's departure for China, comes from the missing chapter, and it is consequently difficult to determine precisely why this sequence was singled out as being so "impressive" (*imiji*). Without any further context the poem cited is ambiguous, although it probably refers to Taishō no Kimi's reaction to news that Chūnagon will be making a voyage to China. Why, we might ask, is this series of events labeled *imiji*? One is tempted to speculate that the way in which Chūnagon learns for certain of his father's rebirth in China, i.e., via a dream, and the implications of that message, i.e., that his father has in fact been reborn to a new life, represent an unusually exciting beginning for a *monogatari*. The validity of dreams and the concept of reincarnation were tenets of Heian belief, and their combined use as a starting point for the story is skillful and impressive. However, quite possibly the *Mumyōzōshi* is simply praising well-crafted scenes in which Chūnagon seduces Taishō no Kimi against their better judgment, and the scenes in which he bids farewell to his mother and Taishō no Kimi. Each of these scenes would be dealing with a familiar *monogatari* motif— a dream, a seduction, a parting—and the drawing of them in the accepted pattern of other *monogatari* would undoubtedly please the reader.

The next scene singled out by the *Mumyōzōshi* is the banquet held shortly before Chūnagon returns to Japan. Here the use of the word *medetaku* to modify *imiji* indicates that the *Mumyōzōshi* views this scene as "magnificent." Presumably the description of these two paragons of beauty, Chūnagon, the superior gentleman of Japan, and the Consort, the most beautiful lady in China, in the setting of a formal banquet the night of the full moon was taken as a picture of ideal human beauty in an ideal natural setting. The reader undoubtedly cherished such scenes, and no matter what emotional doubts or disappointments the characters might be facing, and there are many in this scene, in the mind of the reader the sheer beauty of the setting is captivating.

After these descriptions of scenes that delight the reader, the *Mumyōzōshi* quotes particular scenes and characters that move the reader in a sad and poignant way, the key word here being *aware*. *Aware* is used to describe something that deeply moves the emotions, usually something that is beautiful yet somehow sorrowful. In the scene mentioned by the *Mumyōzōshi* the emphasis is on sorrow, although we should remember that the beauty of the characters both physically and spiritually is taken for granted by the reader.

The scene in which Wu Chün laments Chūnagon's return to Japan is moving (*aware*) because both the characters and the reader know that the two can never meet again, and only the half moon will remain as a symbol of Wu Chün's unsatisfied longing. And, according to the *Mumyōzōshi*, the reader is moved when imagining how Wu Chün must have felt when she received Chūnagon's poem regretting their separation. Regret over what might have been but ultimately cannot be is a significant theme in *Hamamatsu Chūnagon Monogatari*, for the characters, particularly Chūnagon and the women he is closest to, continually find their initial hopes and expectations turning to disappointing failures.

The cutting of one's hair, symbolic of a renunciation of the secular world and entrance into the religious life, is a sad and moving event, particularly when the act is performed by someone as young and full of promise as Taishō no Kimi. It was *de rigueur* to speak wistfully of a desire to put aside the worries of mundane affairs, but actually following through on the wish to renounce the world was considered unfortunate, even unseemly, in one so young. The *Mumyōzōshi* is careful to point out that Taishō no Kimi's behavior is a bit too rash. Although here again the poems quoted by the *Mumyōzōshi* are from the missing chapter, in this case the context is quite clear. She has become pregnant with Chūnagon's child and is in a state of depression. In addition to the regrets she feels for her own mistakes, she is ashamed that she has disappointed her father. He had hoped to marry her to Prince Shikibukyō, a promising young man destined to become the heir apparent. For the reader, the picture of a beautiful young lady suffering such bitter sorrow is, of course, quite sad and moving.

Daini's daughter is also described as *aware*, but this time the word is modified by *itōshiku*, which lends a sense of pity to the sorrow. Chūnagon once promised to claim her for his own, but her mother foolishly rushed her into marriage with Chūnagon's uncle, Emon no Kami. She is an attractive young lady (*rōtaki*, which describes a sort of vulnerable loveliness, is used by the *Mumyōzōshi*) who is victimized by her mother's hasty ambitions, and it is easy to see why a reader is moved to sorrow by her disappointing predicament.

Itōshi is the only word used to describe Yoshinohime. Although this word generally means "pitiful," it can also have the connotation of charm in the sense that a person who is weak and helpless elicits one's sympathy and is thus attractive. Yoshinohime fits both the "pitiful" and "charming" sense of the word *itōshi*. Physically she is attractive, but she has been raised in the country and is completely innocent of the ways of the world. It is precisely this frail and innocent

19

beauty that the Heian reader found so attractive, and the scenes cited by the *Mumyōzōshi* are Yoshinohime at her weakest.

Up to this point in the *Mumyōzōshi* criticism the pattern of analysis has been to associate with the female characters discussed one or two familiar descriptive words: for Wu Chün and Taishō no Kimi it is *aware*, for Daini's daughter *aware* and *rōtashi*, and for Yoshinohime it is *itōshi*. *Hamamatsu* is implicitly praised for its success in depicting characters and scenes in such a manner that they are easily recognized and can be summarily identified and categorized by the above words. After this brief inventory of praiseworthy scenes and characters, however, *Hamamatsu* comes in for direct and rather unfavorable criticism. To begin with, the *Mumyōzōshi* cites two instances in which the *Hamamatsu* story is simply too "unrealistic" (*makoto shikarazu/-nu*). Unfortunately the meaning of "unrealistic" as used in the *Mumyōzōshi* is not clearly defined by the examples cited. Its meaning is apparently quite different from any western sense of literary realism in a mimetic mode, and seems rather to exhibit a concern for the presentation of events that are verifiable either by the experience of the reader or by his or her knowledge of truths based on firm religious beliefs. It would also seem that events in a story should be true to what the reader feels is desirable in or appropriate to a tale.

The first weakness cited by the *Mumyōzōshi*, the intermingling of China and Japan in the person of the Consort, is labeled as "unrealistic," although a more specific reason as to why this is unacceptable is not stated. What seems to be most objectionable is that this woman of mixed blood is able to rise to such a lofty position in the Chinese court. Surely the reader could never imagine such a thing happening in Japan. It should be noted, however, that as far as consistency with earlier *monogatari* themes is concerned, the prototype for the Cinderella-like rise of a woman from humble origins to the role of favorite of the Emperor is found in the *Taketori Monogatari*, a work generally considered to be the progenitor of all tales. The *Mumyōzōshi* objection does not appear to be to the fact that the Consort and her ladies are so Japanese in the way they look and behave, nor for that matter to the fact that so many Chinese speak Japanese, create Japanese poetry, and behave in a courtly Japanese manner—failure to accept these fictions would make the story impossible—rather, the objection is to the fact that this one person is the Consort to the Emperor of China even though her mother and sister live in Japan. According to the *Mumyōzōshi* this mingling of China and Japan into one is "unrealistic." She is one of the leading women in China, her son will become the heir apparent to the throne, but it is her Japanese qualities that attract Chūnagon, and it is her Japanese family, particularly her half sister Yoshinohime, that becomes the important focus of the story once Chūnagon returns to Japan.

It is not clear whether the *Mumyōzōshi's* objection to the Consort's background and position is based on the fact that such a combination is unlikely or simply undesirable. In terms of the construction of the story, the criticism seems inappropriate, for the first chapter is really integrated into the rest of the story based on the very fact that the Consort is half Japanese and half Chinese. Nor is it unreasonable that the mother of the Third Prince of China have some connection with Japan, for in his previous life the Prince was Japanese. Because she and her ladies are so Japanese in their ways Chūnagon feels nostalgic attachment to them whenever he is homesick. Her longing for her mother and sister in Japan and her son's former relationship with Chūnagon in Japan draw her to Chūnagon, and her relatives in Japan eventually become the means by which she will return to him. It would be difficult to imagine how the characters in China and Japan could be tied so closely together were it not for the Consort's unusual background. So even though the intermingling of China and Japan into one is objectionable to the *Mumyōzōshi's* author, it is in fact an important element in unifying the story.

The *Mumyōzōshi* also labels as "unrealistic" (*makoto shikaranu*) the scene in which Chūnagon hears a voice from the sky telling him that the Consort has been reborn in the Trāyastriṃśa heaven. This is immediately followed with the labeling as "nonsensical" (*midarigawashiku*) of the dream in which Chūnagon is told of the Consort's rebirth as Yoshinohime's child. The objection to this is spelled out immediately: everyone knows life in Trāyastriṃśa lasts a very long time, so how could she be reborn as a human so soon? It seems that the objection to the voice from heaven is not so much the content of the message as the manner in which it is conveyed, while the objection to the dream message is just the opposite: it is the content of the message, not the manner in which it is conveyed, that is ridiculous. Perhaps because a voice from heaven was clearly something fantastical, beyond experience or belief, it is objected to as a means of learning something important, whereas a dream, which is clearly within the realm of experience or credulity, is not objected to. But even if dreams are possible and the message contained therein often true, a message that directly contradicts a tenet of faith (life in the Trāyastriṃśa heaven lasts 1,000 years) cannot be accepted.

The objections raised to *Hamamatsu* as "unrealistic" by the *Mumyōzōshi* are, then, to specific facts or situations which contradict the better judgment of the reader. The reader must have accepted certain fictions as essential to the creation of a story—no one, after all, would believe these events actually occurred—but within that fiction certain facts known to be true to the reader must not be distorted or changed.

In addition to the objections to these "unrealistic" elements in *Hamamatsu*, the *Mumyōzōshi* is also critical of the failure of Chūnagon to take a proper wife. While the modern reader might appreciate this as being consistent with the dilemma of Chūnagon's relationships with the women in the story, the contemporary reader views his failure to marry as inappropriate and undesirable. The hero's disappointments become the reader's own, and the failure of the story to end "happily," or at least with some sort of consolation for the hero, is viewed as unfortunate. The tendency to wish for some sort of happy ending, perhaps along the lines of earlier romances, is present, even though consistency with the general themes of the story throughout would argue against such a facile ending. According to the *Mumyōzōshi* the women in *Hamamatsu* were successfully described in the familiar terms of typical *monogatari* heroines, but Chūnagon's failure to have a normal relationship with a woman is inappropriate for the typical *monogatari* hero. In this respect he resembles the ineffectual Kaoru rather than the quintessential lover-husband Genji.

The *Mumyōzōshi* criticism has indicated a number of pleasing aspects of *Hamamatsu Chūnagon Monogatari* and also pointed to some of the shortcomings of the story. By way of supplementing the criticism of the *Mumyōzōshi* it is worth noting the schematic way in which *Hamamatsu* deals with familiar *monogatari* themes, for in the eyes of the contemporary reader the treatment of the traditional *monogatari* subjects and themes was surely a measure of the work's success.

Since the initial chapter of this work is missing, it is impossible to tell if it opened with a formulaic beginning as is found in most tales. Like *The Tale of Genji*, which begins with the words *izure no ōntoki ni ka* ("In the reign of which Emperor was it?"), *Hamamatsu* was also probably placed rather vaguely in a not too distant past, perhaps a generation or two before the era in which it was written. Undoubtedly the first few lines or pages of the work gave genealogical information concerning the major characters, concentrating perhaps on Chūnagon's parents. Since the reincarnation of Chūnagon's father is so important to the story, there was probably emphasis on the closeness of their relationship. Based on information found in various sources, we are able to reconstruct the major events of the first chapter, but the details as to how or to what extent the events of the first chapter conform to established patterns of beginnings found in *monogatari* is beyond our certain knowledge.

In thematic terms, little intrigued the *monogatari* reader more than the plight of young lovers, and in this respect *Hamamatsu* presents some interesting variations of familiar patterns. Unfortunately the start of Chūnagon's relationship with Taishō no Kimi is covered in the missing chapter and we can only speculate as to the details. Since Chūnagon's mother and Taishō no Kimi's father were married after each had lost a spouse, this joining of the two families afforded the opportunity for Chūnagon and Taishō no Kimi to meet on casual terms. Perhaps their original relationship was like that of a brother and sister, possibly even before they were aware of each other sexually. From the regrets Chūnagon expresses later in the story it is clear that he is the one responsible for violating the trust that Taishō no Kimi and her father had placed in him. Perhaps due to the pressure and anxiety caused by Chūnagon's imminent departure to China they let themselves off guard and the fondness they had for each other turned quickly and quite unexpectedly to passion. A momentary yielding to forbidden desires is something a young man is warned of but rarely can resist, and in a *monogatari* the consequences are usually grave. For Taishō no Kimi it meant de-

stroying the future her parents had so carefully planned, and ultimately it caused her to renounce the world.

Chūnagon's affair with the Consort is the result of an "accidental"
meeting clearly ordained by fate. The Consort is in retreat in Shan
Yin on the advice of a Yin-yang diviner, and Chūnagon just happens
to visit the same area in retracing the steps of a famous Chinese poet.
The actual meeting is rich with the formulae of *monogatari* literature
that obviously delighted the reader. Set in a rustic environment, the
house is elegant yet simple in its furnishings. The wall is unfinished
in one corner, and from there Chūnagon peeks inside and sees the
beautiful garden in the moonlight and the lovely ladies on the veranda. The surreptitious observation of unsuspecting ladies through
holes in garden fences and walls is a common occurence in *The
Tale of Genji* and other *monogatari*. Known as *kaimami* in Japanese,
this casual peeking is the first step in the familiar motif of finding a
beautiful lady hidden in an unexpected place. That the lady remain
a mystery to the man is important to the motif, and Chūnagon is
completely unaware that she is the Consort. The Consort's ladies
work to keep their lady's true identity hidden. Although Chūnagon
wishes to take this mysterious woman with him immediately, he is
refused (taboo is the excuse); when Chūnagon returns for her later
she is gone, and her true identity is not known until shortly before
he is to return to Japan. This single fateful meeting binds Chūnagon
and the Consort inextricably together, and their reunion at the end
of the story is the ultimate resolution of this bond.

The third major female character in *Hamamatsu* is Yoshinohime,
the Consort's half sister living in Yoshino. Chūnagon promises her
mother that he will watch over her, and after her mother's death he
takes her to the capital. She is a familiar *monogatari* lady: raised
solely by her mother in the remote forests of Yoshino, she is charming
and musically talented, but utterly innocent of the ways of the world.
She clearly represents the unspoiled hidden beauty so avidly sought
after by the Heian courtier. Chūnagon is prohibited from any amorous designs he might have on her by the interdiction of the Yoshino
monk, but Prince Shikibukyō, ignorant of the monk's warning, steals
her away in what again is a familiar *monogatari* scheme. Shortly
before the abduction she is taken to Kiyomizu Temple to speed her
recovery from some vague malaise. Her guardian, Chūnagon, is

forced to spend the night away from her because of a directional taboo, and the guileful rival who has been secretly following her, Prince Shikibukyō, takes advantage of his absence to steal her away. The Prince's plan is to win her acceptance as she gradually becomes more accustomed to his presence, but her weakened condition—she is virtually in a comatose state—forces him to call on Chūnagon to help revive her.

Chūnagon's relationship with one of the minor female characters in the story, Daini's daughter, also follows a familiar pattern. Chūnagon's first meeting with her is arranged by her parents who hope that he will marry her. Since he is troubled by other matters at the time he initially declines, but then promises to call for her some time in the future. Her parents, particularly her mother, are chagrined at this apparent rejection and rush her into marriage with an older man, Chūnagon's uncle, Emon no Kami. Such a marriage is, of course, a disappointment for both Daini's daughter and Chūnagon, but he manages to meet her occasionally when her husband is away. These secret trysts lead to the birth of a child which the elderly husband takes to be his own. The seduction by the handsome hero of the young, unsatisfied wife of an elderly husband is a familiar motif. So for that matter is the desertion of an elderly wife, and this motif is also tied into this subplot since Emon no Kami deserts his first wife to marry Daini's daughter. Chūnagon secretly observes (again a *kaimami* scene) the rejected wife and pities her, even though it is obvious to him why Emon no Kami rejected her for the younger woman.

As the *Mumyōzōshi* indicates, Chūnagon never achieves a satisfactory relationship with any of the women in his life. When Taishō no Kimi cuts her hair, symbolic of her renunciation of the world, any hopes he had of eventually placating her father's anger and marrying her are dashed. But in the best tradition of the magnanimous hero, Chūnagon refuses to desert her. In spite of her misgivings he insists that they live together so that he might support her, even though their relationship must remain purely spiritual. His refusal to desert her mollifies her father's anger and eventually brings harmony to the household, although Chūnagon must surely wish that he and Taishō no Kimi could be more than just "friends in prayer." Chūnagon's relationship with Daini's daughter is equally frustrating, even though she is not as important to him as Taishō no Kimi is. Once Daini's daughter is married to Emon no Kami, Chūnagon can only hope to meet her occasionally and even then at great risk. There is little future in such a relationship.

For a while it seems that Yoshinohime will be his alone. He sees her as a reminder of the Consort and is willing to wait until her three-year period of taboo is ended. The taking in of a close relative or someone of similar beauty and demeanor as a sort of living memento (*katami* in Japanese) of a lost lover is a significant theme in *The Tale of Genji*. Genji's initial attraction to young Murasaki, for instance, is based on her resemblance to her aunt, Fujitsubo, the woman he secretly desires. Unlike Genji's success with Murasaki, however, the consolation Chūnagon finds in Yoshinohime is very brief, for after her abduction by Prince Shikibukyō and subsequent pregnancy she can no longer be his alone. She rejects his advances once she is returned to his care by the Prince, one reason being that he himself led everyone to believe that they are stepbrother and sister. Here again a similar situation is found in *The Tale of Genji*. Genji secretly desires Tamakazura but because he has led the world to think they are father and daughter she rejects his none-too-subtle hints.

In *Hamamatsu* even Chūnagon's eventual reunion with the Consort will not insure his happiness. Besides the fact that he will be so much older than she and more of an elderly guardian than a potential lover, he must share part of the blame for her having been born again as a woman. Reincarnation as a woman must be considered a mixed blessing; a person may be reunited with her former loved ones, but such a rebirth was surely a detour on the path to Buddhist enlightenment.

The contrasting fortunes of two of the major female characters in *Hamamatsu Chūnagon Monogatari*, Taishō no Kimi and the Ho-yang Consort, were undoubtedly of great interest to the many young women of the aristocracy who were the primary audience for these tales. One of the clearest contrasts is found in the relationship each woman has with the other members of her family, principally her parents. On the surface the Consort would seem to be the more fortunate of the two; she holds a very high rank, is loved by the Emperor, and is surrounded by the luxury and care appropriate for the Emperor's favorite. But all these blessings are of little consolation to her because being in China means being separated from her mother. A good filial daughter, her only wish is that she might be with her mother so that she can care for her. What good, she asks, is the position of Consort if it means being unfilial to her mother? But in the case of Taishō no Kimi it is precisely the position of Consort to the Emperor (of Japan) that her parents wished for her. Neither of the women is satisfied with her position. The Consort may have risen to the position every mother wished for her daughter, but it is of little consolation if she cannot be with her mother. Even the hope of benefiting her father is in vain, for he rejects the vicious life of palace intrigue and retires to a quiet retreat in the mountains. Taishō no Kimi on the other hand is able to be with her parents, but she has difficulty living with the disappointment she has caused her father by her rash renunciation of the world. Chūnagon is in a pivotal position in the relationship of each woman with her parents. He is partially, perhaps principally, responsible for ruining Taishō no Kimi's chance of marrying Prince Shikibukyō, and as such is an agent to her unfilial act. But he is also the one who acts on the Consort's behalf to care for her mother, performing the Consort's filial duties in her mother's final years and after her death.

Since *monogatari* concentrate primarily on the private lives of the characters, it is no surprise that intrafamily relationships, particularly that of parent and child, are of great importance in *Hamamatsu Chūnagon Monogatari*. Chūnagon's trip to China and most of the subsequent complications of plot are predicated on an act of filial piety, Chūnagon's wish to see his reborn father. While Chūnagon's relationship with his mother is not of paramount importance in the story, there are a number of poignant scenes indicating the strain between the two caused by her rather hasty remarriage after the death of Chūnagon's father.

This emphasis on the family is reinforced by the fact that virtually all the major characters in the story constitute one big interrelated family. The marriage of Chūnagon's mother and Lord Taishō makes Chūnagon and Taishō no Kimi stepbrother and sister. Chūnagon and the Hoyang Consort are joined not only as lovers, but also by the fact that the Consort is mother to the Third Prince, Chūnagon's father in a previous life. Yoshinohime and the Yoshino nun are drawn into the circle by their relationship (maternal half sister and mother) to the Consort, and at the end of the story we are told that the Consort will be reborn as her half sister's (Yoshinohime's) child. Even Emon no Kami (Chūnagon's maternal uncle) and Emon no Kami's first wife (paternal half sister of Yoshinohime) are closely related to the major characters. With the focus of the story centering on such a close-knit group it is no wonder extraneous matters such as rituals of court life have little significance in *Hamamatsu*. Even more than *The Tale of Genji*, *Hamamatsu Chūnagon Monogatari* is a story of private lives, a story in which the public lives of the characters have little say.

HAMAMATSU CHŪNAGON MONOGATARI AND *THE TALE OF GENJI*

As might be expected of two works of the same genre and period, and as has already been indicated in the previous section, there are a number of parallels between *Hamamatsu Chūnagon Monogatari* and *The Tale of Genji*. From the title of each work we learn that the focus of each is on a man of high-ranking position and pedigree. Both of the leading characters bear the family name Minamoto, one of a limited number of surnames given to royal offspring. Genji, son of an Emperor, is a generation closer to the throne than Chūnagon, whose father was a Prince. In terms of personal attributes Chūnagon, like Genji, is depicted very much as an ideal hero. His talents in the arts of both Japanese and Chinese poetry and music are unsurpassed not only by his fellow courtiers but even by the experts who were often called to participate in court festivities solely because of their artistic skills. So handsome as to bring tears to the eyes of those who but gaze upon him, he is an understanding companion whose presence soothes the troubled soul of those men and women fortunate enough to spend some time at ease with him. He is a filial son and a devoted father. If he has a fault it is one easily forgiven in men of his class: in the presence of an attractive young lady he has difficulty controlling his emotions.

While the two heroes are in many ways similar in terms of temperament and personality, the two stories are considerably different in the breadth and depth of the depiction of their leading characters.

For one thing, *The Tale of Genji* takes its hero from birth through his renunciation of the world at the age of fifty-two and ultimately beyond his death to the succeeding generation, covering in varying degrees of detail the fortunes of a character in critical moments of childhood, youth, manhood, middle age, and finally old age. Passages in which a mature Genji ruminates on the ceaseless passage of time and the ultimate evanescence of the glories of this world are among the most poignant in the book. The extant *Hamamatsu*, on the other hand, covers a period of less than six years, and neither the reader nor the characters themselves view their experiences through the perspective of age. The strong sense conveyed in *The Tale of Genji* of both the brilliance of its hero and the ultimate ephemerality and futility of his glories in this world is much an accumulative effect garnered from the many episodes in which the author shows the successes and the sorrows of her hero. In *Hamamatsu*, however, the author from the very beginning gives her young hero a seriousness beyond his years, a trait we might prefer the character acquire through the author's showing rather than her telling us. In addition, the way in which Murasaki Shikibu describes the chronological growth of her characters through the remarkably consistent manner in which the male characters are advanced to different ranks and positions is noticeably missing in *Hamamatsu*, where the hero remains a middle counselor throughout the entire story. Even when Chūnagon is appointed Master of the Crown Prince's Household, no mention is made of any change in rank.

This apparent indifference to rank is a reflection of a slight but apparently significant shift in focus between *Genji* and *Hamamatsu* from characters at the very center of the Court to those on the peripheries of power. The major characters of *Genji* are primarily from a very small circle of aristocratic society closest to the Emperor, and the Emperor in both his private and public affairs figures prominently in the tale. The fact that Genji is the son of an Emperor, stepbrother to his successor, ostensible stepbrother (actually father) and the father-in-law to the following two Emperors in the story quite naturally focuses much of the action of that work on the Imperial Court. The characters of *Hamamatsu*, however, are once removed from this innermost circle. Chūnagon is not of as noble birth as Genji, and he seems disinclined to participate in palace politics.

Although the politics of the Imperial Court, especially the maneuvering involved in political marriages and lining up support for potential candidates for the position of Crown Prince, is of far less importance in *Hamamatsu Chūnagon Monogatari* than in *The Tale of Genji*, it would be an exaggeration to say that politics are irrelevant to the tale. For instance, in the first chapter at the Court of the Chinese Emperor we find the essential elements for the making of a subplot involving palace politics similar to that found in the first part of *Genji*. The Hoyang Consort's position at the Chinese Court is analogous to the Kiritsubo concubine's position at the Court of Genji's father, and both stories draw on the story of Yang Kuei-fei, well-known in Japan due to the enduring popularity of Po Chü-i's ninth-century poem "A Song of Unending Sorrow." Both the Hoyang Consort and Genji's mother were raised to their lofty positions solely because of the inordinate affection of the Emperor, and both were victimized by the spiteful schemes of the principal wife of the Emperor and the other jealous concubines. In *Hamamatsu* the Chinese Emperor, like Genji's father, must be careful not to offend his principal wife, the first daughter of an all-powerful minister. Needless to say these characters are similar in position and temperament to Kōkiden and her father, the Minister of the Right. The parallels between the Chinese Court in *Hamamatsu* and the Kiritsubo Court in *Genji* can be taken a step further, for the Third Prince of China is much like Genji as a boy.

There is then an obvious similarity in structure of relationships among the leading characters in the initial sections of both books, but in *Hamamatsu* there is really no further development of the political side of the story. The Third Prince of China is eventually named Crown Prince, but we only learn of this in a final letter which serves to tie up the loose ends of the tale.

The secret seduction of an Imperial consort, particularly when a child is born of the affair, is also a development fraught with political overtones. In *The Tale of Genji* Fujitsubo must be extremely careful that her secret affair with Genji and the true parentage of the Reizei Emperor remain hidden lest all three of them be publicly disgraced and politically destroyed. The Fujitsubo-Genji affair can be read on one level as a son's sins against his father, but never far from the surface are the political dangers to which Fujitsubo seems particularly sensitive. In *Hamamatsu* the forbidden seduction of an Imperial consort also leads to the birth of a child, but the child is kept a secret and eventually returns to Japan with Chūnagon, thus effectively eliminating any further danger. In fact the hero, Chūnagon, is closer to the Imperial family of China than he is to the Imperial family of Japan, and it is primarily in the first chapter which takes place in China that the structure of relationships lends itself to a subplot involving political intrigue. The potential is never developed, however, for the hero returns to Japan and China becomes little more than a dim memory whose presence is felt only in dreams.

With the return of Chūnagon to Japan there is even less potential for the development of a political subplot since the principal characters are not part of the inner Court. The locus for the action of *Hamamatsu* does not center on the Court, and much of it does not even take place in the capital. The action of *The Tale of Genji* takes place primarily in the environs of the capital, the two exceptions to this being Genji's exile in Suma and Akashi, and the final chapters in which the action alternates between the capital and Uji. In *Hamamatsu*, however, nearly half of the story occurs away from the capital, and very little of what does occur there actually takes place at Court. There is only one scene in which the Emperor plays a significant part, and this entire scene is of only minor importance to the entire story. *Hamamatsu* is conspicuously void of court ceremonies, the rituals of the Imperial family, and even the private parties that continually remind the reader that the inner Court—as close as possible to the Emperor (or a leading figure like Genji), the central focal point of Japanese society—was the epitome of the good life in aristocratic Japan. For the elite of Heian society, life hardly existed beyond the boundaries of the capital. Genji's exile in Suma and Akashi is harsh not because he is all that distant from the capital, but because he is separated from the life at Court.

The location of much of the action of the final chapters of *Genji* in Uji is a significant movement from the Court, symbolic perhaps of the debilitation of that court society after the passing of Genji. This is carried even a step further in *Hamamatsu* where the location of the action moves rapidly from the capital to Tsukushi (in the missing chapter) to China, then back to Tsukushi and the capital, and finally alternates between Yoshino and Chūnagon's house in the capital. Court life and the Imperial family, Genji's family, are matters of state, but in *Hamamatsu* the private affairs of the hero do not have such far-reaching repercussions.

Just as the shift in setting from the Court to more peripheral locales is characteristic of the Uji section of *The Tale of Genji*, so too the resemblance of Chūnagon to Kaoru was recognized as early as the thirteenth century in the *Mumyōzōshi*.[28] In terms of temperament they are indeed similar. Both fancy themselves serious, prudent young men not given to the frivolity and adventuresomeness of other men their age; they are approximately the same age and rank; and, as we might expect of a *monogatari* hero, in terms of both physical beauty and spiritual sensitivity to the needs of women, Chūnagon, like Kaoru, comes close to fulfilling "the feminine view of what constituted ideal masculine attributes."[29]

Just as the initial chapter of *Hamamatsu* draws on a structure of relationships in the beginning of *The Tale of Genji*, the pattern of relationships in the Chūnagon-Yoshinohime-Prince Shikibukyō triangle is analogous to the Kaoru-Ukifune-Prince Niou triangle in *Genji*. It must have been a popular *monogatari* schema: a beautiful young lady lacking adequate support and protection, and two handsome suitors, one sensitive, solicitous, and inclined to restraint, the other impetuous, bold, and unwilling to let anything stand in his way. Yoshinohime is represented as a helpless young maiden unwittingly caught up in the rivalry of Chūnagon and Prince Shikibukyō. Just as Ukifune is for Kaoru a substitute for her stepsister Oigimi, Yoshinohime serves to remind Chūnagon of her stepsister the Hoyang Consort, and just as Ukifune is overwhelmed by Prince Niou, Yoshinohime is stolen away by Prince Shikibukyō, an intemperate young man capable of moving quickly, even rashly, in gaining the woman he desires. Prince Shikibukyō is even more willful than Prince Niou, but he is far less effective in winning the heart of the woman once he has taken her away.

In terms of length, the extant *Hamamatsu Chūnagon Monogatari*

28. See page 13 above.
29. Helen C. McCullough, *Ōkagami, The Great Mirror* (Princeton: Princeton University Press, 1980), p. 49.

is approximately one-seventh as long as *The Tale of Genji*. Assuming that the missing chapter was equal to the average length of a chapter in the extant text (approximately fifty-seven pages), then the original *Hamamatsu* was a bit larger than one-sixth the size of *Genji* as we know it today.

There are 125 poems in the extant text of *Hamamatsu*, which is proportionally very close to the number in *Genji*. Of these 125 poems over half (66) are by the hero, Chūnagon. It is unusual that the two women Chūnagon is closest to, the Hoyang Consort and Taishō no Kimi, are responsible for only 8 poems and 4 poems respectively. The Consort's lack of poems is understandable since she is present physically only in the first chapter, but the lack of poems from Taishō no Kimi is surprising. We know that she was responsible for at least two poems in the missing chapter, and most likely there were more by her. Perhaps the lack of poems in subsequent chapters should be taken as a reflection of the prosaic nature of her relationship with Chūnagon as a result of her having renounced the world. Yoshi-nohime, in spite of her natural reticence, is attributed with the second largest number of poems, 16, and Daini's daughter the third largest number, 8. Four of Yoshinohime's poems were written by her in private and are discovered by Chūnagon after her abduction (p. 216). Their presence in the narrative serves as a sort of flashback, revealing to him the secret feelings she was reluctant to express openly.

In addition to the Hoyang Consort, five other Chinese characters are equal to the task of composing Japanese *waka*. As we might expect from an author who surely had no firsthand knowledge of China, the image of China presented in the first chapter bears little resemblance to historical fact. What knowledge the author does have of China seems based largely on the Chinese literature, poetry and the classics, that was popular in Heian Japan, and while the author does on occasion show interest in pointing out differences in customs and language, for the most part the setting is very much like that of Heiankyō.

Among the courtiers of Heian Japan, poetry was a frequently used means of communication. A person was expected to be able to produce spontaneously a poem not only appropriate for the message to be conveyed, but also if possible with imagery apropos to the season and any particular place name figuring in the discourse. Over eighty poems in *Hamamatsu Chūnagon Monogatari*, almost two-thirds of the total, are paired poems in which a poem by one character elicits a response from another. In most instances these exchanges also make use of common imagery.

As is to be expected, the predominant imagery of the poetry is a reflection of the psychological tone of the tale. Autumn, a time of melancholy and sorrow, is the most frequently mentioned season, and the moon the favorite image from nature. A sense of loneliness and isolation is conveyed in the many poems treating the snow and mountains of Yoshino. Dream imagery is mentioned in a number of poems as is this "sad world," (*ukiyo*). None of these images is unusual for Heian *waka*, however, and in general the poetry of *Hamamatsu* is not particularly remarkable. It seems, rather, to be simply a normal and unobtrusive part of the life of the characters. Indicative of the low-keyed presence of the poetry in the tale is the fact that there is very little of the critical reading of poetry as a means of evaluating character that is found in *The Tale of Genji*. In *Genji* both the content and the calligraphy of poems are often commented on by either characters or the narrator as a way of judging the relative worth of the person as a poet, and by extension the poet as a person. This internal criticism is hardly present at all in *Hamamatsu Chūnagon Monogatari*.

DREAMS IN *HAMAMATSU CHŪNAGON MONOGATARI*

Perhaps the most intriguing aspect of *Hamamatsu Chūnagon Monogatari* and the one that distinguishes it most clearly from other *monogatari* is the significant use of dream sequences in the narrative. It is worthwhile to examine in detail the varied ways in which these dream sequences function in the narrative, not only for the purposes of highlighting what is a major motif of the work, but also because the manner in which dreams are presented in the Tale is indicative of a sophistication of narrative technique often overlooked in *Hamamatsu*. For the purposes of analysis I have identified the eleven sequences in which a character is described as having had a dream. Two of these sequences are descriptions in different parts of the story

DREAMS

of the same dream. A brief summary follows of the dream sequences in the order in which they appear in the narrative.

Dream Sequence #1 (Chapter 1, p. 62): In a flashback giving background information on the Hoyang Consort's early life, the narrator tells of a dream experienced by the Prince of Ch'in in which he is told his daughter (later the Hoyang Consort) will be allowed to pass safely from Japan to China even though women were not normally permitted to travel across the China Sea.

Dream Sequence #2 (Chapter 1, p. 67): While in China Chūnagon envisions Taishō no Kimi at his side. She seems distressed and tells him in a poem that she has fallen in a sea of tears and "now wrings her sleeve like a fisherwoman." Chūnagon awakes from this dream in tears but does not understand the import of this dream.

Dream Sequence #3 (Chapter 1, p. 73): While still in China Chūnagon longs to see the Hoyang Consort once again and goes to a temple to pray that he might meet her again. He falls asleep and a monk appears to tell him in a poem that his ties with her are "fated to be deep."

Dream Sequence #4 (Chapter 1, p. 95): Chūnagon has delayed his return to Japan in hopes of seeing the Consort again. The narrator mentions that he frequently sees his mother in a dream. He feels guilty about the grief his prolonged absence must be causing her.

Dream Sequence #5 (Chapter 1, p. 96): As Chūnagon prepares to return to Japan, the Consort is worried about the fate of the secret child born to them. One night as she weeps herself to sleep a man appears in a dream and tells her that the child was not meant to stay in China but must return with Chūnagon to Japan.

Dream Sequence #6 (Chapter 3, pp. 134-35): The Yoshino monk in relating the Yoshino nun's background tells Chūnagon of the Prince of Ch'in's dream in which the Prince is told to take the nun's daughter (later the Hoyang Consort) back to China. This is a second description of the dream described in Sequence #1.

Dream Sequence #7 (Chapter 3, p. 136): Just before Chūnagon's first visit to the Yoshino nun, the narrator relates that the previous night the Hoyang Consort had appeared in the nun's dreams.

Dream Sequence #8 (Chapter 3, p. 144): After Chūnagon returns to the capital from his first visit to Yoshino, the narration turns to a flashback sequence describing the Yoshino nun's state of mind before his visit to Yoshino. In this flashback we learn that she has been praying fervently that someone might relieve her of the burden of caring for her daughter so that she might devote her prayers to her own salvation. A monk appears in a dream and tells her that her daughter, the Hoyang Consort, has been praying for the nun's well-being, and because of this extraordinary exhibition of filial devotion a man the Consort met in China will come to care for Yoshinohime and bring news of the Consort. The narration then turns to Chūnagon's arrival and the changes he brought to the nun's life in Yoshino.

Dream Sequence #9 (Chapter 4, pp. 172-73): Chūnagon is in the capital. The narrator mentions that the Yoshino nun appeared frequently in his dreams. Chūnagon begins to worry about her and hurries off to Yoshino only to find she is on her deathbed.

Dream Sequence #10 (Chapter 4, pp. 201-202): Chūnagon has brought Yoshinohime, the Hoyang Consort's half sister, to the capital. The narrator relates that beginning from the tenth day of the first month Chūnagon frequently sees the Consort in his dreams. She seems sick and in great pain. Shortly thereafter (on the sixteenth day of the third month) Chūnagon hears a voice from heaven telling him that the Consort has cut all ties with the world and is reborn in heaven.

Dream Sequence #11 (Chapter 5, pp. 217-18): Yoshinohime has been abducted and Chūnagon has almost given up hope of finding her. One night he dozes off and the Hoyang Consort appears in a dream. She tells him that because of their affectionate ties to each other she is to be born again as the child of her half sister Yoshinohime, the girl he is searching for.

Even in outline form it should be clear that dreams are an important motif in *Hamamatsu Chūnagon Monogatari*. To begin with,

36

there is the function the dreams perform in relation to the development of plot. Both dream sequences #1 and #5 serve to give direction to the plot in that characters proceed with certain actions based on instructions given in the dreams. In terms of content both sequences are concerned with similar problems, the proper disposition of a child born of a clandestine love affair. The instructions given in the dreams are explicit and unequivocal, and the characters who have the dreams accept the instructions without question, even though in the case of the Hoyang Consort's dream (#5) it means being separated from her son for life.

In addition to being similar in terms of content and the manner in which they give direction to the plot, both of these dreams are in a sense messengers of karmic causality, and together they demonstrate a clear example of the "retribution of fate" (*koto no mukui* in the text). The message the Hoyang Consort receives in the dream telling her she must let her child return to Japan with Chūnagon makes it clear that she must now suffer the same sorrow her mother endured when the Consort (as a child) was taken back to China with her father, a development instructed in the father's dream (#1).

A second group of dreams (#2, #4, #9, and #10) serve to inform characters (and the reader) of events that are occurring in distant places. These dreams are no less important to the development of plot than the first group, but they differ in that they contain no explicit instructions as to what the dreamer is to do. In one sequence (#9) Chūnagon does in fact proceed with certain action based on the content of the dream, i.e., he decided to visit the nun in Yoshino after seeing her frequently in his dreams, but the course of action is more of his own choosing than would be possible in the explicitly instructive dreams (#1 and #5).

Since the import of the messages given in dreams #2 and #10 is not readily apparent in either dream, the character is not free to act upon them. It is clear in these dream sequences and in all the others that what is said is of consequence, but the character must simply wait for subsequent events to elucidate their true significance. To the extent that the message in the dreams is incomprehensible to the dreamer (or the reader) a rather low-keyed sense of suspense is created as we wait for the meaning of the dream to be revealed. For dream #10 in which the Hoyang Consort appears sick and distressed

37

in Chūnagon's dreams, the suspense is only momentary. A few lines later Chūnagon is told by a voice from the sky that the Consort has cut her ties with the world and has been reborn in heaven.

The situation is somewhat more complex in dream sequence #2 in which Chūnagon sees Taishō no Kimi and hears her recite a poem telling that she has fallen into a sea of tears and now wrings her sleeve like a fisherwoman. Chūnagon apparently misses the obvious pun on the word *ama* (fisherwoman/nun) and does not realize that she has renounced the world. Since her renunciation of the world probably was described in the now missing chapter after Chūnagon's departure for China, a contemporary reader with the complete text available would of course know precisely what was meant.[30] Even today when the first chapter is missing, it is unlikely a reader would miss the significance of so obvious a pun. The reader knows that Taishō no Kimi has renounced the world, but Chūnagon does not, and each time he reminisces longingly for the woman he left back home the irony of the situation is readily apparent. The suspense engendered by this dream is that concomitant with dramatic irony in which the reader wonders what this turn of events will eventually mean to Chūnagon and how he will react to the news that Taishō no Kimi has renounced the world.

That the author would seek to sustain the reader's interest in this important storyline even when the setting of the narrative is China and the main focus is on Chūnagon's relationship with the Consort is indicative of both her conception of the work as a unified whole

---

30. Although most scholars are in agreement that the missing chapter is prior to the extant first chapter, an intriguing theory postulating that there are two missing chapters has been argued by Matsumoto Hiroko in "*Hamamatsu Chūnagon Monogatari* no Gensaku Keitai ni Kansuru Kōsatsu" *Ochanomizu Joshi Daigaku Jimbun Kagaku Kiyō*, Vol. 21, No. 3 (March 1968), reprinted in *Nihon Bungaku Kenkyū Shiryō Sōsho, Heianchō Monogatari IV*, Nihon Bungaku Kenkyū Shiryō Kankōkai (Tokyo: Yūseidō, 1980), pp. 181-97. Matsumoto suggests that the events in Japan after Chūnagon's departure for China are described in a chapter narrated after the extant first chapter but before the second chapter. The chapter would constitute a flashback in time to a period prior to or concurrent with the events in China. If this ordering of the narrative were true, then the reader would not be aware that Taishō no Kimi had renounced the world unless he were to read the double meaning of the word *ama* (fisherwoman/nun). Although the evidence supporting this theory is very limited and not persuasive enough to be definitive, to a certain extent this argument is supported by the tendency of the work to rearrange the story (story time) and the order in which they are narrated (narrative time).

and her skill as a storyteller. The narrator is omniscient but her focus is disciplined. By using dream sequences to tell of events occurring simultaneously in distant locales she is able to keep the focus of the story in one place while at the same time revealing significant happenings elsewhere. When the story is taking place in China we learn of events in Japan only through a dream sequence, and likewise when the setting is Japan we learn of events in China through dreams, a voice from heaven, or the final letter which serves to bring the story to an end.

A third group of dreams (#3, #7, and #11) is made up of dreams that serve as omens of events to come. The three categories in which I have placed dreams in terms of their relation to the plot—dreams that give direction to the plot, information on concurrent events in distant locales, or omens of events to come—are not to be considered mutually exclusive. Some sequences might fit into two of the categories. For instance, dream sequence #7 in which the Yoshino nun sees her daughter the Hoyang Consort the night before Chūnagon arrives might be placed in the category of dreams giving information on characters in a distant locale, although I prefer to interpret it as an omen to the nun telling her that she will soon be getting news of her daughter. Likewise dream sequences #9 and #10 which I have classified as dreams of information could also be taken as omens, since the sight of the ill women Chūnagon sees in these dreams might be interpreted as an omen that each is about to die. In terms of giving direction to the plot, dream sequence #7 in which the Yoshino nun sees the Consort and dream sequence #10 in which Chūnagon sees the sick Consort are passive since they call forth no action by the dreamer. However, dream sequence #9, actually a series of dreams in which Chūnagon sees the Yoshino nun, sets him to worrying about the nun and is clearly the reason he chooses to suddenly visit her. When he arrives he finds that she is seriously ill. Were it not for this fortuitous dream, Chūnagon would not have witnessed the nun's miraculous death scene, nor would he have been present to direct the resuscitation of the unconscious Yoshinohime. While this dream sequence is very brief, the immediate effect it has on the development of the plot is considerable.

In dream sequence #8 the Yoshino nun sees a monk who tells

her that the Consort has been praying for her well-being, and because of this extraordinary exhibition of filial devotion a man the Consort met in China will come to care for Yoshinohime and bring news of the Consort. This sequence also gives information on events far away and serves as an omen of things to come. It is important in terms of the development of the plot in that it, along with the Hoyang Consort's letter to her mother, provides the justification for the mother's unhesitant acceptance of Chūnagon's offer of support.

The most significant dream as omen, and perhaps the most important dream in the entire story, is dream sequence #3 in which Chūnagon is visited by a monk who tells him that his ties with the Consort are fated to be deep. Although this prophecy sets the direction of the story, at first neither Chūnagon nor the reader fully understands its meaning. Shortly after this dream Chūnagon chances to meet the Consort in Shan Yin and the vows of love they share that night tie him irrevocably to the Consort and her family. But here again there is an element of irony in the situation, for Chūnagon does not realize that the woman he has spent the night with is the Consort. The confusion in Chūnagon's mind as to who the woman really is, and the reader's uncertainty as to whether they will ever meet again are the important storyline of the first chapter. While it would seem at first that the meeting of Chūnagon and the Consort at Shan Yin is the fulfillment of the prophecy made in the dream, in fact it is only the beginning. Because of that meeting Chūnagon becomes inexorably tied to the Consort and her family in Japan, and the ultimate fulfillment of the omen in the dream does not come until the end of the story when we learn that the Consort is to be reborn as Yoshinohime's child. Unbeknownst to Chūnagon or the reader the message in that dream is an omen not only of an immediate event (the meeting with the Consort in Shan Yin), but also the subsequent development of the plot up to the final resolution, and it is this message that keeps coming back to Chūnagon as he sees his life increasingly drawn to the Consort and her family.

In the final dream of the story (#11) Chūnagon is visited by the Consort and told that she will be born again soon as the daughter of her own half sister, Yoshinohime. Out of context this prophecy might seem difficult to accept, but it is perfectly logical within the context of the story. The fact that every omen in a dream has proven true makes it almost impossible for the characters (or readers) to reject this final one. Even the act of reincarnation has been demonstrated once before in the story, for at the beginning of the story we are told that the Third Prince of China was Chūnagon's father in his previous life. Reincarnation of his father in China is what draws Chūnagon to China in the first place; it is the reason Chūnagon happens to meet the Consort, and the prophecy of her reincarnation back to Japan is what ends the story, fulfilling in an unusual way Chūnagon's abiding wish that they might be reunited once again. That the Consort should be reborn as her half sister's daughter is not completely unanticipated, for when Chūnagon takes Yoshino-hime from Yoshino he is warned by the monk that there will be grave consequences were she to "know" a man before the age of twenty. With her abduction by Prince Shikibukyō and subsequent pregnancy the monk's warning looms ominously, and the import of that prophecy becomes clear with the announcement to Chūnagon in a dream that the child is to be the Consort reborn. The true meaning of the earlier dream in which Chūnagon is told his ties are fated to be deep is at long last clear.

A sense of balance resulting from a return to the beginning of the tale is also effected with the final dream sequence prophesying the rebirth of the Consort as her half sister's child. In a sense the relationship of Chūnagon and the Consort had its beginning in Chūnagon's dream (in the missing chapter) in which he learned that his father had been reborn in China. It is fitting that their story should end with the prediction of the Consort's rebirth in a dream. The parallels between these two events are also symbolic of the fate of humans caught in the circular existence of karmic causality.

In addition to performing various functions in terms of the development of the plot, the manner in which dreams are woven into the narrative varies considerably, an indication of a sophistication of narrative technique that is often overlooked in *Hamamatsu Chūnagon Monogatari*. Let us consider first the intensity of description, the varying degree of detail with which the dreams are presented. In its simplest form the narrator merely mentions that a character saw someone in a dream (#4, #7, and #9). Other than mentioning the appearance of a certain person, there is no description of the dreams themselves, only the fact that they occurred, and this fact is told in a single sentence or less. The only distinction that can be drawn among these dreams is that sequences #4 and #9 refer to a repeated series of the same dream while #7 refers to one single dream. The significance of each sequence would be unclear were it not for the fact that events which immediately follow are closely related to the character who appears in the dream.

Only slightly more detailed in presentation is dream sequence #10 in which Chūnagon sees the Hoyang Consort in pain. Here again the narrator mentions that Chūnagon saw the Consort a number of times in his dreams, but this time mention is also made of the fact that she seems sick and in pain.

All of the remaining dreams are sequences in which a person appears in a dream and actually speaks to the dreamer. These are consequently more detailed than the previously mentioned sequences. In all but two of the sequences the dialogue of the dream is preceded by mention in some manner or other of the word *yume* (dream), indicating that the sequence that follows is a dream. The two exceptions are dream #2 in which Chūnagon sees Taishō no Kimi (the "fisherwoman" dream) and dream #11 in which he sees the Hoyang Consort and learns that she is to be reborn as Yoshinohime's child. Dream sequence #11 is preceded by mention of the fact that Chūnagon first falls asleep and then sees the Consort, but for sequence #2 there is no mention of his even falling asleep. From the language with which the sequence is described it would seem that Taishō no Kimi is suddenly by his side, and it isn't until she has finished her poem and Chūnagon begins to weep that we are told he then awakens. The narrative moves without warning into a dream sequence as easily as if the person who appears in the dream had merely walked into the dreamer's room and what we are hearing are not the words spoken in a dream but rather a normal conversation of the character's waking hours. From context it would of course be impossible for Taishō no Kimi to be right by his side in China, but the unrestrained manner in which the sequence suddenly materializes still takes the reader by surprise. The narrative technique in which the dream blends into the flow of the story is an early indication that to this author the worlds of dreams and reality are not the clearly separated worlds we might expect.

Two of the sequences (#1 and #6) describe the same dream, that of the Prince of Ch'in before he takes his daughter (later the Consort) back to China. In terms of the narrative, these sequences are of interest for how they relate to the sense of time in the story and the order of succession of events.[31] The description of the Prince of Ch'in's dream occurs in a flashback which interrupts the story to relate events that occurred more than twenty years before the primary time frame of the story. The incident is first related by the narrator immediately after Chūnagon and the Consort first catch glimpse of each other the evening he exchanges chrysanthemums with her ladies. After a brief description of the favorable reaction each has for the other, the narrator immediately begins a rather lengthy description of the Consort's background beginning with her birth, then moving quickly to the Prince of Ch'in's dream assuring them safe passage back to China, the courtship of the Consort by the Emperor of China, and finally her precarious position at Court. In a splendid display of free moving narration indicative of the author's skill as a storyteller, the narrator describes, as if it were happening at that very moment, precisely the words spoken in the dream by the Dragon King of the Sea: "Leave immediately. This girl is destined to be a consort in your land. You will pass safely." This dream is an omen of things to come, but in terms of the original time frame of the narrative it is an event which has already occurred. The narrator's description of the Consort's background then covers her coming-of-age in China, the courtship by the Emperor, and the difficulties encountered because of the opposition of the First Empress and the other ladies at Court. This recounting of the Consort's background does not end until it has reached approximately, but not exactly, the same time frame of the story it interrupted to begin her history, that is, when we are told that the amusements the Emperor and the recently arrived Chūnagon engaged in served to divert the unusual sorrow the Emperor felt at not being able to spend more time with the Consort. But this is only a momentary return to the original story time, for the narration immediately moves to a description of the Consort's own feelings during the events since she left Japan. The first flashback was a relatively detached description of her background focusing primarily on her father, who does after all have the

31. The following analysis is partially based on theoretical concepts explicated by Gerard Genette in *Narrative Discourse, An Essay in Method* (Ithaca: Cornell University Press, 1980).

important dream embedded in this narrative, and on the Emperor of China. The second account is a highly personalized description of how the Consort herself remembered the separation from her mother, the Emperor's courtship, her precarious position at Court, and the longing she felt for her mother. Both of these flashbacks have a considerable reach and extent. The first reaches back well over twenty years from before the birth of the Consort and extends up to the time Chūnagon is in China, the second reaches approximately eighteen years to the time the Consort was five years old and extends beyond the point at which it began.

In spite of the length of time covered, a sense of immediacy is gained in each retelling, the former by the vivid description, including dialogue, of the Prince of Ch'in's dreams, the latter by description, here again with dialogue, of the Consort's parting with her mother. What is significant in terms of narrative technique in these flashbacks is the tempo of the story and the fact that time measured as a sequence of events is broken down by the manner of the telling. In terms of tempo, the narrator's initial description of the Hoyang Consort's background is told in the form of summary, where years of the story time are covered in a few lines of narrative time, except for the actual dream sequence which is presented as a scene, where the time in the story equals the narrative time.[32] This scene, the dream sequence, represents a dramatic moment embedded in the less dramatic narrative of summary. This distinction might be considered as a prose parallel to the *ji/mon* (ground/design) distinction so important to Japanese poetics. In the second flashback the Consort's parting words with her mother form the dramatic scene set in the summary background. That this parting is treated in some detail is significant not only for the fact that it serves to emphasize the important theme of the sorrow involved in the relationship of parent and child, but also because the Consort will likewise later be separated from her child in karmic retribution for this event. Because it is treated as a scene it remains a vivid memory in the mind of the reader.

The Prince of Ch'in's dream is described a second time early in Chapter Three by the Yoshino monk in relating to Chūnagon the

32. For the various ways in which story time is related to narrative time see Genette, *Narrative Discourse*, pp. 94-95.

history of the Yoshino nun, the Hoyang Consort's mother (dream sequence #6). Chūnagon has just arrived in Yoshino to deliver to the nun a letter from her daughter, the Consort. Since the monk is telling Chūnagon the story focusing on the mother's experiences, the beginning of his story, that is, the part up to where the Prince of Ch'in returns to China with his daughter, is very similar to the narrator's earlier description of the Consort's background which included the Prince of Ch'in's dream. In the monk's version of the dream the words spoken to the Prince are very similar, but not precisely the same, as the words described in the earlier flashback. As is found in the flashback described by the narrator, the dream sequence here is presented as a narrative scene within narrative summary.

The first two descriptions of the events beginning twenty years before the time frame of the story included a relatively detached description of events by the narrator, and then a more personal description of the Consort's background focusing on her experience. In the Yoshino monk's retelling of this story we are given a detached account focusing on the Yoshino nun, the Consort's mother. Much of what he relates has to do with the mother's desperate condition after the Prince of Ch'in returned to China, including her affair with Sochi no Miya leading to the birth of Yoshinohime. But this, the third account of those events, is not the final one, for just ten pages later, after Chūnagon has left for the capital promising he would return to Yoshino as soon as possible, the narrator describes in even greater detail the Yoshino nun's separation from her daughter, the future Consort, and the birth, described in almost despairing terms, of Yoshinohime. In this summary there are a number of brief instances in which the narrative time slows down to the story time, the most apparent being the moment when the Hoyang Consort left for China, once again serving to place emphasis on the sorrow of separation. In this description the focus is primarily on the unfortunate birth and childhood of Yoshinohime, the beautiful young girl destined to grow up as a stereotypical "hidden beauty" in forlorn and desolate surroundings. The pattern of narration is similar to that used earlier in the description of the Hoyang Consort's background in China. It begins as a flashback to events some twenty years earlier

45

and describes the Yoshino nun and Yoshinohime's life up to (and beyond again) the point at which the flashback began.

It is during the description by the narrator of life at Yoshino that yet another dream sequence is related. In a dream (#8) the Yoshino nun is told directly by a monk who speaks to her in the dream that her daughter, the Consort, has been praying for her well-being and became intimate with a visitor from Japan so that the man would look after the nun's needs upon returning to Japan. This dream is, then, an omen of things to come. But like the dream of the Prince of Ch'in, it is described in the narrative after the event that it predicts has already taken place. Once again the timing of events has been reversed. When narrative flashbacks contain descriptions of dreams that are omens of events that have already been related earlier in the narrative, suspense is sacrificed, but the importance of the dream as experience is not diminished and the reader is left with a very strong sense of the author's complete faith in the veracity of dreams. At the same time the flashbacks serve to break down the linear movement of time measured as a succession of events.

In addition to the use of flashbacks, there are other aspects of the story that point to a resistance to, even rejection of, the effects of the inevitable movement of time: the rather perfunctory treatment of seasonal changes in the natural setting, the disinterest in the annual ceremonies of society (*nenchūgyōji*), the lack of any significant psychological growth in the characters, and, most surprisingly, the fact that the hero remains the same rank throughout the story. And reincarnation as it is depicted in this Tale, rebirth again as a human being, seems to be the ultimate resistance to the movement of time and the aging process. Perhaps this is why Mishima Yukio used *Hamamatsu Chūnagon Monogatari* as the classical source for his final tetralogy, *Hōjō no Umi* (*The Sea of Fertility*).[33]

In conclusion it might be noted that one effect of the unusual use of dreams in *Hamamatsu Chūnagon Monogatari* is a breakdown of the distinction between dreams and reality (*yume/utsutsu*) in the story. As a corollary of this it should be noted that the most important scene in the first chapter, the meeting of Chūnagon and the Consort in Shan Yin, is frequently referred to later in the story as that "spring

33. Mishima Yukio, *Haru no Yuki* (Tokyo: Shinchōsha, 1969), p. 369.

night's dream." In this Tale the distinction between dreams and reality has been collapsed. What occurs in a dream will occur in the reality of the story, and what happens in the story becomes for the characters a dream.

PRINCIPAL CHARACTERS

CHŪNAGON   The hero. Son of Lady Taishō and father who is reborn as the Third Prince of China.

CONSORT   See Hoyang Consort.

DAINI   Assistant Governor of Tsukushi.

DAINI'S DAUGHTER   In love with Chūnagon but becomes Emon no Kami's wife.

EMON NO KAMI   Chūnagon's maternal uncle.

EMON NO KAMI'S FIRST WIFE   Half sister by the same father (Sochi no Miya) as Yoshinohime.

HIMEGIMI   Daughter of Chūnagon and Taishō no Kimi, born while Chūnagon is in China.

HOYANG CONSORT   Daughter of the Yoshino nun and the Prince of Ch'in. Mother of the Third Prince of China by the Emperor, and Wakagimi secretly by Chūnagon. Half sister of Yoshinohime.

LADY NǕ WANG   Lady-in-waiting of the Hoyang Consort.

LADY SAISHŌ   Lady-in-waiting of Taishō no Kimi.

LADY TAISHŌ   Chūnagon's mother. Marries Lord Taishō after the death of Chūnagon's father.

LORD TAISHŌ   Father of Taishō no Kimi and Naka no Kimi. Takes Chūnagon's mother (Lady Taishō) as his second wife after his first wife dies.

NAKA NO KIMI   Younger sister of Taishō no Kimi. Marries Prince Shikibukyō in place of her sister.

NURSE CHŪJŌ   Chūnagon's nurse. Entrusted with Wakagimi when Chūnagon returns from China.

NURSE SHŌSHŌ   Nurse of Taishō no Kimi.

PRIME MINISTER OF CHINA   Father of the first Chinese Consort and Wu Chün. Most powerful minister in China.

PRINCE   See the Third Prince of China.

PRINCE OF CH'IN   Father of the Hoyang Consort by the Yoshino nun (before she takes vows) while he is serving as an envoy to Japan. Later lives in a retreat in Shu Shan.

PRINCE SHIKIBUKYŌ   Only son of the reigning Emperor of Japan.

PRINCESS SHŌKYŌDEN   Daughter of the Emperor of Japan.

SHINANO   Lady servant of Yoshinohime.

SHŌSHŌ NO NAISHI   Lady-in-waiting of the Empress of Japan.

TAISHŌ NO KIMI   Elder daughter of Lord Taishō. Becomes a nun after giving birth to Chūnagon's daughter, Himegimi.

THIRD PRINCE OF CHINA   Son of the Hoyang Consort and the Chinese Emperor. Chūnagon's father in a previous life.

WAKAGIMI   Son of Chūnagon and the Hoyang Consort. Returns to Japan with Chūnagon.

WU CHŪN   Fifth daughter of the Prime Minister of China.

YOSHINO MONK   Protector of the Yoshino nun and Yoshino-hime.

YOSHINO NUN   Mother of the Hoyang Consort by the Prince of Ch'in, and Yoshinohime by Sochi no Miya.

YOSHINOHIME   Daughter of the Yoshino nun and Sochi no Miya, half sister of the Hoyang Consort.

SUMMARY OF THE MISSING CHAPTER

Chūnagon, the hero of this tale, is the handsome and talented son of a Japanese Prince. Chūnagon was particularly close to his father, but when he was still a boy his father died and his mother remarried a widower, Lord Taishō, the father of two lovely young ladies, Taishō no Kimi and Naka no Kimi. This rapid chain of events shocked Chūnagon and he found it difficult to become close to his new stepfather. He longed for his departed father and might well have renounced the world were his mother not dependent on him.

Chūnagon was not averse to an occasional affair with women, but he was always careful to see no harm was done. One night while visiting his stepfather's mansion, perhaps to avoid an unlucky direction, he caught a glimpse of Taishō no Kimi. She had been raised by her father with great care, and arrangements were already being made for her betrothal to Prince Shikibukyō, a man the world felt certain would be the next Crown Prince. Chūnagon was attracted to Taishō no Kimi and found occasion to meet secretly with her, although he was careful not to become too intimate.

Seven or eight years after the death of his father, Chūnagon secretly heard some most extraordinary news: his father had been reborn as the Third Prince of China. Shortly thereafter he saw his father in a dream. Chūnagon asked the Emperor of Japan for three years' leave so that he might travel to China, and although Chūnagon's mother was deeply grieved, permission was granted and preparations for the journey were quickly completed. Shortly before his departure Chūnagon visited Taishō no Kimi. Until now they had contained their passion, but the sorrow of Chūnagon's impending departure proved too strong: that night true vows of love were exchanged. Somehow Taishō no Kimi's father learned of the liaison. He found it necessary to call off her marriage to Prince Shikibukyō and offered in her place his second daughter, Naka no Kimi.

Though Chūnagon found it difficult to leave Taishō no Kimi and his mother, he had already received permission from the Court, and he could hardly cancel the journey at such a late date. He longed to see his father, and went ahead with his plans to travel to China.

Taishō no Kimi soon realized that she was pregnant as a result of that meeting with Chūnagon. She was grieved that she had caused her father such embarrassment and sorrow. Her relationship with her father and stepmother (Chūnagon's mother) was so difficult now that she despaired and decided to cut her hair and renounce the world. Chūnagon, meanwhile, fast on his way to China, knew nothing of her taking of vows.

POEMS FROM THE MISSING CHAPTER

SOURCE: *Mumyōzōshi*

"On the morning after Chūnagon has a dream in which he learns his father had been reborn as a Prince in China, Chūnagon is visited by Saishō no Chūjō who recites this poem:
> Surely she did not expect
> To spend the night alone,
> But now the unexpected sound of waves
> Echoes at her bed.

"Although Taishō no Kimi's behavior was neither prudent nor thoughtful, it is very moving and quite sad when she cuts that beautiful hair of hers and recites these poems:

> What am I to do,
> What can I do?
> To renounce the world grieving
> Would be sad,
> But to stay on is also regretful!

> My parents' loving care
> Was not for this:
> How wearisome the short clipped ends
> Of my dark black hair!"

SOURCE: *Shūi Hyakuban Utaawase*

(#29 on the right) "A poem by Chūnagon sent to the capital as he is about to board the boat for China:

> Blinding tears
> Set my sleeves to disarray,
> For today I have boarded
> The boat for China.

(#30 on the right) "A poem by Taishō no Kimi when she is troubled by many thoughts after Chūnagon has left for China:

> Even though I try not to remember
> It as even wearisome,
> Still the gates of heaven were opened
> At the early morning moon."

SOURCE: *Fūyō Wakashū*

#531, "Spoken by Prince Shikibukyō one moonlit night after Chūnagon has asked for leave of absence to visit China:

> How many tears
> Will darken my eyes
> As I think of you
> When I watch the moon
> Setting in the west?

#532, "Chūnagon's reply:
>And how am I
>To view the moon
>Remembering the hill of Mikasa
>In my old home?

#535, "Sent to a woman by Chūnagon while he is traveling to his boat to China:
>Like the path our boat cuts
>While sailing across the waves,
>Only the memory of you
>Which stays with me
>Is not left behind.

#660, "Spoken by Taishō no Kimi to one who said how sad she would be were Taishō no Kimi to renounce the world:
>Even though no one knows
>Who is shrouded in smoke,
>Are the clouds at evening
>Still not sad?"

HAMAMATSU CHŪNAGON MONOGATARI

Chapter One

THE PASSAGE to China was not so long and frightening as Chūnagon feared.[1] Rather than rough winds and waves, the party seemed to be continually attended by favorable breezes, a consequence perhaps of the deep sense of filial piety with which Chūnagon began the journey. On the tenth day of the seventh month, the travelers arrived at a place called Wen Ling[2] in China. Proceeding along the coast, they dropped anchor at Hangchou in a very pleasant harbor in an inlet. The lovely scene, reminiscent of the view from Ishiyama on the shores of Lake Biwa, aroused in Chūnagon endless memories of Japan.

> I long for the one who lay with me
> In my distant home
> On the shores of the Nio Sea.[3]

From Hangchou the party went to Hsü Pai T'an, an interesting place with many houses where the townspeople, hearing that some Japanese were passing through, made an unusual commotion trying to view the travelers. The party left its boat at Li Yang and proceeded to Mt. Hua where towering peaks give way to deep valleys. With a lingering sense of uncertainty, Chūnagon chanted a verse in the Chinese style,

> "The blue wave path seems distant,
> The clouds a thousand miles."

1. Chūnagon, "Middle Counselor," is the hero's rank, not his given name. As in most Heian tales we never know his true name. He is always referred to by his rank.
2. Most of the Chinese place names are written in *kana* in the extant Japanese texts, and consequently it is occasionally difficult to determine exactly which Chinese characters the Japanese sounds correspond to. In general I have transcribed the place names suggested by Matsuo Satoshi in the headnotes and supplementary notes given in the text I used for this translation: Endō Yoshimoto and Matsuo Satoshi, eds., *Takamura Monogatari, Heichū Monogatari, Hamamatsu Chūnagon Monogatari*, Nihon Koten Bungaku Taikei, no. 77 (Tokyo: Iwanami Shoten, 1964). Where no suggested readings are put forth by Matsuo I have chosen readings I felt would not disturb the flow of the narrative. Unless indicated otherwise, the annotation for this translation is based on Matsuo's notes.
3. "The Nio Sea," *niho no umi*, is another name for Lake Biwa. In this poem Chūnagon is surely thinking of Taishō no Kimi, his lover in Japan.

Scholars accompanying him were moved to tears and responded with the refrain,

"White mist covers the mountain,
The lonely cry of a bird."[4]

Near sunset, the party passed over Mt. Hua and arrived at the border gate of Han Kü[5] where they decided to spend the night. Having read that the guards open the gate when they hear the cock-crow, one of Chūnagon's party, a lover of practical jokes, decided to test the story.[6] In the middle of the night he cleverly imitated the sound of a distant rooster, whereupon the guards woke up and opened the gate. Some in the group criticized the fellow, calling it a humorless prank, but Chūnagon merely laughed at his cleverness in recalling the old story.

The group of officials which gathered the next day at the gate to greet Chūnagon looked just like the illustrations in "The Tale of China."[7] They were captivated by his charming, almost shining demeanor as he adjusted his robes with great dignity before passing through the barrier. Arrangements had been made for Chūnagon to stay in the mansion Wang Chiao-chiang once occupied, its jeweled fixtures carefully polished to full luster.

When Chūnagon was able to settle down and relax, he recalled his homeland; though it lay far beyond the clouds and mist, over mountains and sea, the sorrowful memory of those he had left behind lay heavy on his heart. He was, however, fully consoled by the realization that he would soon see the young Prince.

An Imperial messenger came with an invitation for Chūnagon to meet the Emperor at the Ch'eng Yüan Hall[8] within the Inner Palace.

4. The couplet quoted by Chūnagon and the scholars is by Tachibana no Tadamoto, *Wakan Rōeishū*, #646 in *Wakan Rōeishū, Ryōjin Hishō*, ed. Kawaguchi Hisao and Shida Nobuyoshi, Nihon Koten Bungaku Taikei, no. 73 (Tokyo: Iwanami Shoten, 1965), p. 216.

5. Although the *kana* in the text undoubtedly corresponds to Han Kü Kuan, "the border gate of Han Kü," the author is confused about its location. One would pass through the Han Kü border gate before reaching Mt. Hua when traveling from the coast to Chang-an, the capital.

6. A story from the Meng Ch'ang Chün chapter of the *Shih Chi* in which Meng Ch'ang manages to evade his pursuers when one of his retainers tricks the guards into opening the gate early by imitating the sound of a cock crowing.

7. A Heian *monogatari* no longer extant, *karakuni to iu monogatari*.

8. I have translated the characters given in the text even though Matsuo suggests that they are mistaken.

The Emperor was a young man just over thirty, very handsome and dignified, but even he thought Chūnagon magnificent beyond compare. With men such as Chūnagon, the ministers and counselors mused, Japan must indeed be a remarkable place. They were certain that even P'an Yüeh of the Hoyang District[9] could not have been as charming as this counselor from Japan. And when they tested him at writing poems and playing musical instruments, they discovered no one could excel him. "We should learn from this man. What could we possibly teach him, even of the arts of our own land?" thought the Emperor in amazement. The courtiers found that his constant company assuaged their grief and worry.

The young Prince was living with his mother, the Consort, in a mansion in the Hoyang District near the Imperial Palace. When an invitation came from the Prince, Chūnagon was more than happy to visit him.

The estate seemed so much more splendid than all the others; the color of the water, the placement of the rocks, even the branches of the trees were delightful. Chūnagon was led inside to meet the Prince, a child of seven or eight, charming, yet so correct with his neatly parted hair and smartly fitting robes. Even though the young man's face had changed from his previous life, Chūnagon recognized his father immediately and was soon close to tears. The color of the Prince's face changed slightly, and though he spoke only the usual pleasantries, avoiding more specific subjects, it was clear he had not forgotten their past relationship. When Chūnagon read the Prince's note expressing deeply felt sentiments on their meeting, he was so moved that he could not hold back the tears. Chūnagon's poem in response spoke of his feelings after having traveled so very far through waves of clouds and mist to seek out his father; how, though the Prince's appearance was different from that Chūnagon once knew, the very sight of the boy made him forget his melancholy. These sentiments brought a stream of tears to the Prince's face.

9. P'an Yüeh was a fourth-century poet and magistrate of the Hoyang District, which was north of the Yellow River in what is now the Meng District of Honan. The Hoyang District was close to the Later Han Dynasty capital of Loyang, but a considerable distance from the T'ang capital of Ch'ang-an. Since Ch'ang-an is undoubtedly taken as the capital in this story, later references to Hoyang indicating its close proximity to the capital are undoubtedly due to the author's uncertain knowledge of Chinese geography or her willingness to fictionalize an exotic and distant land.

Chūnagon recalled the serious misgivings he had when he saw what pain his leaving caused his mother and the others. The long, lonely voyage had been a trying experience, and often Chūnagon had wondered what was to become of him; now, as he gazed at the young Prince, he realized how terrible he would have felt had he not come. The Prince was careful not to show his emotions to the others present, even though he was deeply moved by the solace and joyous sense of anticipation reflected in Chūnagon's face. Chūnagon was impressed by the boy's mature behavior.

The Emperor favored the Prince's mother, the Hoyang Consort, and was also partial to the Prince, but the Emperor's desire to be constantly with the Prince made it difficult for the boy to spend any time at his beloved home in Hoyang. Still, the Prince wanted so much to be with Chūnagon, he made frequent excuses to absent himself from Court.

One evening in the middle of the eighth month, as Chūnagon sat in his room staring intently at the garden before him, his thoughts drifted to his distant home. His companions resting within the raised blinds began to reminisce about the capital and a particularly sensitive young man recited a poem.

> The insect's cry,
> The flower's fragrance,
> Even the whisper of the wind
> Are no different from the autumn
> We knew in Japan.

Others tried to think of an appropriate response. Their attempts were collected and about to be recited aloud when, after a brief pause, Chūnagon smiled and said, "Though what you have said is true, there really are many surprising things here." The young man blushed unwittingly. Among the many poems only Chūnagon's was read aloud.

> The morning dew
> And the misty sky,
> The cry of the deer,
> Even the geese in the sky
> Are no different.

On the first day of the tenth month, the Emperor made an Imperial visit to a place west of the palace called Tung-t'ing, [10] the most famous maple-viewing spot in the land. Many people came from faraway provinces in hopes of seeing Chūnagon accompany the Emperor. There was hardly a woman who did not feel slightly faint on seeing him. Those too low in rank to be worthy of his affections were sick with disappointment, while those who felt themselves worthy plotted as best they could to capture his attention. No one among the princes and nobles could equal Chūnagon in composing Chinese verse. Everyone, including the Emperor, was amazed at his talents; they thought he must be from an unusually splendid land.

The next day Chūnagon went to see the Prince, who had returned to Hoyang. It was a dismal, windy evening, and the cold autumn rain made Chūnagon forlorn. As he came upon the Prince's estate, he suddenly heard the sound of a *kin*[11] more beautiful than any he had ever known. Overjoyed, he quietly slipped into a hidden corner of the garden to find where it was coming from. The roof of the building was heavily coated with an indigo paint, unlike the natural cypress roofs in Japan; even the customary furnishings were stained a bright Chinese vermillion, and the blinds were trimmed in brocade. To the southeast, a waterfall descended from a high mountain, and an unusual formation of nearby rocks awaited the gushing mist of the cascade. Near the edge of the billowing stream beautiful chrysanthemums slightly faded by the mist of the waterfall were everywhere to be enjoyed.

Beneath the raised blinds of the mansion perhaps a dozen ladies-in-waiting dressed in splendid garments sat on brocade mats spread

10. "Tōtei" in the text probably refers to either Tung-t'ing Lake in Hunan Province or Mt. Tung-t'ing in T'ai Lake on the border of Kiangsu and Chekiang Provinces. Neither, however, is west of the palace, and both are too distant to be reached quickly from the capital. The author probably knew "Tung-t'ing" as a scenic spot from Chinese poetry and assumed it was as accessible to the Chinese courtiers in Ch'ang-an as the scenic spots in Japan were to the courtiers in the Japanese capital of Heiankyō.

11. A seven-string bridgeless musical instrument resembling a zither. Originally transmitted from China, the instrument went out of fashion in the mid-Heian period and would not have been played much (if at all) in the period *Hamamatsu Chūnagon Monogatari* was written. The close association of the Hoyang Consort with the *kin* throughout this *monogatari* surely lent a sense of "exoticism" to her image in the minds of the readers.

on the veranda. Though their faces were hidden behind varicolored fans, he noticed that their beautiful hair was combed up,[12] and colorful shoulder ribbons and waistbands adorned their clothes.[13] The entire scene seemed no different from a cleverly executed Chinese painting. Near the raised blinds, a lady was playing the *kin*, her decorous ribbons of Chinese weave spread far to one side. A curtain dyed in the faded style, light at the top and gradually darkening to a deep purple near the bottom, was turned back over the arm of its frame. Chūnagon stared at her intently, thinking she might be the Consort. She seemed no more than twenty years of age, with a full well-shaped face, neither too thin nor too plump; her lovely complexion seemed to radiate with a beauty so fair and clear as to dim white crystal jade.[14] She was truly without fault: her lips were crimson, her hair carefully coiffed, and her eyebrows seemed much more elegant than those of the other ladies. She gazed intently at the garden while playing the *kin*. Chūnagon was taken aback to find such a lovely lady in this land. He had always thought the familiar fashion of Japan—the long straight hair falling casually over the shoulders and cheeks—held a certain refined attractiveness, and now he realized this beautiful ornamented style with the hair bound up was also quite agreeable. Perhaps, he thought, this beauty was a

12. *Kamiage* was a formal hairstyle for high-ranked ladies-in-waiting in which part of the hair was tied up in a small bun and held in place with combs. The popular Heian style of *kamiage* was an imitation of Chinese fashion and here the author is quickening the reader's interest by depicting a familiar fashion at its source. A drawing of women in the *kamiage* style can be found in Ikeda Kikan, *Zenkō Makura no Sōshi* (Tokyo: Shibundō, 1967), p. 710.

13. *Hire* (shoulder sash or ribbon) was a decorative sash worn over the shoulder on full dress occasions. According to one explanation, it was originally used in ancient times to shoo away insects, but in later days its only practical use was in waving goodbye to someone. *Kutai* (also *kuntai*) was a decorative ribbon used as a waistband with an open skirt (*mo*). The ribbon was tied in front and the excess ends were allowed to drop to the sides. *Hire* and *kutai* were always worn together. Ikeda Kikan, *Heian Jidai no Bungaku to Seikatsu* (Tokyo: Shibundō, 1966), pp. 226-28.

14. The Consort's fair complexion, a mark of beauty to Heian sensibilities, is here compared to someone or something designated by the word *hariseramu*. Matsuo offers two possible interpretations for this phrase. The first, originally posed by Onoe Hachirō, is that the word should really be *harishiratama*, "crystal white jade." The second interpretation, offered by Yamagishi Tokuhei, is that the word was originally *hansefuyo*, "the Lady in Attendance Fan." In addition to assuming the original text is a miscopy, both explanations have certain grammatical problems. Neither explanation is definitive but I prefer the former.

consequence of high birth. He had never heard such a lovely melody from the *kin*, and the seven or eight ladies on the veranda were what he imagined maidens from heaven to be. Each held a chrysanthemum as, with vibrant voices, they sang the Chinese verse, "The storm in the orchid garden . . . ;" others within the room lifted their voices in response, "After this flower has bloomed. . . ."[15]

Chūnagon had always thought such verses were sung by men, not women; he wanted to know more about who was chanting these verses while viewing the flowers, but the Consort had the blinds lowered and went inside. The brief glimpse left him dissatisfied, as though he had only seen the half-moon. Unable to bear this uneasiness, he left his secluded spot, picked a chrysanthemum, and brought it to where the ladies sat half-hidden on the veranda. As they showed no sense of shock or alarm at his unexpected appearance, he offered the ladies a poem.

> Seeing this flower tonight
> Has helped me forget
> My yearning for home.

Each lady held a fan before her face and listened to the poem just as ladies in Japan would. He was delighted to find that they were not unable to respond in kind.

> Would that this flower
> Remain fragrant and never fade,
> So that no one need be homesick.

When the young Prince appeared on the veranda, Chūnagon turned from the ladies and went to greet him.

"What a splendid evening," said the Prince as he pushed a koto toward Chūnagon. The beauty of the Consort's face, even the lingering hint of her perfume, had moved Chūnagon deeply. He found it difficult to begin playing the koto, for the sound of her *kin* still echoed in his ears. Within the blinds she too was lost in thought.

"This man is so wonderfully talented. How sad indeed it will be after his return when we can no longer see him," she thought, weeping secretly.

15. These two lines are from different couplets in the *Wakan Rōeishū*. The first, #271, is by Sugawara no Fumitoki, the second, #267, by the T'ang poet Yüan Chen. Kawaguchi, ed. *Wakan Rōeishū*, pp. 115 and 116.

The Consort's ancestry could, it seems, be traced back to a certain Prince of Ch'in, a descendant of the T'ang Emperor T'ai Tsung. A man of outstanding talents and handsome appearance, this prince was sent as an envoy to Japan to handle some diplomatic matters. In Tsukushi[16] he met the daughter of a Japanese prince who had died in exile there, leaving his daughter with only a poor nursemaid for support. The Prince of Ch'in became intimate with the forlorn lady and, in due course, a beautiful jewel of a baby girl was born. The child was so preciously charming, the Prince felt he could not possibly return to China without her, yet to take her with him involved great risks.

No woman had made the journey since Sasemaro tried to take the Lady Unawashi across.[17] In that instance, the Dragon King of the Sea was captivated by Unawashi and refused to let the boat pass until Sasemaro cast her off on mats thrown on the sea.

The Prince of Ch'in was at a loss over what to do with his lovely daughter. Having spent five years in Japan, he could stay no longer, nor could he bear the thought of leaving her behind. Time and time again he begged permission of the Dragon King of the Sea to allow her to pass. Finally he heard these words in a dream. "Leave immediately. This girl is destined to be a consort in your land. You will pass safely."

The Prince of Ch'in was overjoyed and returned to China with the girl, now five years old. There, under his careful tending, she grew into an unparalleled beauty, finally coming to the attention of the Emperor, who pressed for her hand. The Prince, however, was reluctant to give his daughter to the Emperor, for he feared the Prime Minister, father of the Empress who had borne the Crown Prince and numerous other children. He felt certain that his priceless daughter would meet with danger in such a hostile environment. In spite of his misgivings, he acquiesced to the urgent pleas of the Emperor

16. The historical name for the provinces of Chikuzen and Chikugo in particular, and all of Kyūshū in general, Tsukushi was the initial point of landing for diplomats, merchants, and scholars from the continent. Being quite distant from the capital, it also became a place of exile for disgraced nobility.

17. The author is apparently unconsciously mixing two legends, that of Ōtomo no Sadehiko found in the *Chikuzen Fudoki* and Ōtomo no Sademaro found in *Fukuro Sōshi*. Both legends are based on historical characters of the Nara era who made voyages to the mainland.

and, at the age of fourteen, the daughter went to the palace at Yangchou. The Emperor favored her to the exclusion of all others, and her father was raised to the rank of Minister. When, at the age of sixteen, she gave birth to a boy, she was immediately given the rank of Imperial Consort and enjoyed unparalleled favor.

The Prime Minister, father of the First Empress, was greatly angered and resentful of her rapid rise at Court. He cursed the new consort and perpetrated many incidents by which he hoped to destroy the Emperor's affection for her. The other consorts and Imperial concubines joined forces in opposing the newcomer, bringing to mind the well-known fate of Yang Kuei-fei.[18] Her father felt all resistance futile, so he resigned his position, and to the north of the capital, in the mountain temple area of Shu Shan[19] he built a fine villa and retired from public life. Realizing that she could hardly serve the Emperor without any backing at Court, the Consort sought to join her father in his retreat. This upset the Emperor terribly. She was, however, tormented by the machinations of others, frequently ill, even faint on occasion, and was obviously no longer able to continue at Court. The Emperor decided that if he could not have her at Court, at least he might keep her close at hand. He built an imposing mansion in nearby Hoyang District where he quartered the Consort, and every two or three days he had her son, the Prince, come to Court.

Though the Court seemed very ordered and restricted, in fact, the movements of the Emperor of China were not nearly as limited as the Emperor of Japan. In times of inordinate longing he was able to quietly visit the Hoyang Consort, though he had to be careful not to go too often or too conspicuously. The Emperor so lamented the limitations of his position he frequently became ill and seemingly was indifferent whether he lived or died. His attendants remained

18. Concubine of the T'ang Emperor Hsüan Tsung, their love story was immortalized in Po Chü-i's poem "A Song of Unending Sorrow," a favorite poem of the Heian court aristocracy.

19. Shu is the name of an ancient kingdom in what is now Szechwan Province, and the author may be referring to the mountains of Shu in general, even though these mountains are not north of the capital and are too distant to be easily reached from the capital. Mountains by the same name in present-day Shantung and Kiangsu seem equally inappropriate, although the latter were made famous by the Sung poet Su Shih (1037-1101). However, *Hamamatsu Chūnagon Monogatari* was surely written before the poetry of Su Shih became known in Japan.

close, ministering to his every need and offering prayers for his recovery. It was just about this time that the Emperor began visiting various places and engaging in poetic amusements with Chūnagon; owing perhaps to the efficacy of everyone's prayers, these amusements successfully diverted the Emperor's sorrow.

Though the Hoyang Consort spent only the first five years of her life in Japan, she had been a good deal more mature than other children her age and could remember her mother quite well. Particularly unforgettable was the day of their separation, when her mother had embraced her and said, "Since this is to be our final parting you will probably never know when I die. Think of today as the end."

The Consort could still recall her mother's weeping face. As she grew older, she would often gaze at the mountains to the east, wondering what had become of her mother. Lonely and depressed, she had no particular wish to remain in the world. When the Emperor brought her into the Inner Palace, he pledged his love day and night, wishing they could be like two birds sharing a wing;[20] this touched her deeply, but she was still sad and easily upset by the harsh vengefulness of palace intrigue. The young Prince, peerless in his beauty and mature behavior, was her only consolation for the sorrows of the world. Surrounded by the splendor of the Hoyang villa, she would sit and stare at the garden for hours; by day she read the Lotus Sutra, and on moonlit nights she played the *kin*.

The sorrow of her position would be too heavy for anyone else, but from the very beginning, the Consort never cared much for life in the palace. Nor for that matter did she consider her relationship with the Emperor an inviolate trust. Her only lament was that her mother was gone forever, she knew not where, and they could never meet again in this world. The Consort was content to live peacefully in Hoyang District where she could pass the time viewing flowers and the moon, though at times she felt it strange that she should accept such a fate. Perhaps because she resembled her mother so much, her appearance, mannerisms, and even her way of speaking

20. Alluding to a famous couplet in "A Song of Unending Sorrow": "we wished to fly in the heaven, two birds with the wings of one, And to grow together on the earth, two branches of one tree." Translated by Witter Bynner in ed. Cyril Birch *Anthology of Chinese Literature*, (New York: Grove Press, 1965) p. 269.

seemed no different from those of the court ladies of Japan. Her grace and genteel beauty bore little resemblance to the ways of women in China, although her own ladies-in-waiting were similar in manner. This was why Chūnagon was surprised by their gentleness—so like the ladies of his own land—on the night they exchanged poems over the chrysanthemums.

Ever anxious to talk with people from Japan, the Consort would even spend time telling her sad story to the many Japanese monks visiting China, and when she heard that Chūnagon had come, she wanted very much to meet with him too. Her son, who was always a bit aloof with the people from her land, seemed to enjoy Chūnagon's company and spent a great deal of time in intimate conversation with him. The Consort watched Chūnagon on his frequent visits to the Prince. Each time she saw him, she tearfully thought of him as a person from the distant land which so obsessed her everyday thoughts. Perhaps because she thought of him, Chūnagon too could not easily forget the night of the chrysanthemums, and his wish to see her again was a source of constant yearning.

One day when the Consort and her son were alone, the Prince found an opportunity in the conversation to make a confession. "People have been remarking about how much I resemble Chūnagon," he began. "Though the comparison makes me look foolish, there is something in it. Until now I have never revealed this, but I was once a native of Japan, and this Chūnagon is my son from my former life. I longed for rebirth into the nine ranks of the Pure Land, but deep affection for Chūnagon, my only child, prevented this. And apparently for that reason I was born here. Word of my rebirth reached Chūnagon, and though the Emperor of Japan lamented and Chūnagon's mother was near death with sorrow, he disregarded their pleas and took a three-year leave of absence to come visit me. Many people have criticized me for so quickly becoming intimate with a person from an unknown land; but, in fact, I am merely following the past sentiments in my heart. I have a great affection for him and always wish to be with him. You too must not think of him as a stranger. Since he will not be here long I am already thinking of the many memories I will have after he returns to Japan."

The Consort was profoundly shocked by the Prince's tearful confession.

"Why didn't you tell me these things before? Even I can plainly see you do resemble Chūnagon, but I had no idea your relationship was this deep. I had merely thought you enjoyed the company of this handsome man. Whenever I see you two together I feel a certain uneasiness over how difficult it will be for you when he returns, but had I known your ties were this deep. . . . I went to Court only with the intention of helping those close to me achieve the fame and power of high position. Because of me, however, my father felt disgraced and quit the Court to live secluded in the mountains. I am unable to serve at Court and, like the ladies shut in the Shang Yang Palace long ago,[21] I am confined alone in my quarters, with no desire to carry on. You are now a mature young man, well versed in the ways of this world. I look to you as my only source of consolation. Of course I will treat him with affection equal to yours; in fact, your story is so moving that I might even meet him myself, if we can avoid the disagreeable stares of others."

The Consort had always wanted to know Chūnagon better since he had come from the land she longed for. Now that she heard the Prince's story, she was even more anxious to speak with him in private, where no one could see them. In her mind, however, she could hear the invidious voices of the court ladies scheming of ways to further disgrace her. She realized that should word spread of secret meetings with Chūnagon, not only would she be ruined, but both the Prince and Chūnagon would be defamed. She therefore decided not to meet him.

Though Chūnagon was not aware of the Consort's feelings for him, he often thought of her. "I would like once again to see her as she was. From afar her ways did seem familiar, but up close I

21. Although the text has *shōkiyō*, Matsuo takes this as a misprint of *shōyōkyū*, Shang Yang Kung, a palace of the capital at Loyang. A similar phrase using *shōyōkyū* appears on p. 312 of the Iwanami text. The allusion apparently is to a line from a poem entitled "The White-Haired Woman of Shang Yang" by Po Chü-i. The Shang Yang Palace was where the most beautiful concubines were locked away once Yang Kuei-fei gained the complete devotion of the Emperor Hsüan Tsung. It is indicative of the author's eclectic use of Chinese allusions that the Consort would compare her situation to that of concubines disdained by the Emperor because of his infatuation with Yang Kuei-fei, when only a few pages earlier the Consort's own situation was likened to that of Yang Kuei-fei.

66

imagine her appearance and words are not at all like a lady of Japan."
While he never ceased longing for his homeland, this preoccupation
with the Consort did serve to divert his attention.

Taishō no Kimi sat staring vacantly, apparently lost in sad thoughts.
Chūnagon went to her side, and just as he was about to express his
unworldly sorrow over their separation, she burst into tears.

> For whom have I fallen
> Into this sea of tears?
> Does he know I must wring my wet sleeve
> Like a fisherwoman?[22]

Chūnagon was so moved by her poem that he found himself
crying, and the tears which filled his eyes suddenly woke him from
the dream. The sense of the dream was still with him, and he was
unable to stop weeping.

"If she thinks this much of me even though we're very far apart,
then our love is indeed out of the ordinary.[23] I was reckless and then
left so suddenly. I wonder what she must think of me now?"

> Tonight I saw her in my dreams,
> As faithful as the pines
> Waiting on the beach of Mitsu,
> The one who loves me still.[24]

How lovely she had been as she wept uncontrollably the morning
they parted. "Should I live long enough to return," he thought, "I
wonder what she will think of me when I try to soothe her resentment
over my long absence. Since Prince Shikibukyō surely visits there
frequently, it must be very difficult for her."[25] For a long time he
could do nothing but think of her.

22. There is a critical pun in this poem on the word *ama* which can mean either
"fisherwoman," or "nun." Chūnagon misses the obvious double meaning and thinks
only that she is wet with tears of sorrow.

23. It was a common Heian belief that a person appears in one's dreams because
he or she was thinking of the dreamer a great deal.

24. The second line of this poem in the Japanese, *mitsu no hamamatsu*, became
the title for *Hamamatsu Chūnagon Monogatari*. "Mitsu" refers to the port of Naniwa
(present-day Osaka), a point of departure for travelers heading for China.

25. A reference to events in the missing chapter. Prince Shikibukyō was originally
betrothed to Taishō no Kimi, but after she became pregnant with Chūnagon's child
the Prince quickly married Taishō no Kimi's sister, Naka no Kimi. The Prince's visits
to his wife, Naka no Kimi, would obviously be a source of uneasiness for Taishō no
Kimi.

The year came quickly to an end. The thought of welcoming the new year in an unfamiliar land saddened Chūnagon, but he found the young Prince's support reassuring. In appearance the young boy did not resemble Chūnagon's father at all, but his heart, unbeknownst to others, had not changed.

The morning of the new year is the same everywhere. The hazy sky and the cry of the warbler served to remind Chūnagon of springtime in Japan, but the memories of the people he had been with last year only made him sadder.

In hopes of dispelling his loneliness he decided to visit a mountain said to be completely covered with plum trees.[26] Even from a distance the wind was heavy with the fragrance of blossoms in full bloom, and with no other trees in sight these flowers made the entire mountainside seem white.

> From afar the mountain abloom with plum
> Seems covered with pure white snow.

The banks of a pond in T'ao Yüan[27] were covered with beautifully aligned rows of peach trees as far as Chūnagon could see. The spectacular sight of the trees in full bloom caught him by surprise and reminded him of a story he had once read.[28] It seems that long ago a lover of flowers went to an area covered with peach trees. No matter how far he walked, he did not reach his goal. Forcing himself on, he came to a place where he heard dogs barking. There were men there. He ate the peaches they gave him and turned into a Taoist immortal.[29]

Chūnagon felt certain the peach trees he was now looking at were

26. Although plum trees were an important component of the well-groomed Heian garden, they are not native to Japan. The opportunity to see a vast number of plum trees growing wild would have been an exotic experience for a Heian courtier.

27. *Tōguen* in the text, apparently referring to the *T'ao Yüan* of *Wu Ling T'ao Yüan*, an enchanted utopia found in an essay entitled *T'ao Hua Yüan Chi*, "Record of Peach Blossom Fount" by the Eastern Chin poet T'ao Ch'ien (365-427). Again, the author of *Hamamatsu Chūnagon Monogatari* is freely using even fictional place names from Chinese literary sources to paint an ideal picture of the China Chūnagon visited.

28. The following story is apparently based loosely on a legend associated with Hsi Wang Mu, "The Grand Old Lady of the West," a mythical character who lived in the Kunlun Mountains and possessed an elixir of eternal life.

29. *Sennin* were mythical Taoists who had gained the secret of immortal life. In Japan they were thought to have wandered in the mountains practicing their magical arts.

the very ones mentioned in the story. Since he had both read the story in faraway Japan and then actually seen the sight with his own eyes, he felt an unusual self-satisfaction in this experience.

At that time there was not a single Chief Minister or High Court Noble who did not wish Chūnagon to meet his daughter.

"Though he is only a foreigner here for a brief visit, I would like to have him come and visit my household while he is in our land. If perchance my daughter should bear his child, wouldn't that be a wonderful way to retain the memory of this magnificent man."

They continually made attempts to entice him to their homes, but Chūnagon refused their advances. He never thought himself the type to partake in such activities even in his own country—how much more inappropriate it would be to become involved in an unknown land! Furthermore, he was fully aware of the difficulties he would have in returning home were he to fall into such a relationship. The young Prince also gave Chūnagon a secret warning.

"There are a number of people making such plans. Do not let them entrap you. This may appear to be a refined and elegant society, but, in fact, people can be quite fearsome. Should they take it into their heads to prevent your return there would indeed be trouble. Besides, it is wrong for a person born to live in Japan to spend his life in China. And the worst thing would be the terrible crime of filial impiety in deserting your mother."

Since Chūnagon was of the same mind as the Prince he was now more adamant in refusing the many temptations.

Among the numerous daughters of the Prime Minister, father of the First Consort, the fifth daughter, Wu Chün,[30] was particularly beautiful and favored by the Prime Minister. After seeing Chūnagon at the maple festival at Tung-t'ing she fell into inexplicable fits of depression which caused her complexion and appearance to deteriorate. The Prime Minister was shocked and worried by this stange illness. He had sutras read and other rites performed, but Wu Chün failed to show any sign of improvement.

30. Wu Chün is known in the original as *go no kimi*, "the fifth daughter." Women in *monogatari* were commonly known by their rank (or that of their parents), place of dwelling, or the order of birth (as in this case). Quite often, however, the subject of a sentence is omitted and the context alone tells us which person is being referred to. I have taken the Chinese pronunciation for the characters for *go*, "five," and *kimi*, "honorable person" or "daughter" in this case, for this lady's appelation.

"What has caused this?" he sighed.

"I would like to hear Chūnagon of Japan play the koto," she told her father. "I think that might alleviate some of my worries. I am not suffering from any great pain, just an annoying weariness . . ."

"Indeed, Chūnagon is just the man. Seeing him will surely arrest your depression and give you new life. What a splendid idea! I'll call on him right away." With a cart so covered with flowers it seemed to glitter he set off for Chūnagon's mansion.

Chūnagon was surprised to see him. He wondered why the highest minister in the land, a man who held the reins of power and could very well do as he pleased, would bother to visit him.

The Prime Minister extended the invitation. "I thought of having some suitable messenger come invite you to my home, but, fearing you might not be inclined to heed their call, I decided to take it upon myself to invite you to my humble abode to view the flowers in full bloom. I would be pleased if you would join me . . ."

Chūnagon could hardly refuse such an invitation. "I am deeply honored. Had you merely sent word I would have come immediately," he said as he arranged his robes upon leaving.

The Prime Minister's house was decorated with the most beautiful furnishings and seemed no less brilliant than the Imperial Palace itself. As Chūnagon entered the main gate, the lively sounds of the flute and drum were signaling the beginning of the festivities. Seven or eight men, all Major or Middle Counselors,[31] greeted Chūnagon with great pomp and ceremony. Large chairs were set up beneath the young willow branches and under the exquisitely beautiful cherry blossoms in full bloom near the edge of the pond. On either side of the pond stood small pavilions for music, dancing, and poetry, the entire scene being one of grandiose display. The Prime Minister had, of course, spared no expense in planning the most delectable cuisine.

Once the festivities had begun, the Prime Minister quietly slipped inside the mansion to where his daughter was seated. The girl, so languid of late, now wore bright jeweled pins in her hair and laughed openly as she watched Chūnagon from behind a curtain of brocade. Seeing her so relaxed the Prime Minister could not help but regret

31. Dainagon and Chūnagon, Major Counselor and Middle Counselor, were high ranks in the Japanese bureaucratic structure but not proper ranks in China. The author has given familiar Japanese ranks to the Chinese characters.

having let his daughter suffer in silence so long when the cure was so simple. How things differ in the world!

After a day of delightful entertainment, the Prime Minister insisted that Chūnagon spend the night at his mansion. After a time the minister's persistent attempts to draw him behind the blinds began to irritate Chūnagon. He had heard that the man could be fearsome, and he wondered what he had in mind. He called for the minister's third son, a Middle Counselor who had frequently visited him, and asked about the minister's intentions.

"Why does your father want me to spend the night here? I'll go in only if I know exactly what he has in mind."

"His fifth daughter is his favorite child," the Middle Counselor replied. "Recently she has been troubled with fits of depression and is unable to leave her bed. This grieved my father deeply. She mentioned that seeing the Counselor of Japan might enliven her. That was all he wanted."

The unusual frankness of the Middle Counselor's explanation took Chūnagon aback. To himself he mused, "It seems it is the custom in this country to speak one's mind directly. This man is a complete gentleman, noble and handsome, no shortcomings in either intellect or demeanor. There mustn't be anything wrong with his speaking so." He could not help but laugh aloud when he thought of his countrymen's tendency to dress and embellish each phrase.

"That is the very least I can do to help alleviate you sister's suffering," he told the Middle Counselor. "Why wasn't I approached earlier about such a simple matter? It is no trouble at all for me to see her like this, but I must tell you that since my stay in China is only temporary, I have avoided intimate contact with women. If it were only for the love of a woman would I have come all the way over here? Please consider my situation. I was drawn here by an inexplicable wanderlust, an impulse quite out of the ordinary. And while I am here I must avoid the ordinary affairs of men and women. If on occasion you should invite me as you did today, then I will come; but was your father perchance thinking of more mundane matters?"

The Middle Counselor explained these sentiments to his father who, remembering that Chūnagon was said to feel this way about affairs with women, readily agreed to his conditions.

"I think it is just as you say," he told Chūnagon. "Young people are always interested in the exotic and the unusual; all I want is that you find what you are looking for!"

He continued to urge him into the inner chambers. No longer able to escape by refusing, Chūnagon finally consented to go inside.

Needless to say the furnishings were dazzling. As many as fifty ladies-in-waiting sat in full dress, their hair coiffed in the upraised style and their faces slightly hidden by fans. Each pillar of the inner room had a glowing oil lamp, and the ladies sat in well-ordered rows between these pillars. The Prime Minister's daughter lifted the curtain surrounding her dais and, toying with her fan as she lay in bed, stared at Chūnagon.

Amazed by her unexpected boldness he was momentarily at a loss. He realized that if she were at all like the Hoyang Consort he would not really care what happened. He moved closer to the dais and began to talk with her. She in turn showed no hesitation or embarrassment in speaking to him. In the dim light she seemed perhaps seventeen or eighteen with a lovely pale complexion, but clearly no match for the Hoyang Consort. Her speech was filled with strange unfamiliar words that left Chūnagon feeling lost in a foreign land. Cooled by her unfamiliar ways he could not help but wonder why she was so different. The girl moved slightly forward and began to play the koto.

Chūnagon was deeply impressed by her playing. Before leaving he vowed not to take their relationship lightly and promised to call on her occasionally during his stay. Leaving his flute as a parting gift he returned home before the break of dawn.

In order not to offend the temperamental Prime Minister, Chūnagon thereafter sent occasional letters to the young lady. Her illness, which turned out to be nothing more than a young girl's pining for a handsome man, quickly abated. Her disposition must have always been rather vigorous, for that brief visit from Chūnagon was enough to ease her depression. From that time on she showed no unusual symptoms. Her father, well aware of Chūnagon's reluctance to become deeply involved with women, had no reason to doubt his behavior; he delighted in his daughter's recovery and constantly thanked Chūnagon for having found the cure. This unusual display of emotion was enough to make Chūnagon pity the old man.

The visit to this young lady stirred in Chūnagon the desire to see the Hoyang Consort once again, but such a meeting seemed impossible. In desperation he visited a temple called P'u T'i Ssu which enshrined a Buddha said to be most effective in answering petitions. While praying to see the Consort once again he fell asleep and dreamt that a priest, apparently from this temple, appeared before him dressed in very beautiful, stately robes. The priest recited a poem:

Is it only for a moment
You wish to see her again?
Your ties are fated to be deep.

Upon awakening, Chūnagon could not comprehend the meaning of this dream.

About this time the Hoyang Consort was visited by ominous warnings of danger. It seems that just when she had decided to reenter the Court at Yangchou, her health suddenly took a turn for the worse and she became subject to frequent fainting spells. Rather than worry the Emperor with her troubles she simply sent word that she was alive, then tearfully took her leave. Wondering what might lie in store for her in such a frightening, uncertain world, she secretly summoned a learned Yin-yang diviner to interpret the terrible signs.

"Leave this place and begin strict abstinence immediately," he warned.

In China the movements of a Consort are relatively unrestricted. Leaving her son in the palace, she had the Hoyang mansion sealed completely for the period of abstinence, and with just a few trustworthy ladies she slipped away to a place called Shan Yin, a day's journey from the palace.

About the same time Chūnagon felt a desire to visit this very area since it was famous as the home of Wang Tzu Yu, a distinguished poet known for composing verse while pleasure-boating on moonlit nights. The moon, hidden by a slight haze, seemed remarkably captivating, and the flowers in full bloom gave the night a beauty beyond compare. Chūnagon could not help but wonder if the sky of his homeland were this lovely tonight; he wondered too if someone might be looking at the moon this evening and thinking of him.[32]

32. The image of Chūnagon in China looking at the moon would remind the reader of Abe no Nakamoro's poem on viewing the moon in China and longing for home, *Kokinshū*, #406.

He recalled the many times he had visited the palace back home to join in musical festivities. Just such a night as this in the spring of last year he had visited Prince Shikibukyō. The memory of the sorrowful Prince reciting his farewell poem, "the moon setting in the west,"[33] now brought tears to Chūnagon's eyes.

> As I look at the moon
> Hidden in a faint green mist,
> I long for the sky
> I knew back in my homeland.

A few houses were visible from the pond where he sat gazing at the moon. By the edge of the pond an old man with a black lacquered cap leaned on a metal cane and stared at the moon beneath the pine and cherry trees. The scene was enchantingly picturesque. A small child with hair tied back held a fan and stood behind him. Chūnagon found the scene fascinating and paused for a moment to watch them.[34] While gazing at the moon the old man spoke this poem.

> Who knows whether I will be alive tomorrow;
> Tonight I will enjoy the view
> Of the moonlit evening sky.

It was truly a moving sight. In response Chūnagon said,

> Ah! How many ages
> Must this water have known
> Before gathering to reflect
> The moonlight tonight.

Near the lake he could hear the lovely sound of a *biwa*. Following the music he came upon a respectable, even elegant, unfinished dwelling at the foot of a mountain alongside a small river. Since no one was at the gate he went to an unfinished corner of the wall surrounding the grounds and peered inside. The flowers of the garden were spectacular in the moonlight flooding the yard. Seated near the veranda of the main building within upraised blinds were several well-dressed ladies, one of whom was playing the *biwa*. The scene

33. This poem from the missing chapter is listed in the *Fūyō Wakashū*, "Separation" poem #531.
How many tears / Will darken my eyes / As I think of you / When I watch the moon / Setting in the west?

34. The description here is meant to evoke the familiar image of a Chinese-style painting (*karae*), a popular art form in Heian Japan depicting landscapes and scenes in the T'ang and Sung style.

was beautiful. Within the main room another lady lay on the floor, her head resting on her hand as she gazed at the moon. Thinking this might be the mistress of the house, Chūnagon paused for a closer look. Though he could not see the lady's face clearly in the moonlight, her beautiful figure reminded him of the Hoyang Consort on the night of the chrysanthemums. But he simply could not imagine finding her in such a place. He felt terribly confused; how could anyone bear such a striking resemblance to the peerless Consort? Was it preordained? Throwing caution to the winds he walked directly to the veranda when the ladies paused in their playing.

"Is this a dream?" they thought, stunned by his sudden appearance. When they realized the stranger was none other than Chūnagon of Japan, they immediately grasped the seriousness of the situation and, as one might expect of such discerning ladies, had the presence of mind to act accordingly. They remained calm and decided there was little they could do but try to conclude the incident without letting him know their lady's identity. The Consort was dismayed.

"That terrible oracle which led me to this unexpected place—is this what was meant to be?" she wondered. "Had I remained in the palace nothing so dreadful could have happened, no matter how wretchedly the other ladies treated me. But what am I to do now? Some unknown bond must have drawn us together. In any event I must not let him know who I am." She tried not to appear too distraught.

He was amazed to find this lovely lady in a land so foreign to his own sense of delicate, subdued beauty. Even up close she was gentle, yielding, and incomparably beautiful, no different at all from the finest ladies of his native land. Weeping he pledged his love.

"I had no idea our karmic bond would be so deep. In all this land I have been joined with you alone. But I must know who you are, for I cannot do without you for a moment. I want you to come secretly to my quarters."

She warned him gently of her predicament.

"Unexpected omens of danger have plagued me lately and I must be very careful in my movements. It would be most difficult for me to do as you say. The unusal fate which has drawn us together cannot be escaped. Surely it will not be difficult to meet again. Please ask the ladies here for further details. They will tell you everything."

Her gentle manner and kind reply showed that she was no ordinary person.

As dawn was soon to come she urged him to leave. "It is dangerous for you to remain here. Please leave quickly."

Chūnagon realized she was right but he could not bring himself to depart so suddenly.

Even in my own land
I have never known
Such a bewildering dawn parting.

"I had such a strange dreamlike feeling when I left my loved ones in Japan. I see now that I was drawn to this meeting by destiny," he whispered tearfully.

In her heart the lady too realized fate had brought them together. Weeping sorrowfully she answered,

Wretched and yet tender
Is the fate which ties me to one
From the unknown land far beyond the clouds.

The pitiful sight of the weeping lady made it even more difficult for Chūnagon to leave, until suddenly he felt a tender longing for Taishō no Kimi in Japan. To leave without knowing more about the lady was unfortunate, but he realized that it was inappropriate to linger too long.

"I will do as you say and leave immediately, but I must see you again this evening. How am I to find you?" he asked.

"Today and tomorrow I am in a period of strict taboo so you must not come here. Two or three days from now come late at night to my mansion in Ting Li. I am to be here for only a few days and the period of taboo must be strictly observed. There are people we must be wary of, so do not send any messages here. I shall see you at Ting Li . . ."

She seemed well-intentioned. She had told him exactly where she would be and when he should visit her. He had no reason at all to doubt her word, and the lady herself gave no indication of misleading him. Clearly her instructions to ask the ladies for further details meant this was not the end. Chūnagon had always found the people of China very straightforward and honest, and he felt certain she would not deceive him. After reaffirming again and again their promise to meet, he finally left. Later he sent one of his men back to investigate the premises.

"The house is indeed under lock," the man reported. "Even the keyholes have been covered up. Guards are posted and there seem to be a number of people within."

Chūnagon pondered the situation as he returned to his quarters. "She does not appear to be a woman unfamiliar with the ways of the world. There must be some good reason for her caution. Even in my own country I would move prudently in such a matter. And in an unfamiliar land—how much worse it would be to get the reputation of a reckless lover."

At night three days later Chūnagon went as instructed to Ting Li (a place similar to the western half of the capital in Japan). The people there, however, had never heard of such a lady. He peeked through the fences but still saw no sign of her. Bewildered and choked with disappointment he sent a man back to Shan Yin where they had met, but no one was there either. The lady had obviously planned her disappearance skillfully. Even in a country where he knew his way around he could hardly hope to find a lady who deliberately hid from him. It was even more difficult in a land where he was unfamiliar with the local customs. As a mere visitor he felt it imperative that no one even dream that he, of all people, was caught up in some sordid love affair. There was simply no way to find the lady. Unceasingly he sent retainers to Ting Li to inquire after the lady, but no one was of any help. In his heart he could not forget her for even a moment, but to think of her made the sorrow more painful.

> I was drenched by many rough waves
> On the voyage here,
> Only to now find myself lost
> On the mountain path of love.

Following this incident Chūnagon was very depressed and his dejection was clearly visible in everything he did. The young Prince felt he understood Chūnagon's problem. "For a while everything was unusual and interesting, but now he is finding it difficult to live in an unfamiliar land. He must be very homesick." The Prince mentioned this to his mother, the Consort.

"Chūnagon tries to hide his grief but he is obviously not happy. He must find life here difficult."

These words brought tears to the Consort's eyes and in her heart she felt crushed. She was frightened and upset by the terrible fate which seemed to direct her life.

"He is a fine person," she thought, "but who would even dream of an Imperial consort carrying on with a foreigner?"

After returning to Hoyang from Shan Yin she was unable to eat much of anything. Within a few months she began to notice peculiar changes in her body. She realized it was something foreordained, a wretched yet somehow wonderful sign of the karma which had drawn them together.

A number of wise diviners had already determined that the Emperor would have no more than three sons. "I have been away from the palace so long no one would believe it is the Emperor's child," she thought tearfully. "What terrible things the other consorts would say. They would surely destroy both me and the Prince. We would be made public criminals. What am I to do?"

As the months passed by she became increasingly concerned about her condition. "The Emperor is sure to come and visit some time. What am I to do it he sees me like this?"

About that time the Empress hatched certain schemes to make life even more miserable for the Consort. Making a pretext of these incidents, the Consort decided to go into hiding.

"I could hardly live a moment in this loathsome world without the Prince by my side, but the Emperor also insists on being with him. It would be frightening to ignore the Emperor's wish that I stay, but foolish to go on living here as if I were oblivious to the vicious intrigues against me."

Palace life was so unbearable she resolved to leave the capital area altogether. Leaving the Prince at Hoyang with an appropriate number of servants and retainers, she took but seven or eight of her closest ladies and quietly withdrew to her father's estate in Shu Shan. The Prince lamented this turn of events and felt very lonely. The Emperor, shocked and saddened by her decision, sent letters daily to her father begging him to intercede.

"I have heard she intends to renounce the world completely," the Emperor pleaded. "Please do not let this happen. In my present position I find it impossible to rule as I would like. Nor can I renounce the temporal world, for until some current difficulties are resolved I must do as others instruct me. If you wait a while longer I will be able to abdicate in favor of the Third Prince and leave the world of palace intrigue behind. Please be patient and wait for the reign of the Third Prince."[35]

Even if the Emperor had not made such a plea, is it likely the Consort's father would permit his lovely daughter to throw away everything? As a matter of honor he did his best to relieve her sorrow. When the Consort was shown the Emperor's letters she shed tears of bitter grief. "If word of my condition were to spread, my life would be worthless," she thought. Refusing to see anyone she spent days and nights reading the Lotus Sutra and performing devotions before the Buddha. Word spread in sympathy that the Consort was no longer able to even enter the capital.

In the meanwhile Chūnagon was grieving in silence over the disappearance of the mysterious lady, and he was thus all the more anxious to meet the Hoyang Consort whom he thought resembled the lady very closely. He was disappointed to learn that the Consort had gone into seclusion. "I had hoped that meeting her might bring some relief. I wonder what possessed her to hide away?"

Whenever Chūnagon visited Hoyang the Prince tried not to grieve openly over his mother's absence. He was delighted with Chūnagon's visits and always behaved very maturely and cordially in spite of his loneliness. He sighed as he told Chūnagon what was on his mind.

"Though the people of this land are enlightened, there are times when they are incapable of discerning the difference between the petty affairs of daily life and the most awesome relationships such as our own. They can even be cruel and indifferent to the feelings of others. It would be a frightening prospect for you to remain in

35. The author obviously imagined the Chinese order of succession to be similar to that in Japan. The Emperor clearly promises to abdicate in favor of the Third Prince, but since his son by the First Empress (daughter of the Prime Minister) is Crown Prince, the Emperor was probably thinking of making the Third Prince Heir Apparent after his abdication (i.e., during the reign of the present Crown Prince). Although it is unlikely the author attached a great deal of significance to the political intrigue at Court, the domination of the Chinese Emperor by the Prime Minister does resemble the Fujiwara dominance of the Japanese Imperial household during the first half of the eleventh century.

this land for a long time, yet I know how terribly lonely I will be when you leave. How do you feel about this?"

Chūnagon was moved to tears by the Prince's words and did all he could to reassure him. The boy begged Chūnagon to stay with him at Hoyang. "Won't you please stay here with me while my mother is in seclusion? I find your company relieves the loneliness of her absence." He had a room prepared and together they soothed each other's troubled hearts with music and poetry.

The Prince spent most of his time with Chūnagon, avoiding whenever possible the disagreeable court life. While his mother was at Shan Yin he was sensitive to what others were saying; with Chūnagon he could now speak freely. However, Chūnagon occasionally seemed troubled and would stare vacantly at the sky, tearfully reciting a poem.

> The spring moon is gone,
> I know not where.
> Now in misery
> I watch the empty sky.

The Prince was discreetly aware of Chūnagon's sorrow. "Something more than mere homesickness is troubling him," he guessed. "But what lady in our land could cause this fine man such grief? Ever since spring he has been acting strangely. There must be something to this line 'The spring moon.' I wonder who it could possibly refer to?"

On the first day of the sixth month, Chūnagon and the Prince joined the Emperor for rites of purification at the great river Chang Ho south of the capital.[36] The river, swift and wide like the Uji and Ōi rivers in Japan, was the setting for innumerable festivities. A large brocade awning shading the spectators' chairs spread along the river bank, and two boats, one fashioned with a dragon head on its bow, the other with that of a rooster, floated in the river. Everyone enjoyed immensely the poetry and musical amusements of the day.

The Hoyang Consort had been driven into seclusion deep in the mountains by the harsh treatment of the other ladies at Court, but the Prince was too refined and handsome to be ignored. The special

---

36. The text clearly indicates that the *kana chōga* "long river" represent the name of the river. Perhaps the author thought this an alternate name for the Wei River which is just north of Ch'ang-an.

treatment afforded the boy by the Emperor on such occasions was extraordinary.

As Chūnagon's sorrow was not diverted even by these splendid gatherings, he merely sat in dejected silence, staring across the river. Most people thought this pose particularly handsome, but the Prince could see that something was troubling him. Moving to where Chūnagon was seated, he smiled and said,

> Perhaps the god of the river
> Will not allow the cleansing of your loneliness.
> The depths of your heart
> Are not yet calm.

Chūnagon was surprised and embarrassed at how well the Prince had fathomed the feelings in his heart. Responding he said,

> I entrusted my heart
> To the god of the river.
> No longer do I possess
> A heart longing for love.

On the seventh day of the seventh month the Emperor called on Chūnagon to participate in a poetry party commemorating the meeting of Hsi Wang Mu and Tung-fang Shou in the Ch'eng-hua Palace.[37] Chūnagon had come to the conclusion that while the Emperor was a man of elegant and fine taste, he was easily dominated by the Prime Minister and court ladies and was far too interested in frivolous amusements to rule effectively. The fact that he could be cut off completely from his beloved Hoyang Consort was further proof of his weakness.

When a cool evening breeze set in and the moon appeared, the

---

37. The seventh day of the seventh month is the Weaver Festival, Tanabata Matsuri in Japan. According to Chinese legend two lovers, the Weaver represented by the star Vega and the Herdsman represented by the star Altair, were put on opposite sides of the Milky Way for having neglected duties out of love for each other. They were allowed to meet once a year on this day but only if the night was clear so heavenly magpies could form a bridge for the Weaver to cross.

Hsi Wang Mu was the "Grand Old Lady of the West." Tung-fang Shou, also known as Tung-fang Man-ch'ien, was a clever retainer of the Former Han Emperor Wu-ti (reign 141-87 B.C.). According to traditional folklore Tung-fang Shou was a practitioner of magical arts. He once stole some peaches from Hsi Wang Mu and after eating them lived a very long time. Matsuo suggests that the *kana hōkaden* in the text are a misrepresentation of *shōkaden*, "the Ch'eng-hua Palace," the name of a palace found in stories associated with Hsi Wang Mu.

Emperor gazed wistfully at the sky and repeatedly intoned the famous lines,

> "In the sky we would be like two birds sharing a wing;
> On earth like two trees sharing a branch."[38]

It was a sad sight, for Chūnagon knew he was referring to the Consort. The Emperor drank his wine then passed the cup to Chūnagon who offered this poem.

> The vows once shared like intertwining branches
> Are now of no avail.
> The distant mountain bird
> Is seen only from afar.

The Emperor could not withhold his tears, for Chūnagon had understood his feelings.

> Our vows may be compared
> To that of long ago,
> But I feel ours still may be
> One of never-ending love.

Although Chūnagon spent many days like this in the congenial company of the Emperor, deep in his heart he kept thinking of the dreamlike meeting with that lady, sometimes even in disdain. "No matter how dangerous the circumstances, a lady of Japan would never sever contact completely. The women in this land can be unintelligible and downright cruel at times!"

Still, he could never forget her weeping face the night she whispered her poem, "Fate ties me to one from the unknown land." He longed to be back in Japan but could not imagine returning without meeting the lady again. He was continually plagued by these thoughts as summer turned to autumn.

He lay awake during the long autumn nights, tormented by the memory of the lady. Finally the frustration became too great. He decided he must at least see the Hoyang Consort, who bore a likeness to the lady, even though such a visit might not seem completely proper.

Bearing a letter from the Prince to the Consort he secretly visited her retreat deep in the rugged mountains of Shu Shan. The flow of a nearby waterfall and the gentle swaying of the grasses and trees surrounding the splendid house of the former minister seemed quite

38. From Po chü-i's "A Song of Unending Sorrow." See note 20 above.

out of the ordinary. Though hardly desolate, a faint sense of loneliness imbued the stillness of the grounds.[39]

Even the gentle whisper of the wind brought tears to the eyes of
the Consort who had grown more depressed with each passing day.
Refusing to see anyone she spent all her time in worship before the
Buddha, mournfully staring at the altar as she did penance for her
transgressions in lives past and present. A sharp pain pierced her
breast when she was told that Chūnagon of Japan had come bearing
a letter from the Prince. Quickly regaining her composure she reasoned to herself: "He does not know it was I that night. I could not
imagine having such an affair even in a dream and yet our unfortunate fate must have been preordained. I must not treat him as a
stranger; my wretched karma is what I resent."

Sorrowfully she pondered her troublesome predicament. "Since
he made the effort to come here I should see him. My son, who is
far more sensitive than most in these matters, suggested I meet with
him. And he must have his reasons." She had a cushion prepared
for Chūnagon near the entrance of the main hall and invited him
in.

Even as he walked in the shade of the mountain he seemed almost
dazzling. Though somewhat inhibited by his splendid appearance,
she was anxious to meet him. Many emotions tore at her heart as
she gently moved forward to accept the letter from his servant. After
a considerable pause she finally offered a poem through an inter-
mediary.

> Casting off the wretched world
> With no clues to my retreat
> I hid deep in the mountains.
> How is it someone now comes to visit?

The lonely setting gave her words a special poignancy.
Chūnagon, unable to restrain his tears, responded,

> Deep in my heart
> I have been thinking of you.
> I care not if the road be near or far.

39. In this sentence and the following two, there are seven blank spots where
characters are missing. The size of the blanks vary but are present in all the different
manuscripts. This strongly suggests that all the extant manuscripts stem from a single
source. Some of the manuscripts have possible interpretations written along side by
the copier. In determining the meaning of the sentences, I have followed some of
these suggested interpretations.

A gentle silence settled in the hall and in the surrounding forest. When the beautiful scent from within the blinds reached Chūnagon, he was suddenly reminded of the dreamlike fragrance of that spring night. It was as if the very fragrance which had soaked his sleeve that night, a scent which could carry a hundred paces, now came back to him.[40] He could not distinguish between the Consort's unusual perfume and the fragrance of tormented love from that spring night. Though unaware that she had been the lady, he could not hold back his tears.

The Consort's father had always wanted to meet Chūnagon and was now surprised to hear he had come. Delighted though the minister was, he was somewhat embarrassed that the provisions in his retreat were inadequate for a proper reception. Nevertheless, he sent a message inviting Chūnagon to visit his quarters.

The former minister was a handsome man of just over fifty. Upon seeing Chūnagon he burst into tears and told him of the years he had spent in Japan. Chūnagon found he could relax in the former minister's presence, for he was like a gentleman of Japan, not at all foreign in speech or manners. The minister spoke in detail of his days in Japan; the story of his parting with the Consort's mother was particularly moving. It was a night for music and poetry, and when dawn came the minister was terribly disappointed that Chūnagon had to leave.

The morning sun had not yet penetrated the lush mountain forest as Chūnagon prepared to take his leave. The Consort's attendants, fully coiffed and lovely as ladies in a fine Chinese painting, opened the Consort's door to watch him depart. Pausing momentarily Chūnagon sent them a poem.

> The morning mist covers
> The hills and valleys.
> Perhaps I cannot find my way home.

In return the ladies sent a poem no different from what one would expect in Japan.

40. The author is probably referring to a particular fragrance known as the "Hundred-Pace Incense." It was made of a blend of eleven different ingredients, buried in the ground for twenty-one days, and when removed and burnt, its fragrance carried, as its name suggests, one hundred paces. The Heian nobility scented their clothes by draping them over a frame and burning incense underneath, thus allowing the smoke to permeate the cloth.

> If the morning mist in the hills and valleys
> Does not clear,
> Please stay with us a little longer.

"The Consort's mother was Japanese and her father knew many Japanese," he thought. "I suppose this is why her ladies act this way. When I am with the Prime Minister and his people I often do not understand what they are doing or saying, and I truly feel as if I am in a different world. The mysterious lady whose disappearance has haunted me was very much like a lady of Japan; I wonder if she is part of the former minister's entourage. No other women are quite like these ladies." With no way of finding the lady, however, only the fragrance lingering on his sleeve often served to remind him of her.[41]

> Why does this fragrance linger even now
> To torment my wretched soul?

With the arrival of winter the Consort realized that the time of delivery was near, but she refused to call either the Emperor or even her son, the Prince. She was lost in grief, certain this would be the end. The birth, however, was unusually easy: without the slightest pain, as simply as if delivering a child from her sleeve, she gave birth to a boy bearing a remarkable likeness to Chūnagon. Two of her most intimate servants, ecstatic over the safe birth, immediately attended to the infant's needs. "This is indeed a child from another world," they marveled. "What terrible things might have happened had it been a difficult birth!"

Though the Consort was saddened when she compared this lonely birth with the great care and joy shown by everyone, especially the Emperor and her father, on the birth of the Prince, she found the occasion particularly moving. Whenever she looked at the child she was reminded of the strength of her fateful tie with Chūnagon. What could she do but be overjoyed at the safe and easy birth of the child? She entrusted him to a few knowledgeable servants who guarded him as they would a personal treasure. Experienced wet nurses fed the baby in secret like a personal possession. He was raised in hiding and day by day grew into an uncommonly beautiful child, yet when

41. When lovers slept together, the sleeves of their robes might bunch together and the fragrance of one permeate the other.

the Consort looked at the child she could not help but worry about his future.

How was Chūnagon to know of this child? He had promised the Emperor of Japan and his mother he would be back within three years, making this the year to return, but he was troubled by a number of things, particularly the idea of leaving without seeing the mysterious lady again. Everyone, including the Emperor, was disappointed to see him making preparations for his departure, and they tried to persuade him to prolong his visit.

"Long ago the emissaries from Japan stayed twelve years before returning. Why couldn't you stay at least five?"

Though he himself was none too anxious to leave immediately he felt uneasy about spending the rest of his days in China. In addition to his concern over his people in Japan, particularly his mother and Taishō no Kimi, at times he found the people of China heartless. They might treat him with the utmost kindness only to desert him and cause him grief. "Once I have returned I am sure to find some consolation for my sorrow," he reasoned.

The Prince, realizing that Chūnagon must have good reasons for returning, did not try to convince him to stay, even though the thought of never seeing him again was very painful. Chūnagon, saddened by the grief his departure was causing the Prince, tried to explain his feelings.

"Perhaps I could spend the rest of my life here, but I cannot help but recall how terribly grieved my mother was when I left her. I am very worried about what might have happened to her." Chūnagon was right, of course, and the Prince could not ask him to stay even a little longer. The Prince realized that his own rebirth in China had spurred Chūnagon to the long and perilous journey. It was quite natural that Chūnagon should worry about his other parent who remained the same person of old. Still, the Prince was so grieved by Chūnagon's imminent departure he could neither eat nor participate in the usual court activities. Depressed, he longed to see his mother again.

The Emperor was so worried about the Prince's condition he sent messengers to Shu Shan requesting the Consort's return.

While the Consort had long considered court life disagreeable, she had gone into retreat only to avoid being seen by the Emperor during her pregnancy and never intended to cast off the world completely. What was there now to keep her in Shu Shan? Anxious to see the Prince well again, she decided to return to Hoyang.

The Emperor went to see her immediately. Owing to the endless hours of devotion and worry she had become quite frail, but this only served to enhance her peerless beauty. He loved her deeply and felt the world a wretched, lonely place because they could not live together in his palace at Yangchou. The Consort was frightened by the ominous implications of her vow with Chūnagon and spoke not a word of it to the Emperor.

The other consorts, once safe in the knowledge that the Hoyang Consort was hidden away with her father in the mountains, were jealous and resentful now that she had returned to the captial area and become the object of the Emperor's constant affection. Once again they devised scandalous and frightening schemes to cause her grief. With the Consort's return the Prince's sorrow abated and he was able to take food, much to the relief of those close to him.

Everyone lamented Chūnagon's impending departure but nothing could be done to make him stay. Day and night the Emperor pondered what he might offer at the farewell banquet.

"For the three years this splendid man has been here no one in our country has been able to surpass him in artistic skills. Were he to return without seeing or hearing some extraordinary display of our finest talent, our country would be disgraced. It seems there is absolutely nothing in this land splendid enough to impress him. Perhaps if he were to hear the Hoyang Consort play the *kin* he might be impressed enough to tell everyone in Japan of her talent. But should word spread among the Japanese that he was entertained by a consort of the Emperor they might view us with contempt. It would also be dangerous were he to stay longer and grow too fond of her. If I were to disguise the fact that she is a consort and merely present her as a lowly lady-in-waiting from the palace, then perhaps the honor of our country would be upheld." That, he decided, would work quite well.

Since Chūnagon was to return the first day of the ninth month, the farewell party was set for the middle of the eighth month, with the full moon the theme for the gathering. The scene of the party, the Wei Yang Palace, equivalent to the Reizei Palace in Japan, was decorated with extraordinary care.[42] The Palace grounds encompassed no less than thirteen ponds, truly a magnificent setting for viewing the moon.

In his instructions to the Hoyang Consort the Emperor gave no indication of what he would ask her to do that night. "Chūnagon's imminent departure grieves me so I have decided to give a farewell party on the night of the fifteenth at the Wei Yang Palace. I am sure you would find the formalities insufferable and the resentment of the other ladies very unpleasant, so why don't you and a few of your ladies come and view the party secretly? Since this is his final farewell he is certain to spare no effort in displaying his artistic talents. It should be magnificent. He will probably never again come to our country, and you would regret not seeing him."

Surprised by the Emperor's proposal, the Consort's heartbeat quickened and her face turned pale. In spite of her misgivings she felt it would indeed be unfortunate to miss Chūnagon's final farewell. "It would be pleasant, indeed," she said, "but even though you say we will be hidden, I am worried that we might be discovered by the others."

"How could you possibly be seen?" he said. "You will be completely hidden from view."

At dawn on the day of the party two court ladies especially appreciative of fine music left the Palace before any of the others. The accompanying guards thought the ladies were simply off for a bit of sightseeing, but the ladies secretly joined the Consort at the site of the banquet.

Around eight in the morning the Emperor went to the Wei Yang Palace to supervise the final preparations for the party, sparing no effort in decorating the palace and grounds to full radiance. The dancing and singing of the ministers, courtiers, and virtuosi trying to impress Chūnagon were particularly splendid. With "Laments for Chūnagon's Departure" as a theme, the finest poets of the land created verses which spoke eloquently of their sadness, and the verse

42. The Wei Yang Palace in Ch'ang-an is mentioned in Po Chü-i's poem "A Song of Unending Sorrow." The Reizeiin, frequently destroyed by fire and rebuilt, was one of the largest and most luxurious buildings in the Heian capital. It was the home of the abdicated Emperor and was often used as a temporarary palace for the reigning Emperor when the main palace was destroyed by fire. The night of the banquet, the fifteenth day of the eighth month, would be the night of the full moon in autumn.

Chūnagon himself composed brought forth the greatest stream of tears.

The Consort, hidden behind blinds, was transfixed by the seemingly shining figure of Chūnagon. The regrettable fate which had drawn them together was, to be sure, a source of lament for the Consort, but seeing him today helped her forget the resentment she normally felt. The thought that she could never see or hear him again brought tears to her eyes.

At dusk, just as a chilly evening breeze stirred the flowers in full bloom, the musical entertainment began. Chūnagon's playing of "Autumn Breeze"[43] on the *biwa* and ten-stringed koto was indescribably beautiful. The Emperor was completely captivated by his fine figure and superb virtuosity. He slipped into the Consort's room and pleaded with her to play for Chūnagon.

"There is no one in our land who can match Chūnagon in any of the fine arts. I tried but could think of nothing impressive enough to catch his eye. In order to save our country's honor please let him think you are a lowly palace lady and play the *kin* for him."

In spite of the Emperor's urgent pleas the Consort felt she should not do it. He pressed her again and again, finally making a solemn promise which caught the Consort by surprise.

"If you play for him and preserve our country's honor, I will be so happy I will in time abdicate in favor of the Third Prince, no matter what trouble it might cause at Court."

The people of China apparently see no need to show reserve.

"Well, in that case, I shall do as you wish," answered the Consort.

Overjoyed, the Emperor invited Chūnagon behind the blinds. Chūnagon was puzzled as he walked gracefully into the room where the Emperor sat next to a slightly raised blind. A dark red curtain inlaid with silver and gold foil and dyed to a deeper hue at the bottom was drawn back enough for Chūnagon to catch a brief glimpse of an indescribably lovely lady sitting in the shadow of a pillar. She was dressed in bright, beautiful robes, waistband, and shoulder sash. Demure in her behavior she seemed no more than a lady in service of the Emperor.

---

43. A tune of the court music (*gagaku*) repertoire usually accompanied by four dancers.

The Emperor addressed Chūnagon.

"Your departure after these three years causes me such inconsolable grief I cannot restrain my tears. As a parting gift I offer you this lady's playing of the *kin*."

There was nothing Chūnagon could say to this. He sat up straight and began to tap with his fan the rhythm for the singing. The beauty of his voice as he sang the words of "How Grand the Day"[44] surpassed even the finest melody produced by a host of instruments played together. When the Emperor offered the *kin* to the lady she set her fan aside and began to play. Somehow her slight, delicate figure, partially hidden by the shadow of the pillar, reminded Chūnagon of the Hoyang Consort the night they met while viewing chrysanthemums, but he could not imagine the Emperor allowing a consort to perform thus. Unobtrusively he looked more closely at the lady and was shocked to find she was the very lady he had met that spring night in the moonlight. When the Emperor called for a faster tempo, the lady played the *kansu* melody,[45] an indescribably beautiful tune.

Chūnagon was bewildered as he tried to compare the sound of this *kin* with the koto music the night of the chrysanthemums. "The sound is similar, but how could it possibly be the same?" he wondered.

The peerless beauty of this lady, like the light of a full moon luminous through a cluster of clouds, turned Chūnagon's thoughts first to the Consort on the night of the chrysanthemums and then to the lady of that spring night dream, memories of endless sorrow. Not a trace of cloud covered the bright, clear moon. The Consort was deeply moved by the beauty of the moment as she followed Chūnagon's cadence, the sound of her *kin* echoing in the moonlit sky above. Surely neither the Nanfu koto nor the Hashifūkoto played by Naishi no Kami in *The Tale of the Hollow Tree*[46] could have

44. A *saibara* song. Originally a folk song, these tunes were adopted by the court aristocrats and often sung at parties to the accompaniment of various musical instruments.

45. Matsuo says the tune is unidentifiable. Could *kansu* in the text be a corruption of *kansuiraku*, a *gagaku* melody?

46. *Utsubo Monogatari* is a lengthy tale written in the last quarter of the tenth century, possibly by Minamoto no Shitagō. In the first chapter of the story a man named Kiyowara Toshikage is blown off course during a trip to China and lands in a country called *hashi* (Persia according to some sources, but probably a land east of India). There he is taught to play magical tunes on the *kin* by three heavenly creatures.

sounded so fine, thought Chūnagon, convinced that there never was, nor ever would be, a sound so beautiful. He struggled valiantly but could not restrain his tears.

The Emperor was pleased to see things going as planned. Looking at Chūnagon, a peerless gentleman of Japan, and the Consort, a matchless beauty of his own land, he felt as if he were viewing sunlight and moonlight together. He was certain Chūnagon would write of this incident and tell everyone of the wonders found in China.

With the Emperor's *biwa* Chūnagon joined the Consort in playing every song he knew. She was deeply impressed by his skill; relaxing somewhat she tearfully played with all her heart. Those listening from outside could not help but weep. When dawn finally came the Emperor and the Consort returned to their quarters.

But how was Chūnagon to know she was the Consort? The lady of that spring night dream had indeed resembled the Consort in her appearance and koto-playing, but unfortunately he had no way of finding her. Once again he sent a man no less sensitive than himself to Shan Yin to investigate the premises carefully. A servant there spoke with Chūnagon's messenger.

"This is the house of the Lady Nü Wang,[47] a highly regarded relative of the Hoyang Consort now serving her as a lady-in-waiting. Because this house is rather far from the capital Lady Nü Wang rarely comes here, but spends most of her time at a mansion in Ting Li."

After hearing this report Chūnagon felt he understood the situation.

Later Toshikage is given a number of precious kotos by the Buddha. Two of these kotos, the Nanfu koto and Hashifu koto, are capable of magical powers, but he or his descendants are only to play them in times of extreme danger or extreme good fortune. Toshikage returns to Japan and teaches the secrets of the two instruments to his daughter (later known as Naishi no Kami). When she and her son are threatened by warriors at their home in the mountains she plays the Nanfu koto. Trees are uprooted, a mountain collapses, and the threatening soldiers are all buried alive. Near the end of the tale, when Naishi no Kami plays the Hashifu koto for the Emperors Saga and Sujaku, heaven and earth shake at the miraculous sound.

47. The text has the characters for *nyōbō*, the designation of a high-ranked lady-in-waiting. Matsuo prefers to follow a number of other texts which have *jo ō*, "the woman Wang." I have given her a name consisting of the Chinese pronunciation for the characters indicated by *jo ō*.

"That would explain why she resembles the Consort," he reasoned. "She spends so much time with the Consort her appearance and koto-playing would quite naturally be similar to those of the Consort. Being so close to the Consort she felt it inappropriate to become too intimate with someone from a foreign land. Perhaps that is why she planned to disappear, leaving me no hint of her whereabouts."

Too anxious to wait for dark Chūnagon set off for Ting Li in the quiet of evening, a time no sensitive man could let pass by. A number of people were apparently enjoying the flowers in the garden when he arrived at the estate. He heard a lady's voice and his heart leaped for joy, for the voice resembled that of a lady who had seen him off that spring night.

Lady Nü Wang was told that he had come. In the past she had concealed her movements to avoid being seen by him; but now, when she considered the secret relationship between the Consort and Chūnagon and his imminent return, she could hide no longer. Since the Consort herself was not present she thought it permissible to meet with him, though she tried to reveal nothing.

Chūnagon, greatly disappointed by the chilly reception, wondered if she were really of such a high rank. Why was she so haughty? Wiping away tears he said to her,

> Even now no one knows my heart's sorrow,
> This autumn evening,
> The last day in this land.

Bitter, resentful, and thoroughly disappointed, he started to leave the mansion. Lady Nü Wang felt pity for the frustrated Chūnagon and began to play a beautifully clear melody called "Do Stay Here" on the *biwa*, beckoning him to return. He paused for a moment then returned to a rock by the garden stream where he sat and joined in the *biwa* melody with his flute. Unable to restrain her tears, Lady Nü Wang had Chūnagon brought within the blinds where her ladies engaged him in conversation while she pondered her next move.

"Ever since the Consort returned from Shu Shan I have cared for the baby. He is growing bigger every day and seems to combine the very best of the beautiful Consort and Chūnagon. It is a delight to see him now taking his first steps, but I worry about what the future holds for him. Since I am taking care of him day and night I cannot be with the Consort as I should. The bonds between a parent and child go beyond the present world. The Consort wished it kept a secret, but it would be a grievous sin to end the affair without letting Chūnagon know of the child."

Even though she knew Chūnagon was soon to leave she wanted him to know. With sensitive, tenderhearted people such as she, can China really be such a fearsome, formidable land? Had this situation occurred in Japan Chūnagon might never have learned the truth. China, however, seems a country of judicious people: such things are not kept secret forever.

When Lady Nü Wang moved closer to Chūnagon, he knew from her speech that she was not the lady who said "tied to one from the unknown land"; perhaps her sister, he thought. The months of frustration suddenly spilled forth in a flood of angry tears. Lady Nü Wang was too moved by this pitiful sight to remain silent any longer.

"Perhaps I should not tell you this; it is frightening and might be better left unsaid, but the bonds between parent and child transcend this world. I am afraid it would be a grievous crime were I not to let you know. It would be most unfortunate if this incident were to become known even in a foreign land, and I trust a sensitive person like yourself will not mention a word of it, even after you leave this country."

She then told Chūnagon the entire story from beginning to end. If she were a Japanese lady and had already gone to such lengths to hide the true story, she would scarcely have told him everything now.[48] To Chūnagon it all seemed no more real than a dream within a dream. He wept uncontrollably. The Consort? He never would have guessed. What must she have thought of his casual visits to Hoyang? Their extraordinary ties were too touching for words.

Lady Nü Wang presented Chūnagon the beautiful child who smiled as he seemed to recognize his father. Chūnagon was deeply shocked, for he now realized that his resolute journey to China had in fact been foreordained for the fateful meeting with the Consort.

48. Following the sentence in the text there is a phrase meaning something like "be numbered among the 990 Wangs (or kings)," *kyūhyaku kyūjūnin no ō no kazu ni irete*. This is probably based on a Chinese legend, but since the source is uncertain, it is difficult to discover the quotation's meaning or relevance to the narrative. I have omitted the phrase from the translation.

What extraordinary karma! And now at last, he understood the significance of the dream in which the priest had said, "Your ties with her are fated to be deep."

"Then the lady who played the *kin* at the Wei Yang Palace was none other than the Consort," he thought. "The Emperor must have been trying to impress me by disguising her true rank." How unlike Japan! His surprise soon turned to tortured sorrow with the realization that, in spite of their deep ties, he might never see the woman he yearned for even though they were in the same land.

From that day on the boy quickly grew accustomed to Chūnagon's daily visits to Ting Li. He was constantly at his father's side and wept longingly when he left. Chūnagon made plans to take him back to Japan, for he could not bear to desert the child.

Weeping he pleaded with Lady Nü Wang to arrange one more meeting with the Consort.

"I will be here only a little while longer and there is something I must tell her. Now that I know her rank I realize full well that any misbehavior would deserve swift punishment. Although I had no idea fate would carry us this far, ever since I saw her viewing chrysanthemums I have had it in my mind to somehow see her again. Surely she realizes our bond is inescapable. Please allow me to meet her while I am still in this country."

Lady Nü Wang listened sympathetically and decided to approach the Consort, disguising the fact that she herself had revealed the secret.

"Chūnagon heard your koto-playing and apparently caught a glimpse of you the night we were viewing chrysanthemums," she told the Consort later. "When you next met he must have suspected something, even if he was not certain it was you that night. Listening to your playing the night of the moon-viewing party at the Wei Yang Palace, he once again got a brief glimpse of you, and putting two and two together, came looking for you at Ting Li where he saw the little boy. Since then he has persistently questioned me in all sorts of ways about you . . ."

The Consort was stunned by this report. She had tried her best to end the incident without letting him know; what a bitter disappointment to be discovered now. She realized, however, that this too was the workings of fate and not something to be blamed on any one person. Still, in her heart she felt it was not safe to meet again.

"As Chūnagon said, I too think our meeting was due to an inescapable bond from a previous life, but for his sake and mine it would be dangerous to meet again. I know how terribly sad and distressed the Prince is over Chūnagon's leaving, but I should not speak with Chūnagon, even though he will be in our land but a few more days. It is a dreamlike bond from a former life."

She resolved not to meet him again. Although she felt a growing affection for him she tried to suppress her feelings and keep her distance.

Chūnagon fully realized the dangers that both he and the Consort faced in this frightening, unfamiliar world if even the slightest hint of their relationship were to leak out, but the thought of never seeing her again was unbearable. He could not imagine simply leaving; secretly he spent most of his time with the little boy, dreading his departure more and more, yet finding consolation for his sorrow in the boy's company.

The ninth month soon came. He could not think of returning, nor could he continue passing the time as he did now. Every night he dreamed of his mother. She had only reluctantly agreed to the trip; he wondered what she must now be thinking, waiting anxiously for his return. Difficult though it was to remain in China, it would be impossible to hurry back without first reconciling that spring night's dream with reality. He was trapped between two worlds. Except for the usual sorrows of this transient life he had been a person relatively free of worries; now he found himself tormented by uncommon concerns in both China and Japan. He was certain he would be swept away by the waves and perish on the trip back home. All preparations for the return voyage were halted as he spent his time sitting and staring vacantly into space.

The Consort occasionally had Lady Nü Wang bring the secret child to her. The child was beautiful but an all too clear reminder of her wretched fate. "Chūnagon has no intention of leaving this child behind," she thought. "How terrible it will be to lose the child, never to see him again in this world, never knowing what will become of him. It would be sadder still were he to grow up in this land, for he resembles Chūnagon too closely. Even without such problems

95

this is a difficult world; how much more so it would be for him!"
Her grief was certainly no less than that afflicting Chūnagon's
troubled heart.

She soon learned that the usually strong Chūnagon was now in
a state of utter despair and dejection. The poem he sent was very
sad.

> What is it that stirs me
> More than a boat
> Tossed by windswept waves?

On seeing this could the Consort's sorrow in any way be ordinary?

> The boat, they say,
> Has a place to harbor.
> I yearn to be the restless waters.

Chūnagon could delay his departure no longer. "It would be most
inopportune if I became so despondent people disdained me and
began to doubt my strength of character," he thought. "I deserted
Taishō no Kimi and left my mother in tears; what must they think
of me now? Was it not that fateful meeting, that karmic bond, which
would not let me quit the journey I had resolved to make? I was
resolute and brave to set out on this voyage; how can I simply while
away my time now? This is no place to sit idle." He secretly made
preparations to take the child with him.

The Consort was grieved but made no effort to prevent this. What
should she do, she wondered. One night as she wept herself to sleep
a man appeared in her dream. "The child was not meant to live in
this land," he told her. "He is to be a guardian of Japan. Let him
go immediately." Sad it was when she awoke and realized it must
be so.

"This is how my mother must have felt when I left my birthland
to come here," she thought. "Even now I cannot forget her face as
she hugged me and wept the day I left. Now I too must bear the
sorrow of losing a child. My mother must have been as sad as I am
now. The retribution of fate truly does exist."

Two nights before he was to return, Chūnagon set off for Hoyang
by the light of the full moon. Not only did he find the Prince's grief
over the inevitable departure heartbreaking, it was even difficult for
him to leave the familiar garden and streams of the Hoyang estate.
There was little hope of seeing the Consort again. When left alone
Chūnagon merely sat and stared vacantly at the sky.

As the quiet of the night gradually deepened, Chūnagon was summoned to the Consort's wing of the mansion. He sat very still on the veranda, appearing more splendid than usual in the moonlight. The Consort, watching Chūnagon from within the blinds, could not restrain her tears. The young Prince was with her.

"Is no one with Chūnagon?" she asked as she edged closer to the veranda where he sat.

Chūnagon was lost in emotion as he recognized the beautiful fragrance covering the lady, an essence no different from the lingering memory of that spring night dream. The Consort spoke to Chūnagon.

"Ever since I learned the Prince's love for you transcends the present world, I have felt closer to you than to the people of my own land. But fear of what others might think has kept me from you. I am sorry to see that your imminent departure causes you such grief, and I too am distressed that you must leave in a few days."

There was nothing extraordinary in her words and distant manner, yet how could Chūnagon fail to be moved by the elegant, radiant figure before him? Struggling to control his all too obvious emotions he responded very formally in words too splendid to repeat.

Once again the Consort addressed him.

"I understand that you have heard about my past. My mother, I hear, is still alive in Japan. I asked a priest who came to China whether he knew of her, and he told me she was living as a nun in Ōuchiyama.[49] When he was to return to Japan I had him take a letter for my mother. I doubt he would fail me; if she is still alive he must have given it to her, but still I am worried and uncertain. Once you leave it will be almost impossible for me to make contact with her. It is difficult for me to ask this of you, but please, promise to visit her and give her this letter. Your countrymen are continually coming to this land. Please find some reliable way to send her response to me. Should you find that she has died please send even that news back in a letter in this box."

The Consort was weeping freely as she passed a large box of sweet smelling aloeswood to Chūnagon. She seemed so graciously charming, no different from the spring night dream, that Chūnagon could no longer restrain his tears, though he pretended her sorrowful tale

49. A mountain in the Omuro-Saga district of Kyoto northwest of the capital.

alone made him weep so. With great difficulty he finally controlled his weeping enough to respond.

"No matter how rough the waves, should my life be spared, I will immediately upon arrival in Japan do all I can to give your mother this letter. I myself will bring her answer back to you, even though a return voyage would be without precedent. And if you do not receive a reply you will know I was tossed to the bottom of the sea and drowned on the trip."

In Japan one would never say such things to an Imperial Consort, no matter how much two people secretly longed for each other, but even in China, a land of strict decorum, there are times of disarray, Chūnagon sensed. But as much as he wanted to pour forth his deepest feelings he could not. This only made him sadder. The Prince left for a moment, and under the din of people speaking nearby, Chū-nagon whispered softly to the Consort,

No longer can I reconcile what has happened;
Could that spring night have been but a dream?

With an expression of unbearable sorrow the Consort whispered her barely audible reply as she retreated behind the blinds.

Why is it you think it even a dream?
Does one really see something in an illusion?

If he were a person who cared not what the others think he might have called her back, but he wisely decided to show more reserve.

The Prince returned to the veranda and began to play the *biwa*. Although Chūnagon was in no mood for music, he realized this was his last night with the Prince and resolved to do his best. Nothing seemed real as he took the *biwa* from the Prince and began to play. The sound of the *kin* accompanying him from behind the blinds was the same as the night at the Wei Yang Palace. The music was her parting gift to him. Though he had firmly resolved to leave, her charming words and image remained in his ears and in his heart, so dizzying him with emotion he was unable to think clearly.

"When I left my mother and Taishō no Kimi soon after the affair," he remembered, "the sorrow of departure, though of my own choos-ing, seemed unparalleled. Yet knowing that if I survived I would return in three years afforded me some consolation. But will I ever come back to this country again?"

Everything seemed sad when he realized he might never see her again. The Consort tried to keep her distance; her attitude to the impending separation was tender yet controlled. This only served to intensify the unusual torment Chūnagon felt. He had no cause to resent the reasonable reserve shown by the Consort, for he well realized that for the sake of both of them they had to be circumspect; a scandal would inevitably follow the exposure of their relationship. But he was perplexed as he wondered what he should do.

"What am I to do when her attitude is so distant, cruel, and coldhearted?" he asked himself. "Perhaps she will not forget me as long as I have the boy with me." Though this conjecture excited him for a moment he soon fell again into a state of despair, seemingly losing the will to carry on.

The days of autumn are a particularly wretched time for parting. The sorrow of the Emperor and Crown Prince seemed greater than that of the people he had left in Japan. And yes, the lady whose illness he had cured, Wu Chün, daughter of the Prime Minister, sent a sad note lamenting his departure. The letter, written in a fine hand on light purple paper, showed signs of true talent. Within the elegant composition was a poem.

> Will you visit soon?
> Will I see you today?
> Expectantly I waited.
> Just being in the same land is consolation . . .

He had heard she was very talented, but he had been unable to think of anyone but the Hoyang Consort recently. Her skill surprised him. As he was soon to leave he sent her a touching note with a poem attached.

> Had I not feared the sorrow after parting,
> Would I have kept you waiting day and night?

He went to Hoyang the day before he was to leave, but this time he did not even hear the Consort's voice. He wept profusely; now that he was to return, the sorrow would remain forever, he felt. Glum and sorrowful, he thought,

> Even if we were not joined unto each other,
> Would she not at least find words to say to me?

Weeping, he left Hoyang, for it was useless to spend the night sulking.

Remembering Wu Chün's fine letter, he secretly went to visit the Prime Minister's mansion. The late evening moon shone brightly in the cloudless sky. The third, fourth, and fifth daughters of the Prime Minister were playing instruments on an island pavilion in one of the vast ponds of the Minister's estate. They invited Chūnagon to view the moon with them. Branches of maple in their finest autumnal color spread from the banks of the pond to cover the pavilion, clothing the landscape in evening brocade. Chūnagon passed beneath the raised blinds and sat near the ladies, separated by only a thin curtain. Are gentlemen visitors always allowed such liberties? The ladies sat overlooking the pond, their fancy hairstyles and elegant garments glittering in the shade of the maple trees with a picturesque radiance indistinguishable from the brilliant moonlight. The third daughter played the *kin*, the fourth the koto, and Wu Chün the *biwa*; the sound of all three together proved very pleasing. Although the playing of the *kin* could not compare with the Hoyang Consort's playing, in this particular setting it sounded wonderful. The koto was lovely, but the *biwa* seemed the very best of all. Chūnagon knew now why the Prime Minister favored Wu Chün. The young men joined the music with flutes, and the sorrow of departure and the beauty of the music combined to produce a sense of delicate sadness in everyone.

As dawn approached, Chūnagon rose and whispered a poem to Wu Chün.

> When I see the moon
> Rise from the mountains of Japan
> I will surely recall this evening.

Choked with tears Wu Chün could find no words to answer him. The music of her *biwa* gave her reply.[50]

> Though every night I watch the moon
> And think of you,
> How can a half-moon
> Satisfy my longing?

The *biwa* music was more beautiful than anything he had ever heard before. "Why didn't I come and listen to her more often?" he thought, chagrined over the missed opportunity.

50. It is not clear whether the author meant that the music of the *biwa* transmitted the meaning of the poem, or whether she spoke while playing the music. The grammar of the sentence implies the former, unlikely as it may seem.

Chapter Two

 ON THE VOYAGE across the vast unknowable seas Chūnagon had been tormented by a number of thoughts sorrowful beyond compare. Still, knowing he would return home in three years should he live so long had afforded some consolation. While he had not spent many years in the foreign land, his parting from even the common grasses and trees of the garden was particularly sad, for he realized he would never return again. And now only the small child was left to remind him of his unusual love for the Consort. Day and night were all the same to him as an endless flow of tears, more plentiful it seemed than even the rough waves of the sea, darkened his spirits for the entire voyage. Finally he heard the cry that they were soon to land in Tsukushi.

The morning of their parting the Consort had held the child in her arms and wept as she instructed Chūnagon to feed the boy a special medicine, since there would be no one on the ship to nurse him. Due perhaps to the efficacy of this medication, the child did not weaken or lose color, but rather seemed to shine more fair and beautiful. He did not cry at all; nor was he inconvenienced or annoyed even amidst the rugged boatmen. The startling beauty of the child, so much like that of a divine being only temporarily assuming human form, sometimes made Chūnagon feel uneasy.

"If people learn he was born in another country they might treat him coldly," he thought. "For the time being I would rather they not know he came from a foreign land."

He wrote his mother for assistance.

"I trust you have been well lately. When I left you I suspected I would not return early, and once the period of my leave had passed I was afraid you might be worried. I was fortunate enough to return safely, and now I can think of nothing more joyful than to see you again. The details of my visit must wait until I see you in person. Please send Nurse Chūjō to Tsukushi immediately, making it appear as if she simply cannot wait to see me no matter what people might think of her unseemly haste.[1] I have someone I wish to place in her care before I arrive in the capital, but no one should be told this.

"The Chinese who accompanied me will soon return to their own country. Please select some unusual gifts, things that are sure to please these people, and send them to me. I will return to the capital as soon as I have finished taking proper care of our guests."

His poem to Taishō no Kimi, discreetly enclosed in a letter addressed to her attendant Lady Saishō, was not insignificant.

> Because of you
> The swift boat crossed
> The vast sea quickly.
> My yearning could not wait
> Until the storm had passed.

His letter arrived just in time, for rumors had spread in the capital that he had been detained in China to serve the Emperor and would not return for a long time. Everyone had been saddened by this talk, especially his mother who was heartbroken and beside herself with worry. When she saw his letter tears of joy so overwhelmed her she felt lost, as if in a dream. She secretly conveyed Chūnagon's request to Nurse Chūjō who was more than happy to go meet him.

"Even if he did not ask I would want to go, no matter what people might think," she said, beside herself with joy.

Those who came to help Nurse Chūjō with the hasty preparations for the trip thought she was simply anxious to see him. "She cannot bear to wait in the capital," they said to each other. "She does not have to go, but even we are not happy waiting. Think how she must feel. Besides, it seems his mother has asked her to go as quickly as possible."

Just hearing talk of his return upset Taishō no Kimi, now a nun. "For the past few years I have felt this house inappropriate for someone of my station, but I thought it would be ungrateful of me suddenly to turn my back on the care my stepmother has so kindly offered me. Now that he has returned I should not stay any longer."

She called Nurse Shōshō.

"My presence in this house is much too conspicuous and quite inappropriate now that he will soon be here and crowds of people

1. Nurse Chūjō is Chūnagon's wet-nurse. It would be unusual for a woman to go meet him in such a distant place.

will come paying their respects. Please tell my father and stepmother that a person of my status should be in some quiet, out-of-the-way place."

Even though she did not say everything on her mind, the reason for her uneasiness was, unfortunately, all too clear. How nice it would be if she were waiting for him in dress other than that of one who has renounced the world, Nurse Shōshō lamented. Her mistress's words made her weep. It was, however, quite understandable that Taishō no Kimi would feel out of place.

Nurse Shōshō conveyed her lady's wishes to Lord Taishō and his wife who were, as usual, doting over the little girl, Himegimi.[2] While Lord Taishō was happy to hear that Chūnagon had returned, it only made him regret even more his daughter's rash behavior. Her request now brought tears to his eyes.

Lady Taishō understood her husband's tears and pitied him. "Why is it Taishō no Kimi feels so conspicuous here? As long as I live I want to keep her by my side, to be with her day and night, for I consider myself painfully responsible for her present condition. It grieves me to think she would feel estranged from me now. Chūnagon will be living in the East Wing. I do not think she should leave. Please tell her to stay here as I have indicated, for there is nothing to be done about her status now."

Lord Taishō, who thought it best to leave such things to his wife, said nothing. He understood why his daughter would feel ill-at-ease in the same house as Chūnagon, but he also knew it would be unfortunate were she to ignore Lady Taishō's wishes and move elsewhere. Since the girl, Himegimi, was living at Chūnagon's mansion, it was not as if she had no connection at all with the household. Chūnagon did not yet know the child, but he would surely not disown her.

2. Heian marriages were usually uxorilocal except for very high-born husbands. In this case Lord Taishō and Chūnagon's mother are apparently living together in the mansion Chūnagon calls home. Lord Taishō has a home of his own but spends most of his time with his wife and granddaughter at Chūnagon's home. It is a bit unusual for Taishō no Kimi to be living in the same house, but not completely contrived since Chūnagon's mother is also Taishō no Kimi's stepmother. As a nun Taishō no Kimi could not be expected to be the mistress of her father's home after the death of her natural mother. Heian marriage customs are admirably detailed in William H. McCullough, "Japanese Marriage Institutions in the Heian Period," *Harvard Journal of Asiatic Studies* 27 (1967):103-67.

"It is probably best if she just remains where she is," he said. "It is unfortunate she feels she ought not live here because everyone knows she is a nun. Her concern about what others might think is genuine, I am sure, but she should just calmly accept the support offered her and not be troubled by the criticism and gossip of a few. If she herself is less glum about the whole matter her faults will be forgotten and her childish charm will prevail. It is, on the other hand, dreary and distasteful to be too severe and haughty in one's penitence."

Nurse Shōshō sensed in his words the deep regret he felt over his daughter's station in life. She realized, however, that he was right. As she left the room Lord Taishō followed her out and asked, when no one else could hear, if they had received letters from Chūnagon.

"We did," she replied. She found his anxious inquiry painfully sad, but showed him the notes Lady Saishō and his daughter had received. The words he read were so tender and sincere it was almost enough to make him forget the unpleasant moment they would soon face. He found it hard to take his eyes off the letter.

"While Chūnagon may be experienced enough not to write a halfhearted note of clever but insincere sentiments," he thought, "he could not write these words if he did not truly care for her." He now found his daughter's childish compulsion to be elsewhere particularly sad.

When Taishō no Kimi was told of her parents' answer to her request she wept bitterly. "So I must remain here. My wish neither to see nor hear any more of this vile world has been in vain. In spite of what my stepmother said, I had hoped at least my father would agree I should not stay."

It seemed her parents were always disregarding her wishes. She really did not have any place to go, however, and it would not do to simply run and hide. Nor did she desire to spend the rest of her life estranged from her parents. How well she knew the sorrow of the mountain pear, living in a cruel world with no place to hide.[3]

---

3. Alluding to a poem found in *Kokin Rokujō*, anonymous, *Zoku Kokka Taikan* #35,111:
   Even though the world / Is said to be cruel, / There are no mountains to hide / The *yamanashi* flowers.
   There is a pun on the word *yamanashi* which means either "the flower of the mountain pear" or "no mountains."

With the worry of the past few years suddenly lifted, Lady Taishō now spent her time preparing everything from the curtains of the bed dais and portable frames to the servant's clothing in anticipation of Chūnagon's arrival. She hastily planned exciting new color combinations for his clothes, both the day and evening garments. She let the Emperor know that outstanding gentlemen of China had accompanied Chūnagon back to Japan, and he assembled a vast amount of gold to present to the visitors. These gifts were sent with the Emperor's personal envoy, Gon no Chūjō, the handsome and gifted son of the Minister of the Left.

Chūnagon was welcomed in Tsukushi with great pleasure by the Assistant Governor, Daini, and all the provincial officials. Among those who came from the capital to meet him, Nurse Chūjō's party traveled day and night to greet him as soon as possible. When she saw the one whose absence had worried her for three long years, she was overcome with joy as her eyes darkened with tears. Chūnagon too was delighted to see her. She had been so young and fresh when he left; now the years of constant tears and worry made her seem thin and tired. The look in her eyes had changed completely. Pitying her, he wondered if his mother too had aged so.

Secretly he told Nurse Chūjō of the boy, but he did not reveal it was a consort's child. "While in China I was presented this child by an unimaginably high-ranked lady. I could not bear to leave him behind so I brought him with me, even though it was difficult to take him from his mother. As he grows older it will be hard to keep his background a secret, but for the time being I would rather people not know he was born in a foreign land. Since it would be impossible to keep this secret for even a short time if I left him among these crude fellows, I asked you to come here to take care of him."

The child in his arms seemed radiantly beautiful, in no way inferior to Taishō no Kimi's girl whom everyone considered peerless. His face looked just like Chūnagon's. The child had retained both his weight and color while among the rugged crew, and Nurse Chūjō naturally wondered how he had fared so well without any milk on the voyage.

"He did not cry at all during the trip," said Chūnagon. "He seems like something from another world, the Buddha transformed." From his description it was clear Chūnagon had a very special affection for the boy's mother.

Nurse Chūjō began to tell him in detail of all that had happened to Taishō no Kimi while he was gone, and when she described her renunciation of the world tears clouded Chūnagon's eyes as he wondered what was to happen now.

"Even then I knew I should not long for that which her father would clearly not allow," he thought. "Once I decided to make the journey we unfortunately let our emotions get out of hand. Our actions were regrettable, but I never thought she would go this far; nor did I expect the results of our indiscretion to appear so quickly. Once our misdeed became apparent she must have felt terrible. I am certainly at fault. Since her father had always been so careful and loving in raising his beautiful daughter, he must have been terribly upset and confused when she suddenly renounced the world. I suppose he thinks me foolish. How could my mother possibly be comfortable knowing how he must feel about me? Be that as it may, what must Taishō no Kimi think? She was so unreserved and sincere in speaking to me, as if I were different from other men. Surely she regrets the unexpected turn of events and is now utterly disappointed. What was it like when all this trouble occurred? Only a very special grief could have prompted her to cut that extraordinarily beautiful hair."

He had not forgotten her even when he fell in love in China; whenever he longed for his homeland he always thought of her. Nothing could surpass his sorrow upon hearing of her actions.

"Long ago I vowed never to cause myself such problems or let myself become infatuated with others, but my efforts were all in vain. I am tormented by love's problems here just as in China, and I have caused others great sorrow. Not just strangers either, for now I am ashamed to face even my own parents. Everything has turned out contrary to my plans."

Hoping to find a note from Taishō no Kimi in Lady Saishō's letter he quickly opened the envelope, only to find a solitary poem by Lady Saishō.

> Even in the morning calm
> The one who but watches

> The fisherwoman in the bay
> Is drenched with tears.[4]

His sorrow and regret seemed overwhelming, for now he understood that dream in China in which Taishō no Kimi had asked, "For whom have I fallen into this sea of tears?"[5] Nurse Chūjō took pity and did her best to be of comfort.

He had considered asking his mother to watch over Wakagimi but now decided she might find it difficult to abandon the child already in her care. Besides, it would be a pity for Taishō no Kimi, who already had enough problems, to have everyone talking of the child, this "fern of longing,"[6] he had plucked in a far-off land while she was suffering at home. The truth could not be concealed forever, but for now he instructed Nurse Chūjō not to tell anyone at Lord Taishō's household of the child.

He had hoped that the grief of his unexpected affair with the distant Consort might be the only burden he need carry in his heart. His wish had been to trust his most intimate thoughts with Taishō no Kimi were she not yet married, and even if her father did not completely approve of their marriage, he had planned to visit her secretly. His only hope of comfort was now lost, and all that remained were bitter regret and love's anguish pressing from his pillow and his feet.[7] His mind could find no peace.

The Assistant Governor of Tsukushi, Daini, a fashionable man inclined to intemperate behavior, was unaware of Chūnagon's feelings. He had long hoped to offer his beloved daughter to him, but until now Chūnagon had shown no interest. Daini felt that such a match might not be impossible to arrange, even though Chūnagon often seemed aloof and unaffected by the normal affairs of this world. It bothered Daini that Chūnagon was like one from far beyond the clouds.

4. There are two significant puns in this poem. The first is the familiar use of *ama* for "nun" and "fisherwoman." The second is on the word *asanagi*, which is the "morning calm" when seashore winds change directions; the *nagi* component of this word also sounds like *naki*, "to weep."

5. See translation, p. 67.

6. *Shinobugusa*, a type of fern or moss, was often used for the image of a child born of a love tryst since *shinobu* means "to long for someone far away."

7. From poem #1,023, *Kokinshū*, anonymous:
From my pillow and my feet / Love's anguish presses in on me. / Nothing can be done but lie / In the middle of the bed.

Chūnagon had grown more manly in the years since Daini last saw him; his handsome presence, it seemed, gave new life to those around him. Daini was determined to introduce his daughter to Chūnagon this time, and even if he were not completely captivated with the girl he might, like the Tanabata herdsman, grace her with his shining presence at least once a year. Since Daini was too embarrassed to court Chūnagon directly he decided to arrange a meeting at an unusual pavilion built in a setting particularly appropriate for musical parties. One night when the moon was very bright he secretly sent his daughter to the pavilion to play her koto. He then sent his cousin, the Govenor of Chikuzen, to Chūnagon's nearby quarters with an invitation.

> I long for Mt. Mikasa my home—
> Won't you come view the moon with us tonight?[8]

Chūnagon had been staring at the moon, thinking of his last days in China. The sound of Wu Chün's *biwa* as she played her poem "how can I be satisfied" that moonlit night under the maples still echoed in his ears. He wondered why he had not visited her more often. Such thoughts had never occurred to him in China, but now he regretted his oversight.

> Why did I not visit her
> To view the moon together?
> Now that I think of it,
> I miss her so!

Even the slightest recollection of the Consort made him lonely and upset. His sorrow seemed aimless and without limit, enough perhaps, to fill the empty sky at which he now gazed so longingly.[9] His sensuous longing was plainly visible when the Governor of Chikuzen arrived with the invitation. Chūnagon felt it would be impolite to refuse; besides, such a visit might help alleviate his grief. He went discreetly to the pavilion, where four or five sensitive young men

8. The poem is by Daini. Mt. Mikasa, one of the three peaks of Yamato, was symbolic of the ancient capital of Nara.

9. This sentence contains allusions to two poems from the *Kokinshū*:
#611, Mitsune
    My longing is aimless / And without limit; / My only hope is / To meet you again.
#488, anonymous
    My longing is surely great enough / To fill the empty sky. / But though I try to clear my thoughts / They have no place to hide.

with slightly forlorn expressions awaited him. They were delighted he had come.

The handsome pavilion, set at the foot of a mountain overlooking the sea, afforded a beautiful view of the shoreline, and the building itself reminded Chūnagon of the mansion of the Consort's father in Shu Shan. Daini offered his guest a thirteen-stringed Chinese koto, he chose the *biwa* for himself, and the Governor of Chikuzen played the six-stringed Japanese koto and the flute. Even provincial officials invited from the surrounding area played well. As the night progressed interesting stories from the past proved an excellent diversion for Chūnagon's sorrow, and he remained on even though the hour was late.

When Daini pressed him to stay the night at the pavilion Chūnagon hesitated a moment, but since dawn was soon to break he decided he might as well go in and rest. Daini was delighted and soon brought a young, slender woman into Chūnagon's room.

"Please allow this woman to massage your legs," he said, then left immediately. Dismayed, Chūnagon wondered who she was and what she was to do. To simply ignore the woman would be harsh, so he called her closer and told her to massage his legs as Daini suggested. There was a certain elegance to her beauty, her clothes were fragrant and her touch delicate, and from her frail yet charming figure he could tell she was no ordinary woman.

"This must be the daughter Daini is always fussing and worrying about so much," thought Chūnagon. "He must think I am just another indulgent young man, but at the moment I could not fall in love even with a celestial maiden from heaven."

Chūnagon quickly became annoyed, for he could not simply tell her to leave. When she drew close and lay her sleeve alongside his, the feel of her robes was not at all unpleasant. But he had determined first and foremost never to become deeply involved with another woman. Besides, many Chinese who had accompanied him back were still in the area, and since he had resisted the Chinese Prime Minister's request to stay with his daughter, it would be disgraceful were the visitors to hear he had become Daini's son-in-law the moment he got back home. Furthermore, he had just learned that Lord Taishō's daughter had renounced the world. What a pity were she to hear her renunciation had not bothered him in the least, and he was now intimately involved with another woman.

The girl could not understand why Chūnagon offered no more than gentle conversation. Stunned at first by his unexpected behavior, she soon found his handsome face and intimate words touching. While she was bewildered by his reluctance to exchange true vows, his company was soothing. He too could not help but be moved by the unabashed way she lay by his side.

It would appear too calculated, he felt, were he to awake and leave before dawn as if vows had been consummated, so he pretended to sleep late.[10] When he finally awoke and opened the door facing the sea, in the morning light he could see that the girl was wearing a light blue woven jacket over many colored robes. She appeared to be seventeen or eighteen years of age, young and delicate, yet elegantly beautiful. Her hair, though hardly overabundant, spread about her evenly and smoothly. It had a faint tint, the color, one might say, of lustrous jade. The ends of her hair were as delicate as the tips of fine pampas grass, and her unblemished fair face was visible amid the hair falling gracefully over her temples and cheeks. There was nothing in the placement of her combs and accessories with which Chūnagon could find fault, and everything about her had a pleasing fragrance. He was now reluctant to depart, for she was surprisingly more attractive than he had first anticipated. Determined to meet her again he offered a poem while leaving.

> I know now I could never, never
> Forget the lower leaves of ivy.[11]

Her response was so faint as to be barely audible.

> If you will not forget,
> Send messages before the wind
> Turns the ivy leaves against you.[12]

10. A prospective bridegroom traditionally made three consecutive night visits to the bride's house. The first two nights he left before dawn, but on the morning of the third he stayed late and the finalization of vows was thus revealed officially. Chūnagon does not wish to appear as if he were participating in such a ceremony.

11. The *kuzu* (kudzu in English, but I have translated it as "ivy") is a delicate prostrate vine with purplish-red flowers. The white underleaves of the plant show when blown by the wind. Chūnagon is likening the woman to this plant.

12. The original is:
Wasurezu wa / Kuzu no shitaba no / Shitakaze no / uraminu hodo ni / oto o kikase yo

Her voice, muffled as she timidly hid her face, seemed young and charming. It was a sign of her fine character that she did not forget to respond with a poem immediately. Duly impressed, Chūnagon paused and spoke a few more words before taking his leave.

Daini, who had spent the entire night worrying, was excited and somewhat relieved to see that Chūnagon had stayed with his daughter all night. After leaving the girl's room, Chūnagon sent for Daini and said lightheartedly, "I had thought the woman you sent to massage my feet would be a servant lady. I was surprised and somewhat at a loss to find she was no ordinary lady."

Daini felt his face flush with embarrassment as he tried to explain.

"For a long time I have fervently wished that I might present her to you for even a moment. I was certain, however, that you would not deign to respond to any attempt I might make to discern your feelings on this matter, so I decided to take this opportunity to have her come massage your feet. I can think of nothing finer than to have you visit her, even if only for a few evening hours once a year. I spent the whole night worrying about my foolish plan."

He burst into tears. Chūnagon felt sorry for him and wondered if he would be bitter that things did not turn out as he had hoped.

"What a strange way to treat one's daughter," thought Chūnagon. "Had he told me what he wanted I might have been able to explain my feelings and avoid this misunderstanding."

He sat silent for a moment, then began to speak to Daini.

"While I was in China the Prime Minister was very intent on presenting his favorite daughter to me. I was wary of becoming intimate with someone in a foreign land; in fact, I ended the incident rather brusquely, for I was afraid I might have difficulty leaving the country if I became involved. Some of the Prime Minister's people accompanied me back to Japan. I am certain they would report everything to the Prime Minister if I were suddenly to visit your daughter regularly. It's the same everywhere: people will talk. The

---

This poem by Daini's daughter contains a clever pun on the word *uraminu* which I have found difficult to translate. Since the underleaves of the *kuzu* plant show white when blown by the wind, this word is often used with the word *uramu*, "to resent" or, as I have freely translated, "turn against." The first two syllables (*ura*) of *uramu* mean "underside." Thus *uraminu* in the poem can mean "not to resent" or *ura minu* "not to see (or by extension "show") the underside."

Prime Minister would soon learn that the man who rejected his daughter was now engaged with another woman.

"If a certain woman here in Japan, one with whom I had but a brief affair, were to hear such rumors, I would feel terrible. Well, the incident did not take place in a foreign land, so I suppose you know what I am talking about. My wish had always been to separate myself from this world and live like a hermit, different from any ordinary person, for I knew I could not live long in a world of many impurities. But I became involved with Lord Taishō's daughter, the girl he loved so dearly and had been so meticulous in raising. While we were unwittingly lost in that dreamlike affair she suddenly took on the unmistakable signs of a woman with child, and everyone was terribly distraught. I have since learned that she renounced the world. The whole affair was ordained, no doubt, by a bond in a previous life, but still, from Lord Taishō's point of view my sin would be difficult to forgive. Deep in my heart I had vowed never to cause even a lesser woman to take that drastic action whereby she would finally be avoided by other people, pitied, and mourned. Now I have enkindled grief and resentment in a person I might consider my own father, and I wasted the life of his daughter. I realize it is all my own fault.

"I traveled over very rough waters to the unknown world of China in hopes of seeing my newly reborn father. Now I feel guilty, frightened, and worried about my mother, for she must find it very difficult to bear with Lord Taishō's sorrow, knowing it is all my fault. Everyone would surely be bewildered, even insulted, if they heard somehow or other I had taken up with another woman right here in Japan. It would be unfortunate for your own daughter and painful for me were we to become intimately involved. I was troubled by these thoughts all night, but do not think you should give up hope and look for another man simply because I am so frank with you. I only wish to avoid being accused of unseemly behavior so soon after hearing about Taishō no Kimi's pitiful situation. In a short while I hope to send for your daughter. I do not know whether this makes any difference to you, but I will be very upset if you should think me insincere."

Daini was impressed by the sincerity of Chūnagon's plea, and he suddenly regretted having devised such a tasteless, vulgar scheme at a time Chūnagon was absorbed with so many other problems. But what was he to do now?

"If like most other people I were one to worry about gossip, I would never have thought of presenting my own daughter to you so unexpectedly. I had merely hoped that some way or other I might bring her to your attention. Now that I understand your feelings for her, even though you did not look upon her as I had originally hoped, how could I possibly consider giving her to another man?

> Why should we have waited
> Like the pines of Hakozaki?
> There was no vow at all.

"I will always regret my unseemly actions," he said.

Chūnagon smiled as he left. "You need not speak so despairingly."

> I wish to vow my love
> In the distant future.
> Do not quit so soon,
> Pines of Hakozaki.

"But, 'she wishes to see you while she is alive,' "[13] grumbled Daini somewhat resentfully and left with his retainers.

Chūnagon felt sorry for Daini, who was apparently quite disappointed. He was, at the same time, somewhat intrigued that he had allowed himself to forego such a beautiful, delicate woman as Daini's daughter. That evening he called on the Governor of Chikuzen and had him take a letter to the girl.

The girl's mother was very disappointed that things had not gone as she hoped; no wonder she began complaining to her husband.

"It is of no avail to us that Chūnagon is so splendid a man. What a foolish blunder it was to rashly force our daughter on someone who was preoccupied with other matters. One would only expect such drastic measures on behalf of a lonely orphan."

Just as her husband was again regretting his decision the letter arrived from Chūnagon, lifting his spirits. Opening it he found a beautifully written poem addressed to his daughter.

13. From poem #685, _Shūishū_, Ōtomo no Momoyo:
After I have died for love / What good will it do? / I wish to see you now / While I am still alive.

113

> As I gaze at the evening sky,
> Why this knowing face of joy?[14]

"Look at this," Daini said to his wife, desperate to soothe her anger. "How could anyone not trust a person like him? Out of pity for the girl and, perhaps, for his own peace of mind, he obviously decided not to become intimate with her while he had so many other worries. The deep concern he has demonstrated by avoiding reckless action shows first and foremost what an unusual man he is. He has gone to great pains to express his true feelings and allay her suspicions. He really is an unusually splendid man."

Daini's wife thought this excitement just more of his wishful thinking until she herself read the letter. She was so impressed she could not set it down.

The girl disliked hearing her mother weep and complain. She had been so tense and embarrassed in Chūnagon's presence she hardly slept the entire night. Now she dozed off in another room while her parents were discussing Chūnagon's poem. Her father quietly entered her room and woke her.

"Answer with something that will capture his interest," he instructed her.

> What am I to make of the evening sky?
> Why sit and watch the clouds disappear?

Chūnagon found the writing innocently attractive. "The resentful, pretentious tone of the poem must be the work of Daini," he thought, pitying the girl.

That evening he quietly visited Daini's house. Although the match was not to be, the inquisitive stares of other people might be bothersome, so Daini did not have his daughter meet with Chūnagon again. Chūnagon had no reason to resent this.

When the Chinese who had accompanied Chūnagon were ready to return home, he presented them with gifts almost too splendid, things they would find unusual and delightful. He also sent letters back with them. The letter to the Prince was very moving. What a pity, he thought, that he could not mention Wakagimi in the letter

---

14. The third line of this poem, *kotowarigao ni*, Matsuo takes as a miscopy of *kotoarigao ni*, "a meaningful look." I have followed the sense of Matsuo's correction in my translation. Chūnagon has a "knowing face of joy" because he anticipates meeting her again, not because of anything they did the previous night.

to Lady Nü Wang, for fear someone might read it. For any ordinary situation he might find in his heart words to express his feelings, but his sentiments far outnumbered the grains of sand on a beach. He wanted to tell her many things but he could not continue writing. He hoped she would understand his feelings, the many thoughts locked in his heart, drowned in his tears; if she could read between the lines she would surely be moved by his letter. His tears flowed unrelentingly until he simply could write no more.

> To what can I compare my thoughts?
> They go beyond the clouds,
> Beyond the sea.

The words alone seemed quite ordinary.

No longer blinded by a veil of tears, he was able to recall in a poem for the Prime Minister's daughter the splendor of their days together and write to his heart's content.

> How sad indeed!
> When will we meet again,
> To watch the early morning moon?

"Unless I am reborn in that world I shall never hear the sound of her *biwa* again," he mused. The sound of her playing now came to mind unprompted; he had missed his chance to listen more carefully while in China and his regrets now were one more reason for tears.

The night before the Chinese delegation was to return, Chūjō, the official messenger from the Japanese Court, along with Daini and the Governors of Chikuzen and Higo, and everyone else from Tsukushi with even the slightest sense of taste gathered for an evening of Chinese and Japanese poetry. When Chūnagon read his Chinese verse, both the Chinese and Japanese guests were so deeply impressed their tears ran red.

Chūnagon wept as he recited his Japanese poem.

> I had only hoped
> To spend more time with you.
> How sad that we must live apart.

Everyone watching this splendid recitation found the verse even more moving than his Chinese composition. Daini in particular was deeply touched.

The Chinese Imperial Adviser who had accompanied Chūnagon

was a man of outstanding appearance and character, smooth and self-assured in all his actions. They had been close companions for the past three years (the Chinese adviser greatly admired Chūnagon) and parting was particularly sad. He had accompanied Chūnagon this far, and now, his eyes filled with tears, he offered his farewell.

> Though rough waves and distant clouds
> May stand between us,
> I shall think of you always.

It was the night before Chūnagon was to return to the capital. He was feeling quite sorry for Daini and his daughter, understanding their thwarted hopes, and he felt himself disposed to see the lovely girl again. Late that night when the moon was bright he stole away to visit her house.

Since Daini himself had first brought them together it would be ridiculous for him now to refuse Chūnagon entry or openly force his daughter to rebuff him. He was instead very fastidious in preparing the meeting place, for he had heard that Chūnagon, unlike most other men, was always painstakingly correct in his behavior.

He invited Chūnagon to sit on a cushion near an open door which afforded a view of the beautiful moonlight. His daughter, however, was seated behind a screen and a curtain of state.

"I suppose this exaggerated effort at keeping us apart is because no vow was made on our last meeting," he said resentfully. "It is truly sad you think I am so difficult to get along with."

He then led her out from behind the screen. In the moonlight the girl seemed more elegant and beautiful than before. Chūnagon was not one to become involved in short-lived affairs, but ordinarily he would not pass up a woman so attractive. He remembered, however, the extraordinary importance Daini attached to such a union: the man was reputed to be very ill-tempered, and there would surely be trouble if Chūnagon's intentions were misunderstood. Chūnagon therefore gave up any thought of seducing the girl that night.

He explained his reasoning to the girl as gently and sincerely as he could. Perhaps because she now realized Chūnagon would soon be far away she seemed to accept his words with sad resignation. This he found particularly charming.

As Chūnagon hurried to leave before dawn, he felt the evening had been no less moving than the moonlit night the Chinese Prime

Minister's daughter had played the song "half a moon" with her *biwa*. Weeping he bade farewell.

> Our parting is sullied
> By teardrops from my heart.
> If we lived together,
> I would not need weep so. [15]

"If your parents try giving you to someone else do not be swayed. I am determined to take you with me later. Do not take my feelings lightly."

The young girl was so moved by his repeated pledges she did not doubt him for a moment. She seemed quite tender as she wept, trying unsuccessfully to hide her embarrassment.

> Had I not seen you
> We could live apart,
> But why do my tears now fall
> Like drops of water from cupped hands? [16]

How strange, how dreamlike, he mused, now finding it difficult to leave the charming girl; when he did depart for the capital Daini saw him off as far as the border.

Nurse Chūjō and the child, Wakagimi, took a separate boat back to the capital. People who did not fully understand the situation marveled at the deep devotion she had shown in coming down to greet Chūnagon. She had once been the wife of a Governor of Sanuki who had died and left her a considerble inheritance. She lived in a large house with her daughters, and it was there that she took Wakagimi upon arriving in the capital.

Lord Taishō and his sons, along with Chūnagon's uncles and many of his old friends among the high court nobles and senior courtiers, came out to greet him. He was deeply moved by the reception, but when he saw Lord Taishō he began to weep anxiously as he wondered how resentful and reserved the man must now feel. Lord Taishō was surprised at how much more splendid and hand-

15. There is a pun on the word *sumaba* meaning either "if we lived together" or "if it were clear," i.e., if our parting were not sullied like a clouded moon by teardrops.

16. The first line of this poem, *kagemizu wa*, could mean either "had I not seen you," or "water carried by a bamboo pipe." Its second meaning is, therefore, related to the last line of the poem.

some Chūnagon had grown in their years apart. He too began to weep as he pondered their predicament.

"People say the excitement of the unknown is lacking when close relatives marry, but had my daughter married Chūnagon I doubt either would have been disappointed. What a shame she renounced the world so suddenly. It must have been fated that she not even marry someone of his rank. Ever since she was a child I raised her with the hope of marrying her to one of the highest rank. My efforts in this world were all in vain."

Troubled thoughts lay hidden in their hearts, but neither he nor Chūnagon let his feelings show as they engaged in small talk on the way to Chūnagon's mansion. Since people were waiting expectantly at the mansion Lord Taishō decided to return home to his own estate. Chūnagon and his mother would talk for a long time. Besides, he thought his presence might prove embarrassing when Chūnagon met Himegimi, his new daughter.

When Chūnagon saw his mother he was surprised to discover that the once youthful vigor of her face had weakened so much she seemed almost a different person. The moment she saw him tears darkened her eyes and she could not speak. He felt frightened and guilty for all the grief he had caused her, and now he could not bear to see her weep. There were many serious matters to discuss, and as they were not likely to finish in one evening his mother first brought out Himegimi and showed her to him.

Now three years old with loose hair reaching her eyebrows, she was indeed pretty. From her grandmother's lap she stared shyly at the unfamiliar man in the lamplight. She was so very precious he began to weep, and it was quite appropriate that he should seem so profoundly moved. Softly he spoke to his mother.

"I pity poor Taishō no Kimi, for her father must think us terribly loose and indecent. I was shocked by the news, but anyone who sees this child will know that the predestined bonds of former lives are difficult to escape. Perhaps that would excuse me somewhat, but since the lady has turned her back on the world there is no way for one as unworthy as myself to atone for this sin." He apparently wished he could say much more.

Secretly he told her of Wakagimi. "While in China I unexpectedly fathered a child. Since I wish to keep it a secret for a while, I entrusted him to Nurse Chūjō."

His mother, who had always thought Himegimi would be inauspiciously lonely without any brothers or sisters, was willing to care for any number of children he might bring home.

"Why didn't you bring him with you tonight?" she asked disappointedly.

"I did not want others to know about him, but you shall meet him soon.

"Now that I have seen you my worries have been put to rest and perhaps we should go to sleep. I wonder if it would be unseemly of me to send Taishō no Kimi a note," he sighed. He decided to have Lady Saishō meet him by the center sliding door of his room.

When Taishō no Kimi saw the ominous bustle, good spirits, even tears of joy of everyone in the household, her unfortunate relationship with Chūnagon distressed her more than ever. "Even though I feel terribly out of place I have to hear all this commotion so near at hand," she lamented, and went behind her curtain and pretended to be sleeping. As she thought of all her problems, particularly her wretched karma, she wept tears enough to float her pillow.

Lady Saishō had no sooner brought in the note from Chūnagon than he himself appeared. Taishō no Kimi was crushed: she felt so much more reserved, restrained, and wretched than before. Rising quickly she tried to move away from the curtain, but he seized her robes and made her stay. This annoyed her greatly. Lady Saishō was startled by his boldness but could not begin to restrain him now, even if her lady was a nun. Instead she moved away from the curtain slightly.

Weeping, he told Taishō no Kimi everything from the morning he had left until that very morning.

"You will never know how terrible I feel in being gone so long without knowing what you had done . . . or the regret I feel over this bond from a previous life. I am afraid you cannot clear a worthless reputation in a moment. I suppose that when Prince Shikibukyō heard of our relationship you then decided you knew the meaning of 'sorrow' and could turn your back on the world and cut your hair. But you must know that he too finds talk of your behavior disgusting."

His words were tinged with scorn and bitterness as he moved nearby to touch her. She seemed the same as before, gentle and elegant, but when he touched her hair he found it had been cut short and swayed easily.

"How terrible," he thought. "What ever could have made her so glum and discouraged as to cut that beautiful hair?" Forgetting all his other worries he wept openly and uncontrollably. His deep concern would surely make all her bitterness disappear.

> Please tell me:
> How could you renounce the world,
> Forgetting all the vows we made?

He did his best to control himself and tried not to let her see his disappointment, but he could only weep. Now that she was right before his eyes he wondered remorsefully how he had found the courage to leave such a beautiful woman behind. Why had he crossed the frightening sea, tortured himself in a forbidden affair, and caused this woman to abandon the world?

She had told herself that she never wanted to see or hear him again, yet now he seemed quite special, sitting before her, unable to hold back his tears. It was as if the very things she wanted to undo, the events of that night three years ago, were now happening to her again. How wretched to once again be seen and heard at such a close distance.

> I thought of what I might have done,
> But life's limit is ordained.
> That you should find me still alive
> I regret most of all.

The refined, elegant, and charming way she wept as she spoke had not changed, and her words moved him beyond measure.

Chūnagon was never one to take any woman lightly, even the kind he might encounter purely by chance. Nor was he likely to become intimately involved except for some extraordinary reason, and it was most unlikely that one so circumspect would be ignorant of the inaccesibility of a heart devoted to the Buddha. Neither of them had the strength to restrain their tears as they spent the entire winter night in intimate conversation. It is impossible to report all they said to each other, for there is no way to describe such strong feelings.

A parent's love is rare indeed. "What were Chūnagon's feelings

when he saw Himegimi?" wondered Lord Taishō. "Maybe he's meeting with Taishō no Kimi now. Perhaps she should have moved
elsewhere. He will, I suppose, be disappointed when he gets a good
look at her. And what a pity for her if he acts indifferently once he
sees what she has become."

He could hardly sleep for worry. Anxious to learn what had happened, he went to Chūnagon's house early the next morning and
questioned Nurse Shōshō in detail. Out of pity she told him everything.

"He had Lady Saishō take a note to her, but when she went into
your daughter's room he followed her right in and spent the entire
night talking with your daughter. It was not, I think, a trivial conversation. He should be leaving her room about now."

Lord Taishō smiled when he heard this. A parent's love is blind,
and it never occurred to him that there might be any wrong to it,
any sin to be paid for in the next life; he was simply pleased that
they still cared for each other deeply, even if she was a nun.

He decided he should at least try to appear more concerned, so
he piously threw several priestly robes over his shoulder, shut his
eyes tightly, and began to recite the Nembutsu.

"Inform Taishō no Kimi she is not to be seen by him any more,"
he told Nurse Shōshō.

"How terribly sad," she thought. "Everything he does is so unexpected."

Chūnagon was not distracted by the bustle of activity in the mansion as people gathered to celebrate his return; instead he would go
directly to Taishō no Kimi's quarters to play with the girl, Himegimi.
He found her delightfully charming, in no way inferior to the child
left as a memento of another deep love. As he held the girl in his
arms he wondered why he should care what others might think, for
everyone already knew of the incident. He opened the doors of Taishō
no Kimi's room and walked in, much to the surprise of her ladies.

Taishō no Kimi had been relaxing, certain he would not dare visit
her during the day. Shocked though she was by this intrusion, she
could no longer hide, so she merely sat with her head turned to one
side. He found her more brilliant than flowers in full bloom, a vividly
proud and charming woman. Her hair reached the floor only when

she was seated now,[17] and the clipped ends swayed gently, spread out like a fan. She was still quite graceful and beautiful. When he caught a glimpse of her face among the luxuriant hair of her forehead, he realized that even with the change she was more lovely than ever. The color of her face, now slightly red with shame and sorrow, gave her presence a beautiful radiance. She wore simple garments of subdued colors, gray and orange; even more than the many-colored robes of formal wear these garments gave her a different beauty, a pious, even august presence. He had feared that she might be reserved and difficult when he came close, but in fact she was quite charming and agreeable.

"Ah," he thought, "even if a woman like this were to become empress her parents would not think it good enough for her. I am responsible for her renunciation of the world. How her father must detest me. Perhaps he tries to curb his anger in deference to my mother. A single lifetime is not enough to atone for my sins. What a shame!"

Even as he stared he felt his spirit drawn to her and could not stop his tears. He was treated politely by her, though she seemed terribly confused as to how she should respond to him. His love for her was certainly no less than the extraordinary affection he felt for the Hoyang Consort whose distinct, unearthly beauty had captivated him even in a land of constant surprises. No one in Japan could be more beautiful than Taishō no Kimi, he felt, but unfortunately nothing could be done about her present condition.

"Well," he mused, "if we keep our inner feelings pure and curb our reckless hearts, the Buddha will look favorably on us. Whatever people might say should not be too painful to bear. If I look to her daily for comfort, perhaps her father's resentment will abate. When Prince Shikibukyō suddenly gave up courting Taishō no Kimi and married her sister, everyone, even Nurse Shōshō, must have been shocked by the abrupt change."

In pity he sent for Nurse Shōshō.

"It is too late to apologize to Taishō no Kimi. She has only my mother with her now; Nurse Chūjō apparently exhausted herself in caring for Taishō no Kimi and spends most of her time at home.

17. The hair of a woman who had not renounced the world would normally exceed her height when standing.

From now on I want you to assist Taishō no Kimi. She will surely appreciate your help."

Nurse Shōshō found his gentle, generous manner reassuring. His devotion made her extremely happy, for she had worried he might be interested in another woman now that Taishō no Kimi had become a nun.

When Chūnagon went to the Imperial Palace in response to the many invitations offered, his train was far from ordinary. He set off in smart-fitting robes of magnificent color, dazzling to the eye, and the unusual fragrance of his clothes carried more than a hundred paces. The snow that had accumulated for the past few days continued to fall, adding even more brilliance to his appearance. People along the palace route looked at him in awe. As he walked through the gate near the guardhouse, even people of no particular aesthetic sense, servants of the bath or kitchen and the like, were moved to tears. Higher-ranking ladies overflowed into the narrow corridors and strained to see him; they were irritated, even upset that he passed with only a glance their way.

Chūnagon was called into the Emperor's room. The Emperor was astonished when he finally set eyes on Chūnagon after all these years. For a while he could not utter a word but merely gazed at him and wept. Awed by the Emperor's presence Chūnagon grew weak. When the Emperor began questioning him in detail about China it became obvious the audience would not be over quickly. Around sunset, even though the snow continued to fall heavily, the moon shone brightly.

"While you were gone I found little interest in playing instruments, and most of the time there was little music at all," the Emperor said.

With this the musical entertainment began. Everything about Japan seemed refreshingly new to Chūnagon, and when he found himself in a situation in any way similar to that spring night in China, his feelings were stirred. After calming his spirits he began to play the koto, and the sound of the music was beautiful beyond compare. His touch was as skillful as ever, and none of the listeners could restrain his tears. Though the setting was not unusual, memories of the Consort made it impossible for Chūnagon to continue.

He received a gift of clothing, as was the custom, along with this poem from the Emperor.

> After you left,
> The moon in the sky was always clouded.
> I never saw it shine
> As brightly as now.

Chūnagon was deeply honored by the unusually kind words.

> How sad it was to watch
> The distant moon in the heavenly plain,
> My only reminder of my home.

He performed a ceremonious bow upon taking his leave of the Emperor.

It was quite late when he arrived at the Empress's quarters. In anticipation of his visit many of her ladies had burned elusive incense which now permeated the halls. He was nervous, for he suspected the Empress might at that very moment be secretly watching him enter the mansion. Suddenly he recalled the night he sat before the Hoyang Consort's blinds; at first she seemed quite distant, but when circumstances changed and he was about to return home she received him kindly. The memory of her graceful beauty now moved him profoundly. As he sat before the Empress he was momentarily at a loss for what to say, and he feared the ladies might misunderstand his feelings. Was he perhaps attracted to the one behind the screen? In his heart he thought of her.

> Were you not tied
> To the purple clouds,
> Might not my thoughts at least
> Go out to you?[18]

Such desires were presumptuous and not befitting his position.

In the midst of the small talk one of the ladies behind the screen cautiously offered a poem.

> Perhaps you did not know
> We thought of you,
> Whenever we saw
> The moon in the west.

---

18. Chūnagon possibly knew the Empress before she reached her present position. "Purple clouds" is actually a poetic name for the position of Empress.

In response he said,
> Who was it
> Who looked at the moon
> Setting in the west
> And wondered if I
> Was alive or dead?

He paused momentarily to recall his past acquaintances, for many of the Empress's ladies were attracted to him. The ladies modeled themselves upon the Empress, and to him they seemed particularly splendid, perhaps because he had not met court ladies for so long a time. He feared talking too much lest his words be misconstrued, so he left before saying all he wished. He was, however, intrigued with the lady who had recited the poem of the moon setting in the west. She was, he later discovered, Shōshō no Naishi, a reputable lady of the Court. Delighted with this discovery he sent a poem.

> I have a mind to visit you
> Even there above the clouds.
> I would like to meet
> And talk awhile with you.[19]

Could her joy on receiving this be commonplace? In return she wrote:

> Your interest in me
> Is but a brief impression
> Of your visit to the Court.

From the clear and charming style of her calligraphy he could tell she was not at all unattractive. Daini's daughter's poem "like drops of water from cupped hands"[20] had a certain innocent charm which he had thought unique among women of that class. He began to correspond frequently with this intriguing new lady.

Taishō no Kimi decided that since she was a nun she and her daughter should no longer sleep in the same room. Since the girl was already three the ceremony of her initial wearing of a skirt was held at the end of the month, whereupon her quarters were moved to the main building.[21] In the western half of the main room a statue

19. "Above the clouds" is another name for the Court.
20. See translation p. 117.
21. *Hakamagi*, "wearing of the skirt ceremony," was performed for both boys and girls some time between the age of three and seven. An auspicious time (usually

of the Buddha was erected and the room was furnished so extensively it dazzled the eye. Taishō no Kimi made the center of this section her living quarters and placed curtains draped with pale figured cloth to the north and south of her living area. The room was very neatly furnished. The eastern half of the main room, where Himegimi lived, was furnished with special miniature utensils and dolls for her to play with. The two nursemaids assigned to her were particularly devoted in their care, much to the delight of Lord Taishō and his wife, and the room was everything a little girl would ever want.

Although Taishō no Kimi still felt out of place in Chūnagon's mansion, any mention of leaving brought sharp remonstrances from her parents. She saw her own life now as difficult, even worthless, and while she bemoaned her unexpected fate continually, what could she do about it? Her parents had entrusted her well-being to Chūnagon, and he was with her constantly, watching after her needs and still behaving quite decorously.

The rooms of the ladies-in-waiting were located in the northwest wing of the house. Chūnagon's clothing and all his personal effects were entrusted to Nurse Shōshō. In order to be with Taishō no Kimi all day Chūnagon would simply push aside the curtains surrounding her room and walk in. Were she lacking in charm he might only pity her, but even in her present station she was elegant, beautiful, and splendid beyond compare. There was nothing disagreeable in her appearance. At night they set their bedding together and talked of the past and present, weeping, laughing, and forever vowing to each other that in the next world they would be born again on the same lotus leaf. On the holy days they copied sutras to offer to the Buddha. Together they performed the Nembutsu and recited praise for the Bodhisattva Samantabhadra. Her father found great relief in their ideal relationship. It was truly like the ties binding King Subhavyūha and his wife Vimaladattā, he thought.[22]

Lord Taishō was relieved Chūnagon did not scorn her simply

---

evening) was chosen and the head of the household performed the ceremony.

In the *shinden* style of architecture, the main building faced south directly overlooking the garden. Although Taishō no Kimi and Himegimi both move into the main building, their living quarters are on either side of the room and separated by curtains of state.

22. Based on a story found in Chapter 27 of the Lotus Sutra. King Subhavyūha became a follower of the Buddha through the efforts of his wife and two sons.

because their families were so closely tied. Chūnagon's reassuring devotion to her was, in fact, quite a contrast to Prince Shikibukyō's behavior; the Prince's infrequent visits to Naka no Kimi made her feel uneasy and inferior. It was apparent, much to Lord Taishō's delight, that Chūnagon and his daughter had vowed themselves unto each other in this world and the next.

Many of the ladies who had ungratefully deserted Taishō no Kimi when she became a nun had a change of heart. Now she seemed the ideal mistress and they hurried back to serve her. Lady Saishō, however, had never wavered in her devotion to her lady and for this Chūnagon was deeply grateful. He treated her as special, apart from all the other ladies, and had her act as foster mother for the child. [23]

He moved ahead quickly with plans to build for Taishō no Kimi a splendid new pavilion in a remote location nestled between a mountain and a pond. On certain occasions, when the morning moon was still very bright and they had spent the night together in worship before the Buddha, he would wonder somewhat mournfully why it was that in spite of their youthfulness they had been praying all night for the happiness of a life together in paradise, when in fact they might have "slept side by side not knowing the dawn."[24]

At first the young woman had loathed living where she felt exposed and shamed before the world. Even though she loved her parents dearly and they had always been generous in their support, how could she stay with them if it meant not performing the meritorious acts necessary for her own salvation? With Chūnagon she could now devote herself entirely to prayer, and in her heart she was no longer disturbed. She was delighted to have found a friend in prayer; together they could pray with one heart for their life in the next world, and as she grew more accustomed to his presence she no longer felt so distant and gloomy.

Not only were her beauty and charm without flaw, but her character was accomplished, discerning, and versatile. Though he could

23. Since Taishō no Kimi is a nun and, theoretically at least, separated from the worries of this world, she cannot fully care for her daughter. Until now Lord Taishō and his wife have been watching after the child's needs.

24. Based on a poem in the Ise Shū (Poems of the Lady Ise, ca. 877 to ca. 939). The poem is by the retired Emperor Uda:
We might have slept side by side / Not knowing the dawn; / How was I to know / I might not see you even in my dreams?

see she left nothing to be desired, he did occasionally wish her station in life were that of an ordinary person. But even if she were not a nun, he wondered, could they live as an ordinary couple? Probably not. There would undoubtedly be times when she would resent his overly modest ways. And were they less diligent in their prayers they might lose sight of their hopes for the future world. Their present relationship, even with its difficulties, was such that neither he nor she had any obvious cause for bitterness, and the more they prayed together the greater this devotion grew.

His willingness to talk with her of society or personal matters any time she wanted made her feel as if she truly had someone to rely on. For years her nursemaids had cared for her, but the comfort they gave her had its limits, and sleeping alone was very lonely. She was now satisfied with her station in this life and her hopes for the next. This served to lessen the sorrow and resentment of those around her, and made it easier for them to accept his constant presence in her room.

Nurse Chūjō ignored the affairs of Chūnagon's household to spend her time caring for Wakagimi. Her single-minded devotion assured the child proper care. Since Chūnagon's house was nearby he came to see the child nearly every day, sometimes even staying the night. As he watched the boy grow he cherished him more each day, and his affection was surely no less than his love for Himegimi. He thought of the child as someone from another world and loved him so much he found it difficult to take his eyes off him for even a moment. He kept him hidden, however, for he still thought it best people not know of the boy.

Chūnagon's mother, always anxious to see the child, would visit whenever she left home to avoid the interdictions of an unlucky direction. Could she conceivably disdain the boy? On the contrary, she wished to take him home and keep him by her side along with Himegimi. Chūnagon, however, had other thoughts and kept the child with Nurse Chūjō.

On sleepless nights, when Chūnagon told Taishō no Kimi stories of this land and China, only the story of the Hoyang Consort remained hidden in his heart. He knew it would make interesting conversation—her appearance on the night of the chrysanthemums, the sound of her *kin*—but before he could say anything he was overcome with tears and could not continue. While he could never forget the Consort, the kind company of his mother, Himegimi, and Taishō no Kimi kept him busy and preoccupied; he became settled and more at ease, no longer tortured by the grief he had felt upon leaving China.

Whenever he thought that he would never again meet the Consort his longing seemed great enough to fill the empty sky.[25] Since he had already been in China for three years he might have stayed a little longer in hopes of seeing her again. She had not for the most part been too distant. In fact she had treated him kindly. But he had feared his love for the woman might become known to the people of that foreign land had he proved unable to control himself. Since that would surely have led to trouble for the Consort, the Prince, and himself, he had suddenly set sail and returned to Japan. Now, however, he was left with a sense of longing and regret.

He took out the large aloeswood letter box which the Consort had entrusted to him. The sweet fragrance of the wood lingered on his hands as he opened the box and found a long letter addressed to the Consort's mother inside.

"As long as I can remember I have anxiously wondered what became of you after we left you in Japan; my wish to know seemed all in vain, for not even the whisper of the wind brought news of you. Every day as I watched the sun and moon rise in the east I wept with the realization that only these would remind me of you. What sin in a former life has forced us to live in the same world without being able to see or hear each other?

"I now live so far beyond the distant clouds neither of us can tell if the other is still alive. I might find joy in living a full life if I had even the slightest hope of somehow crossing the mountains and clouds to see you once again. But I despair of knowing how or when I will ever see you again, and my life until now has been nothing but bitter regrets.

"Had you not made me remember so well the day we parted perhaps I could cope with my sorrow, but the sight of your weeping face the morning you told me to consider that parting the end has not left me for a moment. I fervently prayed to the gods and the

25. See note 9, above, for the source of this allusion.

Buddha that I might have word of you. I was overjoyed that my daily petitions to the Buddha were answered, for I met a priest from Japan who knew you well. You have seen, have you not, the long letter I had him take you when he returned to Japan?

"Before many years had passed Chūnagon came to China, as I am sure you know. My very own child was Chūnagon's father in his previous life! Chūnagon came to China to see his reborn father. Since I received no answer for the letter I entrusted to the monk I was worried you might no longer be alive. I have written everything in this letter because I am sure Chūnagon is to be trusted. Travel from your country to mine ceased for a long time and only recently began to flourish again. That, unfortunately, is all I have to show for my daily prayers to the Buddha. Even the rank of Consort of China means nothing to me. I would not begrudge my life at all if I could be reborn as even a grass or tree of the land where you live. Chūnagon will be visiting you. Please meet with him and ask him in detail about my country. Now that you have renounced the world is there any reason to be embarrassed?

"I heard from the monk something about your having had another child. I want so much to see the child. I am envious and delighted that she is able to be with you when you feel lonely. If it were a boy I could wait expectantly for the day when he might come to this land; how sad and regrettable even this is impossible.

"Chūnagon considers his relationship with my son very unusual so I hope you will not treat him indifferently. Do not doubt his sincerity; rely on him for everything as if he were I. That is my request. Do not think of him as a stranger."

A poem and a postscript were attached.

There is nothing like it
In this land or in that—
The tie between parent and child.

"It is fruitless and insufferable to be born a human being. Day and night I think of you; whenever I hear the sound of the wind or rain, or see the blossoms or leaves fall, I can only wonder where you are and how you are faring."

As Chūnagon finished the letter the whole world seemed to turn dark; he could not think, and the flood of tears might, it seemed, sweep his whole body away. Again and again he read over the part where she told her mother to rely on him: "think of him as if he were I." To say he was deeply saddened would not do justice to his sorrow.

"To think that such a splendid person as she would actually ask her mother to think of me as herself; she must care for me," he thought. She has a sister somewhere, he now realized. He opened a tightly folded letter which was apparently addressed to that sister.

"You would not know me, but I have been thinking about you ever since the priest told me of you. Unless I am reborn in Japan I must abandon all hope of meeting you. What a sad, cruel fate.

> Though you do not know me,
> Look for me in the fragrance of the flower
> Come blown with the wind.

"I find it hard to forget the child Chūnagon took back with him. If you have a chance to look after the child, please treat him kindly."

It would be all too commonplace to say he was once again overcome with sorrow.

He returned the letters to the box and closed the lid tightly, but his breast was choked with emotion over what he had read. He wanted nothing more than to be a bird so he could immediately fly to the Hoyang District.

When he finally settled down he began to inquire after this monk who had traveled to China. Someone said the monk had built a retreat in a place called Miyoshino on the far side of Yoshino and now lived in seclusion there.[26] Chūnagon decided to visit this monk before looking for the Consort's mother, but he first spoke with Taishō no Kimi.

"The Prince of China gave me a letter to deliver personally to a monk who just recently returned to Japan from China. He is living somewhere in the inner recesses of Yoshino so I thought I would take the letter there myself. I hope to return immediately, but these things have a way of taking time. I once left you to go all the way to China, but now that I have spent some time with you I feel uneasy

---

26. Yoshino is a mountainous area in the present-day prefecture of Nara. The *mi* of *miyoshino* is generally just added for poetic effect, but in this tale it often refers more specifically to the remotest part of Yoshino. Throughout the story, however, the words are occasionally used interchangeably.

about leaving you for even a short time. Please devote yourself completely to prayer while I am gone."

She was moved by the tears he shed while giving these instructions.

"The monk's retreat seems the sort of place a nun like myself would wish to visit."

> Since I took my vows
> I have longed to live in Yoshino,
> Cut off from this vile world.

She was beautiful as she began to cry, and Chūnagon reasoned that a man less mindful than himself of the Buddha's wishes and the dangers of sin might well take advantage of her. His own forbearance he attributed to his pure heart, when, in fact, it was probably because he cared only for her.

> If you lived there
> I too would hide away in Yoshino
> And no longer wander like this in the world.

"In recent years only my mother's needs kept me tied to this world, but now I must care for you. It is sad that this bond too must keep me from renouncing this world."

It was only a brief journey, but he found it very difficult to leave; he was extraordinarily considerate in telling everyone of his plans.

He visited Wakagimi and told him time and time again how worried he was about leaving for even a short time. How could he restrain his tears as he remembered how fondly the Consort had written of this child?

When he told his mother she burst into tears and asked, "Where are you going this time?"

"How about China?" he said in jest.

"Oh! I cannot understand you," she wept. "These peculiar, wild notions of yours cause me nothing but worry and grief. I would be better off not even seeing you again."

He felt sorry for her, but knew she had reason to feel mistreated.

Chapter Three

THE MOUNTAINS of Yoshino are well-known for their seclusion, but the monk's retreat took Chūnagon into the even more distant recesses of Miyoshino. Since he was traveling incognito with only a few close retainers the trip seemed lonelier than the heavily escorted voyage to China across the distant seas.

He arrived on the twentieth day of the third month. The snow was no longer piled high, but patches remained in the lower parts of the valleys, and the branches of the cherry trees, already green in the capital, were here in full bloom. What a pity the wind seemed to know of blossoms not yet scattered.[1] Chūnagon's thoughts turned only to China.

> My yearning does not wane;
> She lies buried in my thoughts,
> Deeper than the deepest mountains of Miyoshino.

He arrived to find a splendid prayer pavilion near the mountains, but the monk's living quarters were no more than a temporary corridor off the main building, a modest house surrounded by black bamboo. It was the kind of place where one might never hear the sounds of the everyday world, not even the songs of the birds. How, Chūnagon wondered, could anyone live in such a place?

The monk was astonished to see him enter the grounds. His disciples hastily cleaned a room and prepared the finest cushion for the visitor.

The monk was approximately sixty years old and apparently not of ignoble birth, for he carried his frail body with dignity, unlike some old men who seem utterly emaciated. He kept his living quarters clean, and the pavilion seemed an ideal place for worship. For a few moments the monk watched Chūnagon very closely, and then suddenly he gave a look of surprise, as if the Buddha had appeared before him. He wept as he told Chūnagon what had happened in

1. An allusion to a poem by Shōni Myōbu, *Shūishū*, #66:
Cherry blossoms hidden / In the mountain shade— / Do not let the wind know / You have not yet scattered.

the past few years. Chūnagon in turn related his experiences in China to the monk.

"The Imperial Consort of China, mother of the Third Prince, once told me she was wondering what had happened to a letter she entrusted with a certain monk. She insisted I meet the monk to see if her mother was still alive. She gave me a letter which, unfortunately, I was not able to deliver immediately. What with all the bothersome distractions since my return it was only recently that I finally heard you were living here. It is a pleasure to meet you at last."

"While in China I heard about the Consort and had occasion to meet with her," the monk replied. "Often she wept and told me of her mother; she insisted I take a letter back, which I did without fail. Her mother has been very upset, but how could she answer that letter? We did not receive word that you were going so we missed the opportunity to have you take a letter. That was a pity, but I am certain she will be delighted to see you now."

"Where is she?"

"She is living in the building to the east."

Chūnagon was surprised. "How can she live in such a remote area? Who or what led her to this fate? What an unusual bond it must have been."

"Perhaps you have already heard of her family background," answered the monk. "There was a certain Prince of Kōzuke,[2] wiser and more learned than most men. He was, however, charged with some offense against the Emperor and exiled to Tsukushi. He had a daughter whose mother had died earlier and, since he could not abandon her in the capital, he made the painful decision to take her with him into exile. While they were in Tsukushi the Prince died and the girl was left in the care of an unreliable nurse. Shortly thereafter she met a man who was in Tsukushi as an official from the Chinese Court. Somehow or other—perhaps the nursemaid let the envoy into the woman's room—this lady gave birth to the Consort. When the child was five her father was scheduled to return to China. Since he realized women were not allowed to cross the sea he did not know what to do with the girl. One night after praying

2. Kanzuke in the text is probably a corruption of Kōzuke, an ancient province corresponding roughly to present-day Gumma Prefecture.

fervently to the Dragon King of the Sea, he had a dream in which he was told: 'Your daughter is to be a consort in that land. Take her with you immediately.'

"After they had left, the mother's uncle, Hyōe no Kami, was appointed Assistant Governor of Tsukushi. He looked after her and took her back to the capital when he returned. There the Governor of Tsukushi, Sochi no Miya, secretly but quite persistently courted the lady. She, however, considered herself the unfortunate victim of a most unusual fate and would not consider marrying anyone, so she became a nun and went into hiding. Grieved though he was, Sochi no Miya could not visit her so he stopped his courting.

"The child conceived during that brief courtship, a girl, was born after she became a nun. Even though the mother thought this world wretched, she could not easily free herself from the bondage of the human affection she had for her daughter. Since no one else would care for the girl she decided to take the child with her, even though her retreat deep in the mountains offered little in the way of comfort. After the birth the mother shaved her head completely and has since prayed devoutly like a master of the Law. She looked to me for support, so when I built this prayer hall in the mountains she came with me, saying she too could no longer remain in society. Since I had formerly served her father, the Prince, she has come to rely on me for everything, especially from the time I gave her the Consort's message. I find her trust in me quite moving.

"Though we might say her fate was preordained, her experiences in this world seem without parallel. Thus it is truly wonderful that you had the opportunity to see the Consort blessed with Imperial favor in China. Her mother thinks that it must be retribution for something she did in a former life that has kept her from enjoying the support of a daughter in such high position. People who meet such a pitiful fate in this world will surely get their wish in the next. Woman that she is, she has been very serious and devout in her prayers; she is quite learned too."

Chūnagon found the monk's story most intriguing. With such unusual experiences it was only fitting she should renounce the world, he thought in pity.

"What with the difficulties I had in merely coming to see you, I was worried about making a separate trip to see her if she were living far away. I am delighted to hear she is nearby. Would you please give her this letter and tell her why I have come?"

He handed him the Consort's letter.

Letter box in hand, the monk walked through a bamboo grove to the nun's lodging. The previous night the nun had seen the Chinese Consort in her dream, and though she spent the day in earnest prayer and devotions her thoughts frequently turned to her daughter. When she received the letter box she felt choked with emotion; was this too but a dream? she wondered. Needless to say she was deeply moved as she read the note. She now realized how difficult it was to free herself from the cares of a world she thought she had abandoned completely.

"What fate is it that ties us together as mother and child, yet keeps us from each other, separated like the parting of the swallows?"[3] she wondered, resenting her karmic bonds from a previous life.

The monk spoke to her.

"There is apparently nothing ordinary in the intentions of a man who would come alone to mountains most people would not even consider visiting. I think it best for you to invite him in and listen to the details of his story."

She was not inclined to agree.

"This grass hut I have chosen for my final years on earth is shamefully wretched," she thought. "Were he to see me in such straits it would be a disgrace for the Consort's patrons, even though they live in another land."

The letter, however, specifically directed her to befriend him and speak with him. It even said she should think of him as the Consort herself. This would be reason enough to meet him. Her heart was so removed from the everyday world she decided there was no need to feel embarrassed, and the joy of receiving the letter might help her forget her shame. She had the south end of her room prepared and asked the monk to show him in.

"She has asked you to come in," he told Chūnagon.

"With a sense of anticipation and joy, Chūnagon approached the nun's quarters; this, he thought is where he might rekindle the distant, elusive memory of the Consort. Dusk had passed, and though

3. Alluding, perhaps, to a poem entitled *Yen Shih Shih Liu Sou* by Po Chü-i, which tells of the mother swallow's sorrow when its child leaves the nest.

it was difficult to see clearly in the shadow of the mountain, he could distinguish her lovely presence. Apprehensively he entered the room and sat down near her. In their hearts each saw the other as a link with the incomparable Consort, and for a while neither could find words to speak. At long last the nun calmed herself enough to talk.

"You can surmise my station in life without my telling you. Even though my life is far from ordinary, I am saddened and shamed when I consider what my daughter must be thinking as she awaits my response. One can renounce the world but because of a child still be unable to sever the ties to this world of darkness. I have been downcast ever since I received her message from the monk, even worse than when I had heard nothing at all. And now with your letter I feel completely lost here in the mountains where even the birds are not heard. I do not know what to do."

> Waiting for what
> I thought was not real
> I saw her letter.
> What is it? A dream? An illusion?

Chūnagon would not even dream the words were from one who had cast off the world to live as a recluse deep in the mountains. She still seemed young and beautiful. When he noticed how closely she resembled the one who had said "tied to the one from beyond the clouds,"[4] he could not hold back his tears.

> It cannot be called
> Either dream or reality—
> This place I have sought
> Is not of this world.

"I undertook the long journey to China in order to visit a Prince of that land. There were many heartrending experiences, but I remember best the time I was invited to Hoyang just before my return. The Consort and the Prince praised me for the unusual determination I had shown in leaving my loved ones in Japan to undertake a journey no ordinary person would even consider. She pleaded with me to bring this letter to you. If I were ever to think of her, she said, I should consider the anguish she felt over not knowing if you were

4. See translation p. 76.

137

dead or alive. Had your retreat been even more remote I was still determined to visit you. It is like a dream that I am able to come here myself and talk with you."

His moving description of the Consort's request was too beautiful for the nun to bear.

"Perhaps I should be embarrassed that you heard of our most unusual karma," she said, "but someone who lives like a hermit in a desolate mountain can harbor no hope or shame in this world. The letter said I might look to you for support, and with good reason, I feel. For the few remaining years of my life I hope to rely on you."

Chūnagon felt she might have more to tell.

"She must have been quite beautiful when she was young," he thought. "What an unusual life she has led." He was not at all disappointed in her appearance.

"Considering the remoteness of this location," he said, "journeys here cannot be made on a whim. Since I have come this far I think I will stay awhile with the monk. Think of me as your night guard. Call on me freely anytime."

The moon was coming out as he left the room. Looking around the grounds, he noticed a small building in the *shinden* style[5] set against the mountain. Part of it, the north wing perhaps, was barely visible beneath a pine grove. The surroundings were desolate and still. In spite of the remoteness of this mountain people seemed to be living here. The roar of a mountain waterfall nearby mingled with the cry of the wind in the pines to give the locale a terrible sense of loneliness. He wondered as he looked about how she could bear to live in such a disheartening place. The Consort was sheltered with great care in magnificent surroundings in Hoyang; what a pitiful contrast was her mother's fate. As he stared at the surroundings he wished he could be transformed at this very moment into that golden-winged bird,[6] and fly off to China to tell the Consort how her mother was living. He went to the monk's quarters, but it was uncomfortably crowded with disciples and low-ranking priests.

---

5. The popular architectural style of the Heian period. Single-story wooden buildings were covered with gracefully sloping roofs made of bark shingle or wattle. The main building faced south overlooking a garden and pond. Secondary buildings were connected to the main building by long covered corridors.

6. A mythical bird of enormous size from India.

"And this monk is the only person she had for support," he thought. He asked the monk if the girl was living there.

"Yes indeed," the monk replied. "Where else could she go? The child was born after the nun took vows. At first the nun was depressed and said the child should be hidden, and she would have nothing to do with it; but the baby grew into such a beautiful girl she could not forsake her. When her prayers are finished the nun shows such concern for the girl it makes everyone feel sad. I have heard the girl is particularly adept at playing the koto."

A retreat such as this may be fitting for someone who has renounced the world, Chūnagon thought, but it is a terrible place for a young lady to live. To hear of such things in tales of old is one thing; to see it for oneself is truly pitiful. Tears filled his eyes as he remembered that all this came from his ties with but one person.

He could not bring himself to leave this lonely household and return immediately to the capital. Even though there had been no particular mention of her wish in the letter, the Consort had said that should Chūnagon find her mother still alive he might tell her many things. The nun's life now seemed all the more noble to him. He told the monk he would like to stay a while longer and sent letters to that effect to the capital.

Chūnagon also sent messengers to his nearby estates. When the managers of his holdings in Yoshino heard he was in the area they brought provisions and gifts to the retreat. As the monk's quarters were soon filled to overflowing with resplendent gifts, Chūnagon had appropriate items sent to the nun's room, making it seem like the work of the monk.

The long spring days were difficult enough in the capital and even worse here where one rarely heard the song of the birds. The flowers and the ever-present mist made him feel quite lonely; this was indeed the proper place for someone who would renounce this world to think only of the next. He settled in almost as if he were going to stay forever. His recitation of the sutras and daily devotions were so awe-inspiring the monk thought he looked more splendid than even the Buddha might were He to appear before their very eyes.

All day long the monk wondered sadly what outstanding deeds in a former life had allowed this man to be born such a handsome person, and what terrible transgression had forced him to be born in this world of squalor.

As there was no need for reserve in such a place Chūnagon often visited the nun. At night the surroundings seemed appropriate to her station in life. Traces of a brushwood hedge were too dilapidated to even hold the dew. How could she live here? Not only did the grounds seem antiquated, but her own room was enclosed by thread-bare curtains in the pattern of decaying wood. Still, the fragrance from within the blinds mingling with the incense before the Buddha made him realize that the lady within was elegant, even if a nun.

In a gentle voice she asked about Wakagimi.

"The Consort mentioned in her letter that I should see the child you brought back to Japan, the one she could hardly bear to part with. Where is he now?"

Chūnagon was reluctant to tell her the whole truth.

"That beautiful child belonged to a very close friend of the Consort, but there was no one this friend could look to for support, so I took the child. The boy frequented the Imperial Court—did she mention that in the letter? I will bring him here when I can."

The evening sky was clouded in a heavy mist and no voices could be heard within or without, only the faint sound of the temple bell ringing vespers.

> The sound of the bell
> Heightens the loneliness of evening
> Deep in the mountains.

He seemed remarkably handsome as he gazed at the estate in the evening glow.

"You realize that only the ringing of the bell tells us here another day has passed," she wept.

> In the shade of the mountain
> We cannot tell dawn from dusk;
> Only the vesper bell reminds us.

As they wept together Chūnagon's messenger to the capital returned. He brought with him gifts the Consort sent for her mother as well as many of the necessities of daily life which Chūnagon himself had ordered. The monk was given flaxen garments; his disciples, lower-ranking priests, and even the novices living at the foot of the mountain were also presented with gifts.

To the stewards of his estates in that province he detailed new orders.

"From now on do not take my proceeds to the capital. Everything is to be brought here. Each night three or four of you are to direct the guards, seeing that the night watch is properly positioned. Be prepared to serve the people here in whatever they might ask."

He sent the same message to the managers of his holdings in the nearby provinces of Izumi and Kōchi. Some of his most trusted servants, all sensitive and considerate people, he had stay to serve the nun. His subordinates in the neighboring provinces were ordered to repair the living quarters, rebuild the roof and hedge, and beautify the stream and rock garden. While it was hardly like the "village of Fushimi"[7] he could conceive of spending the rest of his life here. Difficult as it was to leave, however, his inescapable commitments in the capital were many and he knew he must return.

"This location is so remote," he told the nun, "even with daily letters I could not dispel my never-ending concern for your safety. With a heart as devout as yours it really does not matter where you worship. Why don't you move to a slightly more accessible location?"

"Ever since I realized the futility of life," she wept, "I have longed for a place even more distant from the everyday world than this, for I have no desire to live in the usual dwellings of this world. With your support I could possibly follow you anywhere, but I never have lived as others do. Since I previously cut off contact with the world and no one really knows if I am dead or alive, it would be painful for me to return now. Though my station in life would not change, I would feel sorry for the Consort in China, for what would people think . . ."[8]

He knew she had a right to feel as she did.

"But since I am not a follower of fashion," he said, "no one would start rumors questioning for whom or for what reason I was doing this. Even if I do everything for you, you need not worry about the Consort's reputation. Rest assured all will go well."

7. Alluding to poem #981, anonymous, *Kokinshū*:
Perhaps I shall spend / the rest of my life here; / Even the desolate plains / Of the village of Fushimi in Sugawara / Are difficult to part from.
8. The Yoshino nun apparently fears people might start rumors about her daughter, the Consort, and Chūnagon, were his support to become well-known.

He offered many words of comfort, but when he was leaving he looked back tearfully and wondered if she would really be all right.

"I shall return later; you needn't fret about not seeing me again."

After instructing the monk to see that her days were comfortable, he left for the capital.

As long as a Buddhist monk lives in this world even he cannot completely disregard his earthly needs, and this retreat was almost too remote a mountain forest for the monk's disciples. They found it unsuitably lonely. But the timely support of Chūnagon seemed like the expedient intervention of the Buddha himself, and everyone wept for joy and prayed in thanksgiving.

The nun's father, a Prince, was the son of an aging concubine who had never met with much success at Court. The Prince too had very little support at Court; only his scholarship and skill with the flute and koto were outstanding. When he was charged with a crime against the Court and exiled to Tsukushi his situation became even more precarious and his whole world was shattered. His house in the capital went to ruin and he himself soon passed away in some unknown part of the provinces. His daughter, the nun, was left adrift in the charge of an unreliable nursemaid before being taken in by the Assistant Governor of Tsukushi. While he did take her back to the capital, he had so many responsibilities of his own he could only offer the basic necessities. She never knew any moments of splendor and soon lost even her uncle, the Assistant Governor. Alone in a sad world she became involved in an affair with Sochi no Miya, but her karmic bonds were too unusual: no longer did she wish to marry anyone. Thoroughly distraught, she renounced the world and went into hiding. Upon discovering that she was with child she felt so shocked and depressed she wanted to throw herself into a deep river and die. But the length of one's life is preordained and she lived to give birth to a beautiful girl.

"Throw this child into a deep river," she said bitterly. "I do not want to see or hear it."

Her attendants, however, cherished the baby and would not think of even letting a stranger take her. Each helped in raising the child, and by the time she was five she would toddle about exactly as the Consort had at the age she went to China.

The parting from the Consort had been so difficult. Just when the nun realized she would never see or hear her daughter again the girl tenderly hugged her around the neck and said, "Mama, come with me!" The boat was already late and their final farewell was hurried.

The nun's sorrow over that parting and her fear and anguish over the karma directing her life abated with time. She worried, however, that her second daughter, Yoshinohime, might some day hear of her half sister in China. Even though the nun had renounced the world again and again, she could not forget her first child, and her second bore a striking resemblance to the first. With the passing of the years, she sadly accepted the fact that in spite of the parental bond she would never see her first daughter or even hear news of her. Only Yoshinohime would be with her in the lonely years ahead. Even though she had gone to great lengths to disown the child, she now loved her; after her prayers, the nun would go to the girl's room, caress her gently, and see that she was well cared for.

As the child developed into a flawlessly beautiful girl she became a comforting diversion for her mother's constant sorrow. If the girl's beauty were only more commonplace her mother's regret that the child must live at the foot of a mountain among the birds and beasts might be less intense. But what was to become of this child, more beautiful this year than last, today more lovely than yesterday?

"I may dress in moss-covered rags and eat pine needles, but what of the girl?" the nun lamented. "She is buried away with me in a mountain so remote even the cries of the birds do not break the silence. She lives in a hut so shabby the dew seeps in . . . she has no furnishings; her clothes are faded and worn. And what of attendants? What decent lady would be willing to cut off contact with the world to come serve in such a desolate location? Anyone who could be of help would not stay long. The occasional servant who might come, women with no hope of finding a mistress in a normal household, would be of no use to her."

Yoshinohime's nursemaid had three not unsightly daughters, but each of them was well past her prime. The eldest had become a nun. The other two, already showing signs of age, did not want to abandon Yoshinohime and stayed with her out of pity. The younger of the two was occasionally visited by a low-ranking page from the province of Yamato, and he was the only man Yoshinohime ever saw. The nun was no longer bitter that she herself led this pitiful life so out of the ordinary, but how, she wondered, could she go on providing for her poor daughter?

"If this girl were not here, my prayers and devotion would not be inferior to those of the Dragon King's daughter who became a Buddha.[9] It is as if a demon were born in her to frustrate my hopes for the next life."

Forsaking her prayers for Paradise, she spent all her time imploring the Buddha to relieve her of the burden in this life. Bad karma, she felt, had kept her from finding someone to look after the girl. In desperation she even began to wonder what it might be like if the girl were to die first. This distressed her even more and she began to sleep late in the morning and nap at noon, dangerous omens indeed for one presumably devoted to the Buddha.

"What is to be done?" she prayed woefully. "No matter what I do it all seems for naught, and it is useless to hope for better in the next world. Please send a sign, at least, that someone might come and care for her. Then I can put my mind to rest and devote my prayers to a future life."

For three full years this alone was the focus of her prayers. At long last an august monk spoke to her in a dream.

"The Consort in China is so worried about your well-being she has been praying day and night that she might somehow hear from you. Her devotion is very impressive, but being in a foreign country she cannot hope to realize her wish. She became involved with a visitor from Japan, capturing his affection and using his singular devotion as a way of persuading him to look after your needs. Your wish to have someone care for Yoshinohime so that you might pray peacefully for a place in Paradise has been joined with your daughter's wish for your well-being: this man is to be Yoshinohime's support."

As she watched this magnificent man in her dream she prayed to him and said, "Surely the one who helps me will be a transformed Buddha."

Soon thereafter Chūnagon appeared in Miyoshino and she was given a detailed account of the Consort's well-being, news she had thought forever beyond her reach. After the letter arrived her whole

9. In Chapter 12 of the Lotus Sutra. Though the girl was only eight years old, she was wise and mastered the knowledge necessary to attain Buddhahood. Before a vast multitude she instantaneously turned into a man and sat upon a lotus blossom.

situation seemed to improve remarkably as the retreat became alive with activity. The grounds soon overflowed with people refurbishing the dilapidated buildings, adding new buildings, and constructing storehouses for the autumn harvest of rice brought in by the managers of Chūnagon's estates. Because of the expedient works of the Buddha she felt refreshingly assured beyond doubt of her salvation in the next world.

The four or five attendants with her had almost given up hope. "Where are we to get support in such a lonely, isolated retreat? It is unfortunate for our mistress, but how can we hope to stay here much longer?" With the startling arrival of Chūnagon their lament gave way to joy.

While Yoshinohime was still a child she came to pity the constant laments of the low-ranking people about her. But where was she to find the better side of life? How was she to get hold of even an illustrated romance for diversion from the weariness of that remote mountain? There was no one of like mind to share the seasonal change of colors or the cries of the birds. She would awake and sit alone, staring at the mountains, the brush with which she practiced calligraphy her only friend. She learned the *kin* from her mother and soon surpassed her teacher in skill, but with no one to listen she was forced to play alone while gazing mournfully at the lonely grounds. There was nothing to her life but waking and sleeping when Chūnagon arrived.

Everyone seemed overjoyed with his presence, but she felt ashamed.

"This mountain is not even visited by commoners; what must this magnificent man think of our wretched home? The houses in the capital could not be like this."

> Everyone thinks this
> A mountain in the world of sorrow,
> But what mountain is not?

She longed for a location even more remote. Whenever she played the *kin* in the dim light of evening the people about her were particularly impressed. "The past few years her playing had a chilling clarity to it," one said. "Now it seems to have a certain warmth." Their spirits were lifted by her music; Yoshinohime alone thought her life shameful and wearisome.

Shortly after the tenth day of the fourth month packages of apparel and furnishings, apparently meant for the semi-annual change of wardrobe,[10] arrived from Chūnagon. Enclosed were two four-foot curtains of state; a three-foot curtain; rolls of cloth in the withered leaf combination of yellow and green, three-foot and four-foot in length; crimson silk beaten to a lustrous shine; robes in wysteria color combination of light purple and green; layers of figured fabric of the same color; and underrobes of the pink and green *nadeshiko* color combination. The nun's provisions included a light gray robe with undergarments dyed dark orange and a shirt of silk decorated with gold and silver foil, all neatly folded into two packages. Her attendants were given robes of figured cloth and material dyed a bright red. Even split-bamboo blinds and straw mats were included. The clothing box contained many packages of incense, and a small Chinese-style incense chest with drawers filled with fine colored paper and high quality inks and brushes. In addition, there was a collection of illustrated romances which had been carefully chosen for Yoshinohime to alleviate the tedium of living in the mountains. A letter from Chūnagon was also included.

"I had hoped to visit you again soon, but duties in the capital have kept me busy. Forgive me for being blunt, but I am so worried about your well-being I have hardly had a moment's rest. I would be much happier if you were somewhere closer to the capital.

"Enclosed are some picture scrolls which are usually considered amusing diversions from the tedium of everyday life even in the capital. I imagine they will be particularly useful in your situation."

He had thought of everything. In fact, the nun had the uneasy feeling he was perhaps overattentive. Considering her dream and the letter from the Consort, however, she decided it must simply be the expedient workings of the Buddha. Everyone was understandably delighted when they gathered to read his letter.

The nun knew that whether a man is of high rank or low, once he has heard a young lady is living in some unexpected place his curiosity will be aroused. Chūnagon had obviously learned of the girl, yet he showed no sudden desire to see her. In fact, he went to all the trouble to send her picture scrolls to pass the time, and his

10. On the first day of the fourth month, which marked the beginning of summer. Summer clothes were used until the first day of the tenth month, the beginning of winter.

unusual concern for the girl impressed the nun. Rather than send return gifts with Chūnagon's messenger, which might seem too immodest or consciously fashionable, she thought it best to write a simple letter appropriately detailing her gratitude. This by itself was becoming.

"My daughter has found the picture scrolls a happy diversion from the dreariness of our daily routine."

When Chūnagon read this he wondered what the girl was like.

"She probably looks like the Consort, but since she lives in a secluded mountain with a mother who has forsaken the world completely, she wouldn't be too discriminating or graceful in her manners."

He felt no sudden desire to approach her more closely, but he could not stop worrying about her, for she was his closest connection with the Consort.

"Come what may, she is someone I should watch over, my only connection with the unfortunate person now far beyond my reach." He felt a deep personal responsibility for the girl. "I would like to show Wakagimi to her, but the long trip would be too difficult for a small child," he lamented.

Daini of Tsukushi, meanwhile, sent his wife and daughter to the capital before he himself arrived. In the capital his wife heard rumors that Chūnagon was living with Lord Taishō's daughter, a woman who had renounced the world, and would take notice of no other woman.

"I thought so," Daini's wife grumbled to herself. "He turned a deaf ear on our well-laid plans only because he had someone else in mind. But there was nothing spurious in the deep affection he showed for our daughter, was there? Why need we be reserved? We should visit him right away."

Chūnagon, however, was in Miyoshino and had not even left a letter for them. Quite put out by his apparent neglect, she decided to act immediately.

"He had shown such affection for my daughter, how could he leave without writing a single word when he knew full well we were coming to the capital? He's a good deal more callous than most people think."

Daini's wife was a stubborn, vain woman anxious to take matters into her own hands. She knew that when her husband arrived he might vacillate, so she decided to arrange a match herself.

Emon no Kami, son of a former Captain of the Inner Palace Guard, was Chūnagon's uncle.[11] His wife, daughter of Sochi no Miya,[12] was a distinguished lady, but well past her prime. Emon no Kami never cared much for her to begin with, and as she grew older there was really very little keeping them together. As his affection waned Emon no Kami began to wonder how he might find a new woman to whom he might devote himself fully.

He had chanced to see Daini's daughter one night when her family was away from home because of construction taboos,[13] and he was intrigued. She was precisely the sort of woman he was looking for. He feverishly pressed his intentions with letters of intimacy, letters that suggested to the girl's mother that Emon no Kami's wife was old and no longer loved.

"He is a handsome, well-bred man," she thought. "Even though he has a wife he would certainly not mistreat my daughter. Some of the high court nobles who might promise to devote themselves exclusively to her are really without any promise or character, but this man has both. Chūnagon would hear of the match too. Even if Emon no Kami has a wife he is still handsome and highly regarded in society; we should be thankful he has shown such interest in the girl. His suggestion that we arrange the marriage quietly is quite correct. It would perhaps be too much like treating his first wife as if she did not exist at all were the match made with great display."

She arranged immediately to have him come visit her daughter. Although the girl was told of her mother's decision, she could not believe the marriage would happen so quickly. Emon no Kami was thirty-five or six, in the prime of his manhood, but his attentiveness could not approach the gentleness she had found in Chūnagon, nor could his strained attempts to win her affection compare with the

11. His mother's brother.

12. Since Sochi no Miya was also Yoshinohime's father by the Yoshino nun, Emon no Kami's wife and Yoshinohime are half sisters.

13. On certain days it was advisable to avoid construction work so as not to disturb the god of the earth. When the work was unavoidable, one could be spared the ill effect of the taboo by executing a *katatagae*, leaving one's home and spending a day or two at some locale in a favorable direction.

casual, yet effective charm of Chūnagon. Each morning she awoke in grief and anger.

When Chūnagon heard of her marriage he was very upset.

"I had hoped to keep that lovely, gentle woman as someone I could visit secretly and be at ease with. It would not do for people to say I was captivated by her the moment she arrived in the capital. But now there is too much activity at her place for me to visit. After she had settled in a bit I wanted to meet her alone and tell her of my love. I had hoped, perhaps, to fix her quarters in some quiet mountain village."

He regretted immensely the tardy way he had pursued the affair. Curious about what she must now think he sent a poem.

> Time and time again
> I wish you would remember,
> We did not vow to change so quickly.

When she saw his beautiful handwriting she was reminded of the morning he left Tsukushi. Even when she was with her new husband she could not forget Chūnagon's anguish on parting, or the sincerity of his words. He really cared for me, she thought, her sorrow deepening. Her response included these tender words.

> I did not forget our vow,
> But what now can be done?
> If only I could turn the past
> Into the present. [14]

The handwriting was lovely and there was nothing pretentious or coy in her expression: the words came from her heart. Impressed by the note, Chūnagon began thinking of ways to visit her.

One day when Lord Taishō was suffering from a severe cold his family and attendants all gathered at his house to keep watch. Emon no Kami, who was also present, slipped away in the dim light of

---

14. The last line of the poem in the original, *shizu no odamaki*, actually means "a spool of (traditional style) cloth," the traditional woven cloth as opposed to the imported Chinese style. The line is an allusion to a poem in the *Ise Monogatari*:

As often as the spool of cloth / Spins time and time again, / I wish I could change the past / Into the present.

In the *Ise Monogatari* poem, the line *shizu no odamaki* is a preface word (*joshi*) for the line "time and time again," since a spool spins around many times. The mere mention of this line in *Hamamatsu Chūnagon Monogatari* would immediately bring to the Heian reader's mind the final lines of the Ise poem which I have used in my translation in order to convey the true meaning of the *Hamamatsu* poem.

early evening, apparently to inform certain ladies he would not be making any extended visits that evening. Shortly thereafter he returned to his guard position at Lord Taishō's mansion. Chūnagon decided it was a good opportunity to excuse himself.

"There are enough people here now," he said. "I will rest at home tonight and take the watch tomorrow evening."

He went directly to the quarters of Daini's daughter where he had his retainer knock at the gate. Since the moon was not yet out the guards at her gate could not see very well; they apparently thought Emon no Kami had returned, for they let the visitor in immediately. Chūnagon went to her door and tapped his fan lightly. Her sleepy-eyed attendants also mistook him for Emon no Kami and let him in. He felt sorry for deceiving the servants but walked silently over to her dais. Everyone was quietly sleeping and the oil lamps gave off only a faint flicker. Pushing aside the curtain surrounding her dais he could hardly restrain his laughter as he walked directly to where she lay sleeping. She awoke and was shocked to find the man was not her husband. Her fear soon gave way to anxious joy when she discovered it was the very man she longed for day and night.

"I waited anxiously for you to come to the capital," he said. "When I heard you had arrived I was waiting for the right moment when we could meet together quietly, but I was left with only the bitter regrets of the salt maker's smoke.[15] Why? Had you only hinted of what might happen I would never have allowed it. I would have taken you away secretly."

Even though the passion he felt for her could not compare with the love he experienced that one night in China, he was chagrined that she had arbitrarily allowed another man to take her away. Ignoring his own negligence in the affair he placed all the blame on her. A more experienced woman might have been able to return his accusations, but she was overcome with shame. She seemed so helplessly beautiful he could not wait for a second meeting to complete the vows of love.

15. Alluding to poem #708, anonymous, *Kokinshū*:
In the bay of Suma / The salt maker's smoke / Is blown by the wind / to unexpected quarters.
The last line expresses the poet's regret that his lover has now turned to another.

She knew it was wrong to spend the night with him, but, grieved that he should resent her so, she meekly submitted.

"As long as I must live in this world," he thought, "I wish I could keep her as a secret source of comfort for my troubles." His deepening sense of regret only intensified the flame of love. The girl seemed worried as the chirping of birds signaled the approach of dawn.

"The vow I once made to you," Chūnagon said, "was not one to make you think less of me than him."

He was, however, in a hurry to leave for he knew her husband might be returning soon; last night at Lord Taishō's mansion Emon no Kami seemed anxious and ill-at-ease, and it would be unfortunate to be seen thus by one's own uncle. He led the girl to the same door he had entered the night before. The lower branches of nearby trees were hidden in darkness even though the moon still shone brightly. The song of a *hototogisu* in a fragrant orange tree nearby seemed particularly beautiful as he spoke his poem.[16]

> Hototogisu—
> Stay hidden in the orange tree
> And do not stop your secret singing.

Any commonplace lover would do his best to capture the tenderness of an early morning parting. If even such a man could make his exit without disappointing his lady, how much more moving Chūnagon's departure must have been. She found his gentle charm incomparable.

> Even at other times
> The fragrance of the orange is powerful.
> How can the bird hope
> To persevere in hidden song?[17]

She seemed so compliant he found it difficult to leave.

"I would like to take you now to hide away with me. What would you think of that?" he asked.

She nodded her head faintly and moved a little closer, now even more beautiful than before.

"Emon no Kami is more mature than I, and perhaps more difficult to be close to," he explained gently, "but he is my uncle and has

16. *Hototogisu*, the name of a bird, is often translated as "cuckoo."
17. Daini's daughter is warning that Emon no Kami's watch, "the fragrance of the orange," is severe, and secret meetings would be difficult.

always been kind and helpful. I feel sorry for taking advantage of him even this one time. But then again, I did know you first, and I wanted to see you again so badly I did not think it wrong. If I were to take you away with me now rumors would spread and he would hear of it. That would be a pity. Were it not for him I would take you with me. It is still fairly dark out; seeing you like this I find it hard to leave."

He led her back into the room, however, and then left under the cover of darkness without another word.

"What an uncommonly beautiful woman," he thought. "When it comes to women of the middle ranks, those I need not exhaust my heart completely for, it is just such a pliant, gentle woman as this I find most attractive." That he would think so shows his intentions were not frivolous.

No one had yet awakened when he arrived home. In spite of her station Taishō no Kimi disliked performing her devotions rigorously when he was present. The task was much simpler when he was absent. He went immediately to the Main Hall where she had spent the night in prayer.

The delicate light that summer morning was no less moving than the haze of springtime or the mist of autumn, and the light green tips of branches spread effortlessly throughout the garden. Taishō no Kimi was seated in prayer next to a pillar at the edge of the building. Chūnagon seemed unusually handsome in robes slightly disheveled for having been slept in. As he lifted the blinds and sat down near the pillar separating the open veranda from the inner rooms, she suddenly became very flustered and tried to hide her rosary.

The light gray robes of her everyday clothing for some reason or other seemed to fit her particularly well. Though she wore no makeup, in the morning light her proud, handsome face had a lovely hint of color, as if she had just finished her toilette. He found it even more attractive than the moonlit face of the woman he had just visited. Overcome with emotion he soon lost his composure; the uneasiness he felt on leaving Daini's daughter gave way to weeping.

She seemed deep in thought as she sighed and greeted him with a poem.

> Whenever I see you
> My mind is put in disarray,

Even though I look
To the lotus flower for comfort.

She was so beautiful he could not let her go, even if an escort
from Paradise were to come right now to take her over the clouds.

You might have given
Even this vile world a chance,
Had not the dew settled
On the lotus leaf.

Taishō no Kimi would on occasion try to make light of the endless
weariness she felt for this world, but the true sorrow evident in her
poem today made Chūnagon quite sad. When two charming nuns
dressed in humble robes offered water to the Buddha, it was brought
home to him that her station in life and her devotions were different
from the layman's.

"My sins must be grievous indeed," he said, "for I feel so much
sadder than usual. I am quite troubled. Please meet me in your
quarters this morning."

When he arrived at her living quarters the attendants awoke and
busily prepared the room. He sent messengers urging her to come
immediately. She came quickly, for it would be too much like an
ordinary woman to coyly delay her arrival. Removing the small
curtain which usually separated them, he had her sit down beside
him. He had told her before of Daini's daughter; this morning he
described in detail the uneasy cry of the *hototogisu* during his restless
sleep.

"If you were able to await my visits like any other woman I wouldn't
have to make such unseemly excursions. It upsets me even to think
of it," he said resentfully. After a brief massage from one of the
servants he lay down beside Taishō no Kimi for a morning nap.

The attendants at Daini's mansion, mistaking Chūnagon for Emon
no Kami, told the mother that Emon no Kami was so frustrated at
spending the night on guard duty he had apparently returned to visit
her daughter. This, of course, delighted the mother.

"No matter how splendid a man might be, it matters little if he
does not really care for a woman," she smiled. "My husband thinks
this Chūnagon is so splendid, but in what respect is Emon no Kami
inferior to him?"

Her daughter was frightfully worried that someone might have ascertained the visitor was Chūnagon. When a letter arrived—everyone thought it was from Emon no Kami—she herself unexpectedly went out to get it. Worried that others might see the letter first, she hastily seized it and retreated to her room. The servants thought her behavior quite strange.

"I was frightened when you appeared in my dreams."

> The brief night
> Disturbed by the cry of a bird
> Now seems like a hundred nights of autumn.

Before finishing the letter she quickly took a brush and scribbled on the paper to disguise the handwriting. Just then her mother entered.

"This is the letter that just arrived, isn't it? What a foolish thing to do. Why did you make such a mess of it?"

Though disturbed by her daughter's strange behavior she smiled contentedly.

The girl suddenly blushed. As she hid her face the smooth flow of her hair decorated with combs was particularly beautiful. How could any sensible person ignore this girl, her mother wondered, still annoyed that Chūnagon had suppressed his obviously strong attraction for her. She urged her daughter to write a quick reply, but the girl seemed in no mood to comply. When the mother took the letter the girl suddenly lay down saying she was ill.

"This is a shame," her mother said. "Why don't you send a reply? You are as stubborn as your father. You let yourself become infatuated with an insincere man like Chūnagon and make a hideous mess of this fine note from Emon no Kami."

The girl was so disturbed by her mother's scolding she could not listen any longer. Seeing that any further words would be futile the mother returned to her quarters.

That evening the girl received a secret letter from Chūnagon.

> I cannot dispel my gloom.
> Must I simply sigh with the setting sun?
> Dare I wait hopefully?

Strained by her unsettling day she wept freely while writing her reply.

My tears flow
Like rafts on logging rivers,
For I know not what to ask of you.[18]

Chūnagon's sentiments were stirred by the note, perhaps because he truly cared for her. He showed the letter to Taishō no Kimi.

"She was so disheartened I could not help but feel attracted to her. Since she cannot escape her ties with Emon no Kami I fear what might happen if word of our relationship were to leak out. Still, it would be cruel of me to end it right now. Men who are accustomed to such affairs might know peace of mind, but I feel ill-at-ease in such unfamiliar matters."

Taishō no Kimi pitied him.

"You should have claimed her before Emon no Kami."

"And whose fault is that?" he said. "Even though you have really forsaken me, because of what others might think I feel I must not marry another woman."

All she could do was blush, for she was not one to make excuses. Her noble acquiescence made Chūnagon realize what a rare woman she was, and he could almost feel his heart beat in loving sympathy.

From then on opportunities for Chūnagon to see Daini's daughter were scarce. Each lover longed deeply for the other, but it was difficult to meet. All they could do was think of each other in the evening twilight or the early night, their memories evanescent as a bridge of dreams.

One day Emon no Kami paid a visit to Chūnagon.

"I have, as you know, entered into a certain relationship with Daini's daughter," the visitor confessed. "I know people wonder why I would ignore my wife of so many years to start this affair, but it is something which had to be. I cannot simply suppress my feelings and ignore the girl. Visiting her has become an embarrassment, however. Were she a forlorn girl in a house surrounded by sagebrush, people would understand, but she is well-off and I don't want to seem like a fortune hunter. If I continue this relationship I suppose it will all amount to the same thing anyway; in any case, I am thinking of bringing the girl to a wing of the Ōidono mansion."

Chūnagon listened without showing the pity he felt that the man

18. The first two lines of the original poem "rafts that flow on logging rivers" are a preface for the word *ika*, 'how' (or in my translation, 'what').

need solicit advice so plainly. He wanted to suggest that taking the girl so suddenly might appear too brazen, but he thought it unwise to advise against something Emon no Kami had obviously set his heart on. Chūnagon agreed to the plan.

After the tenth day of the sixth month Emon no Kami had the west wing of the Ōidono mansion made ready for the girl. Chūnagon, hoping to catch a glimpse of the festivities, lingered about the mansion. From the ostentatious train of five carts and numerous forerunners with which Emon no Kami brought the girl, it was clear he really cared for her.

"Her mother was right," thought Chūnagon as he left for home. "It is a fortunate match. No matter how much I care for her, I could never treat her so regally. All I could do is hide her in some distant village and visit occasionally. That would be quite a lonely life."

The home of Emon no Kami's first wife was along Chūnagon's route home. Feeling sorry for the lady, he peeked through the unguarded gate. The blinds were up and ladies sat on the veranda enjoying the cool evening. Their voices sounded bitter as they talked disparagingly of Emon no Kami's actions. A woman with a cranky old voice came out from the inner room.

"I heard they have arrived at the Ōidono mansion. Our master went to get her early this evening; then they rode in the same carriage. The procession had over twenty footmen and five full carriages with open blinds. He obviously spent a great deal of effort on the preparations. He even gave the guards from our house commemorative gifts. It is simply terrible, doing such things right before our very eyes."

Perhaps this weeping woman was an old nursemaid. All the ladies were complaining bitterly, and Emon no Kami's wife was apparently nearby.

"There, there, let's hear no more of this. Complaining won't help." Her gentle voice seemed quite elegant.

"But why shouldn't we complain? If one simply accepts these insults silently as you have what do you end up with? This fine mess. People should be able to say what must be said. The more you accept such affronts, the worse fate you will meet."

"If crying would help, I could cry like the *hototogisu*,"[19] she sighed.

19. Alluding to poem #107, *Kokinshū*, Naishi no Suke Anameiko no Ason:

Chūnagon judged her to be old, yet quietly sensitive to the sorrows of life. On the verge of tears he considered offering his condolences to the lady, but decided such an unexpected intrusion would be inappropriate at this moment of grief. Furthermore, Emon no Kami might hear of it and think such an unusual visit, coming on the day he made public his relationship with Daini's daughter, was meant as some sort of criticism. He left without visiting the old woman.

"Emon no Kami is really being selfish and inconsiderate," he decided. "It is easy to see how a man like him could be attracted to Daini's daughter, for she is young and attractive. She seemed so vulnerable even I grew fond of her and I am not one to follow the usual ways of this world. Still, it is sad the way he goes from one woman to another." Perhaps because his own heart was so pure he was quick to criticize the wrongdoings of others.

He told Taishō no Kimi all about the ceremony for Daini's daughter and the reaction of Emon no Kami's first wife.

"After seeing her resentment I have decided that as long as you are alive I will never lavish attention on another woman the way he did. I know you think it doesn't matter to you since you renounced the world, but I am thinking of your father's feelings and the heartbreak it would cause Nurse Shōshō. Even though in truth our relationship is not that of husband and wife, for appearance's sake I will never marry another woman."

Swearing before the gods and the Buddha he made this solemn promise, even though he did not know what the future held.

She still believed it was wrong to be living with him. Everyone else must think so too. She would not suffer if he took in another woman, but their living arrangement did indeed give people reason to think they were deeply involved. If he wanted to bring some young lady to his house it would be better for her to leave before that happened. The new woman would surely feel uncomfortable living in the same household. Chūnagon should not go on like this, she thought, preferring to escape to a quiet place before something happened. It was not for her to worry about what would happen if he found a new woman, that did not bother her, but she felt guilty about how it might affect her father, for he would certainly be concerned about her. She wondered how she could continue to cause

---

If crying would stop / The flowers from falling, / Would I weep any less / Than the *hototogisu*?

her own father such sorrow, but when she tried to hint at her feelings to Chūnagon, he became upset.

"What troublesome thoughts. Let us continue quietly as we have up to now and deal with the problems when they arise."

The fervor in his promise frightened her, but she lacked the will to oppose him further. After he left she pondered her predicament.

"I have no choice but to accept whatever might come. At least Himegimi will be taken care of, for my father and stepmother are too fond of her to leave her for a moment. Nor will Chūnagon forget the girl. People must think I am a fool. No matter how pure our hearts are, as long as we are this close to each other something improper is bound to occur. I hope to die before that happens."

It was sad to see how fervently she petitioned the Buddha to take her to Paradise.

When the altar in the Fishing Pavilion[20] was completed, all the statues in the mansion were moved there and decorated with offerings of lotus flowers. Chūnagon, unusually solicitous of Taishō no Kimi's needs, planned to have the eight readings of the Lotus Sutra performed there. The structure of the altar and the decorations on the statues seemed from a different world, beautiful beyond imagination. On mornings of special worship Chūnagon had the room opened completely so Lady Taishō and Prince Shikibukyō's wife could also participate. Each was given a specially furnished seat for the occasion. The pond before the prayer hall was crystal clear to the bottom, and lotus flowers of many colors bloomed on a surface reflecting the surrounding verdure. One could imagine that the Pond of Eight Merits in Paradise[21] was like this. The entire room reflected the high thoughts, charm, and elegance of Chūnagon, the owner. The devotion and unusual fervor manifest when he himself led the prayers was so magnificent, what need had Taishō no Kimi for the exalted position of Empress? His solicitude alone was enough for her.

Her father's past grudges too were all swept away in tears. "Chūnagon never cared much for me after I married his mother," he thought. "Even when he was with her he would rarely look at me.

20. A building occupying the southwest corner of the *shinden* complex overlooking the pond.
21. A pond in the Pure Land Paradise made of seven treasures and holding the water of the eight virtues.

Often I was upset by his strange behavior. After his return from China he seemed constrained in my presence, worried, I suppose, about my reaction to my daughter's situation. What a delight to see them together now. After she became a nun most men, even if they did occasionally pay a secret visit, would never ignore other women completely to see to her needs. What a rare, unusually splendid fellow."

His admiration and affection knew no limits and he loved him more than he would his own son.

Chūnagon's mother was saddened that Lord Taishō felt rejected by her son, and she was shamefully grieved that Chūnagon so clearly thought her remarriage inappropriate. Now that everyone's bitterness had passed her face reflected her joyous feeling of relief.

Senior courtiers and high court officials were often present for the eight lectures on the sutras.

During the cool, moonlit nights of the sixth month,[22] Chūnagon held impromptu concerts at his mansion. It was reassuring to see everyone relaxed and enjoying the music, but the events preceding the journey to China still haunted Chūnagon. It had been difficult to leave Taishō no Kimi when he had just come to know her intimately. Still, to suddenly cancel without cause a long journey for which he had already received official leave would have been strange indeed. He chose to go in spite of his misgivings. And even when he was wondering how she would accept his decision it suddenly became clear she was pregnant. What a pity it had been, he thought. How people must have grieved. He returned soon enough, however, and, while she had forsaken the world, he was happy to watch over her now and allay the misgivings of her people.

But what of the Hoyang Consort, now so far away that she seemed but a dream? Even though she might not be thinking of him she must long for their child, Wakagimi. When Chūnagon met the Third Prince he realized that the bonds between parent and child remain unbroken even though one of them might be reborn in a new world. The Consort had found it difficult to lose her son, and surely she realized there was no way ever to see him again. Her grief must be

22. The text actually has the "eighth month" but since events of the seventh month are described a few pages later, the text has probably been miscopied.

inconsolable, Chūnagon thought. He knew it would be impossible to see the Consort again in this world, but he hoped that by following the example of Śākyamuni, he might gain enough merit to meet her in the next.[23]

The only way he could ever be near her would be for one of them to be born again. That spring night's dream in Shan Yin was the last he would see of her in this world, he thought, almost faint with grief. Putting aside all thoughts of Paradise he prayed that they might see each other again, even if it meant being reborn in this world. He begged to meet her once again, just as he had seen his father, to learn what she really thought of him. It was distressing to find his prayers being devoted exclusively to his wish to see her. Had he ever imagined he would abandon himself to sinful ways and lament so? On the contrary, he had restrained his love for the attractive Taishō no Kimi precisely to avoid such sorrow. How people would laugh and make a fool of him were they to hear how futile was his resolve. His whole life would now be spent grieving over a dreamlike vow exchanged with an untouchable lady in an unfamiliar land. He lamented bitterly the vows he had made in Japan and China, for they now seemed to amount to nothing.

Since he could not go himself he sent letters every four or five days to the girl in Miyoshino. His meticulous concern for her left nothing to be desired; it was his way of trying to control the flame which burned in his heart for his love across the sea. But even if he devoted himself entirely to caring for the girl this was not the same as meeting the Consort and could not soothe the pain within.

The breeze was cool and the many colors of the garden were beautiful when Chūnagon visited the Imperial Palace on the evening of the seventh day of the seventh month. Prince Shikibukyō was also in attendance. When the Emperor was told of Gen Chūnagon's arrival,[24] he sent for him at once. Chūnagon's figure approaching in the faint light of dusk was a sight worth seeing; the Emperor thought him unusually handsome, though hardly for the first time.

23. The text has "the example of the one on the rock," based on the popular belief that Śākyamuni attained enlightenment while sitting atop a rock beneath a *bodhi* tree.

24. Chūnagon's father was a Prince, but Chūnagon himself was given a surname, Minamoto (Gen by the Sino-Japanese reading), and made a commoner like the hero of *The Tale of Genji*.

With few people present the Emperor decided it was a good time to ask about the trip to China.

"Did you find anything in the everyday life particularly superior to life here?"

"Everything I saw at first seemed unimaginably intriguing, but soon I realized there were similar things in Japan. There really wasn't anything different."

What could he say was different? he wondered. Whenever he considered telling of the Hoyang Consort's *kin*-playing at the full moon banquet at the Wei Yang Palace he sensed tears in his eyes and remained silent. Such inquiries call for a gossipy tale, but for love of the Consort he could not tell; he regretted that the truth of that shining example of beauty need remain hidden in his heart. With a great deal of deliberation he said, "I expected to find men of China quite intelligent and perceptive, but I was surprised to meet some extremely intelligent women."

"That's interesting. I'd like to hear more."

"Among the Prime Minister's daughters, the First Consort, mother of the Crown Prince, was very talented. She gave wise advice in affairs of state and was well thought of at Court. Her sisters were no less talented, and the youngest, Wu Chün, was particularly accomplished. She knew characters and *kana* better than most;[25] her Chinese poetry was lucid, the meter and composition far superior to that of the ordinary scholar."

When he recited parts of the letter she had sent him, all, including the Emperor, were so amazed they could not restrain their tears.

"Then there was a consort, daughter of the Third Minister, who lived in a place called the Hoyang District. She was famous for her beauty and, like Yang Kuei-fei, dominated the Emperor's affection until the jealous bickering of the First Consort and others finally drove her from Court. The people in her service at Hoyang spoke and acted no differently from the people of our own land. One rainy evening in the tenth month, when I was particularly homesick, I went to visit her mansion. Within the raised blinds I saw a lady viewing chrysanthemums while she played the *kin*. The music, her

25. Characters are used to write Chinese, but *kana* is a system of syllabic writing found only in Japanese. Wu Chün wrote some Japanese poems in *kana* in Chapter One.

appearance, and the whole atmosphere were unimaginably beautiful."

"Was that lady the Consort?"

"I don't think so, but I couldn't be certain. I do remember thinking that this is what we mean by the phrase 'dazzling light.' Seven or eight ladies-in-waiting dressed in elegant robes sat among the chrysanthemums singing "The Moon of P'eng Lai Tung"[26] with young attractive voices. It was one of the most elegant sights I saw during my visit.

"Once on a fine misty evening in the third month I saw a most beautiful lady among the people enjoying the moon and flowers in a place called Shan Yin.

"And shortly before I returned to Japan a banquet was held on the night of the full moon at the Wei Yang Palace in honor of my departure. Scholars and masters of the many arts attended; the poetry and music were outstanding. When a perfectly full moon appeared in the sky, the Emperor had one of his ladies come forward to play the *kin*. Both she and her music were more beautiful than anything I have ever seen in our land or theirs."

In his heart he was thinking of only one person.

"That's fascinating," the Emperor said. "Women in China are apparently quite exalted. Long ago there were many famous ladies—Yang Kuei-fei, Wang Chao-chün, Li Fu-jen.[27] The woman confined to the Shang Yang Palace was said to have eyes like lotus blossoms and breasts like jade. I wonder if there were any men of such renown."

"Long ago there lived in Hoyang District a famous man named P'an Yüeh.[28] The woman who lived next door spent three years watching and waiting for him, but he never deigned to visit her. While in China I saw many lovely women in the capital, but none

26. From the second line of the couplet mentioned in Chapter One, p. 61.
After the storm in the orchid garden destroys the purple flowers, / The Moon of P'eng Lai Tung illuminates the frost.
The couplet is by Sugawara Fumitoki, #271, *Wakan Rōeishū*.
27. Wang Chao-chün was a concubine of the Han Emperor Yüan-ti, and Li Fu-jen (the Concubine Li) a consort of the Han Emperor Wu-ti.
28. See note 9, Chapter One. The legend of the woman waiting three years for her neighbor to notice her is associated with a man known as Sung Yü, not P'an Yüeh. Since both were handsome and accomplished men of letters, the author might easily have confused the two.

could compare with the ladies-in-waiting I mentioned. Yang Kuei-fei and Wang Chao-chün were reputedly superb, but women said to resemble them could not compare with the ladies of Hoyang. They were elegant and proud and had about them an unusual charm and amiability which seemed to radiate from their presence."

The Emperor could see from the change in Chūnagon's expression that he had been captivated by these ladies. They must be extraordinary women, he thought, his curiosity and imagination aroused.

"They sound like unusually rare beauties. So this is what you saw on your visit."

"I wouldn't have come back if it meant leaving such women," said Prince Shikibukyō.

The Prince felt that Taishō no Kimi, to whom Chūnagon still held fast, was the loveliest woman in all Japan, and this fondness still caused him great pain and regret, even if he did not let it show. Now, however, he wished he were a bird to fly off to China immediately.

Chūnagon felt that if the Prince truly were to see the Consort his life would be changed. Only Chūnagon's peculiar resolve and forebearance allowed him to live through the incident.

On the verge of tears his sad thoughts then turned to Wu Chün, daughter of the Prime Minister, and he began to tell the Emperor of her. She was not so beautiful as to gain a widespread reputation, but she was far more charming than any ordinary lady. Her calligraphy, composition, and traditional scholarship were outstanding. He told of the letters she sent before he left and of her *biwa* music and Japanese poetry. The Emperor was impressed.

"Do show me that letter sometime. It is a shame I haven't heard these unusual things until now," he said, slightly resentful.

Though the Emperor had but one son, Prince Shikibukyō, he had many daughters. He was particularly troubled over the future of the Princess born to the Lady of the Shōkyō Room, who, unfortunately, had no reliable support at Court. Chūnagon, still unmarried, would be the perfect husband for this Princess. Taishō no Kimi, being a nun, would not make a fuss, he reasoned. He found Chūnagon's intimate, moving story of his stay in China so splendid he decided in the course of this serious conversation to broach the subject.

"My reign will soon be over," he said to Chūnagon, "and I am worried about the future of my many daughters. In spite of some misgivings I occasionally feel, I imagine that those who now have sufficient backing will continue on without much difficulty; but Princess Shōkyōden, I fear, has no one but me for support. I pity her and thought of asking you to care for her."

What could Chūnagon do? He merely sat in solemn deference before the Emperor's request.

Returning from the Palace he went directly to Taishō no Kimi's room to rest, but, troubled by the Emperor's request, he could not sleep.

"He assumes my interests are like those of any other man," thought Chūnagon, "but long ago I vowed not to become involved in amorous affairs. Ever since that unimaginable moment with the Consort I haven't been myself; my emotions are in such disarray I don't see how I could be a suitable match for such an august person. Even before that incident I became recklessly involved with Taishō no Kimi, only to suddenly desert her for that far-off land. How sad and humiliated she must have felt. And it wasn't just a private grief either, for when her shocking condition became apparent her younger sisters were quickly married off to Princes before her. The grief she felt on seeing and hearing what others were saying when her own situation changed so drastically must have been inconsolable. What terrible sorrow must have possessed her to cut off that beautiful hair.

"Considering her father's bitterness toward me for having caused his lovely daughter to forsake this world, I cannot be absolved of my sins. Had I merely accepted her renunciation of this world as the end of our relationship the matter might have ended, but even now I look to her for comfort. This has pleased her father and she too has come to accept her fate and feel comfortable in my presence.

"If I were now to accept the extraordinary proposal of the Emperor, even if deep in my heart my feelings for Taishō no Kimi did not change, surely she would regret not having left earlier for some quiet, secluded place. I can imagine how sad she would be to learn her fears were justified. I weep just to think how her family would feel merely to hear of my plans. All I really want in this world is to be left alone to spend my time in devotion to the Buddha, a wandering monk in the mountains. I would have difficulty always being deferential and complaisant as the Princess's husband; it's not in my nature. But what can I say? The Emperor made a personal request."

He felt beset with a myriad of problems. Weeping he told Taishō no Kimi of the Emperor's request and his own thoughts on the matter.

She had always felt she should not be living with him, and though rumors and gossip were unpleasant, she felt helpless to resist. She had worried people might think her headstrong were she to refuse Chūnagon's kind assistance and run away, so she had continued as before. She could accept her position as simply fate no matter what might happen, but it bothered her that others would worry, unable to understand the situation.

"This is worse than if I had moved away in the beginning," she thought. But what could she say?

"Why should you hesitate?" she told him. "Even if I were like everyone else, there would be no reason to feel reserved on my account. And now that I am a nun it makes even less sense."

Though her response was gentle and dispassionate Chūnagon could imagine the sorrow in her heart, and suddenly he felt the need to pour forth all the resentment he had felt since finding her a nun. He told all that happened in China save the incident with the Hoyang Consort.

Concerning the young child in the care of Nurse Chūjō, he said, "When I heard that a child had been born to a lady I saw but once as in a dream, I went to see the baby. He was so charming I took the child and brought him back with me. I was going to entrust him to you right away, but I hid him since I thought it best not to let people know he was from a foreign land."

He had Wakagimi brought to her secretly. She found him simply delightful, especially since she rarely saw their own child, Himegimi; her stepmother had taken the girl and seldom let her out of sight. Chūnagon wished he could let Wakagimi stay with her, but unwilling to reveal the child to so many people right away, he only brought him over occasionally.

Because he was unable to forget his experience in China Chūnagon continued to worry about the people in the mountains of Yoshino. Commitments in the capital kept him busy, and he was unable to make the distant journey as he had hoped. When his concern became too great he left for Yoshino around the tenth day of the eighth month. During the entire trip he wondered for whom he was making this journey into unknown mountain roads. If only there were some way the Consort could know what he was doing. When he entered the lonely inner recesses of the mountains autumn was in the wind.

The change of season was apparent everywhere; the colors of all the flowering plants seemed lovelier here than in the capital, the transient beauty of autumn more pronounced. As he approached the temple the sound of a *kin* carried by the wind in the pines seemed to echo through the sky. Though the music sent a lonely chill through his heart he was suddenly reminded of the night of the chrysanthemums in Hoyang. Unable to restrain his tears he paused in the shade of a tree to listen secretly to the music. The playing stopped and all became silent. He wished for more.

The grounds were now well cared for, but still seemed like the lonely dwelling of an ordinary person. For years the nun had lived in a forlorn home unaccustomed to the visits of even lowly folks; now she awaited eagerly this magnificent gentleman, for he alone could bring back the memory of her daughter in China. He arrived just as the mist was settling on the garden that lonely autumn evening. Her heart seemed somewhat confused as she watched the handsome man approach her quarters.

> Though rarely visited
> By even the cries of the birds
> I now wait for you;
> When did people's sojourns
> Come to interest me so?

"I suddenly feel so strange . . . ," she said. Pitying her he replied,

> How many times
> Has my heart made the trip
> Along the steep paths of Miyoshino?

He entered a long narrow corridor which was a recent addition to her building to sit and rest after his journey. Officials from his Yoshino estates brought supper. This time the course of the river and the placement of the rocks, well-groomed by his men, seemed even more picturesque and charming than before. The moon was clear and bright: it was the night of the full moon! Last year at this time he was enjoying the festivities of the moonlit banquet at the Wei Yang Palace. Now in Yoshino he felt as if he could see the Consort playing the *kin* and hear her music. More than ever his tears flowed without end as he chanted again and again the verse "Beyond Two Thousand Li."²⁹ His voice penetrated the wilds with such beauty it seemed to rouse the birds in the mountain.

Perhaps because the lonely setting moved him so, that evening more than ever he exhausted himself with tears. He returned to the nun's room where they talked freely of things past and present; on this occasion each felt fully at ease in the other's presence as they touched on all subjects without reservation.

"I have no hope of remaining long in this world," wept the nun. "I sought this remote location only to pray for my life in the next world. I am ashamed that you should see this wretched life I live, but it is fate, just as your unexpected visit too was fated. What need have I of reserve? I will tell you everything. Perhaps you have already heard my story from the monk.

"I wanted so much to abandon this vile world, but it has been impossible. I am bound to this life by my strong tie to Yoshinohime. My father's prospects in this world were never too promising, but he stayed with me, supporting me while he could. Soon he died and I was left alone, without help.

"My daughter accompanied me to this desolate mountain where my robes are moss-covered, my food nothing but pine needles. Here we live buried deep in the snows of winter. The girl's fate is not felicitous; our life in these mountains may seem no different from that of wild birds, but she has been cared for. I will not be in this world much longer, I fear. Her life, however, will go on and I am terribly worried about what will happen to her after I am gone. I prayed that I might be able to devote myself exclusively to finding the guiding light of Buddha and not be forced to divert my attention to things of this world for the brief time I have remaining. When you came to visit our wretched hut I knew it was a sign from Buddha

29. Possibly from couplet #242, *Wakan Rōeishū*, Po Chü-i:
The color of the full moon that just came out! / What thinks my friend now far beyond two thousand li?

in answer to my earnest petitions. My mind is refreshed and at ease; now I can give myself exclusively to prayer."

"You seem to think that my sudden appearance was something my own shallow heart conceived," Chūnagon answered. "It was not so. Were I to tell you all the details, however, it would be too tedious. It was the deep feelings we both have for a certain person which led me to search for you. You must not for a moment make light of our connection. When I first saw you in this harsh, lonely setting, I thought that you as a nun must be most devout to live in such a place, but I wondered how a young girl could possibly survive here. I hoped from the beginning she might come to a place not so distant. I wanted to gain your trust so that I might care for the girl as long as I live. From now on do not for a moment worry about your daughter's safety."

"I can understand the sincerity of your intentions, but unfortunately it is difficult to forget my worries. This girl is but a remnant of my wretched fate and I dare not hope she might live in normal surroundings. She should stay here; as long as you know she is still alive I only hope you might make inquiry—if only by the wings of a bird or the howl of the wind—to see she hasn't been crushed by the wind in the pines or buried beneath the deep snows. I dare not expect her to live in the world as an ordinary person."

Indeed, the child would seem the sort of person found living in extraordinary places.

"Please do not think me a licentious man of the world. Ever since my loving father died I wanted to quit my present life. I hesitated to take vows because my mother had no one else to turn to. Though I now appear to live like anyone else, in fact, in my heart I want to be in a place even more remote than this mountain. I wandered as far as China, but now I would like nothing better than to hide in this mountain and disappear from the world. No matter what, I would never leave the girl."

Their heartfelt talk might have continued on without interruption, but dawn was approaching. Before going to the temple for predawn prayers the nun met with Yoshinohime.

"It is inappropriate for people living in a place like this to be unreasonably coy and reserved with strangers: it only depends on who the visitor is. This Chūnagon is truly not the sort of person we need worry about. If he should talk to you, please answer directly."

With the approach of dawn the moon shone ever more clearly and the sound of the waterfall and the echo of the wind seemed to play together. Chūnagon sensed the girl was nearby. What must she feel as she looks at this scenery night and day, he wondered.

> What do the people
> Who live here think?
> How moving the moon
> At the edge of the mountain.

She had no servants capable of giving a response. Too shy to answer directly, she took up the *kin* and played as she gave her reply.

> Each time I see the moon
> Between the trees deep in the mountains
> My loneliness increases.

Both the poem and music were well done. She quietly pushed the edge of her kimono out from under the curtain when she finished. Other than the two occasions when he heard the Hoyang Consort play, he rarely had the opportunity to listen to the music of the *kin*. Its faint sound seemed unusually beautiful at the foot of a remote mountain under the clear moon. He felt as though he could faintly hear the voice of the Consort, and the very memory of her drained him emotionally. His heart was heavy with grief and longing.

The girl had accompanied her poem with the music of the *kin* because she apparently disliked speaking in a plain voice. Chūnagon was impressed: she was no simple country girl.

"Is that all? Let me hear it once again," he asked impatiently, but all was silent. After pleading in vain, he took the *kin* himself; the well-tuned instrument was perfumed with the fine scent of its owner. It was still in tune when he began to play. As he recalled the times he had heard the Consort playing, the moonlight seemed to cloud over with tears.

> Ah! To listen to a voice
> Like the wind in the pines
> Over the Chinese hills of Kirifu. [30]

Just then the sound of the Nembutsu in the main hall ended and the nun appeared.

30. Kirifu in the text is probably a place name, but the corresponding characters are unidentifiable.

Chapter Four

 IF CHŪNAGON were so inclined, he might pursue in the customary fashion the source of the music carried by the wind in the pines. He could envision finding satisfaction for the yearning in his heart, but even in these mountains his spirits might still wander and his soul remain uneasy. The Emperor was, of course, unaware of the troubles plaguing Chūnagon; although the marriage had been mentioned but briefly by the Emperor, it was to take place during the current reign, and Chūnagon would probably be called to the palace before the year was out.

The Emperor blithely assumed the ceremony would be a grandiose affair certain to impress everyone. Receiving a princess as a wife would be a great honor for Chūnagon; his father's wish would be fulfilled, and he himself would surely find satisfaction.

It was apparent to all, however, that Lord Taishō was crushed to hear of the proposal. He regretted having scolded his daughter when she expressed her wish to leave Chūnagon's house and move to some quiet spot. He now realized she could not continue living with Chūnagon as she had when no other woman demanded Chūnagon's attention, even if Chūnagon's deepest feelings remained unchanged.

Taishō no Kimi's feelings were not changed by the news of Chūnagon's engagement, for she already felt she did not belong with him. Still, she was distressed to see the people about her worry so, and she herself at times seemed pained by the constrained, miserable station of her life. She spent more time than usual alone in her prayer hall.

Chūnagon pitied her. "Well, if I took the normal view of life, I might be concerned about meeting the expectations of society. For now I will simply let things be and try not to cause myself and Taishō no Kimi further grief. When I heard Emon no Kami's first wife trying to hush up the complaints of her ladies while she herself was grieving I thought it a great pity. Would Taishō no Kimi do likewise?"

What should have been a noteworthy honor—marrying a princess—now seemed quite disagreeable.

The woman in the Palace with whom Chūnagon had once exchanged poems about the moon, Shōshō no Naishi, served the Emperor as well as the Empress. One day while Chūnagon and she were talking he told her something unusual.

"When I was in China wise men told me many times that my twenty-fourth, twenty-fifth, and twenty-sixth years would be very dangerous. I myself had suspected I was not meant to live long in this world, and since my life had always seemed uncertain, the diviners, I felt, had read my fate well. I am resigned to constant prayer and devotion from the age of twenty-three to twenty-five. When that time has passed I can feel some assurance that I am meant to live on in this world, and only then can I decide on my future. Many people hinted they had plans for me, but I ignored them. The Emperor's proposal, of which I am not worthy, I heard with trepidation, for I am reluctant to marry the Princess until my years of danger have passed. I do wish, however, the Emperor would make me an official so I might serve day and night at Court until I know whether or not I am meant to survive."

"So he has no heart for anything but the wretched fisherwoman's hut,"[1] Shōshō no Naishi guessed. "She must be an extraordinary woman. Even though she renounced the world she is apparently impressive enough for him to ignore all other women and even disdain an Imperial request."

Bewildered, she said to him,

What is wrong?
Waves pound the seashore island,
Yet do not touch
The beach near the rapids?[2]

He laughed a moment then explained his sad predicament. "It's quite a shock," she grumbled on leaving.

The beach is long,
But can you wait

1. "The fisherwoman's hut," *ama no tomaya*, refers to Taishō no Kimi, based on the double meaning for the word *ama*, "nun" or "fisherwoman."
2. The "seashore island" is where the fisherwoman (nun) lives and refers, of course, to Taishō no Kimi. The "beach near the rapids" refers to a person of exalted rank since the first two syllables of *takase* (rapids), *taka*, mean high.

While dangerous waves
Come pounding in?[3]

Shōshō no Naishi recalled how moved Chūnagon was when he told the Emperor of the many splendid women he had seen in China. She told the Emperor of her meeting with Chūnagon.

"Since meeting the ladies of China, the women of our land apparently no longer interest him, except for the attractive nun, Lord Taishō's daughter. He told me that after seeing such beautiful ladies in China, Taishō no Kimi is the only one who can keep alive the memory of that visit. He then mentioned a diviner's warning and how he must not marry until the time of danger has passed. During this period of waiting he wants to help support the Princess by serving loyally at Court."

The Emperor thought this very strange, for he had heard Chūnagon was delighted with the marriage proposal and had no second thoughts. Publicly, however, the Emperor accepted this explanation.

"Indeed, people do say he is apparently not meant to live long in this world. It might be so."

Privately he had his doubts. "Even though Chūnagon is still young and low in rank, I had hoped, because of his outstanding character, to advance him while I was still Emperor. But if he feels so reluctant I will not press him."

The Emperor went ahead with preparations for the Princess's coming-of-age ceremony,[4] but no more mention was made of the engagement.

Chūnagon guessed that Shōshō no Naishi had talked to the Emperor, so he told Taishō no Kimi what had happened. Even though people were obviously criticizing his seemingly foolish behavior, he ignored them completely, for it would be inappropriate to act now as if gossip bothered him. Instead he devoted himself exclusively to prayer. Taishō no Kimi's father was moved to tears by the singular magnificence he saw in this man's heart.

When the nun in Yoshino began to appear frequently in his

3. The meaning of this poem is difficult to unravel, but I believe Shōshō no Naishi is saying that Chūnagon may be patient, but he will have difficulty resisting the pressure from the Court to marry the Princess.

4. This ceremony usually took place when a girl was between the ages of twelve and fourteen. An open, pleated skirt (*mo*) was tied in front and the girl's hair was bound up in the Chinese style. The ceremony often took place just before the girl was to be married.

dreams, Chūnagon worried about her even more than usual. Early in the tenth month he suddenly decided to leave the capital to visit her. When he arrived in Yoshino he discovered she had been seriously ill since the middle of the ninth month, and he was surprised to discover how weak her voice had become.

"Your people may be watching over you carefully, but why didn't you tell me you were sick?" he said resentfully.

"It didn't seem so bad, just a cold, and I thought I would soon recover. The pain has gotten worse, however, and this may be the end. I was hoping I might see you again."

Her weeping voice was feeble.

"If you were worried so why didn't you tell me it was not an ordinary ailment? Had I not come now, you might have died before I even knew you were ill."

He sent for a highly respected monk from the Yamashina Temple[5] and had him preach to her. Offerings were made and disciples of the Yoshino monk were instructed to read the penitential Amida Sutra day and night. Chūnagon positioned monks with inspiring voices near her pillow to read the sutras incessantly. He gave her all the help she could possibly want. Like a child he remained constantly at her side, offering his tender support and solicitous care for her needs in this world and the next. The expedient ways of the Buddha are like a miraculous dream, she thought lovingly, for Chūnagon was a true reminder of the Consort in China. During pauses in the Nembutsu prayers she called him to her side.

"My mind is at peace now that I know you will care for Yoshinohime. I am overjoyed that I can fulfill my true wish to devote myself exclusively to the Nembutsu."

The joy in her faint voice touched him.

"I wish she would remain in our world a little longer," he thought earnestly. "She has taken the place of her daughter, the Consort, who is now beyond reach; if I could do everything possible for her my soul might find some peace. Were she to die now, my hope for peace of mind would be in vain. If only I could keep her alive!"

5. Yamashinadera is the original name of the Fujiwara clan temple. The temple originally was in the province of Yamashiro (present-day Kyoto), but it was eventually moved to Nara and renamed Kōfukuji. Even after the move it was often referred to by its original name.

Early in the morning of the fifteenth the nun told Yoshinohime not to visit her at bedside. There was a reason for this request, she said, sending her to a different room. The nun then sat before the statue of Amida and prayed intently, her frail body supported by an armrest.

This delighted her attendants who said to each other, "She must feel better today. She's using the armrest."

When the evening sun began to cast its shadow she called for the monk.

"The music of Paradise seems close at hand. Have the Nembutsu performed ceaselessly."

After directing the many monks to begin the prayer, she herself intoned the Nembutsu. The moment she seemed to breathe her last, still leaning on the armrest, an indescribably beautiful fragrance permeated the room and a purple cloud trailed off to the nearby mountains, startling everyone. The people who had delighted in her good spirits earlier now wept uncontrollably, oblivious to the joyous realization that she had now ascended to the Pure Land.

Chūnagon went to the garden for a moment and leaned against the railing.

"I had heard people talk of the trailing cloud and the rich fragrance of Amida's welcome to the dying, but to see it with my own eyes! What a rare, miraculous, moving event," he marveled, grieving, yet envious of the nun's final parting.

Inside, Yoshinohime had collapsed and her frenzied attendants did not know what to do. An old lady cried out desperately to Chūnagon.

"What are we to do?"

"Perhaps anguish over her mother's death caused her to faint. There is no reason to become overly excited; the years of the girl's life have been predetermined."

He tried to calm them. He remained outside the house but directed monks to the girl's side to perform exorcism.

"All this must have been determined in a previous life," he thought. "I searched out the girl for reasons I myself never fully comprehended and did all I could to see that she and her mother were well cared for. I worried about them constantly, yet for a while could not come visit. Then, for some reason or other, I anxiously made the trip here, just as the nun was dying. Witnessing her death is a momentous experience, even if some people would think it outrageous and foolish of me to defile myself so recklessly in these remote mountains.

"There are many people in this world, and many have made the trip to China, but no one had the inspiration I had. I was drawn by something unique, the karma that created a bond between me and the Hoyang Consort. Breaking all precedent I made the trip; the karma of our meeting stretched quite far but it was strong. I see that in the child born of this vow. The Consort, now reveling in glory amid the flowers and maples, may not know her mother has died, but if she does not follow the rules of abstinence her sin is still serious. I will take it upon myself to perform the filial services on her behalf, for I have never cared for anyone as I do for her and I probably never will.

"I could become thoroughly captivated with a lady here in Japan and still cope with my feelings. If, however, that love were at all like my love for the Consort, I could lose my rank, be charged as a public criminal, and still not grieve over the loss. Why then should I care if people think my behavior foolish and eccentric? Since I feel so strongly it is a shame to wait outside the girl's room."

Unmindful of the stares of others he headed for Yoshinohime's room. He sat right down beside her curtain, for there was no need to feel reserve here.

"How are you feeling?" he asked. "Are enough people attending you?"

She remained in a daze and there were no dependable ladies in attendance. He moved closer, but she seemed unaffected and could not respond properly.

"This is strange," he said. "Can't anyone answer my questions?"

He lifted the curtain and looked inside. She was wearing a soft dark red robe over white silk cloth. Alongside the prostrate form— only her clothes were visible—her luxuriant hair lay tumbled in a pile. He moved within the curtains and felt her pulse; her hands were cold and she showed no sign of breathing. Chūnagon was shocked. He regretted having to move so close, but there was absolutely no one else to deal with the situation. Fearing she might be dead, he immediately sent for monks and instructed them to perform incantations, read sutras, and make petitions. In the dark room he could not see clearly, but he sensed that she was delicate and lovely, and his attraction for the girl grew stronger.

"Why are you standing so far away?" he asked the servants. "It's dark in here. Bring the light closer."

He then took the lamp himself. Even if the servants were confused and reluctant to expose the girl directly to a handsome man like Chūnagon, any sensible person should have known how to assist her. These women were of no help whatsoever. The lady they had served for so many years in the distant retreat was dead, her daughter lay unconscious and unbreathing, but the servants were all too confused and powerless to do anything. Chūnagon moved next to the girl.

"Please let her live," he implored the Buddha with all his strength, but when he held the light close her face was blank and did not flinch. She lay still as a corpse. She was astonishingly beautiful, especially her face which was flawlessly white. None of her features could be called inferior. The way her hair was parted, its luster, even the bangs on her forehead were lovely. Deeply touched by her unexpected beauty, he stared at her and wept.

He threw himself down beside her and prayed intently. Even when he splashed water in her face she was unmoved, completely lifeless.

"How could both these terrible things happen to me at once?" he wondered. The girl was, he noticed, truly precious, charming, and incomparably beautiful.

When the better part of the evening had passed, her body gradually began to warm and she appeared to be reviving. Overjoyed, he prayed even harder while watching her closely. She moved her body ever so slightly and managed to open her eyes. In the light of the nearby lamp she found herself face to face with an unfamiliar man who lay by her side weeping. As she finally came to her senses she slowly looked away and hid her face in her robes. He was delighted that she had now recovered her senses.

Since the servants had been unable to help, the poor girl was now tended by a stranger she would normally be embarrassed to find so near. When she regained full consciousness she buried her head deeper in her robes and wept profusely. Chūnagon was so worried she might faint again that he refused to leave her side. He had the servants bring warm water, but she would not lift her head at all.

"It is to be expected," he thought in sympathy. "Didn't I break down when my father died, even though I am a man and the circumstances were not nearly so severe? People offer sympathy, but they don't really understand. Having been raised in such a forlorn retreat, how could she keep her senses when the nun, the only person she could rely on, died and she is left alone?"

He realized that she now was the only reminder of the one he longed for endlessly. He knew he could never treat her coolly or neglect her, even if she were frightfully ugly with horns on her head! He stared motionlessly at her hair which lay in thick profusion along her side. From top to bottom it was flawless, shining richly like lacquer inlaid with gold, and spread out like a great fan at least seven or eight feet in length. She seemed very beautiful and charming as she lay there with her head hidden in her robes.

"Even though they had the same mother," thought Chūnagon, "the Chinese Consort, perhaps because of the unusual bond we shared, seemed superior to this girl. What is she like? I don't suppose she can compare with her sister." Though somewhat disdainful, he watched her tenderly and would not think of leaving.

Before many days had passed, the nun was buried on a distant mountain ridge in accordance with her dying wish. During the period of mourning many enlightened monks of outstanding scholarship participated in the ceremonies, and no one doubted that her wish for the next world was fulfilled. Her final days were those of a holy, blessed person, and Chūnagon did all he could to assure her a place among the Bodhisattvas.

He sent a note to his mother and Taishō no Kimi in the capital.

"I have come across a strange and unexpected defilement. Do not mention it to anyone; just say I am worshipping in a mountain temple."

A reply soon arrived from his mother.

"What sort of defilement? I am sure you feel it ominous and unlucky, but your strange behavior troubles me. If only I could quickly renounce this world!"

"Why should my mother feel unfortunate?" he wondered. "Taishō no Kimi might well regret this world and feel lost. But her concern for her next life is impressive."

Day and night he devoted himself completely to prayer.

Though spring and autumn might be tolerable in Miyoshino, the winter was very difficult. The brief interludes of calm were fewer and fewer as the harsh storms of winter moved in, howling in the pines and scattering the few remaining leaves. No one but a mountain hermit could hold back his tears in the loneliness of those cold dreary days. Chūnagon regretted the Consort did not know what he was doing.

"If even in a dream she were somehow to learn I was neglecting both public and private matters to do her filial duty, she would be deeply moved. But she probably passes each day playing the *kin*, completely unaware of what has happened."

Would I had a wizard
To tell her I alone
Perform the mourning she should do.[6]

He had ignored so many women of his own land only to suffer lonely grief over a vow pledged in a distant dream. Unable to divert his thoughts to other subjects, he spent his nights wondering about the Consort.

"Though she was an outstanding woman, I have had my share of grief because of her. If I wei• not here poor Yoshinohime would be so lonely and helpless. She may be too embarrassed and ashamed to even move in my presence, but as long as I am with her, she has someone to rely on."

Gently he tried to reassure her.

"Ours is a transient world. Who has never known the grief of losing someone close? Since everyone must die we can do nothing but try to console those left behind. It pains me to see you so distressed. I have left everything to be with you. You may think it imprudent, but couldn't you make my effort worthwhile by showing at least some appreciation?"

He seemed quite handsome as he wept. No longer dazed as before she could now hear and see what was going on about her, and she

6. The reference to a wizard is an allusion to a poem in the first chapter of *The Tale of Genji*:
And will no wizard search her out for me, / That even he may tell me where she is?
Translation by Edward G. Seidensticker, *The Tale of Genji* (New York: Knopf, 1976), p. 12.

felt terribly embarrassed as she wondered what this handsome, charming man was doing so close at hand. She was mortified to think how wretched she must seem to him. The harsh wind blew from all directions; she had experienced it for many years, but now it seemed particularly cruel.

Frightened and dispirited, she knew not where to turn. At times when he was with her, talking or reciting the sutras, she realized how very fortunate she was to have him for support. But when she remembered her mother and the grief of her death, she sank into sorrow, unable to think at all. These fits of despondency caused him great pain. Pushing aside the curtain he would sit with her and stare at the garden. The leaves had all disappeared, snow was falling, and birds active in the garden were a touching sight.

"Birds make promises to the forest, but when the forest has withered, the birds . . ."[7] he sang gaily, trying to cheer her. He was impatient to gain her trust.

"If only I could comfort her," he thought, "she might be less reserved. Then we could enjoy the sky and the singing of the birds together."

> Winter in the mountains of Yoshino
> Amidst the falling snow;
> Have people stopped coming here?

Mountain villages are many, but some, to be sure, are closer to the capital and more hospitable than this. The nun's fate was extraordinary, and Chūnagon felt she must have had a reason for finding such a remote place.

"Hers was truly a miraculous, holy death," he remembered. "Even male hermits rarely depart this world with such auspicious signs. She was so enlightened she could break the shackles binding her to this world. How pure she must have made her heart."

Her death was truly splendid. Needless to say, he took charge of the preparations for the forty-nine days of mourning after her death.[8] Who else would see that the proper ceremonies were performed?

The snows increased with each passing day as the period of mourn-

---

7. The source of this allusion is uncertain.
8. The forty-nine days after a person's death were set aside as special days of mourning, since it was believed that a person's soul might be wandering about during that period. By the forty-ninth day, the soul would have settled in its new life.

ing drew to a close. He considered returning to the capital, for he could not remain in retreat forever.

"How could I leave the girl behind?" he asked himself. "There isn't anyone here capable of taking charge. No matter how much I care for her, it would be impossible to return quickly through the snow-covered mountain roads. When she was in her mother's care she could get by, but now she could not survive a minute alone."

He could not bear to leave her behind but felt it would be unsightly to take her to the capital himself. He decided, therefore, to send for her after securing for her a proper place to live, even though he worried how she would survive in the meantime.

Nurse Chūjō, who was caring for Wakagimi, had a younger sister who was once married to the Governor of Kōzuke. He was an incompetent official, however, and soon lost his fortune. Bemoaning his poverty he deserted Nurse Chūjō's sister and married the daughter of a rich man who offered support. The sister, grieved at this desertion, wanted very much to live in some hidden mountain path; but in the meantime she and her seventeen-year-old daughter sought refuge in Nurse Chūjō's household. Chūnagon guessed that the sister and daughter were sensitive people who would surely not mistreat Yoshinohime. He sent messengers asking the sister to come.

"You may think it strange, but I will explain the details myself when you arrive. Please bring your daughter with you. I will not cause you any worry."

She wondered what this unusually sudden request could mean. From Nurse Chūjō she knew Chūnagon to be a reliable person, and even if he were to ask her to plunge headlong into a pool of darkness she would not refuse.

Nurse Chūjō urged her to go. "Would he possibly ask anything evil or inappropriate of you? He has sent for you. Please go at once."

Chūnagon told Yoshinohime of his plans.

"These past few days I have been with you always like a shadow, but unfortunately you treat me as a frightful stranger. I cannot remain secluded here forever. I will leave soon to find an appropriate place for you to live and then I will send for you. Since I was worried about leaving you in such a weakened condition for even a moment, I sent for someone who will stay with you. She will remain by your side in place of me while I am gone. She has a daughter who is not uncomely. Be friendly, treat her as someone special, and let her help you."

Yoshinohime, uncertain how to answer, simply hid her face in shame and wept. This Chūnagon found quite charming.

"It is understandable," he sympathized. "What woman could respond cheerfully and readily if an unfamiliar man who was no relation at all were suddenly to be continuously at her side?"

As he began telling her of his inordinate concern Nurse Chūjō's sister arrived with her daughter. When they were settled in their rooms he went to see them.

"There is a poor lonely girl here with no one capable of looking after her, but I cannot bring her to the capital without trustworthy ladies. Her former servants thought they were missing out on things in this wretched mountain retreat, and they all deserted her. I want you to care for her as Nurse Chūjō cared for me. Comfort the helpless child and do not leave her until I come to take her to the capital."

When the women heard this earnest plea they wondered what sort of person could be living in this strange snow-covered locale. How did he find her? She must be someone special, they surmised. Although they had misgivings, they were delighted that he trusted them enough to request their help.

"For my part, keeping a constant watch is simple, just like serving at Court," said Nurse Chūjō's sister. "She, however, might shun us as strangers. Please tell her to feel at ease with us."

"I was so sure you would not fail to come that I already told her everything."

Once again he spoke with Yoshinohime.

"The people I mentioned have come. Do not treat them as coldly as you do me, for they might be offended. Be considerate and try to understand their position."

He sent for Nurse Chūjō's sister. Yoshinohime was stunned by the suddenness of these events, but what could she do? She felt more at ease with this lady than with the man who had been with her the past few days. The flame beyond the curtain gave off a gentle light. Lifting her head slightly she answered the lady's questions in a faint voice. Nurse Chūjō's sister found her young and charming, and realized that Chūnagon must care for the girl deeply to be so concerned.

181

Chūnagon supervised all the services on the forty-ninth day after the nun's death. The girl spent the entire time in tears wondering how she could possibly survive, but the length of a person's life is preordained, and she could not weep endlessly as she had soon after her mother's death. The women with her now, both the older woman and her young daughter, were respectable, attractive ladies. Each time she saw them she felt embarrassed, ashamed to think of the unsightly ladies she once associated with. But even when something had upset her in the past, she was not one to change her servants' ways. Her innocent, unsophisticated behavior was charming.

When only Chūnagon had been with her she was unable to do anything but weep, but now she was ashamed to hide beneath her clothes and shun these two ladies as if life with them were unbearable. She made herself relax and on occasion even let the daughter loosen and rearrange her hair. The daughter was beautiful, and Yoshino-hime gradually grew accustomed to having her nearby.

Though Chūnagon was delighted to see Yoshinohime more at ease, he still worried about leaving her to return to the capital. He spent every night by her side, soothing her loneliness and promising to care for her. Even as he was preparing to leave, his desire to be with her grew, especially since he could see each day how she now delighted in his visits. He instructed a number of reliable people to stay with her, time and time again warning them to remain close while he was gone, but still he could not tear himself away. He promised to send for her, but just imagining her loneliness when he was gone made it difficult to depart.

> How can you gaze
> Alone at the sky?
> The one we knew has become
> The moon amidst the smoke.

She wept freely and could not respond to his poem. She had grown accustomed to his companionship and steady words of comfort for the past few days, but now even he was to leave and she would suddenly be alone. Never had she known such grief and sorrow.

> Did she become the moon
> Darkened by the cloud of smoke?
> I cannot even see the sky.

182

She held her drab, black robes of mourning to her face and turned her head aside without the slightest suggestion of coyness. Her face was lovely and the glistening lines of her dark black hair seemed remarkably attractive. Had he ever seen such youthful charm as he now saw in the faint aura which surrounded her? He stroked the smooth, radiant hair. Not a single strand was out of place and the ends which reached to the fringe of her outer robe spread out like a multilayered fan. She was indeed a rare beauty.

"Whenever I read in the old tales of such beautiful girls being born at the foot of a mountain, I wondered how it could possibly be," he thought. "Here it has really happened! Prince Shikibukyō searched everywhere for women to satisfy his desires, yet he could not find one like this. What a delightful work of fate that I should find her before anyone else. But would I have found her had I not been looking for the Hoyang Consort's relatives?"

He was saddened as he recalled the one person tying them together. She would now be wearing multicolored robes, not these drab garments of mourning. How incomparably beautiful she was! Her person seemed to shine, so proud and handsome. Yoshinohime was gentle, elegant, and attractive. The Consort too was like this, and it was a great consolation to him that they looked so much alike. Of course he had no intention of becoming closely involved with the girl in some mundane affair. How frightened and ashamed he would feel were the Consort to hear, even in distant China, that he had been so infatuated he now used her sister as a source of consolation. The Consort was the only person he really cared for, and nothing could make him forget her. Even if he found comfort in harboring the girl because she reminded him of the Consort, the love he had discovered that dreamlike night in China would not change. And if his prayers were answered and he was born again with the Consort, his heart was so pure that she might still care for him. Yoshinohime was beautiful and she did resemble the Consort, but she only intensified his first love. He felt no urgent need to turn to her to satisfy his longing.

"What is it that ties the Consort and me together?" he wondered. "It must be fate that makes me long for her so. But if that is the case, why can't we be fated to meet again?"

183

For a moment he forgot his grave concern for the girl before him as he recalled the infinite charms of the Consort whispering "tied to one from beyond the clouds." But this only reinforced his attachment to Yoshinohime and made his sorrow that much more extraordinary. He returned to Yoshinohime's room to offer further words of comfort.

As he left she pushed aside her curtain to see him off. Snow, already piled deep, continued to fall so heavily it darkened the sky. Chūnagon wore light purple trousers of Chinese damask with a yellow shirt lined in red. His hunting jacket had a flat white figured design. As she watched this incomparably handsome man make his way through the deep snow she thought how embarrassing and distressing it was to have had him so near. But when he was with her she was not afraid; now that he was leaving, the home she knew so well would not seem the same. Feeling sad and lonely, she wondered how she could continue living there.

> It is hard to go on living
> In the snows of Miyoshino,
> But what mountain could I find now?

The sight of the girl weeping as he left was touching.

The women Chūnagon had sent for felt lonely now that he was to leave, but just being with the lovely girl was a comfort. They promised to stay with her and from time to time read her interesting tales they had brought from the capital. The daughter was young and beautiful, and the way she spoke to Yoshinohime made Chūnagon feel a special attraction for her too. He stopped to talk with her on his way out.

He also visited the old nun's prayer hall. Everything was as it had been while she was alive—the daily prayer book, her rosary—only she was not to be seen. Everyone said she must now occupy an exalted station in Paradise. Indeed, her rank now might be magnificent, but the resentment her poor daughter must still harbor, left behind in the world, lonely and without support, would not soon disappear.

The sky darkened as new snow fell atop the old. The daughter of Nurse Chūjō's sister stared listlessly at the completely overcast sky.

"What a lonely view," she sighed.

Yoshinohime nodded and wept.

Day and night I stare
Into the snow darkening the sky;
It never stops.

She was so beautiful and charming the daughter found her company greater comfort than serving in a jeweled palace.

I have no wish to live
In this vile world.
Now I have come to rest
In the snowbound mountains.

Together they offered each other comfort.

Chūnagon's thoughts were entirely with the girl in Yoshino. On the way home he constantly considered going back to see her, but, worried and anxious about his mother and his children, Himegimi and Wakagimi, he urged his horse toward the capital.

The children had grown surprisingly in his absence, and Taishō no Kimi showed neither her former reserve nor any new resentment over Chūnagon's unexpected period of seclusion in the mountains.

She wore simple dress and no makeup at all for her many hours of prayer. Even without powder her face was proud and fresh; indeed, she seemed more lovely than the girl he had just left. From her radiant beauty he concluded there could not be a finer woman in all the land; whenever he saw her thus his disquieting sense of regret was no less than his feelings for the Consort.

"Ah—if we could marry," he sighed, "would I wander aimlessly into the mountains even if the ties that sent me there were deep?"

He wished he could go back to the days before she became a nun, for he felt that he himself had caused that momentous decision. But now deep in the mountains there is another woman; how, he wondered, had such a rare beauty grown up there?

"I could not avoid an unexpected defilement," he told Taishō no Kimi. "And with my very eyes I saw a moving, holy sight."

He told her in detail of the trailing purple cloud he had witnessed. She began to weep, envious of the nun's final parting.

"I too probably would have been moved. I have always wanted to escape to a remote mountain and die like that, but in my present state that is impossible."

"It doesn't matter whether you live near or far; no matter where

185

you are, it depends solely on your heart. True monks can become Bodhisattvas in a crowded marketplace."[9]

"But my heart is shallow and I am swayed by where I live."

"Yes, yes," he chided her. "I know your sagacious concern for immediate enlightenment. Please be patient a while. I will watch after Himegimi until she is old enough to care for herself; then I will take you to a place like the Yoshino Mountains. But it's hard to tell how long my frail life will last."

With deep affection they vowed, come what may, to wait together for the music of Amida, just as in the *Tale of Ōi*.[10]

The relationship between Chūnagon and Lord Taishō, once so cool and distant, was now very close. Lord Taishō, acting like a father, even scolded Chūnagon for his absence.

"You're acting very strange lately—going off on some reckless mountain retreat. It seems almost perverse."

Such admonitions Chūnagon now found quite painful.

At first Chūnagon considered settling the girl from the snowy mountains in the east wing of his mansion. He could win Taishō no Kimi's understanding with a moving description of the girl. Those sympathetic to him would be reassured and all might go well. People who did not know the truth might gossip, however. They would accuse him of bringing in a rival, even if he still seemed to care greatly for Taishō no Kimi.

The gossip would be painful and Taishō no Kimi's ladies too might feel uneasy. His behavior would seem strange and improper since he had only recently delayed his marriage to the Princess for the period of taboo. What would the Emperor think on hearing that Chūnagon had suddenly taken a new woman into his house?

---

9. Matsuo suggests that the allusion is to Kūya (903-972), who preached Amidist ideas to the common people in the streets. The allusion may, however, be to the first two lines of "In Refutation of the Invitation to Hiding," by the fourth-century poet Wang K'ang Chū:
Little hiders hide in the hills and groves, / Big hiders hide in the city market.
Translation by Burton Watson, *Chinese Lyricism, Shih Poetry from the Second to the Twelfth Century* (New York: Columbia University Press, 1971), p. 75. "Big hiders" refers to great hermits or sages. A similar line is found in a poem entitled "The Middle Hider," by Po Chü-i:
The great hider lives in the marketplace.
10. A Heian *monogatari* no longer extant. It apparently concerned two lovers who renounced the world and spent their time together in prayer.

Chūnagon decided to forego his own mansion and keep her in the spacious, clean house of Nurse Chūjō's children where his own boy Wakagimi was hidden. Eager to send for her before the year ended, he hastily had a room equipped with appropriate furnishings.

"I'm sure everyone will say I am up to the usual philandering," he told Taishō no Kimi. "The girl was left behind by a mother who never could provide much support. I must send for her, as her mother was terribly worried about leaving her alone in that remote mountain. I think of her as a sister and hope you will too.

"Since I just declined the Emperor's urgent request, please understand that what I say about other women is true. You can see, I am sure, how much I think of you."

"You tell me this as if you think me jealous," she responded. "How could any such thing upset me in the least? Since life is sometimes tedious here, I do wish you would bring the girl to me."

"I thought of that, but the gossip would be loathsome. What if the Emperor were to hear of it? For your sake and the sake of others whose feelings we must consider, I decided to keep her in a secret place. I won't even let my mother know."

As usual he spoke tenderly to her.

He sent a messenger to Miyoshino with a letter telling the women of his constant concern for Yoshinohime.

"Comfort her and do not leave her side. Before long I expect to send for you."

He was even so thorough as to caution the servants on how the preparations should be handled.

To Yoshinohime he sent a poem.

> How could you know the many times
> I have succumbed to grief,
> Thinking of the deep mountain snows?

Her reply came on bluish gray paper.

> As time goes by
> My grief grows more intense.
> Who would come visit
> This wretched world of Mt. Yoshino?

The form and rhythm of the characters were correct, skilled, and charming. Virtuous merit from a former life would account for her fine looks, but how did she learn to write so well under the guidance of one whose renunciation of the world was absolute? He could not take his eyes off the poem.

At Yoshino the women had servants prepare for leaving.

"He will surely be coming for us soon," Nurse Chūjō's sister said, "and he'll probably bring some clothes for her. We should prepare some attractive bedding."

The mountains were so lonely and frightening to the girl that one would expect her to "go willing should a stream entice her on."[11] But what would happen, Yoshinohime wondered, if she were to leave this mountain with no one to rely on for some unknown destination? She had her doubts but was not firm enough to make them known to others. Even among the servants who had been with her from the beginning there were none she could talk with intimately. She pitied these lonely, desperate women: without even bothering to inquire about the destination they would be delighted to leave a place like Yoshino. But she was worried.

When the kind daughter began telling her what they would do when Chūnagon came, Yoshinohime broke into tears.

"While in mourning for my mother I had hoped to find a more remote place. How could I move closer to the capital?"

The daughter must have reported this to her mother, who told everything to Chūnagon when he arrived. He immediately went to Yoshinohime's room and pushed aside the curtain.

"I was so worried I struggled over steep roads to reach you, and now you act depressed and want to find a more distant home? I would search for you even if you hid deeper in the woods."

Embarrassed by his charming smile she began to perspire and could not speak. She knew in her heart how difficult it was to leave her only home but was ashamed to say so herself. She would place her trust in him and keep her reservations to herself. Now all she could do was weep.

Chūnagon went to see the old monk.

"Truly the enlightened support of her mother enabled the girl to

11. Alluding to poem #938, Ono no Komachi, *Kokinshū*:
I that am lonely, / Like a reed root-cut, / Should a stream entice me, / Would go, I think.
Translation by Arthur Waley, *The Nō Plays of Japan* (New York: Grove Press, Inc., 1957), p. 148.

survive in this strange location. But I am worried about what will happen to her now. I think I should secretly take her to the capital."

"For the past few years the old nun was very concerned about her daughter," said the monk. "She prayed that the Buddha might send someone to care for the girl so that her own wish to be born in Paradise could be fulfilled. She also had me offer prayers for this petition. It was then that you came to Yoshino. She was pleased that her prayers had been answered so that she could then think only of the next world. Her final moments were truly magnificent.

"The girl, as you can see, seems destined for incomparably splendid heights in the future, but I must warn you of her frightful karma: if she should know a man before the age of twenty her life will be destroyed. I have been carefully observing her recently; it seems that if she were to become pregnant before the age of twenty she would have a great deal of difficulty surviving. It is very inauspicious. She is now seventeen years old; if she is very careful for three more years, it will probably be all right."

What a pity, thought Chūnagon. It shocked him to think what might have happened had his emotions gotten out of control.

"I had no intention of suddenly becoming intimately involved with her, and now that I have heard this I will be especially careful for the next three years.

"Well, there isn't any reason to leave these rooms as they are. I have thought of making them into a prayer hall. When spring comes I will see that the reconstruction is carried out forthwith."

Chūnagon's generosity brought tears of joy to the monk's face.

The daughter of the old nun's nurse was a nun approximately sixty years of age. She chose to remain at Yoshino.

"What good would it do for me to leave this mountain now?" she wondered tearfully.

Yoshinohime's furnishings and old clothes were divided up among the monk and this nun, and the stewards Chūnagon had called to support Yoshinohime were ordered to care for the people being left behind.

The house Yoshinohime knew so well, even the familiar pillars, now seemed like an illusion before her very eyes. Unexpectedly and unwillingly, she now was leaving them. Blinded by tears, she was unable to climb into the cart.

My tears flow somewhere ahead of me,
Though I myself know not where I go.

By midafternoon, when the snow was still falling heavily, they arrived at a way station where Chūnagon had previously stayed. He approached the carriage to help her down. For the past few months she had grown accustomed to his presence, but only in the inner confines of her own room where she could remain half hidden from view by screens and curtains. To crawl out of the carriage in full view was distressing, like wandering aimlessly in a dream, but it would be wrong to sit and vacillate. Oblivious to the world around her she hid her face behind her fan and crawled out of the carriage.

The makeshift room readied for her at the front of the house was embarrassingly exposed and she collapsed in tears the moment she entered. Her predicament was pitiful, and it was only natural she should feel so distraught after suddenly leaving her familiar mountain home to travel through a world of uncertainty.

It was still snowing but the moon shone brightly. The eaves were narrow and moonlight fell directly into her room making the poor girl even more visible. In an effort to comfort her Chūnagon led her out to the veranda. While she seemed unduly modest in hiding her face, she did not act aloof. Delicate and supple, she moved like a young willow in the wind as she struggled to hide her many tears. Chūnagon sensed that the attractive girl gazing at the garden was not insensitive. As she turned her head this way and that in the full moonlight he watched her carefully and marveled at her unusual beauty. With everyone else asleep the night was quiet. He lay down beside her with only their sleeves touching and made comforting promises of support. She was still too reserved to respond directly, but the way in which she nestled close brought back unbearable memories. He decided to tell her everything, even the one great incident he had hoped to keep hidden in his heart, the one thing he could not even tell Taishō no Kimi, with whom he was completely open. Nor did he have the heart to keep from her the story of Wakagimi. The letter from China had hinted of the boy's background, and once she understood, Chūnagon thought it would be good for her to see him.

He told her of his inspiration for the trip, the journey itself, and his arrival on the distant shores of China. He then described the first meeting with the Consort on the night of the chrysanthemums, her playing of the *kin*, and the forbidden thoughts that plagued him but remained hidden until an inescapable bond drew them together for a single meeting in the spring dream of Shan Yin. He did not see the woman again until their brief encounter shortly before his return, and after that there was no way to ever meet again. Only Wakagimi who came back to Japan with him remained as proof of that dreamlike meeting. His tears flowed freely as he told her of the Consort.

Anyone listening to this splendid man's story, especially since it occurred in a foreign land, could not help but weep, and Yoshinohime was particularly moved. Even as a child she had known of a sister living in a foreign land. Her mother, the one person she could rely on, had renounced the world to live in a remote mountain beyond the cries of the birds. Life was tedious. She had no one with whom she could enjoy the moon or the snow, no one to talk to in times of sorrow and loneliness. If only her sister were with her in Japan, she lamented, it would be consoling to live together even in that lonely mountain. Just seeing the letter had made her wonder if there would be a time when she could see her sister other than in a dream. The lonely events of the past few months had not lessened her sorrow. Would she be forced to live this wretched life, unsure of what comes next, if her sister were a consort in Japan? With Chūnagon's description Yoshinohime felt she could see before her very eyes the sister she so constantly thought of. Forgetting all shame and reserve she wept with Chūnagon.

"How would I have heard of my sister," she wondered, "if I had not met him?" The tears they shared brought them even closer together.

"I came to you because of your relationship to the Consort," Chūnagon told her. "We must think of each other as reminders of her. When you start living with her child, he too should remind you of her."

He spent the entire night comforting the girl. The early morning moon stood alone in the pale green sky above the shining snow, and the sight of Chūnagon talking as they watched the morning sky was incomparably beautiful.

> I searched for someone
> Who might be my link

To that restless night's dream;
How sad that we now talk together.

"It does not seem real to me," he added.

From your words
I know my trifling worth:
An illusion of the memory of a dream.

Her weak and pitiful voice seemed truly charming to him.

Gon no Kami,[12] the industrious son of Nurse Chūjō, had been charged with preparing Yoshinohime's room, and everything was completed as ordered when the girl arrived. The southeast section of the main room held a curtained dais with elegant furnishings while the north section was made ready for Yoshinohime's ladies-in-waiting.

Having lived at the foot of a rugged mountain visited only by the wind in the pines, Yoshinohime found the unusual journey to the capital incomprehensible and no more real than the dream Chūnagon spoke of in his poem. She tried hard to understand what was happening, yet found she could do nothing but abandon herself completely to his care.

When they arrived in the capital, Chūnagon first showed her the beautiful boy Wakagimi, who was running about the house playfully.

"This child is proof of what was in the letter," he said. "I do not consider a life contrary to the dictates of my heart worth living, and if I continue my hypocritical ways I cannot expect to live much longer. I would like to entrust the boy to you."

Since Yoshinohime had entrusted herself completely to Chūnagon just when her future seemed hopeless, she was saddened to hear that he did not expect to live long in this world. Unable to answer she merely wept and gazed fondly at Wakagimi.

"This is your mother," Chūnagon told the boy, who seemed to know instinctively that Yoshinohime was a relative. He called her "mother" and from that moment on would not leave her side. At night he would sleep next to no one else. The company of this charming child brought relief from the sorrow and uncertainty which plagued Yoshinohime's heart, and somehow she managed to pass the days.

12. The title means "Provisional Governor," but the province in question is not mentioned.

The daughter who had come to help at Mt. Yoshino was given the name Shōshō and acted as a sort of nursemaid for Wakagimi, staying with him constantly. Her room was in the eastern wing of the house. Some of Yoshinohime's former ladies returned to serve; Shōshō gave rooms to those who might be of assistance and did her best to see that the girl was well cared for.

Nurse Chūjō went to visit Yoshinohime. She had thought Chūnagon cared only for Taishō no Kimi, but now there was this girl. She was surprised at Yoshinohime's tender beauty. Once when Chūnagon was away she got a very close look at her, and just the sight of the girl seemed to give her new life.

"This girl looks so much like Wakagimi," she thought fondly. "I wonder where he found her."

Chūnagon treated Yoshinohime like an only daughter, worrying and fretting whenever he had to be away and doing everything possible to see that she was well cared for. When Yoshinohime saw how really splendid a room and furnishings could be, her shame at having been seen by Chūnagon in the wretchedness of Yoshino intensified. But as it was useless to say anything she innocently accepted all his help.

As Chūnagon became accustomed to the girl's charming ways his love for her grew stronger. Many times he came very close to losing control of his emotions, but he feared the monk's warning about the girl's unique karma. There were other considerations too. Lord Taishō and Taishō no Kimi were deeply appreciative of the unusual devotion he had shown in delaying his marriage to the Emperor's daughter, and they accepted his decision openly in the belief that no one at present was more important to him than Taishō no Kimi herself.

If his devotion to the Princess were somewhat weak it might not matter, for she had others to rely on, but it would be a pity to leave Yoshinohime alone at night now that he had become so close with her. Even though their relationship was not the ordinary one between a man and a woman, each time he saw the extraordinarily beautiful girl he realized it would be terrible to leave her all alone. However, he was accustomed to spending his days and nights with Taishō no Kimi, and even if he did not desert her completely for Yoshinohime, it would be apparent to Taishō no Kimi from his constant coming and going that there was someone else attracting his attention. But now Yoshinohime had come to rely on him. Though he had no intention of arousing the resentment of Taishō no Kimi, what would she think if he were absent for even a few nights? He would be hurt were she to resent his behavior. Bearing in mind the warning from the monk in Yoshino, he suppressed his desire to be with Yoshinohime and continued as in the past to spend the nights at Taishō no Kimi's room. After the situation was explained to Taishō no Kimi, she assented and frequently offered advice to Chūnagon on caring for the girl.

While Lord Taishō's mansion was under construction his entire family, including Prince Shikibukyō's wife, moved to Chūnagon's home at the end of the month. Chūnagon's mother was moved to the east wing, away from the main room which was taken over by Lord Taishō's family.

On the first day of the new year everyone looked splendid. When the ladies all gathered together the scene was stylish and gay. From a nearby corner Chūnagon surreptitiously watched his mother, Taishō no Kimi, and Prince Shikibukyō's wife dote on Himegimi, now a year older.[13] His mother was wearing at least eight white singlets under a robe so richly red it seemed almost black. She moved with ease among the ladies; her clothes seemed radiant, her face young and fresh, and the hair falling neatly over her shoulders was particularly splendid.

Prince Shikibukyō's wife wore figured robes of red plum combination[14] over singlets of the same color and a wide-sleeved gown of white and dark red.[15] She seemed much more mature than the spring evening when Chūnagon first saw her. Her elegant and gentle bearing was quite impressive.

Taishō no Kimi tried to avoid the religious garb her father found so distasteful. For this occasion she seemed particularly proud and graceful in eight-layered singlets covered with a wide-sleeved gown of dark gray, figured but without ornamentation. Her radiant, even overwhelming beauty surpassed all the others. Her hair reached to

13. In the traditional way of counting age, a person was one at birth and a year older with each new year.

14. Light red on the outside, dark red on the inside.

15. The white and dark red of Prince Shikibukyō's wife's gown are a color combination known as *ume* (plum). It is a different combination from the "red plum combination" in the previous note.

the floor when she was seated, seemingly no shorter than before she became a nun. She is really incomparable, he thought, as he watched affectionately the beautiful face visible beneath the thick but neatly trimmed hair that fell over her forehead. He hardly even glanced at her sister's fully powdered face, his indifference, even disdain, due no doubt to his complete infatuation with Taishō no Kimi.

"If Taishō no Kimi could dress as before with fully colored robes and hair the length of other women's," he mused, "now at the prime of her womanhood she might shine with a radiance to dazzle the eye." In spite of the new year's festivities he began to weep with a deep sense of sorrow and regret over her unfortunate situation.

When Lord Taishō, handsome in his best clothes, entered the room ceremoniously, he looked at all the women and took notice of the difference in Taishō no Kimi's dress. His eyes filled with tears, inauspicious though they were, as he stared regretfully at his lovely daughter.

Chūnagon pitied the poor man. "It was my foolishness which led her to this," he lamented. Even though she was now a nun, he vowed that nothing must be done in any way to slight her.

He observed that Prince Shikibukyō's wife, while clearly less enchanting than her sister, still was charming and elegant. The child Himegimi was as beautiful as a freshly blooming flower. Lord Taishō took her to his lap and fondled her tenderly. As he showed her the new year's rice cakes he offered a solemn prayer: "May this child take the place of her mother, now in such a sorrowful state, to become the joy of my life." His prayer was not unreasonable.

"The crowning with rice cakes[16]—Chūnagon should do it," Lord Taishō said. "It is already getting late. Tell him we are waiting."

Chūnagon stepped out from his hiding place and one of the servants told him of Lord Taishō's request. He declined deferentially.

"Lord Taishō himself should perform the ceremony. That is how it was done last year. My rank is too humble."

Upon hearing this Lord Taishō agreed to perform the ceremony.

16. Prepared for special celebrations, these rice cakes were known as "mirror rice cakes" since they were round in the shape of a mirror. As part of the new year festivities they were placed on a child's head while prayers were offered for his or her good fortune.

He went to where Chūnagon was standing and had him hold the girl while he placed the rice cakes on her head.

Lord Taishō's sons gathered at Chūnagon's mansion before going to the palace. Chūnagon, however, delayed his departure so he could cap young Wakagimi with the ceremonial rice cakes.

The boy's room was neat but somewhat somber in the subdued colors of mourning.[17] The light blues and grays of the clothing and furnishings were distinct but far from festive, a decided contrast to the splendor in Chūnagon's mansion. Although Yoshinohime was partially hidden by the curtains of her dais, she seemed lovely as a picture. She wore white robes over gray, and her hair, spread abundantly like a fan, stood out handsomely against the grayish clothing.

"Please try to feel at ease here this year," he urged. "I hurried here even before visiting my own mother in hopes of finding you in good spirits."

Pushing aside the curtain, he caught a glimpse of her face tilted gracefully behind a fan. She seemed particularly beautiful in dress more elaborate than usual. She was petite and charming, and a radiant splendor seemed to surround her presence. He imagined that the fairy-tale princess likened to the autumn moon would have looked like this.[18] Yoshinohime's gentle, supple manner was, much to his surprise, not inferior to the many charms of Lord Taishō's daughters.

"It is only natural those women should be so attractive," he told himself, "for they were raised with the utmost care. I would, in fact, be quite disappointed if they were somehow lacking. But how could a girl raised in the mountain wilderness turn out like this?"

He felt that Yoshinohime's story was even more unusual than that of the shining Princess found in the bamboo grove.[19]

"Prince Shikibukyō searched the whole country, even the distant provinces, for an outstanding woman, but never found one like this though he looked everywhere. But because of my longing for the Consort I visited her mother, the nun, and there I found Yoshinohime. The karma of my life is unusual indeed. She is surely

---

17. Mourning for the Yoshino nun, Wakagimi's grandmother.
18. Possibly from a *monogatari* no longer extant, the source of this allusion is uncertain.
19. Referring to Kaguyahime, heroine of *Taketori Monogatari*, "The Tale of the Bamboo Cutter."

meant to be a private consolation for the grief I have suffered over Taishō no Kimi's actions."

Delighted with this thought he stared at her, unable to turn his eyes away in the least. He began to recall the Chinese Consort, her unusually proud demeanor and seemingly radiant presence. Tears soon filled his eyes, though he felt no sense of ill omen.

"I should be able to live with this lovely reminder of the Consort to soothe my troubled heart. But my yearning for her must be tempered by the fateful warning of the old monk. Perhaps I can best show my unlimited devotion to the Consort by treating Yoshinohime as only a fond memory of the Consort. If our relationship were to follow the normal course of lovers my heart might be consoled, but I would then certainly regret having violated the monk's admonition. If, however, I restrain myself and regard her as a mere reminder of the Consort, then the girl will surely be moved by my upright devotion." His love for Yoshinohime deepened.

"As long as I restrain myself," he thought, "the nights we spend apart need not upset us. If we were man and wife even a single night apart would be cause for regret, and her heart might turn to jealousy. Even though Taishō no Kimi is a nun I have grown so accustomed to spending the nights with her I cannot desert her for Yoshinohime. No matter how I feel about the girl I can think of no one in this land equal to Taishō no Kimi."

His affection for Taishō no Kimi, in spite of her unfortunate station in life, surpassed in intensity even the great pity he felt for Yoshinohime. It would be impossible to leave Taishō no Kimi, for there was never a moment he did not think of her as a truly unique person in his life. As he looked at Yoshinohime he decided that in times of overwhelming yearning he might spend a night with her, sleeping close without violating his trust. How strange to feel that way, he thought.

Wakagimi grew more handsome with each passing day. From the time of Yoshinohime's arrival he virtually ignored his wet-nurse to spend day and night with "mother." The sight of him clinging to her skirt moved the servants deeply.

When Chūnagon returned home the evening of the third day of the new year Prince Shikibukyō was there on an unofficial visit. Chūnagon, as host, greeted his guest and saw to it that even the

197

carriage lackeys were well fed. When Lord Taishō's sons gathered in the main hall toasts were offered for the royal visitor and everyone reveled in the excitement of greeting the new year. Later the Prince drew Chūnagon aside and, in the course of polite conversation on all the usual subjects, began to speak his feelings openly.

"For a long time I have wanted to be better friends with you, but you always avoided me as if I were inappropriate company or some kind of fool. I find that most unfortunate, but everyone knows why you avoid me. Perhaps I'm not the ascetic you are . . ."

As his words contained no bitterness, Chūnagon laughed in response.

"On the surface an ascetic, underneath I'm just a common fellow."

"Yes, indeed. You fooled everyone by going off to China and meeting all kinds of women. Others like myself are confined within the boundaries of this land.

"It's strange that I should be criticized for leaving no stone unturned in searching for a woman. More than a goddess from Ama no Iwaya[20] I want simply to find an ideal woman who meets my fancy, one I can settle down with for the rest of my life. I've looked everywhere, ignoring the gossip and criticism of others and even scoldings by the Emperor, and I must say that none of the women I discovered was really bad. Each was splendid in her own way, but it is difficult for me to find true love in this world. People think I am a philanderer, but I have grown weary of spending the nights alone, sleeping on a single sleeve. I have even thought of going to China to find a good wife!"

The Prince's lament seemed sincere, and Chūnagon wondered what he would think were he shown either Taishō no Kimi or Yoshinohime. Chūnagon was secretly delighted that both women were under his protection, fated to be his personal possessions beyond the grasp of the zealously inquisitive Prince.

"There surely must be an acceptable woman hidden in some

20. Amaterasu Ōmikami, the Sun Goddess, hid in the cave of Ama no Iwaya (in present-day Kyūshū) when she was insulted by Sosa no wo no Mikoto, causing darkness to cover the earth. She was eventually enticed out of her cave by the sound of celebration and dance. Donald L. Philippi, trans., *Kojiki* (Tokyo: Princeton University Press and University of Tokyo Press, 1968), chap. 17, pp. 81-86.

mountain village," he said. "Bad luck has kept you from finding her."

"I have heard there are such women," the Prince responded, "but on close inspection they are usually disappointing."

The Prince's mood aroused in Chūnagon a sense of both awe and pity. It had been a long time since the Prince's last visit to Taishō no Kimi's sister, but even now he showed no inclination to visit her immediately. Chūnagon thought it unseemly and cruel for the two men to talk the entire night while the Prince's wife was waiting.

"It's getting late," he said and stood up as if to leave, even though Prince Shikibukyō apparently wanted to continue the discussion.

In consideration of the feelings of the Prince's wife, Chūnagon urged the Prince to her room and then went himself to Taishō no Kimi's rooms. The Prince was terribly curious about Taishō no Kimi: what did she look like? How could she command such deep devotion from Chūnagon?

Since Taishō no Kimi was spending the entire month in special devotion in her prayer hall and seemed to begrudge any time taken from her prayers, Chūnagon decided to go elsewhere. Snow was falling and the weather was taking a turn for the worse. The sharp wind made him feel lonely so he went to visit Yoshinohime. She was sleeping with Wakagimi held close to her bosom and Shōshō at her side. When the attendants awoke and left, Chūnagon took their place at her side and talked with her as they lay together. Close at hand she seemed particularly beautiful, for she no longer felt distressed as when they first met.

Chūnagon ruminated over the conversation with Prince Shikibukyō.

"Even after hearing of Taishō no Kimi's renunciation of the world, he apparently still cannot forget her," he thought. "Were he to hear that I have another fine woman in hiding, with his insatiable curiosity, he would surely do anything to see her. How terrible if he felt he had to make her his own, no matter what other people might think. My love for Yoshinohime knows no limit, but I must not think of her as a lover—the monk's words are too frightening. Just being with her for these three years should be my consolation, and I must control my overwhelming passion. If the Prince discovered the girl there would be trouble. He might misunderstand my inten-

tions and assume that I do not care for her. Were he then to beguile
her with his many charms she would surely respond to him."

The mere possibility of such a seduction caused Chūnagon a great
deal of consternation.

"I wanted to come sooner," he told Yoshinohime, "but Prince
Shikibukyō came to talk about all kinds of people and things, and I
could not leave until it was quite late. You have been sleeping quite
well, I see. I am disappointed you did not think enough of me to
wait up."

He was inexplicably cross and irritable. Continuing he said, "The
Prince is sure to visit here sometime. Once he has seen a woman
he sends guileful letters which cannot be ignored; he is remarkably
skillful in seducing women. If he but hears of you he is certain to
ply his charms."

He cautioned her about a number of dangerous possibilities, but
she in her charming innocence seemed oblivious to his warnings.
He slept by her side until late the next morning.

When they awoke an elegant letter was waiting for him. Perhaps
from Taishō no Kimi, he thought, but on opening it discovered it
was the Prince's letter.

"You seemed anxious last night, and the reason why was clear to
me."

> Of course you wish to hurry home;
> Do not the waves of Toko Bay
> Have a place to rest?[21]

Although the writing was not consciously affected there was a
certain charm in the shape and style of the brush strokes.

"It's a letter from the Prince I told you about," he said, showing
Yoshinohime the note. "What woman would not be moved by such
skillful words and writing?"

Without embarrassment she brushed aside her beautiful hair still
disheveled from sleep and glanced at the letter. Chūnagon stared at
her lovely face beneath the luxuriant hair falling over her forehead
and could not pen his reply immediately. Prince Shikibukyō had
obviously misunderstood Chūnagon's reason for urging him to his

21. Toko Bay was on Lake Biwa near the present-day city of Hikone, Shiga Prefecture. *Toko* also means "bed," and the Prince is clearly suggesting that Chūnagon
was in a hurry to meet a lady friend that night.

wife's room. Perhaps the Prince even had Chūnagon followed last night.

"He's a dangerous Prince," warned Chūnagon. "Though no one else noticed, he apparently guessed from my behavior that I was harboring you."

In reply he wrote,

> The divers of the Nio Sea
> Do not conceal their movements.
> Why does the wind
> Blow seaweed to expose them?[22]

"You will find I did not deceive you. My deepest respects."

Chūnagon wondered why the Prince questioned his behavior. He instructed a servant called Shinano not to leave the girl's side when he was absent. Yoshinohime, however, turned a deaf ear on his attempts to picture the Prince as a dangerous philanderer willing to do anything to get a woman.

Chūnagon occasionally made brief visits to a number of different women, but whenever possible he chose to spend his nights with Taishō no Kimi. She cared for him and always treated him gently when, in times of particular distress, he found it necessary to be with her. He too understood her moments of grief and sympathized with her.

In spite of the many distractions of his heart, the moment he thought of the Chinese Consort he forgot everything else. Why, he wondered, was he not fated to see her again? With the passing of time the memory of the night they spent together grew more faint, and even when he spent day and night with Yoshinohime, a close and touching reminder of the Consort, his longing was not soothed. He grieved, as if watching the moon on Mt. Obasute.[23]

From the tenth day of the first month his restless sleep was punctuated with frequent dreams of the Hoyang Consort. She appeared much more worried than usual, evidently troubled by some agonizing pain, and the sight of her in such distress was difficult to bear.

---

22. The Nio Sea is Lake Biwa. Chūnagon likens himself to a diver and denies he had a secret tryst. Why, he asks, does the Prince try to expose what did not happen? There is a pun on the word *mirume*, which means seaweed or eyes that see something.

23. Alluding to poem #878, *Kokinshū*, anonymous:
I cannot be consoled / Even as I watch the moon / Of Sarashina's Mt. Obasute.

He saw her each night as he dozed off; her appearance had changed very little but now she lay sick in bed. What, he wondered, has happened to her?

On the sixteenth day of the third month Chūnagon and Yoshinohime sat on the veranda beneath the raised blinds and stared at the lovely moon among the clouds. It was the very night, he recalled, of the dream of Shan Yin, and even now he could almost hear her reciting her poem "one beyond the clouds."

> Ah, that dream I saw;
> Only the moon tonight
> Is a knowing reminder of that time.

With tears in his eyes he took the *kin* at his side and began to play while staring at the sky. Later that night a patch of clouds trailed across the sky, deepening the mist over the moon. The restlessness tormenting his soul seemed great enough to fill the empty sky. While staring entranced at the face of the moon he suddenly heard a voice out of the sky: "The Hoyang Consort has today cut all ties with this world and is reborn in heaven."

"What is this madness?" he wondered. "Did I hear this for thinking of her too much?"

But he clearly heard the same words three times. Wakagimi was terrified and began to weep uncontrollably. The servants hurriedly awoke and tossed rice about to ward off evil spirits, and the sound of the voice was lost in the commotion.

Chūnagon was overcome with grief.

"Indeed, how could I expect her life to match that of a thousand-year pine," he lamented. "Even in a different land the transiency of life is the same. Were this but a dream I might be consoled, but there is no doubting a voice of revelation heard from the sky." He knew it must be true.

He remembered the times with her—the evening of chrysanthemum-viewing, the spring dream of Shan Yin, the full moon banquet at the Wei Yang Palace—and when he recalled her playing of the *kin* he could almost see her before his eyes. The rest of the night he wept until his voice gave out and he collapsed in exhaustion.

"I cannot bear the sorrow," he told Yoshinohime. "Please massage my chest."

She thought his condition pitifully strange and moved closer to comfort him. Though she avoided facing him directly, the beauty of her face and hair made him weep uncontrollably. Perhaps she understood what was troubling him, for her expression changed to a look of sudden surprise. She was so charming he could not help but lean against her as he wept.

"For the past few nights, whenever I dozed off, the Consort appeared in my dreams. I was so worried and then I heard a voice tonight. It grieves me to think what might have happened."

Without answering, Yoshinohime buried her face in her sleeves and wept, for she knew his feelings.

He was thankful that she, at least, was with him.

> Had I not found this link to her,
> I would be lost in weeping
> With no way to remember her.

He could not send someone to find out what had happened, nor could he wait for travelers returning from China to tell him what it meant. He realized he should have followed the advice of those who urged him to remain in China for five years, but there was nothing to be done now.

The very next morning he began a thousand days of fasting and prepared to have the Lotus Sutra read ten thousand times. There was no need to tell everyone what had happened. Strict seclusion was out of the question, but he decided to appear at Court only when it was absolutely necessary. To Taishō no Kimi he said: "I have in a dream seen things which lead me to believe my days are numbered. I felt so helpless I decided to start this fast and recite sutras."

Recently people had been whispering about the extraordinary care Chūnagon was showing for the new woman he had brought home. Taishō no Kimi could surmise from his expression that she must be truly special, but there were also times when it was clear, as he often claimed, that their relationship was not that of man and wife. Since he apparently could not settle down with this girl, perhaps, she thought, he really was not meant to live very long. She had no desire to go on living if she were to lose the one she had relied on, her closest companion day and night. Chūnagon's unusual condition made her too feel sad.

People thought his excessive weeping day and night quite strange. His mother and her husband, Lord Taishō, were visibly upset by his condition and inquired about the cause of this strange behavior, but he apparently thought it too difficult to explain.

He told Taishō no Kimi he would have to absent himself occasionally.

"Recently I decided I must find a secluded place in which to recite the sutras in tranquillity. It is annoying to have people fussing, and Lord Taishō and the others always questioning why I have begun this period of fasting. I think I will find a place where people will not always be watching me."

He left his house and went to Yoshinohime's quarters where he spent an inordinate amount of time watching Wakagimi romp about. Unable to sleep a wink at night, he would mournfully read the sutras until dawn.

While Yoshinohime had never met the Consort, she often imagined this sister of hers living in another land, and the realization that she might now be dead made her feel terribly forlorn. She was upset and saddened to see her only benefactor in such despair, but did her best to hide her tears.

Chūnagon was touched by the deep concern reflected in her face, and his affection for her grew even stronger. With the usual screen no longer separating them, he would lie by her side day and night, reciting the sutras and talking endlessly of the Consort's words and appearance. Together they wept a constant stream of tears; he offered her words of comfort and was, in turn, charmed by the deep concern she showed in sympathizing with his sorrows.

"I really want to renounce this world and find a retreat in the mountains," he told her. "You alone keep me tied to this life, unable to fulfill my wish."

He vowed his deep and everlasting affection as she lay quietly by his side, listening intently to his words. Taking a brush she casually wrote a charming poem.

> I fear we may part
> Before our time has come,
> Even though we know each other
> As reminders of her.

He replied tenderly,
> With this grief
> I cannot expect to be here long.
> Do you know
> For whom I struggle on?

The exchange was serious and yet delightful, and they wept, then smiled together. The deep affection of this exchange served to lift their spirits and soon they felt much more at ease in each other's company. She was beautiful and far more genteel than one would expect of a person raised in distant mountains. Though timid, she was no less appealing than a clever woman with many charms; he could not find fault with her, for she was superb in every way.

In temperament she was much like Taishō no Kimi. But the latter was, in spite of her closeness to Chūnagon, so irreproachably correct in her behavior that she often made Chūnagon feel embarrassed. For the most part Taishō no Kimi was friendly and candid with him, but her innermost feelings were often difficult to comprehend. At times she seemed aloof and distant, and she turned her back on his impassioned advances, rejecting them as unreasonable and inappropriate for one in her position. Even when he felt overwhelmed with emotion and ignored for a moment her guarded reserve, he could not forget that she had already entered into the path of service to the Buddha, and it was not possible to follow the simple dictates of his heart. He could, on the other hand, be more at ease with Yoshinohime, for he need not fear treating her lightly.

"My life is one of grief," he thought, "but as long as I must endure in this world, she is the only one I can turn to for even the slightest comfort." Indeed, she was the only comfort for his endless tears and sorrow.

While he kept his affection for the Hoyang Consort deep in his heart, he always treated Yoshinohime with the utmost kindness. Even a person with a heart of wood or stone could see he loved her. In time Yoshinohime came to place absolute trust in him, and this only served to increase his affection.

"For a long time I wondered why I never had a sister," he thought. "Often I imagined what a joy it would be to watch over her carefully and talk of anything that troubled us. But even with a real sister there are limits: it is hard to be as close as one would like! This girl is different, for together we can speak our deepest thoughts. Were it not for her I might not have lived to see this day, for when I left my dearest love in China and returned to find the only person I cared for in my own land had turned her back on me, I felt I would not live to see my grief go away. Life has a limit set by fate, but I did not expect to live through those days. Though I cannot forget the Consort or Taishō no Kimi for a moment, Yoshinohime's company has sustained me. Her unsurpassed beauty has been a small consolation for my troubled heart."

Ever since Prince Shikibukyō suspected there were "hidden places for the waves of Toko Bay" he had kept a close and curious watch on Chūnagon's behavior. He was particularly intrigued by words from a reliable informant.

"Chūnagon found a woman in the mountains of Yoshino," the man reported. "He was defiled by the death of the woman's mother and stayed in seclusion for a long time before bringing the woman back to the capital. Now he has her hidden and seems very fond of her."

The Prince was interested.

"What sort of person could he have found in Mt. Yoshino?" he wondered. "I suppose she is not undesirable, because he would not bother over an ordinary woman. He has seen the best women of China. She must be an extraordinary woman for him to struggle through the snows of Yoshino. Come to think of it, he did say extraordinary women are sometimes discovered hidden in the mountains. Why didn't I consider the mountains of Yoshino?

"The women I believed would meet my fancy, even the ones I searched hard for, have been disappointing. Chūnagon always seems so unaffected, yet he was fortunate enough to find this woman in such an unexpected location.

"It was the same with Taishō no Kimi. I had spent many years pursuing her with all my heart, and the marriage was set; but then he wooed her without any hesitation, even though he was a close relative, and caused her to renounce the world. That did not seem to bother him and even now she cares for him deeply. When I heard they were still together I wanted very much to get a glimpse of her, even though she is a nun. I tried everything to meet her, slipping into her mansion, eavesdropping, peeking through the fence, but I never heard a single word from her. I could not even see her ladies-in-waiting when they came out of the house. Her behavior was really quite irritating. It pains me to think that he alone now has her as a private source of consolation. I hope at least to see this new woman."

His closest retainers soon bore the brunt of the Prince's anger which arose from his insatiable curiosity. They were, in fact, dismayed that they had not searched in Yoshino. Soon they inquired discreetly about the girl and sent some men to find out where she was, but these men found it difficult to speak with anyone connected with her.

During the fifth month Yoshinohime became quite ill. Chūnagon fretted over her and tried every sort of prayer and incantation, but nothing seemed to work. With the coming of the summer heat she grew more thin and pale, but this only served to enhance her beauty. Chūnagon wished that he could suffer in her place, but the sixth month passed with no change. When her condition failed to improve he decided to take her on a retreat to Kiyomizu Temple in the seventh month. Prince Shikibukyō's men, who had been shadowing her, got wind of the move and reported to their master.

"She has gone to Kiyomizu Temple. It is impossible to approach her at home because of all the people, so this is your chance!"

They took the Prince to Kiyomizu Temple where, somehow or other, he caught a glimpse of her. How could he fail to be enthralled? He was surprised to find that such a lovely woman existed, for she was far more beautiful than he had imagined. He noticed that the boy referred to her as "mother."

"She seems so very young and frail, yet already she has a child. Chūnagon obviously did not just meet her recently!" he thought knowingly. "There can be only one reason for keeping this child hidden so long: he does not want to hurt Taishō no Kimi. What unusual devotion he must have for her to keep this beautiful young lady hidden so long."

The Prince's sudden desire to see Taishō no Kimi made him forget for a moment the lovely girl before his very eyes. Such are the ways of a man obsessed with love.

"No matter how well I plead my case it would be difficult to win the girl's love now that she is so accustomed to Chūnagon's deep devotion. I might feel ashamed and pity Chūnagon if he were to hear I had stolen her away, but what else can I do? A person should only worry about criticism and gossip in minor matters; this is something special. I must take her for my own."

Chūnagon, ignorant of the Prince's plan, arrived at Kiyomizu Temple. The girl had been suffering so long during the heat she was now painfully weak and fragile, but the frailty of her face simply enhanced her radiant beauty. The delight she showed at Chūnagon's visit was quite charming. He had considered joining her in seclusion, but that might make his concern seem too exaggerated. He decided instead to ask the Buddha to protect her in his absence. He told her how worried and lonely he would be away from her, then met with her attendants who were disturbed by her condition.

"She hasn't had a fever for the past four or five days, but night after night she seems in pain," they told him. "She hasn't eaten, not a bite, not even fruit or things like that."

"Continue the rites of incantation a while and try to keep her in good spirits. Then perhaps she can return in a few days."

He turned again to the girl.

"Wretched as I am, if I can feel more at ease on your account I shall have a reason to go on living. If you want me to go on living please try to eat something. You can cheer up, can't you?"

Being away from her the past few days had made him despondent; his longing and uncertainty were unrelenting and difficult to bear. The sight of her beauty now made him shed genuine tears of sorrow, and this moved her deeply.

She was always embarrassed by the presence of strangers, yet now she found herself unexpectedly in their midst. It was lamentable yet unavoidable, for there was no one else to turn to. Chūnagon was the only person she felt comfortable with. She too was grieved by the uncertainty of the past few days spent apart, and touched that their sentiments were so alike. The sight of her weeping face buried in her sleeve would have brought tears to even a wild barbarian. She seemed almost painfully attractive and lovable.

Chūnagon spent the day by her side, talking and caring for her, but that night, the twenty-first, he was forced to leave because of a directional taboo. The echo of the evening bell in the cool mountain breeze seemed like that of Mt. Yoshino. He paused momentarily, unable to leave abruptly.

Do you remember?
Now is no less sorrowful
Than that evening
In the shade of the mountains.

Though in pain she lifted herself enough to see him off. Her poem made it even more difficult to leave.

How sad that the wind should sound
Like the pine breeze in the peaks
I knew so well.

The affection binding these two together was extraordinary, but unfortunately the sun was setting and he had to leave. Just then, as might be expected, Prince Shikibukyō was making reckless plans to steal the girl away that very night.

One wonders what will happen next.

Chapter Five

ALTHOUGH there never was a moment when Chūnagon did not regard Yoshinohime with unusual affection, that night the memory of her sad farewell lingered in his heart and stirred his breast. After a night of prayer he sent her a note with the first light of dawn. The reply came from Shinano: "Something terrible has happened and we are bewildered. I must tell you the details personally."

The writing was an agitated scrawl. Puzzled, he secretly hurried to Kiyomizu Temple where he found every one of the servants dazed and weeping. Shinano explained what had happened.

"After you left, the girl complained of feeling worse than usual and seemed quite despondent. Thinking it might be a fever I had the priests perform incantations. She did not seem in pain and finally fell asleep. Everyone else dozed off, but when we awoke the next morning she was gone. I have no idea what happened."

Chūnagon was shocked. "She would never have slipped away on her own," he reasoned. "Someone who caught a glimpse of her must have spirited her away, someone who knew when she would be unguarded. Some of her servants could have been in on it. They might have planned it secretly, then executed the scheme when they didn't accompany her to Kiyomizu Temple."

The servants still present were weeping so violently he assumed they were ignorant of the scheme. But then, one or two might have known.

"She could not have disappeared into thin air. Someone must know where she is," he groaned, but it was useless to simply sit and talk about it.

"The gossip will be unbearable; I'll look like a fool," he told Shinano. "But what can I do? It was fate. You, however, must not say anything. Just leave at dawn as if she were going back with you."

For a moment he seemed to get a hold of himself, but as soon as he remembered her tender farewell of the night before he could no longer restrain his tears nor calm his troubled heart.

He was further tormented by Wakagimi's searching cries for his "mother," and the very sight of her room and furniture made him feel inauspiciously wretched. Though people were certain to become suspicious, he could not conceal his grief. Day and night he pondered what had happened, trying as best he could to control his weeping.

Some likely suspect must have kidnapped her, but who? He suspected Prince Shikibukyō or one of the Chancellor's sons—no one else would think of such a scheme. No matter who it was, once the man saw her he would not treat her unkindly. She was not one to be abused. Chūnagon had devoted himself to caring for the girl, even while he was lost in tears over the ill-fated vows with Taishō no Kimi and the Consort. In Yoshinohime his heart had found the comfort and solace necessary to persevere. But even if the girl is terribly distraught by her abduction, once the vows of love are sealed, she might grow fond of her captor. Perhaps she now dismissed Chūnagon as an ineffectual fool. His heart was breaking, but she might have already forgotten him.

Annoyed and irritated, he felt as if his life were now coming to an end. He tried to hide his feelings from others by treating the matter lightly when he found her ladies weeping and talking of the incident.

"We're sure to hear from her soon. You must not think she has disappeared completely."

But nothing could compare to the unspoken grief in his heart as he mourned the loss of the girl.

"Although my experiences in China were long ago and in a distant land, I will never know another love like the Consort. Yoshinohime brought the memory of China to life, but now even she is lost."

He was near death with worry yet managed somehow to continue on. Convinced that one or two of the ladies-in-waiting must have known what happened to her, he bore with his grief. He prayed unswervingly for her safe return; not for a moment could he forget her lovely face the times they sat together, he intoning the scriptures in a strong, intense voice, she resting her writing brush to listen carefully. Now whenever he dozed off for only a moment she would appear in his dream, lying by his side and weeping heavily as if on the verge of collapsing.

"For a while she is certain to be beside herself with fear, no matter who abducted her. I wonder if she thinks of me?" His heart beat faster and his chest tightened with grief almost too painful to bear. When he was troubled in the past she had always been close at hand; together they would laugh and weep, finding consolation for their unusual sorrows. Now he was alone and sad, cast in utter darkness with no desire to continue in the world. Nurse Chūjō grieved to see him in such despair. Discreetly she investigated Yoshinohime's disappearance and reported her findings to him.

"A recent addition to the girl's attendants, Kochūjō no Kimi, is young and attractive, and she has received letters from Ōidono's son San'i no Chūjō.[1] I understand his page brought the letters here. After Yoshinohime went to Kiyomizu Temple, Kochūjō no Kimi became ill and has not returned from her home for a long time. Perhaps it was their doing."

"Perhaps it was," Chūnagon said softly. Not surprising, he thought, considering how beautiful she was; but still, what a selfish, insatiable philanderer the man was. If an ascetic monk living in a cave were but to hear of Yoshinohime's beauty or see her in a dream, he could not help being stirred. How much more so a young gentleman such as San'i no Chūjō! What others think after the fact would not disturb him in the least. While Chūnagon expected such behavior from a man like San'i no Chūjō, it still irritated him and nothing could calm his troubled heart.

"Somehow I must search for her and bring her back, even if people think me insane," he decided.

His once tranquil mind was now in complete disarray, his thoughts always sad. He had presumed himself different from others, but now found a single tie with the Consort had led to grief in both China and Japan. It was disquieting.

> Why must I grieve so
> In a world no more constant
> Than the shimmering of heat waves?

While preoccupied with these concerns, Chūnagon had not visited Daini's daughter for a long time. From the twelfth month she had

---

1. Ōidono is a general name of respect meaning "Great Minister" and was usually limited to the Prime Minister and the Ministers of the Left, Right, and Center. San'i no Chūjō is a title meaning "Third-Ranked Middle Captain of the Inner Palace Guard." The rank was specified here because the Middle Captain was normally of the fourth rank.

been suffering the symptoms of pregnancy. Others would never have guessed, of course, but in her heart she felt certain the child was Chūnagon's.

Except for an occasional letter she heard nothing from him after the second month of the new year. As her time drew close Emon no Kami would not leave her for even a moment. He was worried about her health and prayed and cared for her, but she paid little attention to his ministrations. She was thinking only of her seemingly indifferent Chūnagon. Yearning to see him once again she sent a note.

> What is to become of me
> In this web of grief?
> No one bothers to ask
> If I am alive or dead.[2]

"I might expect to live on in this world . . ."

Chūnagon was so engrossed with Yoshinohime's disappearance he had neglected to write for a long time. With pity he quickly sent his reply.

> Though I may not always ask in words
> How you are,
> Never do my thoughts stop reaching out
> To encircle you.[3]

Daini's wife was with her daughter that night, thus making it impossible for Chūnagon to visit, so he spent the night at his grandfather's mansion.[4] But when Emon no Kami went early the next morning to greet the Chancellor returning from Ishiyama, Chūnagon took the opportunity to visit Daini's daughter. The tall and slender figure of the young woman now swelled unattractively at the abdomen. She seemed in great pain, sad and disconcerted, but this only enhanced her delicate charm. Gazing at her, Chūnagon could

2. The first line of this poem, *sasaganino*, is a pillow word modifying the first syllable of *ika* (*i*). *Sasagani* means "spider," and *i* means "web."

3. In the fourth line of this poem, *kumode no omoi-*, Chūnagon takes up the spider imagery of the girl's poem. A literal translation of the last two lines might be,

Never do my thoughts not reach out [to you] / Like spider legs.

4. Daijō no Taishōdono in the text is probably a corruption of Taishō no Ōidono and refers to the mansion of Chūnagon's maternal grandfather (now surely deceased). Since the man is also Emon no Kami's father, Emon no Kami might have spent his time there when he was not with Daini's daughter. This would explain how Chūnagon was to discover that Emon no Kami had gone to greet the Chancellor the next day.

not help imagining that the missing girl too was quite this vulnerable. His pity for Daini's daughter was greater than usual.

"You may have heard that I am troubled by a dream indicating I might not be in this world much longer. I vowed to spend my time solely in fasting and prayer until I pass away. Not for a moment did my concern for you diminish, but if, in this small world, we were seen together, my close relative Emon no Kami would surely think my behavior despicable. That would be unfortunate for you as well as me. Only this kept me from seeing you."

His deep concern, evident in the tears which filled his eyes, was more tender and moving than usual. How depressing it will be, she thought, to be left with only the memory of this man once he leaves. Even though she knew how disgusting she must appear to him, she wept unceasingly as she stared listlessly outside. In the moonlight at dawn she seemed noble as usual, yet gently approachable. He watched her tenderly, but with the coming of morning he felt obliged to leave.

> Would that this were not
> The way we meet.
> Why in this world
> Must there be partings at dawn?

"Will the day come when we can meet quietly without always hurrying to part?"

He paused on leaving to give her one more poem.

> I know how cruel
> These dawn partings can be.
> Still each time I feel lost.

On the way home that morning his thoughts lay particularly heavy on his heart. The road led him past the home of Emon no Kami's first wife, where he heard the faint sound of the thirteen-stringed koto.

The music was beautiful. He remembered well the woman's words the night Emon no Kami took his new wife. "If crying would help . . . ,"[5] she had chided her ladies.

It occurred to him that since this woman was the daughter of

5. See translation, p. 156.

214

Sochi no Miya, she would be related to the missing girl.[6] Unable to pass by, he slipped into the grounds and from a spot where the earth embankment was crumbling peered into the house through the early morning mist. The woman seated near the raised blinds had apparently been up all night. She played the koto with casual familiarity as she stared at the garden. Perhaps it was the setting that made her seem so splendid. She was quite relaxed, not for a moment suspecting someone was watching. Her figure, faintly visible, was slim though not bedraggled, her face seemed slender and pale, but she bore no likeness at all to the lovely girl he sought to compare her with. Disappointed, he now understood why Emon no Kami had switched his affection so unabashedly, for Daini's daughter in the moonlight was far more beautiful than this woman. Still, as she plucked absentmindedly at the koto she did have a certain elegance about her. Chūnagon was confident he could never abandon a woman so completely, leaving her to waste like scattered weeds. Emon no Kami's heart, however, was apparently drawn only by the beauty that meets the eye. Chūnagon pitied the poor woman. While he could understand Emon no Kami's desires, he wondered how a man could treat a woman so cruelly. He found it difficult to leave this field of grass.

> These weeds bear no resemblance
> To fields of violet,
> Yet I feel affinity
> For one of the same root.[7]

"Sochi no Miya must have raised this lady carefully in hopes that he might give her to the Emperor, even though she is truly without charm. She is nothing like the daughters of the Yoshino nun, born here and in China. The nun's fate was indeed quite extraordinary. Only Yoshinohime can remind me of the Consort."

Obviously nothing could be done about the Consort in China, but the worry and longing he felt for the girl lost in his own land caused him incomparable anxiety.

6. Emon no Kami's first wife and Yoshinohime had the same father, but different mothers.
7. Alluding to poem #867, *Kokinshū*, anonymous:
Because of one single *murasaki* plant / All the grasses of Musashino / Are dear to me.

Yoshinohime had, he remembered, considered Kochūjō no Kimi one of her closest attendants. He sent for her and asked if she had seen the girl receiving letters from suspicious characters.

"I saw no letters other than the ones you yourself sent," she replied.

Kochūjō no Kimi seemed as troubled as anyone about the girl's disappearance, but he was still worried enough to look through Yoshinohime's letter boxes himself. There were drawings and practice sheets of calligraphy, but nothing suggesting any clandestine affair. Two poems apparently referred to the falling of spring blossoms.

> The flowers of the capital
> Scatter as in a storm—
> I am too familiar with
> The snows of Mt. Yoshino.

> Imagining those distant hills
> I wonder if the snows
> On the road to Mt. Yoshino
> Have melted yet?

There was a letter he had sent from the palace when she was ill.

"Are you perhaps feeling a little better today? Right now I am terribly upset and worried about you. If you care for me you must know how happy I would be to hear you were eating and getting some rest."

She must have been moved by the letter, for at the bottom she had added a poem.

> How could I have thought
> This world so vile
> I would not go on living?
> At times my heart thinks only of him.

"Though my life is worthless . . ."

This and another poem she had scribbled over and over again in the margin:

> Even if I were
> Among the clouds
> From the smoke of Toribeno
> Could I forget you for a moment?[8]

---

8. Toribeno is a place of cremation and burial in the Higashiyama district of Kyoto.

Her practice poems were all in the same vein.

"She cared for me deeply," he mused, his eyes darkening with tears. At first she had been too mortified to face him directly, but as she grew accustomed to his presence and entrusted herself to him completely she came to care for him deeply; perhaps she thought there was nothing else to do, no one else to care for her. He felt terribly lonesome as he recalled the nights she would wait up late, thinking he would come. As he wiped away the tears with her scraps of writing paper, he noticed that since coming from Yoshino she had secretly tried to imitate his handwriting; her calligraphy resembled his closely, but still had her own charming touch.

"How magnificent she is at everything. And I thought she might belong to someone else!"

His painful regrets were overwhelming. The moon was bright and the sound of the wind gentle as he sat alone in thought. How difficult it was to bear with his yearning for nights like this when they lay together looking at the moon.

"If San'i no Chūjō was the one who took her they certainly wouldn't be looking at the moon tonight. They would be sleeping together in pleasant intimacy. She is so compliant I'm sure he's getting his way. Perhaps it has not even occurred to her that I sit here alone lost in sorrow."

He felt terribly depressed, but could think of no one but her.

> She does not even remember me,
> Yet in her old home
> The moon shines clear to amuse me.

"Dreams after a night of frost[9] . . . ," he murmured to himself before dozing off. In a dream that night the Hoyang Consort appeared as she did the night of the chrysanthemum-viewing and spoke to him.

"Because of your prayers that we be together in the same land even if it meant rebirth, my life ended earlier than expected and I am now in heaven for a brief time. Because I too long for you, I am soon to be lodged in the womb of the girl you now grieve for. I followed the example of the Medicine King religiously, but both

9. From couplet #702, *Wakan Rōeishū*. Wang Chao-chün:
The sound of a horn flute after dreams of a frosty night; / the Han Court is ten thousand miles away as I watch the moon anxiously.

you and I were fettered by a strange, unyielding passion: I must be reborn as a woman."[10]

He then awoke, his eyes drowned in tears. When he realized it was but a dream he felt frustrated, and could not restrain his tears even when fully awake. His mind seemed to be drifting in a sea of tears and he felt terribly confused.

"I have misgivings about dreams and illusions," he reasoned, "but maybe she really has died. My wish had been that I might be reborn with her. I never wanted one so luminous and beautiful as she, the very light of this world, to change."

Still disturbed when dawn arrived, he had sutras read in various temples and renewed his own prayers more vigorously.

"Will I ever see her again?" he sighed. "The young girl who caused me such grief is fated to be loved by someone else! I never imagined Yoshinohime could belong to another man. In what sort of person's house would she be now? No one knew of her but me; how could he have heard of her and found her? She is so compliant, if he but stays with her and treats her kindly he will surely gain her confidence. And even if she causes him grief, I suppose he will still try hard to care for her."

After that dream he could think of nothing but Yoshinohime, worrying day and night what might become of her.

In the meantime, Daini's daughter had with little difficulty given birth to a boy. Emon no Kami's proud rejoicing merely saddened her, for she remembered too well the secret dawn meeting with Chūnagon. Chūnagon too felt pity for Emon no Kami when he heard how the child delighted the supposed father. Publicly Chū-nagon sent appropriate congratulations, but secretly he sent the mother children's clothes with a poem attached.

> With whom do you suppose
> That vow was tied?
> Have you forgotten
> The dream we shared?

This time she was particularly vexed at not being able to respond immediately. A full week after the birth she still worried about what to say to him, for she was ashamed to respond too directly to the

10. The story of the Bodhisattva Medicine King is found in Chapter Twenty-three of the Lotus Sutra.

implications of his poem. She could not have one of her ladies reply, but it would be a pity to keep Chūnagon in doubt too long. In a delicate, faint script she sent her answer.

Even considering that dream
From which your note awoke me,
What I find truly sad
Is my fate in this life.

She felt so disturbed she could not tell dream from reality. She did not, however, lack affection for the child who reminded her of the handsome Chūnagon.

With the death of the heir apparent it was certain Prince Shiki-bukyō would become the new Crown Prince. The Emperor gravely warned him about his profligate behavior: "It will not do for you to be indulging in this wanton behavior at your mansion."

In the seventh month he had Prince Shikibukyō move into the palace, thus making it more difficult for the Prince to spend time with Yoshinohime. The Prince had hoped to take her directly from Kiyomizu Temple to the palace, into the Plum Room of the night duty quarters, where people might mistake her for one of the many ladies-in-waiting living in that area.

The night of the abduction had been terrifying. After Yoshinohime had seen Chūnagon off, she lay for a while staring blankly into space. She felt unsettled, weak, and distressed. Just after she fell asleep a cloth was thrown over her face and she felt herself being carried away. Something seemed to be attacking her and yet she felt certain she must be dreaming. When she was being lifted into a cart, however, she awoke gradually from her dream.

She wondered what was happening. Faint and unresponsive from almost the beginning, she seemed on the verge of dying. Prince Shikibukyō suspected that she was so frightened because she did not know who he was. Out of pity he decided to reveal his name.

"Since you will probably find out anyway, I will tell you: I am Prince Shikibukyō."

The very man Chūnagon had warned of! She had been told time and time again that he would surely try to sway her. On hearing his name she thought first of Chūnagon's reaction.

"This is terrible. Just as he feared. What will Chūnagon think?"

She had been ill for so many months, how could she now find

the strength to bear the anguish of this abduction? Any number of times her breathing seemed to stop.

Prince Shikibukyō had caught a faint glimpse of her before, but up close she seemed a thousand times more beautiful. No wonder even Chūnagon, who had loved the brilliant Hoyang Consort, would on finding this girl watch her constantly as his life's consolation. And what of Prince Shikibukyō who had searched everywhere for such a beauty? Hearing of some outstanding woman he would investigate closely only to discover she was not exactly what he was looking for, even if she had no conspicuous faults. He had, however, never seen a woman with such limitless beauty. Her face was not powdered and her hair fell casually over her shoulders, but not a single strand seemed out of place. It flowed like water and spread out abundantly like a fan. Her face was covered with a stream of tears, but the beauty of this young lady hovering between life and death seemed to Prince Shikibukyō more stunning than if he had actually seen a celestial maiden descend from the heavens. This, he thought, must be Chūnagon's "secret of Toko Bay."[11] But still she seemed unfamiliar with the ways of love.

"How could this be?" he wondered. "Except for one's own sister, how could a man have such a beautiful woman close at hand, be intimate with her day and night, yet not love her? Even a Buddhist monk would find that difficult. But I did hear the little boy call her 'mother.' What could that mean? Perhaps I have taken the wrong person—a sister perhaps who only resembles Chūnagon's lover." He was all too familiar with his own incontinent ways to think of any other possibility.

"I must have taken his lover's sister by mistake. I didn't notice anyone else, but perhaps one of the women was hidden when I watched them. With that brief glimpse I could only tell that she was very beautiful; to be sure, I could not see her clearly. Perhaps I did take the wrong girl. But beauty has its limits: the other one could be no better than this one." He did not feel worse off for his mistake.

The love once bestowed so widely now came to concentrate on this girl alone. But when would she regain consciousness? he wondered. She was so incomparably beautiful that he could not leave

11. See translation p. 200.

her for a moment, but when he tried to soothe her with promises of love she was not consoled. She thought of Chūnagon every day.

"Has he heard what happened?" she wondered. "Perhaps right now he is thinking: 'So she did it! In spite of my warning she gave her heart to the Prince and was stolen away.' Since he told me this might happen, he must be particularly irked. And if he doesn't know who took me, he must wonder where I am. He once vowed that if he could not see me often he would surely die. Perhaps he is already dead!"

She recalled his words with childish affection and concern. Her life seemed fragile as a bubble, but she was too dejected to take medicine. Prince Shikibukyō grieved for her but felt helpless; he tried to console her with every possible promise of devotion, but she was for the most part unaffected by his words and oblivious to his care.

As she lay half conscious in what seemed not quite a dream she often sensed Chūnagon was near, but when she opened her eyes to see if he were there, a stranger sat weeping at her side. In the end she seemed beyond hope, no longer able to distinguish dreams from reality. Prince Shikibukyō lamented helplessly; in spite of his many experiences with women he was unaccustomed to spending himself so thoroughly on one woman. He simply did not know how to care for her.

"This may continue for a while," he tried to tell himself, "but in time she will warm to me and be consoled like any other woman." But the girl grew weaker and seemed beyond saving. Though determined not to let anyone know of her, he alone was unable to help her. He even thought that perhaps the Buddha and the gods had decreed this outcome in anger over his dissolute behavior.

In the meantime, everyone was hoping he would soon be designated Crown Prince. The Chancellor's daughter was to undergo her coming-of-age ceremony in the tenth month, and the whole country was busy in preparation for her anticipated betrothal to Prince Shikibukyō. He, however, could think only of Yoshinohime.

"If she dies I will immediately renounce this life and go live in the wilds. What would the rank of Emperor mean to me?"

Seemingly incapable of continuing without her, he too lay sick in bed unable to eat anything. His nurse and closest attendants

221

understood the problem, but the Prince had thrown such a veil of secrecy over the whole affair they were reluctant to discuss it with anyone. All they could do was pity him.

The Prince's condition finally came to the attention of the Emperor. Attributing this unusual behavior to a possession, he had many prayers said on behalf of the Prince. This sudden burst of activity in itself caused such a stir Prince Shikibukyō's nurse finally had to talk to her master.

"Now that you yourself are so despondent, even if you can keep this a secret today, you cannot conceal it forever. It is a most inopportune time to be in this predicament. You must get hold of yourself. Surely there is someone in her home the girl would like to have notified. Why don't you have whoever it is come comfort the girl?"

Her suggestion was reasonable, for he did not know how best to care for the girl. Indeed, he thought, perhaps she is upset because she doesn't have anyone familiar with her. Moving his face close to hers, he spared no tears in pleading with her.

"Every day I waited, hoping that your illness would eventually abate and you might find some comfort, but your condition has only worsened. This is very sorrowful indeed. It is particularly sad for me to wonder what bonds in a former life have brought this terrible fate upon us. I thought of running away and hiding before I would be forced to witness the nightmarish fate which is sure to befall you, but it would be cruel to desert you and die while you are lost and all alone. I want to notify someone at your home, someone who might be worried about you, but whom shall I look for, and where?"

She understood his words but could not answer directly, for she hoped to die before Chūnagon discovered she had been abducted by this man. "When Chūnagon finds me buried in a plain of weeds," she fretted silently, "his feelings for me will not be shallow, even though I have disappointed him. I am sure he will have lost all sense of disgust and estrangement by then."

Truly she seemed too weak to live through that very day. Still, it was a shame to drift off endlessly, for she did want to see Chūnagon once again and be seen by him. When she was drifting aimlessly after the death of the parent she relied on, Chūnagon had looked after her with unusual affection and devotion. In her frail heart she knew how sad it would be to die without seeing him again. She could not bear to pass up the opportunity Prince Shikibukyō offered her.

"Please tell Chūnagon," she whispered under her breath. For the past few months, even in his dreams, the Prince had not heard a response from her for all the words he spoke. She was still terribly weak, but he was delighted to see that the lovely way she spoke was no less attractive than when she was silent.

"I should have asked sooner. But there are many Chūnagons. Which one should I contact? Gen Chūnagon?"

Though barely moving she seemed to nod faintly.

"What is he to you?" he asked sharply. "For my own sake I should know before telling him."

She was on the verge of fading away, like snow scattered on water, and could not answer him. It was senseless to press her anymore. The Prince considered her request.

"Even though she is not married to Chūnagon, when she is this distraught she asks for him. What is the extent of their relationship? Apparently she is not bothered by what he might think of her predicament. If she were, she would not want him to see her now. There must be some reason for her answer."

He entrusted one of his closest retainers with a note to Chūnagon which read: "I have something very important to tell you right away. Please come immediately."

The retainer was given strict instructions for delivering the message. "I haven't heard anything of Gen Chūnagon's whereabouts these past few months, but find out where he is and tell him I have something I must tell him in person before the day is out. Bring him here immediately."

The man bowed and left immediately to search for Chūnagon.

Chūnagon meanwhile had grown weary of his own mansion and gone to Yoshinohime's quarters where he hoped the fields surrounded by the familiar bamboo fence might remind him of her. It was a night in the ninth month: the garden vegetation was withering, the sky seemed lonely, and the pampas grass swayed with the wind as if beckoning Chūnagon to follow. His heart pounded faster as he entered the familiar house.

Since I have no way to find her,
I'll let the flowers of the pampas grass
Be a sleeve to beckon me.

He had grown accustomed to the aura of beauty that seemed to surround her, and the loneliness which he now felt only increased his longing. Every day Wakagimi would ask for his "mother." "When will she come back? I want to go to Kiyomizu Temple," he cried. These words made her inexplicable disappearance even more difficult for Chūnagon to bear.

"She must still be alive," he thought. "When I find out where she is, and I don't care who has her, I will tell him I am the only one with unbreakable ties to her. Even if he were someone who knew about the girl, and no one other than the monk of Mt. Yoshino really knows her true past, could anyone question my right to take her back? No matter what might have happened to her, if I get her back and take care of her, watch after her closely, I will be content." These thoughts were reassuring if not completely convincing.

"In spite of my devotion, the dark side of her spirit might be swayed, and she could become enamored of a man who exchanged true vows of love with her. What a pity if he were to tell her I was just a false and foolish friend. But surely she is too kind and gentle to believe that. Perhaps this man who took her will fail to become intimate with her."

Day and night, waking or sleeping, he could think of nothing but her. That evening he sat staring emptily when Prince Shikibukyō's man arrived.

"The Prince has something he must tell you in private."

Chūnagon was surprised. "What is it?"

"Prince Shikibukyō instructed me to give you this letter and take you to him right away, before the day is over."

Tilting his head slightly in bewilderment, Chūnagon wondered about this hasty summons.

"I have been ill since the seventh month," he reflected, "and have not been going out much; there have not, after all, been any special ceremonies demanding my attendance. It has been quite a while since I saw the Prince, but I wonder why he went to the trouble to send for me? Where is the Prince?"

"In his palace," the retainer responded.

Chūnagon sent the man back to tell Prince Shikibukyō that he would soon be there. He arrived around dusk, still mystified as to why the Prince sent for him directly. He was led into the Prince's private chambers.

"As I tell you what has happened," the Prince began, "I am all too aware that the consequences of my foolish and irresponsible negligence are unavoidable, but that cannot be helped now. For the past few months I have been caring for a woman whose name I do not even know. It is like a dream.

"Is there any woman who would not feel wretched if she found herself in such an unexpected situation? Probably not. But even when a woman feels distraught, my experience has been that as the man gets to know her better, she will eventually become resigned to her position. But I do not know about this woman. From the time I first saw her until this very moment she has lived each day almost as if she were dead, barely breathing or moving. I waited, thinking this could not go on for long and the time would come when she, like anyone else, would respond normally. But her condition only worsened and she seems beyond saving. Perhaps, I thought, there is someone at her home she wishes to contact, but I had no way of even knowing her name.

"The length of a person's life is difficult to determine and I feared she might die soon. Still, it was not something to tell strangers. If I could find her family, I thought, her troubled heart might find some comfort. I knew that they would be disturbed that so much time had passed without their knowing her condition, and I expected their indignation to be troublesome, but today she seems to be near the very end. I begged her to tell me whom I should approach, and how and where I might find them. She was finally able to say under her breath, 'Tell Chūnagon.' I said, 'There are so many Chūnagons—which one? Gen Chūnagon?' She was barely able to nod her assent. I feared what you might think of me on hearing this, but I realized you must be told. 'Indeed,' I thought, 'she must be known to you. Here she is, completely distraught, virtually unconscious, and with all her heart she wants you to be called.' I could not stand it any more, so I sent for you."

He tried to suppress his emotions, but his endless stream of tears bore witness to his unusual concern for the girl.

Chūnagon had been under the impression that Prince Shikibukyō had mended his ways and was living peacefully. He had suspected only San'i no Chūjō and could hardly believe the Prince's words. As he collected his own thoughts, he wondered how very precious she must have been when in that moment of distress she asked the Prince to find him.

"Prince Shikibukyō is probably unaware of the girl's background," he reasoned. "When he sent me the poem about Toko Bay he must have surmised that she was with me, and then he decided to steal her, just as I feared might happen. I suppose he wondered what it meant when he found that she was chaste. She had him bring me here because she does not want to leave me; even though she has been taken by him I must not let him think I feel the slightest bit estranged from her."

Many thoughts passed through his mind before he finally answered the Prince.

"While I was in China, the Prince of T'ang described aspects of our country so vividly it was as if he were seeing them in a mirror. He told me that while he was secretly frequenting the house of the daughter of a Prince from Kōzuke, she bore him a daughter.[12] The child was very dear to him, but her mother became angry about something and disappeared, taking the girl with her, and the Prince of T'ang never saw her again. After he was reborn in China he worried about his daughter. He said that if I remembered him and cared for him, I should fulfill his one request: find the girl if she is still alive and protect her. When I returned I learned that her mother had renounced the world and was living at the foot of Mt. Yoshino. While I was there, during the winter of last year, the mother died. Since I could not leave the girl alone in the snowbound mountains I brought her to the capital. I knew I could not immediately reveal her story to everyone, but I kept her nearby as a tender reminder of the past, day and night worrying how one so incapable as myself could care for her. Since the fifth month she has been troubled by chills and fevers. She went to Kiyomizu Temple but her condition continued to deteriorate. Soon after that she was unexpectedly discovered by you, much to my shame; she is still very weak. I had

12. Chūnagon's fabricated story makes Yoshinohime his half sister.

hoped to show her to you after she became a bit more sophisticated in her ways."

Prince Shikibukyō did not doubt this explanation in the least. "It must be so," he thought, "for that would explain why he did no more than provide for the girl. Indeed, they do have a certain common beauty." It was interesting that he thought they looked alike!

He hurried to the girl's room, forgetting for a moment his shame and resentment that Chūnagon had found such a splendid person while his own searches had been in vain. The two ladies-in-waiting with her withdrew when Chūnagon entered the room.

"Chūnagon is here. Do you remember him?" Prince Shikibukyō asked.

She did not appear to be breathing. Her hair flowed abundantly off to her side and her frail body seemed almost nonexistent beneath her robes. Chūnagon was deeply disturbed by her weakened condition.

"Come closer to her," the Prince urged him.

Chūnagon moved next to her and lifted her head from the pillow. Though she seemed unconscious and completely beyond help he pressed close and called repeatedly.

"I'm here. Do you recognize me?"

She looked at him weakly and appeared to shed a tear, and this made Chūnagon's eyes darken with pity. He did not wish for her to see him in such anguish but his grief was beyond control.

"I never thought it would come to this," he said. "You poor helpless child. A person's fate is truly inexplicable. Your stay here has been unfortunate, but tonight I will take you back with me."

As Chūnagon ordered preparations for departure, Prince Shikibukyō, lost in tears, could do nothing. "My own selfish excesses have brought this upon us," he said. "My sins are unforgivable."

"All things happen as they must. You need not brood too heavily on it," Chūnagon reassured him. He sent a man to Shinano's with orders to bring a cart immediately. Even if he took her now he could not prevent the Prince from seeing her in the future. But as there was no way for Chūnagon to care for her at the palace, he decided to find a quiet place to minister to her needs.

A servant reported that Shinano had come for the girl. As Chūnagon prepared to leave quietly the Prince made as if to go with them. Chūnagon asked him to stay.

"Given your present position, your good name would suffer if you were discovered. Do not worry about the girl. It would be irregular for you to leave with her tonight."

It seemed but a dream when Chūnagon finally took her in his arms and carried her gently away. He was apprehensive of the monk's warning: fear that that prediction might now hold true loomed even greater than before Chūnagon had recovered the girl. When they arrived at Nurse Chūjō's house he took her inside without telling anyone and quietly drew a torch nearby to examine her closely. She was shockingly thin, like a shadow, so weak she seemed a different person, but the terrible ordeal had only increased her frail beauty. Helpless and depressed, Chūnagon noticed she was on the verge of losing her breath, completely unconscious. He sent for monks from his mansion to read sutras and pray that his request be heard. As he tearfully invoked the Nembutsu he wondered what bonds of karma had drawn him to the Consort's family and led him to this over-whelming sorrow.

Once the girl had left, Prince Shikibukyō grew more troubled over her condition. One night his uneasiness became too great, and he threw on a shabby disguise and secretly went to visit her.

Chūnagon awoke and let him in. Deferential niceties were for everyday situations; there was no need for ceremony in these circumstances. With a light at her bedside they wept together, ministering to her needs until dawn. Prince Shikibukyō would not leave her for a moment, but his position dictated that he guard his reputation carefully. Chūnagon saw him off with every assurance he would watch the girl faithfully. Once she had recovered, Chūnagon hoped he alone would determine the girl's future, but at that moment he felt a kinship of tears with the Prince. When it grew light he ordered the rites of incantation to begin.

The monk of Mt. Yoshino had not visited the capital in ten years, but Chūnagon sent for him and explained the situation. The monk was deeply shocked as he sat down near her pillow. Yoshinohime's mother had looked to him as her only support for this daughter. It was now clear to the monk how restricting were the nun's bonds in this temporal world. While intoning the awe-inspiring Lotus Sutra he recalled his own fervent prayers that someone would support the girl so her mother might find the path to salvation in her next life. Perhaps Yoshinohime heard the words of the Sutra, for even though she was still near death she seemed to recognize the monk's voice, as if in a dream, and tears formed in her eyes. She must know his voice, thought Chūnagon tenderly.

"Now is the period when you should be concentrating on rites of purification,"[13] he told her gently, "but you are in such a hopeless state. . . . I worried so while looking for you I completely neglected my other duties at a most inopportune time. You should try to bear with your illness and think about performing the proper rites."

Her mind was hardly clear enough to remember when the rites were to be held, but with his words she could faintly recall that the time was near at hand. She buried her face in her sleeve and wept profusely, for she did not know whether all this was real or a dream. Chūnagon, delighted to see she could now apparently remember some things, exhausted all possible means of prayer for her recovery.

Prince Shikibukyō came secretly each night and returned at dawn, worrying all day long about her uncertain condition. His complete neglect of his other ladies caused considerable consternation in many quarters. He tried in vain to conceal the anxious nights of prayer and ministration he spent at Chūnagon's.

Lord Taishō and his wife, who had known only that Chūnagon secretly kept a woman he cared for deeply, learned he had been grieving over the loss of that woman.

"Prince Shikibukyō is visiting him secretly every night," they told themselves. "He too shares Chūnagon's grief."

The two men had tried to hide their grief, but, like ducks in shallow water, it was apparent to all.[14]

Lord Taishō and his wife were confused and anxiously queried Chūnagon. Chūnagon was reluctant to tell them the same story he had told the Prince; but, on the other hand, it would be risky to change his story now, even if Lord Taishō and his wife were sworn

13. Possibly the rites of purification marking the end of the period of taboo on the first anniversary of her mother's death.
14. Alluding to poem #672, *Kokinshū*, anonymous:
In a pond there lives a duck / Known as the regretful bird; / It tries to hide in shallow waters, / But is visible to all.

229

to secrecy. He decided after all to tell them what he had told Prince Shikibukyō.

Chūnagon's mother had little reason to doubt the story of her former husband's lost child. "The late Prince loved me dearly," she reasoned, "but he did have many places of diversion. She could very well be his daughter. Strange that Chūnagon did not tell me until now."

Lord Taishō tried to reassure Prince Shikibukyō's wife: "The Prince knows everyone thinks highly of you. He is sure to learn of your feelings and mend his ways."

Since she was in no position to question her husband, the Prince, unreasonably about his behavior, she carried on as if she had heard nothing at all of his new infatuation. This was the first Lord Taishō had heard of his daughter's stoic resignation, and he pitied her greatly.

When first abducted, Yoshinohime was terribly frightened, seemingly set adrift in unknown spaces with only strangers at her side. It was particularly difficult to think that Chūnagon would suspect her feelings of straying toward another man. Her weakened condition was further exacerbated by her inability to eat even the slightest food. Day and night she was sunk in a torrent of tears, her soul seemingly drifting from her body. She was near death when Chūnagon finally brought her home. With the solicitous care of familiar people her spirits were gradually calmed and her troubled heart found comfort. She could not remain despondent for the rest of her years; life seemed to return to her, and while she was still perilously weak she was far better than before.

Prince Shikibukyō joined Chūnagon in delighting over her improvement, but he was perturbed that he could not spend his days with her. "I wish I could see her in a cheerful, normal mood," he lamented, but the nights he was with her she acted extremely shy and would not speak a word. When only partially conscious she seemed to look to Chūnagon for support, entrusting herself to him as he lay by her side. As she gradually regained her senses, however, she could not bear to be seen even by him, for she was ashamed that the very danger he had warned of had come true. It was impossible for her to cheer up with that in mind.

Chūnagon, meanwhile, began preparing for her mother's memorial service. With singular devotion he spared no effort in decorating the rooms and readying new colors for the change of clothing. Yoshinohime realized that what her mother had said was true indeed: the Buddha's divine guidance had brought Chūnagon to them. Her weakened condition did not change; she hovered at the edge of death yet somehow managed to survive.

One day when her attendants were resting and few people were present (only Koshōshō no Kimi was at her bedside). Chūnagon moved very close. As she quietly hid her face in her sleeve he began to remonstrate.

"Why do you hide your face, treating me even worse than before? You may well have reason for feeling so reserved now, but it goes against my feelings for you and is really most regrettable."

As he drew the sleeve away from her face she knew it would seem strange to resist unreasonably. Deeply embarrassed, she lifted her head slightly but quickly hid it again. Her face had such a helpless expression he began to weep. What a joy it was to see her even for a moment. From the moment he had departed from Kiyomizu Temple, leaving his heart with the girl, all through the days she was missing, he was deeply disturbed at losing her. He had decided to search for a reasonable period of time, and then if she were truly lost he would leave this world, for how could he go on living? The emotion pent up in his heart now burst forth in a flood of bitter tears as he told the girl everything, even the dream he had seen of the Chinese Consort. When finished he stroked her hair gently and added: "Still, I never thought I would find you in this shocking condition."

> The promises we made
> Were not like this;
> Our vows were for this world
> And the next.

Tears flowed across Chūnagon's handsome face as their eyes met unexpectedly. She knew not how to answer him, so once again she covered her face and collapsed weakly to the floor. In pity Chūnagon quickly lay down next to her.

"There, there, do not fret so," he said. "The smoke of the salt maker may have drifted elsewhere, but it was not of your own volition. This bitter regret over our karma may give my mind no peace, my heart no rest, but I cannot think it due to your negligence alone.

Had I merely heard that you had been taken thus and were among the clouds, I surely would have died.[15] In spite of your grave condition you felt you could not go on without notifying me, and at your insistence Prince Shikibukyō sent for me. Of all the memories in my entire life only one is important to me: in your time of need you turned to me. This wonderful memory will be with me even in the next world. As long as I am alive I want somehow to devote my heart and soul to caring for your needs. I have been a wanderer, drifting even to China, but I shall consider you, the one who cried out for my help, my only bond with this world I so wish to renounce."

She did not have the strength to answer, but she could not brood silently. Under her breath she managed to whisper a reply.

> I lost the strength
> To cross the mountain of death
> While waiting when you could not find me;
> Now I have returned.

Chūnagon was deeply moved that she had directly asked the Prince to send for him and that she had been so worried he might not find her. Any resentment he might have against her soon disappeared.

"If you really care for me at all," he wept, trying to ease her sorrow, "then please get well again quickly. That might add some years to my life which has been torn by grief recently."

She tried her best to recover, for she did not want to seem inconsiderate. While she was far better than before, her spirits were never completely rejuvenated and she was still fragile as dew before the wind.

Prince Shikibukyō, ever anxious about her condition, continued to visit secretly each night. Even when he had been with her day and night he could not see enough of her; his longing was much greater now that their time together was limited, and he felt a sense of uneasiness and want. His elevation to the position of Crown Prince was imminent, and for a while it would be impossible to see her even as little as he did now. When he considered how difficult the separation would be he found no joy at all in his forthcoming appointment. Using directional taboos as his excuse he made a last secret visit.

15. "Among the clouds" usually refers to the Court and here, by extension, it means "into the hands of the Prince."

"I risked my life for you and yet you ignore me. This unexpected separation will make my life miserable." He pleaded with her, unable to restrain his tears.

In her heart she felt the tender loving care of the magnificent Chūnagon was all she ever wanted from a man, and the Prince's behavior she found rash and cruel.

"Even if he reaches the pinnacle of power," she thought, "how could I bear becoming his charge? Yet for a while we were as man and wife because of that perplexing bond which joined my soul to his." Her shame grew greater still.

She was by nature gentle and charming, and while she wept as strongly as before she no longer succumbed to fainting spells. The signs of recovery became more apparent, and with her improved condition she even stopped turning away when Prince Shikibukyō looked at her. This gentle yielding intensified the love he felt for her.

"How could I survive for even a moment without seeing her?" he wondered anxiously, his devotion almost frightening.

If the Prince were to continue spending nights with her Chūnagon's jealously would know no ends. In spite of his hidden fears Chūnagon served the Prince as best he could, seeing to it that even the ladies who waited on the Prince were extraordinarily attractive. His gentle solicitude was greatly appreciated by the Prince.

The Prince always found it difficult to leave Yoshinohime's room at dawn; on parting he would weep into his sleeve as if he were traveling all the way to China.

> Since we are assured
> Of a long life together,
> Why is it I grieve so
> At these momentary partings?

Though she was by now accustomed to his presence everything was still like a dream, bewildering and unexpected. His anxious, often irritable preoccupation with her convinced her of the hopelessness of her future, even if it made her feel slightly attached to him.

> Your words may endure a lifetime,
> But my life is like
> The disappearing dew by the wayside.

233

Wiping his tears with his sleeve he left her. He realized that now when he turned to her she might show him some small sign of affection. This helped him forget all his grief, even the resentment he felt on not being able to see her for a while.[16]

He was named Crown Prince but found no joy in the many celebrations that marked his elevation. He appointed Chūnagon Master of the Crown Prince's Household, even though it meant passing over others closer to him. Many people wondered why the position went to a man who rarely even visited the Prince; those who did not know the real reason simply assumed that Chūnagon's outstanding talents had earned him the appointment.

Shortly thereafter, just past the tenth day of the eleventh month, the Chancellor's daughter had her coming-of-age ceremony. That very night she was taken with a great deal of fanfare to be betrothed to the Prince. The unusual ceremony was carried out with grandiose display no other ranking noble could hope to match; the girl was accompanied by no fewer than fifty ladies-in-waiting, eight pages, and eight servants. She was just thirteen. Young, plump, and charming, she showed promise of becoming a beautiful woman. Her abundant hair touched the floor when she stood, and she had evidently been served with great pride and affection by her many ladies. Even her innocent childishness could not be faulted. Prince Shikibukyō, however, was at the height of his infatuation with Yoshinohime and could find no comfort in other women when separated from the one he loved.

All day long he wrote her letters. The nurse who had served her from the beginning was ordered to stay with her constantly, but Chūnagon was often called to the palace to be with the Prince. At times Chūnagon was asked to bring the girl secretly to the palace. He sympathized with the Prince's needs, but wondered what it would mean for Yoshinohime. For one thing, Lord Taishō's second daughter, who was the Prince's wife, had no intention of leaving him, even though the Chancellor's daughter was recently betrothed to the

16. The final clause of this sentence contains a quote from a poem by Suō no Naishi. Since the brief quote does not translate easily into English, I have incorporated only the essential meaning into the translation. The date of Suō no Naishi's poem is taken by some scholars as evidence suggesting that *Hamamatsu Chūnagon Monogatari* was not written by Sugawara no Takasue's daughter.

Prince. And it really would be inconvenient to hastily bring Yoshinohime into the palace, trying to keep her presence a secret so
as not to offend the Chancellor. Chūnagon did not know when she
could be brought in, for it was by no means so easy a task as when
Prince Shikibukyō had taken her in from Kiyomizu Temple. While
the Prince understood Chūnagon's reluctance, he felt so wretched
without her that he started to make room for her eventual arrival.
All his ladies in the palace were called before him; those with sufficient backing were allowed to stay, but the less powerful ones, and
there were many of these pitiful ladies, were sent home.

The activity at the palace seemed to Yoshinohime no more than
distant rumblings beyond the clouds; she was worried about her own
uncertain future. The rash advances of the Prince, she felt, were
but a dream which troubled her a brief time; she had no wish to see
or be with him again. She did not even bother to glance at his
lengthy letters. Life to her was frailer than gossamer, and she had
no heart to ponder what might come next.

From the beginning of autumn her morning sickness was particularly severe, even though her condition was not at first perceptible
to those around her. When the signs of pregnancy became clearly
apparent to all, however, Chūnagon was told of her condition. He
was choked with regret now that his hope of sharing true vows of
love with her was futile, but when he remembered his dream of the
Consort tears of joy and sorrow filled his eyes.

Yoshinohime's quarters at Nurse Chūjō's were sufficient when her
existence was still a secret; a slightly inferior house was no particular
problem then, but what about now? Everyone seemed to know that
Chūnagon had found the daughter of his late father, and it would
not do to leave her in such poor surroundings. He visited her as
often as possible but felt quite uneasy when he had to be away for
a day or two.

He decided to take her to his own mansion. Now was the time
to bring her out in the open and care for her as he saw fit, without
worrying what others might think. The room north of the eastern
half of the main room along with the adjoining corridors were furnished brilliantly for her ladies-in-waiting. Wakagimi would not
leave Yoshinohime and Nurse Chūjō could not bear to be away

from him, so she became one of Yoshinohime's ladies and was given a large room when they all moved into the new quarters.

Chūnagon's mother still wondered about this new girl. She had never heard of her until recently and still felt uneasy about the whole affair.

When she had the opportunity to visit Chūnagon's quarters she asked if she might see the girl. Chūnagon decided it would not do to keep his mother away from the girl now that everyone knew of her.

"You are welcome to visit her," he said. "You always wanted a daughter. Wouldn't it be wonderful if you could think of her as your own."

She went into the girl's room. Yoshinohime was terribly embarrassed but how could she object; though mortified to be seen in her condition she always did what Chūnagon asked of her, for she had entrusted herself completely to him. By the light of the oil lamp Chūnagon's mother could see her clearly. Considering the great devotion Chūnagon had shown for the girl, his mother fully expected her to be without fault; still, she was surprised by the peerless, flawless, truly unusual beauty of the girl. She suddenly began to weep.

"Chūnagon is my only child and he cannot be with me all the time," she gently told Yoshinohime. "As the days we spent together grew more infrequent, I often regretted I did not have a daughter. If only he had told me of you sooner. But even now I want to think of you as my own. Please do not regard me as a stranger."

The girl's reply was deliberate, but the tone and manner left Chūnagon's mother wanting to hear more.

"How could there be such a magnificent girl?" she wondered. Lord Taishō's daughters are far superior to any ordinary person; Taishō no Kimi, needless to say, is beautiful and her sister is far better than most women, but neither could compare with this girl. No wonder the Crown Prince feels so strongly about her. And what a pity for his wife."

She was understandably concerned about her stepdaughter's feelings.

With her frequent visits during the day they soon became very close to one another. She had the girl play the koto and could hardly hear enough of her pupil's playing: she could listen until a woodman's

236

axe handle would rot.[17] On such days it was difficult to return home. When Chūnagon brought his daughter Himegimi to visit, Yoshinohime would bear with the suffering and weakness she felt to join in with the others. Such diversions helped her pass through the most difficult days.

Whenever Chūnagon's mother had occasion to visit Yoshinohime she was always surprised at how beautiful the girl looked, and she could well understand why Chūnagon cared for her so deeply. His mother was, however, much older than Yoshinohime who naturally felt somewhat reserved in her presence.

One evening Yoshinohime caught a glimpse of another lady in the moonlight, a woman she took to be Taishō no Kimi. While the lady was for the most part dressed in the casual manner of one who had renounced the world, her appearance and manners were youthful, somewhat reserved, yet gentle and attractive. She was far more beautiful than Yoshinohime imagined; no wonder Chūnagon wished to spend his life with her, even if she had left society. Yoshinohime envied her, for the lady was extremely beautiful and had renounced the world to lighten her burden of sin.

When they met they wept together, each serving to alleviate the other's agony. Chūnagon quietly observed them: neither was inferior to the other and together they seemed to shine as one light, strikingly magnificent figures of unworldly beauty. Even now he was taken aback by Taishō no Kimi's beauty; he had known her for years and she was dressed in the well-worn robes of a nun, but still her charm was not dimmed even by that of Yoshinohime, even though the latter was now carefully tended by diligent ladies-in-waiting. His enthusiasm for these two women waned, however, when he remembered that the Chinese Consort bore a different beauty, one even greater than the shining examples before him. The thought of her brought tears of sorrow to his eyes.

During the dreary days he had kept Yoshinohime in hiding his heart had known no peace, torn as it was between these two women. Now that he had brought the two together and could think of them as one, he was happy. For a long time he had wanted a sister who

17. The metaphor has the basic meaning "a very, very long time," and is based on an incident associated with Wang Chih of Chin. While Wang Chih intently watched a game of chess, his axe handle rotted away.

felt as he did, someone he could do everything for, someone to visit day and night, someone he could talk with. Such a person would be a magnificent consolation for the sorrow and weariness of life. He had envied men who had such sisters. He could now do everything for Yoshinohime, but he was not completely content; her beauty was truly peerless—were it not so, he might feel less regret—but now that she responded to his every wish he found that caring for her each day and night came all too effortlessly. The pure unfettered desires are most easily fulfilled.[18]

Taishō no Kimi was now finally able to entrust herself completely to Chūnagon for all her needs. Her attitude no longer caused him the constant worry he had once known.

Even though he watched over Yoshinohime like a personal possession they were not as husband and wife. This unusual relationship in which he cared for her morning and night as a brother for a sister proved more painful with each passing day, but what could be done about it now? He still wanted her as his wife. Although Prince Shikibukyō would not be likely to desert her, it would not be impossible for Chūnagon to have secret trysts with her. She was close at hand, but everyone in the land—those both near and far—assumed she was his father's daughter. Even if he were extremely discreet, were he somehow to err and be discovered, such seemingly incestuous behavior would cause a terrible scandal and his name would be disgraced. Since he was responsible for both the girl's reputation and his own, he alone would have to bear the onus of his indiscretion. Such an affair would be far more serious than one with any other lady.

Such a tryst would be most difficult. But the way of lovers is to risk anything, even to be reborn in order to meet one another. Why, then, should he be overly concerned about what others might think? Still, if he were to approach her amorously she herself might be dismayed. That, he thought, would be a pity.

"If I were to have an affair with her," he decided, "my own mind would know no peace, and if I do not control my passion our reputation will be sullied." These thoughts occurred to him again and again.

18. This sentence is probably a proverb although the origin and exact meaning are uncertain.

When no one was around he tried to make his irrepressible passion known to her, but she pretended not to understand. In all other matters she was absolutely submissive to him; only on the path of love did she refuse to follow. When he tried to press his love she wept and lamented so bitterly that again she seemed close to death. Chūnagon reflected that her behavior was, in fact, quite natural. Soon his thoughts would turn passionately to the Consort in China.

"Thinking of Yoshinohime day and night has caused my heart this grief; my sorrow and heartaches all come from a single tie with the Consort."

Yoshinohime herself secretly felt that if their relationship had been as before, Chūnagon could do as he wished with her; but everyone now assumed they were brother and sister. In comparison with her early years in the snows of Yoshino, the unstinting support he now afforded her made her feel as if she were already in Paradise. This world seemed hardly real. When no one was around she wept bitterly over the painful burden on her heart.

"Were it anything but this," she thought, "I would die before causing him such sorrow."

To her the idea of sleeping with him now was foreboding, troublesome, and loathsome. She wished she could hide away in the mountains where no one might see her, but she could never bring herself to treat him so coolly.

To her ladies she said, "When the master comes to see me remember that he once said I should have people with me; there are often too few."

Considering her unusual condition her ladies agreed it should be so and stayed with her constantly, thus thwarting Chūnagon's chance to plead his love. His mind knew no peace and he felt disappointed, but as long as she refused to sleep with him he had no intention of forcing himself on her.

"I may shatter into a thousand pieces, but not a speck of dust must dirty her," he vowed. She understood full well his gentle kindness and affection, and she herself was grieved it must be so. The situation in which each suffered for the other's sake was quite extraordinary.

As Yoshinohime mourned her troublesome condition her spirits became even more depressed and she could hardly raise herself from her sickbed. Chūnagon saw her weak and pained condition as ominous, and he wondered what could be done. He became even more frightened when he remembered the warning of the monk from Yoshino. With all his energies he prayed for her well-being.

Yoshinohime's pregnancy came as a shock to the Crown Prince. He thought it a profoundly joyous occasion, however, and had prayers and incantations performed on her behalf. The nursemaid who had served her from the beginning was ordered to stay constantly at her side. In a day he sent a thousand messengers, more abundant than the rain, to inquire after her health. With so many of the Prince's people there it was difficult for anyone else to come or go with ease. When Chūnagon visited Prince Shikibukyō he had mixed feelings about the Prince's unusual devotion; the Prince was somewhat of a dandy, the sort of person always inclined to switch quickly from one woman to another. The singular devotion he now showed for Yoshinohime was surprising.

"If in the future he should ever desert her," Chūnagon mused, "I would have her for my own, even though she would be hurt." There were many things to consider; it pained him not to be able to think of her in only one way.

The new year came without incident. Many visitors came from China that year, and Chūnagon learned through Daini something that disturbed him deeply. There was a letter from the man who had accompanied him to Tsukushi from China, a letter that told a very sad story.

"Last year on the sixteenth day of the third month the light of the Hoyang Consort passed from this world. The whole land was in mourning. The Emperor renounced his throne, took Buddhist vows, and went to the Kunlun Mountains. The Crown Prince assumed the throne and now the First Consort rules the land, although the Third Prince has been made heir apparent. Wu Chün, daughter of the Prime Minister, was to enter the palace as a consort, but she cut her hair, dyed her robes, and went into the mountains leaving this poem.

I long for one not in this land,
What good is a jeweled crown to me?

When he saw this letter Chūnagon realized that this was just as he had seen in his dream. His spirits darkened and his soul seemed on the verge of disappearing as he sank into a torrent of tears.

Works Cited

Abe Akio; Oka Kazuo; and Yamagishi Tokuhei, eds. *Kokugo Kokubungaku Kenkyūshi Taisei 3, Genji Monogatari Jo.* Tokyo: Sanseidō, 1960.

Birch, Cyril, ed. *Anthology of Chinese Literature.* New York: Grove Press, 1965.

Endō Yoshimoto, and Matsuo Satoshi, eds. *Takamura Monogatari, Heichū Monogatari, Hamamatsu Chūnagon Monogatari.* Nihon Koten Bungaku Taikei, no. 77. Tokyo: Iwanami Shoten, 1964.

Genette, Gerard. *Narrative Discourse, An Essay in Method.* Ithaca: Cornell University Press, 1980.

Hanawa Hokinoichi. *Gunsho Ruijū.* Vol. 11. Tokyo: Keizai Zasshisha, 1906.

Hisamatsu Sen'ichi, ed. *Shimpan Nihon Bungakushi: Chūko.* Tokyo: Shibundō, 1971.

———. *Shimpan Nihon Bungakushi: Chūsei.* Tokyo: Shibundō, 1971.

Hochstedler, Carol. *The Tale of Nezame: Part Three of Yowa no Nezame Monogatari.* Cornell University East Asia Papers, no. 22. Ithaca: China-Japan Program, Cornell University, 1979.

Ikeda Kikan. *Heian Jidai no Bungaku to Seikatsu.* Tokyo: Shibundō, 1966.

———. *Zenkō Makura no Sōshi.* Tokyo: Shibundō, 1967.

Ikeda Toshio. *Hamamatsu Chūnagon Monogatari Sōsakuin.* Tokyo: Musashino Shoin, 1964.

Inaga Keiji. "Keishikiteki Shori ni yoru Hitotsu no Baai—*Nezame, Hamamatsu* ni Kanshite—." *Kokugo to Kokubungaku* (December 1950), pp. 38-50.

———. "Suō no Naishi Denkō, Tsuku: *Hamamatsu Chūnagon Monogatari* Makkan no Hikiuta to no Kankei." *Kokugo to Kokubungaku* (August 1954), pp. 17-26.

Kawaguchi Hisao and Shida Nobuyoshi, eds. *Wakan Rōeishū, Ryōjin Hishō.* Nihon Koten Bungaku Taikei, no. 73. Tokyo: Iwanami Shoten, 1965.

Komatsu Shigemi. *Kōhon Hamamatsu Chūnagon Monogatari.* Tokyo: Nigensha, 1964.

Masabuchi Tsunekichi. *Monogatari Shōsetsu Jo.* Nihon Bungaku Kōza, no. 3. Tokyo: Kaizōsha, 1934.

Matsumoto Hiroko. "*Hamamatsu Chūnagon Monogatari* no Gensaku Keitai ni Kansuru Kōsatsu." *Ochanomizu Joshi Daigaku Jimbun Kagaku Kiyō,* Vol. 21, no. 3 (March 1968). Reprint. Nihon Bungaku Kenkyū

Shiryō Kankōkai, *Nihon Bungaku Kenkyū Shiryō Sōsho, Heianchō Monogatari IV.*

Matsuo Satoshi. *Hamamatsu Chūnagon Monogatari.* (See Endō Yoshimoto and Matsuo Satoshi, eds., *Takamura Monogatari, Heichū Monogatari, Hamamatsu Chūnagon Monogatari.*)

————. *Heian Jidai Monogatari Ronkō.* Tokyo: Kasama Shoin, 1968.

————. "*Sarashina, Hamamatsu, Nezame* ni egakareta Kashōmi ni tsuite." *Kokugo to Kokubungaku* (August 1935). Reprint. Matsuo Satoshi, *Heian Jidai Monogatari Ronkō.*

McCullough, Helen C. *Ōkagami, The Great Mirror.* Princeton: Princeton University Press, 1980.

McCullough, William H. "Japanese Marriage Institutions in the Heian Period." *Harvard Journal of Asiatic Studies,* 27 (1967):103-67.

Mishima Yukio. *Haru no Yuki.* Tokyo: Shinchōsha, 1969.

Morris, Ivan, trans. *As I Crossed a Bridge of Dreams.* New York: The Dial Press, 1971.

Nakano Sōji. *Kōhon Fūyō Wakashū.* Kyoto: Yūzan Bunko, 1970.

Nihon Bungaku Kenkyū Shiryō Kankōkai. *Nihon Bungaku Kenkyū Shiryō Sōsho, Heianchō Monogatari IV.* Tokyo: Yūseidō, 1980.

Philippi, Donald L., trans. *Kojiki.* Tokyo: Princeton University Press and University of Tokyo Press, 1968.

Richard, Kenneth L. "Developments in Late Heian Prose Fiction: *The Tale of Nezame.*" Ph.D. dissertation, University of Washington, 1973.

Rohlich, Thomas H. "*Hamamatsu Chūnagon Monogatari*: An Introduction and Translation." Ph.D. dissertation, University of Wisconsin, 1979.

Sakakura Atsuyoshi. "*Yoru no Nezame* no Bunshō." *Kokugo to Kokubungaku* (October 1964), pp. 144-56.

Seidensticker, Edward G., trans. *The Gossamer Years.* Tokyo and Rutland, Vt.: Charles E. Tuttle Co., 1964.

————. *The Tale of Genji.* New York: Knopf, 1976.

Suzuki Hiromichi. *Heian Makki Monogatari ni tsuite no Kenkyū.* Kyoto: Akao Shōbundō, 1971.

————. "*Yowa no Nezame, Hamamatsu Chūnagon Monogatari* no Seiritsu Junjō." *Ronkyū Nihon Bungaku* (June 1945). Reprint. Suzuki Hiromichi, *Heian Makki Monogatari ni tsuite no Kenkyū.*

Suzuki Tomotarō; Kawaguchi Hisao; Endō Yoshimoto; Nishishita Kyōichi, eds. *Tosa Nikki, Kagerō Nikki, Izumi Shikibu Nikki, Sarashina Nikki.* Nihon Koten Bungaku Taikei, no. 20. Tokyo: Iwanami Shoten, 1957.

Tomikura Tokujirō. *Mumyōzōshi Hyōkai.* Tokyo: Yūseidō, 1954.

WORKS CITED

Waley, Arthur. *The Nō Plays of Japan*. New York: Grove Press, Inc., 1957.
Watson, Burton. *Chinese Lyricism, Shih Poetry from the Second to the Twelfth Century*. New York: Columbia University Press, 1971.
Willig, Rosette Friedman. "A Study and Translation of the 'Torikaebaya Monogatari.' " Ph.D. dissertation, University of Pennsylvania, 1978.

Index

Library of Congress Cataloging in Publication Data

Sugawara Takasue no Musume, b. 1008.
Hamamatsu Chūnagon monogatari.
    Translation of: Hamamatsu Chūnagon monogatari /
Sugawara Takasue no Musume.
    Includes bibliography and index.
    I. Rohlich, Thomas H., 1946-   II. Title.
PL789.S8H313 1983   895.6'31   82-61380
ISBN 0-691-05377-4

Thomas H. Rohlich is Assistant Professor of Asian
Languages and Literature at The University of Iowa.
This is his first book.

DATE DUE
